I0762315

Where Skies Fall

BRAVERY. BREATH. BRINE.

PAPERBACK ISBN: 9798367929843

HARDBACK ISBN: 978-1-0880-1248-2

Book Cover designed by
The Illustrated Author Design Services
Character Art Illustration/ Hard Case Cover by
Art by Steffani / Steffani Christensen
Trailer and Interior Formatting designed by
The Illustrated Author Design Services
Edited by
The Girl with the Red Pen

WHERE SKIES FALL

PRAISE FOR WHERE SKIES FALL

"Woven from harsh winds and magical brine, the Where Oceans Burn duology is a thrilling and heart-wrenching tale of opposites that can find peace – if the right hearts find each other." – Angelina J. Steffort, award-winning author of *The Quarter Mage*

"I loved this book. Such a unique magic system and complex characters. Beautifully done!" – Alisha Klapheke, *USA Today* Bestselling author of the *Kingdoms of Lore* series.

ALSO BY CASEY L. BOND

Where Oceans Bleed
Where Skies Fall

Valor

House of Eclipses
House of Wolves

When Wishes Bleed
The Omen of Stones

Gravebriar
With Shield and Ink and Bone
Things That Should Stay Buried
Glamour of Midnight

The Fairy Tales
Riches to Rags
Savage Beauty
Unlocked
Brutal Curse

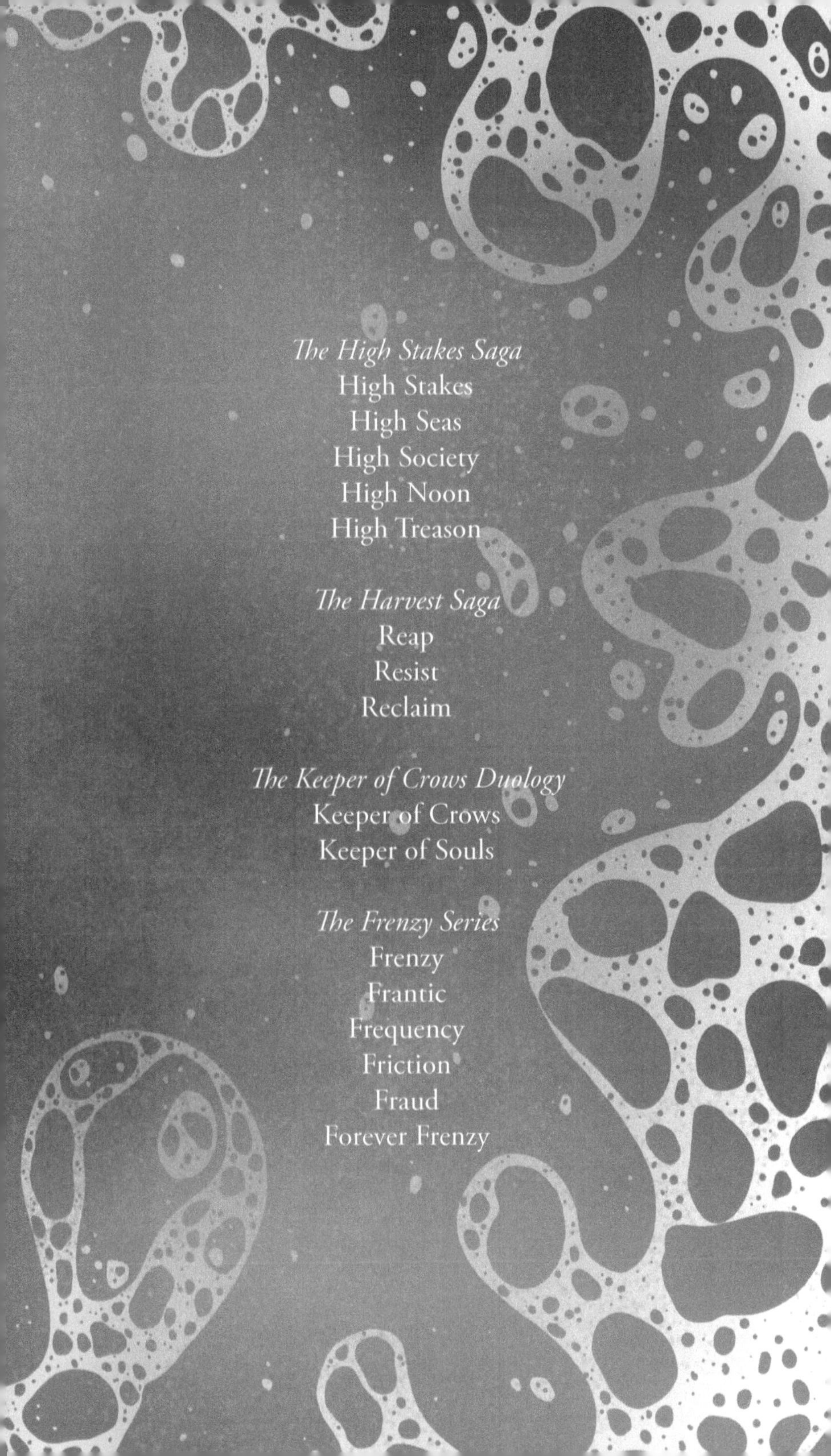

The High Stakes Saga
High Stakes
High Seas
High Society
High Noon
High Treason

The Harvest Saga
Reap
Resist
Reclaim

The Keeper of Crows Duology
Keeper of Crows
Keeper of Souls

The Frenzy Series
Frenzy
Frantic
Frequency
Friction
Fraud
Forever Frenzy

For anyone brave enough to fly through burning skies
with hope in their heart…

EMPYREAN

Village of the Scholars

The Elders

Scribes

Library

House of the Clipped

The Sanctum of Neera

Hatchlings

The General's Command

Younglings

Nests of the General Populage

The Warrior's Quarter

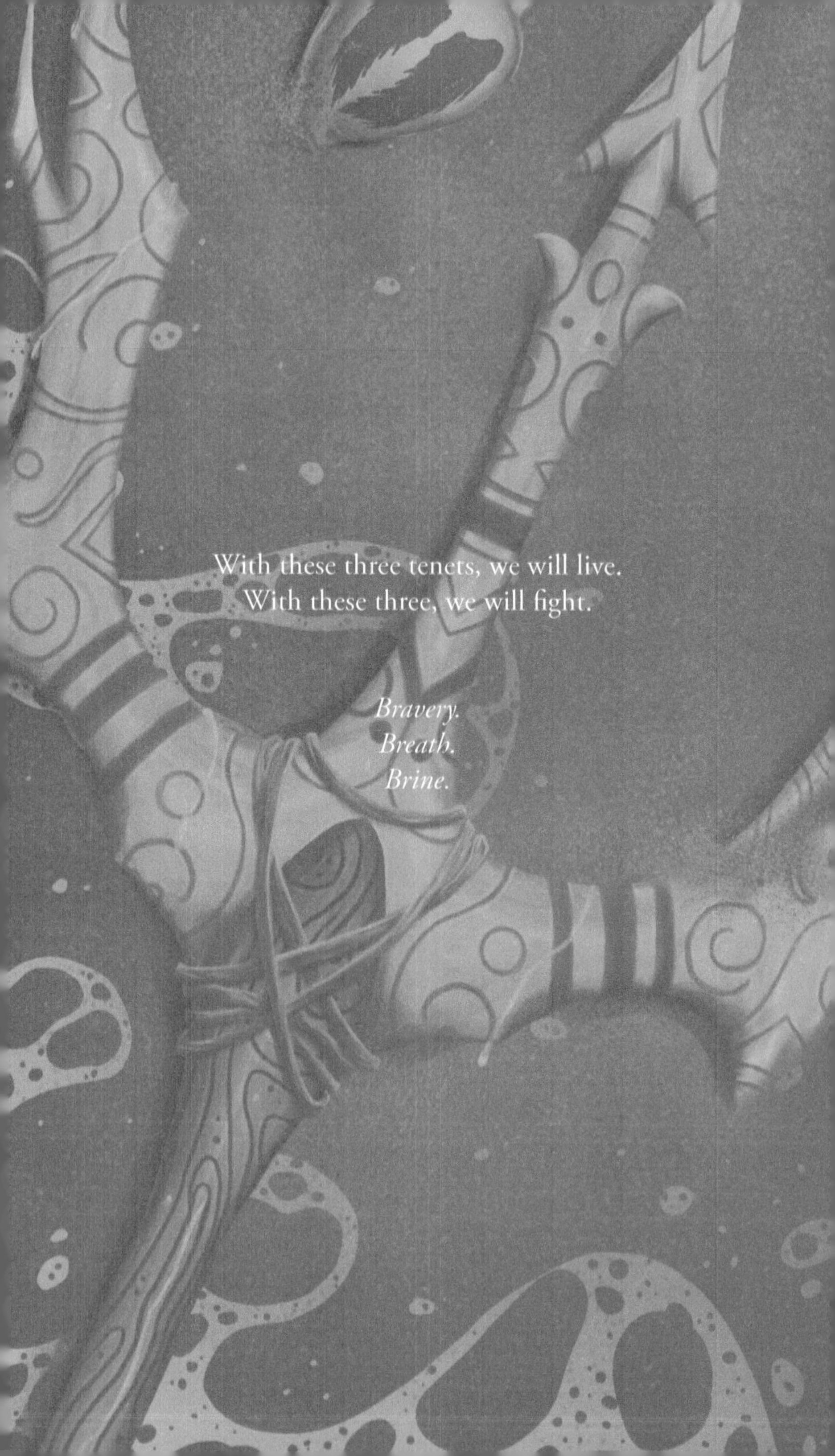

With these three tenets, we will live.
With these three, we will fight.

Bravery.
Breath.
Brine.

The Grove
West Village
Talay's
Temple
East Lagoon
The Falls
The Vines
The Guardians
Isle of Kehlani
The Salt

I

BRAVERY

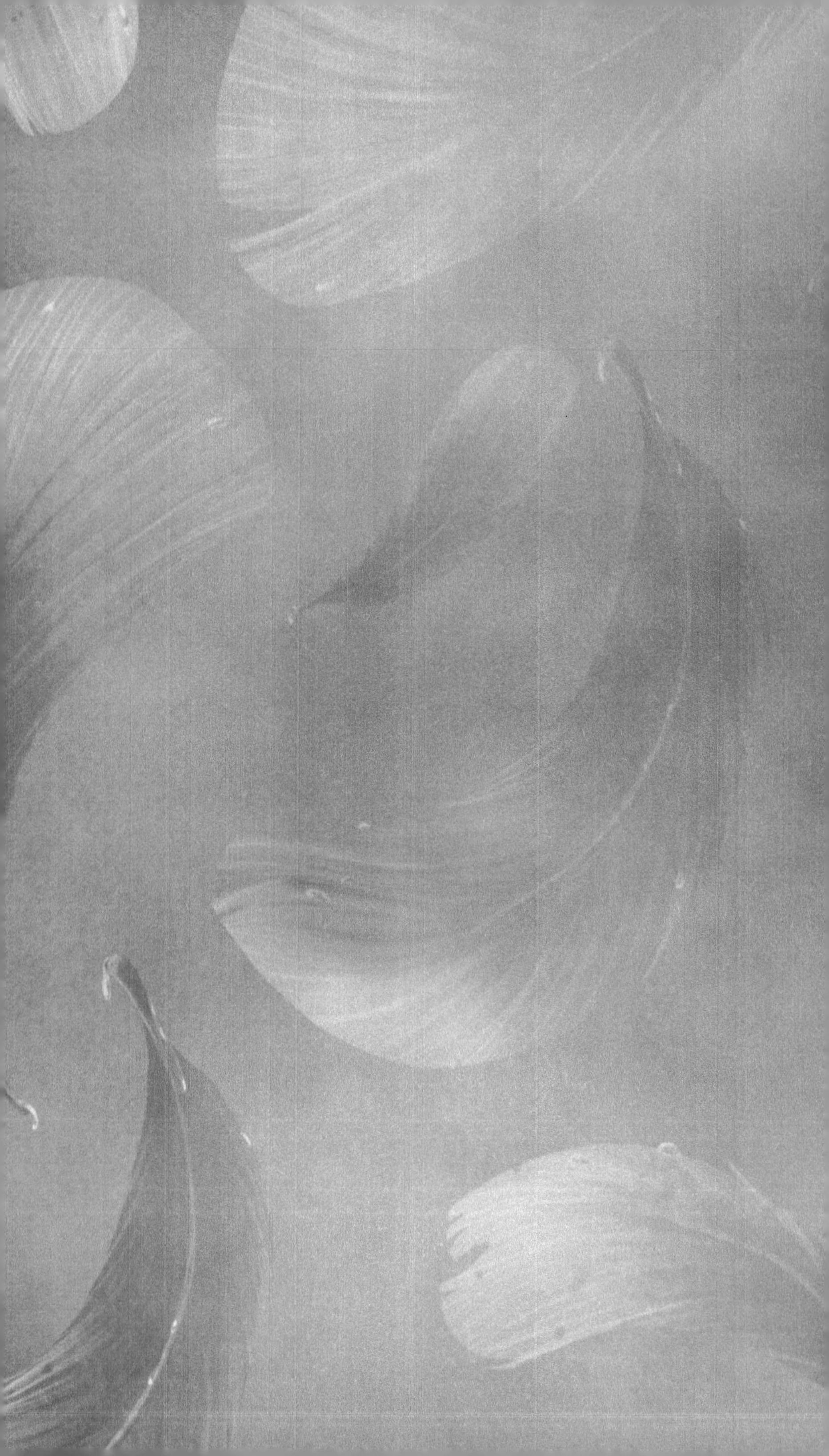

CHAPTER ONE

In my dream, as the rising sun slowly eased into the tranquil ocean, every facet of the water reflecting gold, orange, and lavender, *she* circled above the waves in the place where *she* thought I had died.

She saw my blue feathers, dull and bobbing lifelessly atop the jeweled sea. *She* swept low… The need to be sure tempting her closer…

Closer…

Until finally, *she* hovered just above my wings and pushed her hands into the cold water. Her fingers curled around the strongest of a wing's bones, but as *she* lifted and dragged the appendages from the water, *she* realized that my wings were the only part of me *she* would find. They had been cleaved from my back.

She stared at them for a moment, water cascading down every feather, then relaxed her grip and watched them splash heavily into the sea. Talay spread my blue feathers wide.

I smiled as he drowned her confidence in fear.

She noticed *him* then.

The Shark lurked nearby with his oceanic eyes just above the surface. Water sluiced from his short, dark hair, wending down his skin like serpents. There was a moment when their gazes collided and *her* eyes narrowed. *She* pulled an arrow from *her* quiver as he lifted his trident and drew it backward, stretching her bowstring to its limit, calming each of her breaths. This shot had to be perfect. *She* could not miss. Not now.

Focusing on him, *she* didn't notice me hiding beneath the surface. But *she* saw the triumphant moment I emerged. Then *she* tasted my revenge and her death as my trident's sharp barbs speared *her* treacherous heart.

When *Soraya* splashed into the sea that evening, I swam circles around her until her hands fell weakly from my trident's handle. Until her pupils stilled and bubbles stopped trickling from her mouth; until her muscles stopped twitching. Gripping the end of my trident's long stem, I towed her through the water to Crest, who dragged her into the deep blue.

She wasn't worthy of resting at the bottom of the trench, comfortable in Talay's dark, heavy heart, but she would nourish the creatures who lived within its boundary.

While he disposed of the one who had once tried, and failed, to kill me, I stood on the shore alone watching the distant, darkened sliver where the sky met the sea. Water trickled from my clothes and hair, dampening the sand at my feet.

I remembered Crest saying that he came to the shore when he needed solitude, but didn't want to be alone. At the edge of the ocean, sometimes Talay spoke. And when his god's voice was unclear, he could swim within the fathomless water and pour his heart out to the one who filled his gills with brine and his lungs with the breath he stole from the sky to balance the water Neera siphoned from the sea.

What an irony. That to conjure the storms that displayed her great power, she needed Talay's water.

I hoped I might find Talay here, too. That he might answer the questions haunting me.

In my dream, Soraya was dead. I should've felt a sense of relief. Of finality. But I couldn't feel anything beyond fear and worry because Soraya wasn't the only enemy I'd left behind in Empyrean. She wasn't even the most powerful.

Instead of the gentle, calm words of a god I'd only just met and begun to understand, I found the harsh goddess I knew all too well. The one who planted the soul that took root in my body. Who stirred the Great Wind for my people to fly upon. Who blessed me with wings and her power in my blood.

The goddess who threatened to rip me from the land and drag me back to Empyrean.

Talay had claimed me the moment I splashed into his sea, but the goddess did not care that the god of the ocean welcomed me among his kind.

My blood and wings, my future and my past, all belonged to her.

Neera moved along the thin seam of wind and water, keeping to the far corners, staying in the shadows like she had in her sanctum. I felt her looming presence as she walked just above the waves, taunting the god who ruled them. I begged Talay to protect and hide Crest from her as he swam under her feet.

To Neera, the horizon was just another scale, and it demanded far more than my feathers.

In one of its expansive pans was a glimpse of a future I would kill for.

And in the other, a vision of a future I would kill to prevent…

A feeling of dread washed over me like a heavy wave, and a current stronger than any wind I'd flown through tugged me toward the sky. It felt like she'd reached down and closed her fist around me, squeezing. Displeasure rippled through her Empyrea-laden skin and my blood echoed her anger, writhing in my veins.

She knew my heart. Knew it wasn't loyal to her anymore.

And *I* knew she didn't allow disloyalty.

CHAPTER TWO

The Shark of the Sea came to my tent just before dawn this morning and asked if I wanted to accompany him to the shore to watch the sun rise. I told him about the dream I had last night that started with Soraya… and ended with Neera.

I thought about keeping it to myself and just couldn't. His opinion on the matter was important.

My descriptions unsettled him. He didn't say as much, but I could see it in the way he shifted his weight, the way he studied the waves as if they might know the meaning of it before finally looking away. "You should tell The Salt," he advised.

I hesitated. It wasn't that I was opposed to seeking her counsel, exactly, but this dream felt visceral. Like it was crafted by someone who knew me as well as I knew myself. Like it was meant just for me, and so was its message.

When I thought of how the dream made me feel, I wasn't even sure why I shared it with Crest.

The dream made me feel like I was every bit the monster I had been before splashing into Crest's world – ruthless and cunning with a craving for causing the deaths of my enemies. Only in my dream, I wasn't fighting for the sky anymore.

I didn't have wings.

I fought for Crest, and after him, Talay and his people. The moment I saw his hair and glittering eyes breach the surface, a fierce sense of protectiveness rose within me. If Soraya touched him, if her arrow flew in his vicinity, I would rip her apart and leave the pieces of her scattered on the sea for the birds above and beasts beneath to feast upon.

I'd plunged my trident's barbs in deep, then jerked her back to alter her arrow's trajectory. It struck the sea far over his head, but too close for my comfort.

It felt so real. The fear that I hadn't been strong or fast enough to keep him safe.

"Do any of those among your people have visions? Besides The Salt, I mean."

His blue eyes squinted at the rising sun. "I don't know for sure, but I think gods as powerful as ours could do almost anything they wanted."

Almost anything.

I wondered if he was right. Was there a limit to Neera's terrible power? A place Talay's brine could not flood?

Soft sunlight kissed and slid over Crest's tanned skin. The planes of his arms, chest, and face were bathed in it. He was magnificent. Beautiful was too shallow a word to describe him. Oh, how glorious it would be to embody the sun on the days she shone upon The Shark!

"Elira," he began, his intense stare focused on me, "I'd like you to teach my people how to defend themselves against the Empyrean warriors."

I dug my toe into the sand, twisting and digging like a knife into pliant flesh. "Self-defense isn't enough. I'll teach your people how to kill them."

He stared quietly at the sea for a long moment. I wondered if he was somehow consulting Talay.

Crest had seen enough death to carefully weigh the counteroffer I made. But if he didn't accept it, he would live to see the shore and sea alike stained red and be forced to escort more into the depths than his heart could likely bear.

His eyes flicked sideways. "Thank you, Elira, for helping them."

Warmth spread over me, though it had nothing to do with the sun.

The people of Kehlani brushed it off when The Salt told them Talay had sent a cowrie with an impression of blue wings and confirmed it was mine. They scoffed at the idea that the god himself welcomed me into his sea, onto the soil he had inherited, and into the lives of his people. Though he was revered, that small, curled shell wasn't enough for them to accept the presence of their greatest enemy.

Maybe the shell's pattern, they could reason, was nothing more than coincidence. In refusing to believe Talay's Seer, the people questioned The Salt's integrity, and in turn, challenged the god of the sea himself.

He found a way to erase any doubt they might have harbored.

When I pressed my lips to Crest's the first time, Talay spoke, revealing us as lacunas. There was no denying the irrefutable voice and word of the god of the sea. No one was brave enough to refuse what he insisted upon.

Everything changed after his declaration.

That seemingly simple, but unquestioningly profound moment sparked curiosity in every soul the ocean had crafted in its fathomless blue heart. Fear and anger ebbed away every day I spent among them. On this afternoon, they gathered to watch me and Crest ready our bows and arrows to take aim at coconuts he'd placed in crooks of the sturdy branches of nearby trees.

His people were proud and stubborn. They wouldn't allow me to line them up as I would have my quad. Would have balked if I dared to criticize their skill with a bow, even if it was true that they would die if they kept shooting the way they were taught. Would have walked away the second I left them to practice with the guidance I'd given.

These weren't regimented warriors. The Guardians protected the sea because it was their home and their duty to do so. That was also how they defended the land and the lives upon it. But defense wasn't enough in war.

Like I told Crest, they had to kill, or they would be killed.

They had to fire better, from farther away, and faster than the Empyreans who'd trained since youth to do exactly that.

So, Crest brought me into the village, then the Guardians' Hall, and then to the tents scattered between Talay's Temple and the grove, at each spot openly and very loudly challenging me. Between Kehlanian and

Empyrean, we would see whose archery skills were superior that afternoon.

With his lure secure and the line cast, he waited for them to take his bait.

They were proud of their Shark, Talay's favored. They wanted him to win almost as much as they wanted to see me lose.

But even he knew he wouldn't prevail. He'd seen me shoot. The water was nearly the only thing that impeded me. It would catch my arrows in its great fist and send them to the bottom of the sea, burying them in fine silt.

Crest knew the hearts and minds of his people and his people loved him for it. He was taking the time to learn mine moment by moment, day by day. But our time, I knew, was swiftly coming to an end.

I lightly stretched my back, trying to push the tension from my wings as his people laughed at his playful antics. As we strung our bows, they watched our parrying banter and well-matched skill carefully, curiously. But more than anything, they seemed to marvel at the miracle of how the mighty sea had befriended the turbulent sky.

"How long has it been since you drew your string?" he taunted. "You're quite unpracticed. How many moon cycles have passed since you fell from the sky and splashed into the brine? Five? Six?"

The Shark had forgotten that I wasn't prey, but a predator in my own right. I would thoroughly enjoy proving it to him. I gave a throaty chuckle at the thought. If only joy could be wrung, fill its own earthen void, and become its own sea.

My bow was an extension of my arm. The smooth, sculpted wood was part of me, almost as intimately as the feathers fletching my arrows that were once seated in my wings. It didn't matter how long it had been since I tested its weight or how long since I'd plucked her string. My bow would answer me every time. She had and always would see me victorious.

The earth sweltered beneath the risen sun. While I still hadn't acclimated and perpetually threatened that I would melt into the sandy soil, today's searing heat even affected The Shark.

Sweat trickled down his forehead and slowly careened down his sun-kissed skin, streaking down the tattoo now settled and at home beneath his skin. Droplets slid down the valley separating the muscles in his back. As he pulled back on his bow string, muscles flexing and going taut in too many places to count, I tried not to stare too long.

That would only draw his knowing smile and swell his ego.

I found Crest attractive, but that didn't mean I was happy Talay had emblazoned over his heart the fact that he'd chosen me as the lacuna of The Shark of the Sea. I was The Scourge of the Sky. We hailed from completely different worlds with distinct customs and values and yet… somehow, when we were forced together, we'd grown to tolerate one another. Tolerance grew into respect, and respect now flirted with the friendship he'd offered but that I knew fell short of what he truly wanted.

Lacunas, to the people of Kehlani, were sacred. They were lifelong mates, the bond between them sealed with equal portions breath and brine, lasting until one of the pair perished and was given back to Talay.

My people did not mate for life. Only when necessary to produce an offspring, and never any longer. There was little love to be found in Empyrean, the unforgiving kingdom of the sky. Intrinsically beautiful, yet bitterly cold.

His mark was proof that even gods weren't infallible.

Talay made a mistake in choosing me, and I hated it for Crest.

Crest – who watched his brother Breaker and his lacuna simper over one another at every opportunity. Whose lips curled upward at their constant affection, and whose smile fell when he realized I'd noticed him admiring their easy, passionate love.

I once thought he was a monster. Now, I knew we'd both been monsters to one another for our own reasons. My predicament had given way to a new understanding, and my new understanding shifted my perspective in ways I never knew were possible. Now I wanted him free of my mark. Talay needed to send someone who would love him like Breaker loved Katalini.

But that would have to wait.

Before he was captured and killed, my father had descended to warn us that my people were preparing an attack unlike any they'd attempted before. The people of the sea had been preparing to rise to the challenge and meet them, when they needed to be preparing to win. I hoped to help them do exactly that. It would begin here, today, with Crest and coconuts, aim and arrows.

His brother Breaker, the leader of the Isle, sought an end to the war and thought I might play a part. For a while, my plan was for Talay's people to trade me. Empyrean's first soul would be returned if certain conditions were met. The trade was still on the table as far as I was concerned.

Crest, however, vehemently opposed.

Wars can be ended in other ways, he said. They could be won, instead.

To win something of this caliber, one must be willing to risk everything. To risk everyone. Everyone they loved. Everyone for whom they were responsible.

The Shark – the man who saved my life when he should've let me drown, who justifiably hated me when he was given the task of guarding me – now wanted me to stay by his side. Surprisingly, I wasn't ready to leave. Not that I wasn't still considering it; I just wasn't sure that those who ruled the sky now would be open to negotiation.

I needed to be sure…

Crest closed one eye to focus on the target – a bright green coconut he'd propped on a fallen log.

Quietly, I told him, "When you close an eye, you sever your field of vision by half. Why would you want to do that?"

His fingers tightened a fraction. His lip gave a little twitch. "Stop."

"Two eyes focus more accurately together than one eye does alone," I whispered.

"Stop," he growled.

"Stop what?" I said innocently.

"Stop trying to get into my head. This is how *I* focus to shoot. Not everyone's vision is as keen as yours."

"I believe you asked for my help, Shark. But go ahead and show me how you shoot so I can pick apart your form."

Snickers erupted around us. Bets were quickly made on whether he would strike true and whether I had truly unnerved him.

"She hasn't," he bit at whomever spilled those particular words.

I grinned, knowing he heard them and cared enough to refute the claim. I'd definitely gotten under his skin.

Crest refocused, then released the string. His arrow flew, spiraling and wobbling through the air toward the coconut, but it struck the tree's trunk just beneath his target. To add insult to injury, the fruit didn't even teeter. I tried not to look smug or victorious, but Crest knew that inwardly, I was both.

"Don't you dare say I told you so," he playfully seethed, wiping the sweat from his face.

Frey and Koa watched from behind us. They were Crest's best friends and his most trusted warriors – Guardians of Kehlani. Ever mischievous and loving the tension stirring between Shark and Scourge, Koa began to chuckle. A matching laugh from Frey made his laughter bubble even louder. He flung a hand toward me as he talked to Crest.

"You need help, bro. Look at the difference in the targets. She actually hits them – every single time. The Scourge is offering you advice. Maybe you should take it."

My arrows' heads were embedded in the centers of every coconut. A few of his had struck true, but most were off by a few inches, and not in only one direction where a simple adjustment would correct them all.

"Is it harder to aim while flying?" Koa asked, an awe-struck but ornery grin still on his face.

"I learned early to make adjustments."

He shook his head. "I bet you did. Can't wait to see that..."

Crest growled at his friend, who shrugged a tanned shoulder.

Koa's golden scales glinted as he sank back into the sand, propping himself up with his elbows. His long, brown hair was twisted into a knot at his crown. Koa was always calm; fluid, even when dragging a leviathan to the shore. I envied his easy demeanor and was grateful for it. He kept Crest grounded when the weight of the sky fell on his shoulders.

Crest's older brother Breaker was responsible for the Isle and everyone on it, but even he depended on Crest to lead his Guardians in the deep. Breaker was born with scales, but no gills. I still hadn't figured out why they were different.

Frey sat beside Koa, thoroughly enjoying our banter. Her burgundy hair swayed in a light westerly wind.

Crest turned to her. "You close one eye, don't you?"

She grinned. "I did until today. Sorry, Crest, but Elira's results speak for themselves."

Crest waved her off and turned to his brother, who was busy swaying with Katalini, the pair's hips keeping time with the fronds overhead. They smiled at one another as though nothing else existed. As if no trouble stalked them. Like death might not find and part them tomorrow.

I hadn't known them long enough to know if they were like this before I fell, or whether their incessant displays of affection had intensified in response to the threat we knew was promised.

Crest watched the couple for a few heartbeats, then turned to me. "Show me," he relented.

I stepped forward, nocked my arrow, lifted my bow, and fired. He jogged to new position after new position, trying to see if my aim faltered. It didn't. He only stopped challenging me when the coconut, now skewered with so many arrows I could barely see its green hue beyond the fletchings, rolled backward off the log.

Whistles and claps erupted from the small crowd we'd drawn. Even people from the nearest village had come to watch the contest. It was strange to see them applauding my proficiency when only weeks ago, they wanted to tear me limb from limb.

Crest's brows kissed. "How accurate are you when you have to shoot fast? Or with moving targets?"

I smiled and shrugged to irritate him, confident I could hit any piece of fruit he presented. The Warriors of the sky spent hours each day practicing their archery skills. Even hatchlings were given small bows to play with, and once a child became a youngling, excruciating lessons on accuracy began.

The people of Kehlani only seemed to shoot when a threat emerged. They were undisciplined, unpracticed, and unorganized. They chose to react instead of being the aggressor. If they wanted to win this war, they could be and do none of those things.

Empyrean Warriors had already mastered everything they lacked, but there was still time to teach them. Time for them to learn and adapt. To prepare.

He jogged across the sand to the trees and began tossing coconuts into the air. I hit them all in rapid succession.

Crest wanted his people to hone their skill with a bow, and while coconuts were a fun way for them to practice, Empyreans would not be so easily struck. My people were careful of distances. They knew how far Kehlani's arrows could fly, and they were practiced at evasive maneuvers.

The only reason so many fell in the last battle was because The General had ordered the quads to fly low to form a protective shield before my quad. I couldn't fathom then why he would make such an order, but now, I knew he wanted nothing more than to keep me from falling, from dying. A father would do most anything to protect his offspring, which was why the Elders of Empyrean kept parentage secret and discouraged familial bonds.

The Oracle went to him with word of a vision; she'd seen calamity and he had the authority to mobilize the entire army in an attempt to prevent such a fate. They did as he ordered and ignored mine to fall back, and calamity came all the same.

There is no protection from destiny.

I was meant to fall, to be here for a time until I could rise again, a phoenix from her ashes after those she trusted set her on fire.

"And now that you've tested *my* accuracy, I wonder how brave *you* might be, Shark. Brave enough to place a coconut on your head and let me take aim?"

His ocean eyes met mine and held. "Of course."

His people shifted uncomfortably, whispering that it was never a good idea to fire at another person who wasn't a threat. They shouted that he didn't need to prove himself to me. Someone reminded him of the nickname I had earned: Scourge.

No, Crest *didn't* have to prove himself to me, but he *wanted* to.

He and I were almost equals again now that I was nearly fully healed. I might rule the sky and he the sea, but when our feet struck land, the scale between us balanced. We once battled one another to tip the scales. I never imagined wanting the pans to sit evenly.

More sweat trickled down his chest, the tiny movement drawing my eyes down to the ring of feathers.

When he took Talay's mark, it seemed to knock him off kilter. As if to offset the jolt, the kiss we shared did the same to me.

I met his eye again. Let one of my brows rise in challenge. A dare. A question. Did he trust me?

Koa's laughter chased Crest to the trees where he took up one of the green orbs. A couple wobbles and falls later and the fruit balanced on his head.

"What are you doing?" Breaker asked uneasily, finally having surfaced from Katalini's lips.

Crest's gaze told me to fire, and fast. Before his brother stopped us.

He trusts me.

He trusted me and I trusted him.

I fired before Breaker forbade it.

The Shark's eyes slowly lifted to the shaft wobbling just inches above his scalp. His hands barely had time to catch the target before it rolled forward into them. When he held the fruit up over his head and let out a cheer, his people joined him. The Shark of the Sea rewarded me with a brilliant smile, one I coveted and committed to memory. Like beams of sunshine streaking defiantly through heavy-laden clouds, they were rare, but oh, how glorious they were when they shone…

Breaker sternly told me to put my bow away as he passed by, abruptly declaring our practice over even though I hadn't harmed a hair on his brother's head. The black scales on his legs absorbed the heavy sunlight as he marched across the sand.

I wondered if he now regretted insisting that Crest's good-standing reputation would somehow help others warm to me. Maybe he regretted that The Salt – their Seer – had insisted that Crest guard me instead of appointing another.

Would Breaker reconsider allowing me my own tent? Confiscate my offending bow once again?

Crest, his deep blue eyes on me, grinned proudly at his angry big brother. I caught a few of the words and phrases the brothers flung at one another: *Careless. Overreacting. Insane. Never in danger. Wipe that ridiculous smile off your face. Never.*

But one word from Crest's lips ended their argument at the same time it erased my grin like the tide wiped away messages written in sand.

Lacuna.

Tension flooded the air after that. Crest's eyes fixed on Breaker's and his smile morphed into an angry scowl. I hated when they fought like this. It wasn't worth it.

I walked away, scanning the clear blue sky for any anomaly, my stomach tense though I found nothing. Waiting and worry, hand-in-hand, always spun in my stomach. Not even Crest's brilliant smile could completely push away the fear I felt now.

My wings were almost free from their bindings. Daily, they felt stronger. More capable. Over time, my pain had eased into ache. Now even the ache waned.

I walked beneath the sun seeking shadow, keeping myself and my wings hidden as best I could. The former General of the Sky, my father, committed treason when he descended to warn me. He told me to stay on Kehlani until I healed and could fly, and he had the chance to discern friend from foe.

He was livid when Breaker suggested using me to broker peace between our people. As a father, he loved me, though I never knew it until he landed before me, voice cracking because I wasn't dead, which he'd feared despite the Oracle telling him I was very much alive.

He wanted me to be free. To be safe. He thought the Isle could provide both.

I think he hoped that in time, things would settle back into their former patterns. That the Oracle would stop seeing visions of me walking on the sand. That those who hunted me would begin to think I truly died the evening I fell. Or perhaps that I'd succumbed to injuries sustained in that tragic battle.

But when he returned to the sky that night, his life was ended. I didn't know how or what his last moments were like, but I knew in my marrow that they weren't peaceful. If he was caught and apprehended, then dragged before the Elders, the Oracle likely read his feather and knew I lived and that I had come to an understanding with my enemies. Just like they would learn my siblings, only hatchlings, were hidden somewhere on Kehlani.

I just hoped she didn't tell them the truth he tried to keep safe and hidden.

Because he was gone, I had no allies in the sky. No one I trusted.

The General said that two of the three members of my quad were hunting me. Not because they wanted to save me from Talay's kind, but to finish what they started. To make sure I couldn't return to the sky.

My commander died from wounds she received during the battle in which I fell. I didn't know the state of things in Empyrean or who had been elevated to her position. Didn't know who paced the floors in the General's study and had access to his great stone tablet that depicted the sea and every creature on it. It showed the Isle and every soul.

If things were different and I wanted to return to Empyrean, and the Elders didn't want to clip and bind me to the firmament… If I would be welcomed and honored among the clouds, it would be *my* right to spar for the position of General and to declare vengeance on the traitors who tried to kill me.

I couldn't deny that I'd thought about doing just that.

Flying back into the clouds, veering toward my nest. Landing in the piazza, blue wings flared menacingly. Malice in my eyes. Vengeance at the tip of my nocked arrow, eager to sink into anyone who tried to touch me.

The Oracle would meet me there, her lavender eyes deepened into amethyst. She would say she'd anticipated my arrival, but the Elders wouldn't have. Oh, the look on their faces. Surprise. Terror.

And I would, before everyone, challenge Soraya and Talon each to a duel – a fight to the death. I would publicly declare their treachery, end their lives, and cleave them into pieces suitable for the hatchlings to devour. Once I was spent and covered in their blood, I would claim the position of General and watch as the Elders schemed to stop me… tried and failed.

The leaf of a broad plant brushed my calf, ripping me from my musings. Reminding me that daydreams were not reality.

Just ahead, my new home came into view.

Breaker had agreed to give me a little more freedom by providing me with a modest tent. He didn't completely unleash me from Crest. I could throw a stone and strike The Shark's home. But he was perfectly content to put some distance between the Scourge and his brother now that things had changed between us.

Crest insisted I have a wooden floor like his, even when I told him that a sand floor like The Salt's – the Seer of Kehlani – would be fine. He, Koa, Frey, and Wade had worked an entire morning to quickly build a frame before laying the planked floor. Then, they helped me raise the tent and secure it on the poles that held it aloft. Ropes anchored it to long copper spikes driven into the ground. The same storms that rocked Empyrean blew across the sand here.

Driving rain.

Unceasing wind.

They were a clash between Neera and Talay. Crest told me that the surf sometimes grew so high it broke over the dunes and flooded the Isle in a rush of seawater and savagery.

Familiar footfalls came from behind me a moment before Crest appeared at my side, holding out one half of a split green coconut as he sipped the sweet water from his half.

The flaps of my tent rapped in the warm wind. This wasn't the first home I'd had. It wasn't the first I'd lived in alone. But it was the first on the sand among these people, besides the one I'd lived in with The Shark right after I crashed into the sea. Small and simple, I couldn't have loved it more if I tried. Because here, even if I was alone, I never truly felt it. Not like I did in the sky.

I accepted the coconut and drank its sweet water. "Thanks."

He nodded.

"You and Breaker quashed your bickering much faster than usual."

His lips started to raise at the corners and I waited… Waited for that brilliant smile to shine on me, as a flower cranes her long neck to the sun. But his smile stalled, then fell.

His gaze was drawn to the ocean.

"What is it?" I asked.

"Did you hear someth –" He tilted his head into the wind. "Someone's calling for help." His half of the coconut fell to the ground as he took off running toward the shore.

I followed with my bow at the ready. "Where is your trident?" I shouted from just behind him, having caught up with him despite the differences in our strides.

"I left it with Koa!" he shouted back. "You need to get inside."

"Is it *them*?" I asked. The Empyreans. My people. Was this it? Had the war finally come?

I reached back for the feel of a feather affixed to wood and found no fletchings. Nothing at all. I cursed. The quiver between my blades was woefully empty, because I'd left our exhibition before recollecting my arrows.

"I don't know," he answered. The land broke apart into sand and it sprayed behind him, arcing with each of his quick steps.

No one and nothing filled the blue sky above. Where, then, was the threat?

Down the beach, Koa and Frey splashed into the water, both using their ear-splitting calls to communicate with Crest before they dove into the waves.

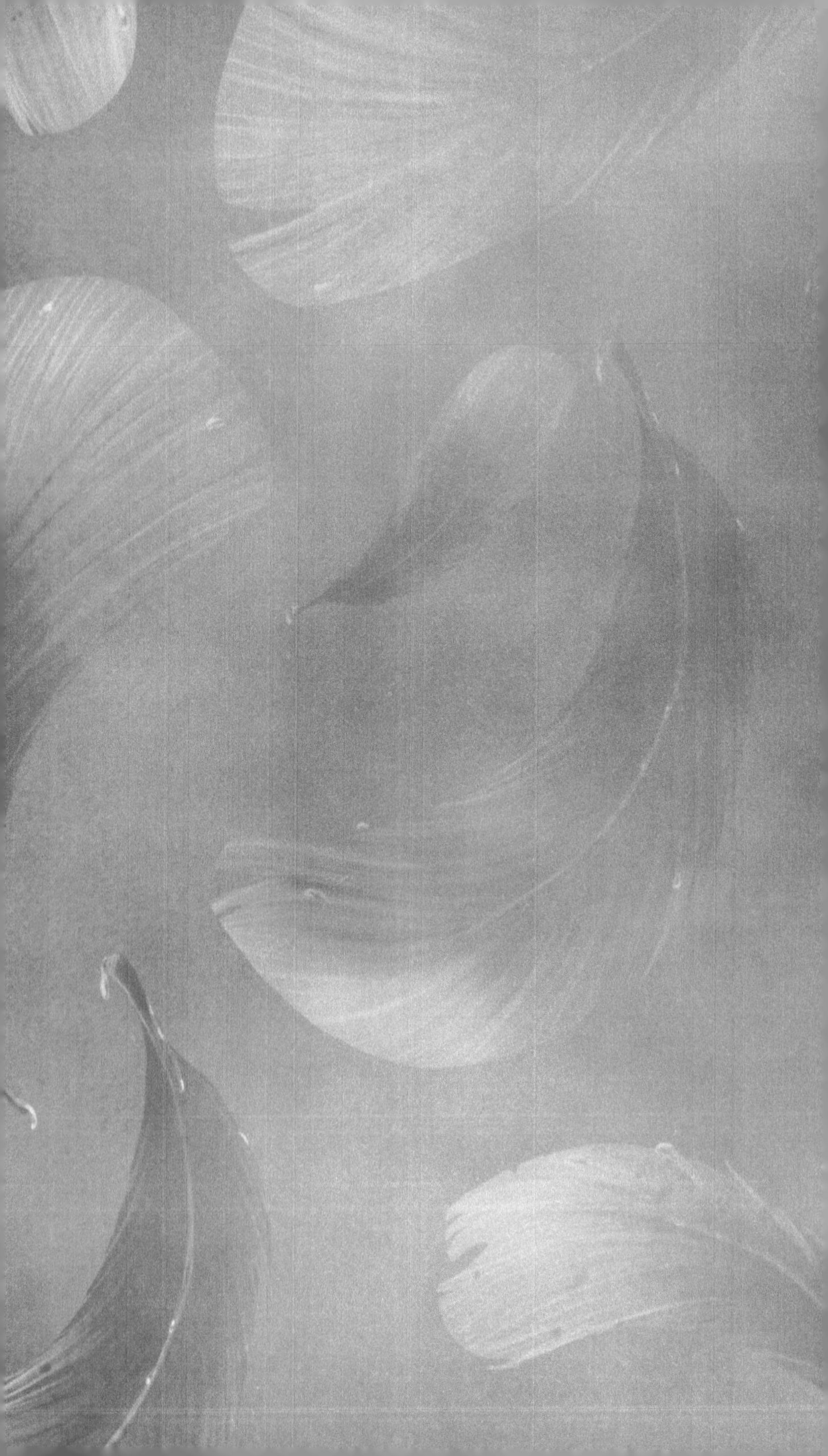

CHAPTER THREE

I tucked my wings in tightly against my back and wondered what was happening and what I could do to help. If I pushed into the sky, the more delicate bones might break again, and if they did, I'd have to begin the healing process anew. I'd be even farther from flying…

But what if they were healed and I was just afraid to test them out and take the next step forward into my future? Afraid that in flying, I might become The Scourge once more.

Farther up shore, a group had gathered. I ran to join them and found Magma standing in their midst, worrying her hands. Crest's grandmother, the Mender of Kehlani, was upset. I knew from her nervousness that someone was hurt and she was waiting to get her hands on them. To help them just as she'd helped me.

She tied her long, silver hair back, preparing to help whoever needed it. "It's Wade," she told me.

Wade? Wade hated me, but he was one of Crest's friends – a fellow Guardian. He was among the best swimmers in the sea.

"Did the attack come from the sky?" I asked nervously.

She shook her head. "Shark attack."

Breaker strode forward from the waiting group. He sensed his brother before anyone else. Crest's head surfaced first, followed by Koa's, Frey's, North's, and a handful of others I couldn't name. They carried Wade from the water. Arms tightly crossed over his chest, his entire body quaked. Magma guided them to a wide blanket I hadn't noticed lying on the other side of the crowd.

There she had cloths, a few basins of fresh water, and threaded needles waiting.

The pale blanket washed red the moment they laid him on it. His entire body trembled violently. His face was extraordinarily pale, and his right leg… was mostly gone. The remaining deep green scales dangled like leaves on a sickly vine.

A wound like this couldn't be stitched. I wasn't sure how Magma could help him at all.

The older woman wasn't deterred or intimidated by the sight of her newest patient. She leapt into action and Crest helped her tie the tourniquet tightly around his thigh. "He's losing too much blood!" she shouted before sending Breaker to her tent to get half a dozen things, some of which she shouted after he'd crossed the dunes.

Wade hyperventilated and sucked in air desperately as if he was a fish on the shore, trying to get water into his gills. His icy blue eyes were wide and brimming with panic and tears. "Help me!" he cried, lifting his head to see the Mender hovering over him. "Magma… am I going to die? I'm dying, aren't I?"

She didn't answer him, other than to tell him to hush and stop raising his head and shoulders. The healer kept a firm hand on his chest. To ground him. But also to reassure him she was there and he wasn't alone.

"Can I help?" I shouted to Magma over the din of panic.

I bit into my palm until it stung and the taste of blood met my tongue, then conjured a cloud of Empyrea in my hands, the power of Neera fidgeting within. Magma hadn't heard me, so I knelt across from her and held the bright Empyrea up to her face. Her eyes lifted to mine, questioning.

The clamor of voices went still, until only the wind and Wade's harsh panting remained.

"It's Empyrea; it's what our kingdom is made of. I think it might help him. I don't know why, but I just… I need to put this on his leg. Will it hurt him?"

Her mouth dropped and her blood-soaked hands went still.

My eyes were feverish, pleading. "I don't want to hurt him, Magma. What do you think?"

For the first time since I'd known her, she uttered the words, "I don't know."

"Try it," Crest insisted. "I held it, and it didn't bother me."

"You weren't wounded, though," I argued. "I don't know whether it will help or –"

Magma's gaze met mine. "It can't hurt him now."

Wade's trembling, I realized, had stopped. His eyes blinked slowly, heavily. He was close to death. He had nothing to lose in taking the risk.

I expanded the cloud, shaped it so it would fit over the end of his injured leg, and applied it, wincing when Wade let out a low moan that even the sound of the surf couldn't muffle.

The Empyrea cloud flooded crimson.

Fingernails piercing the cloud, I urged the lightning inside to intensify. Bright flashes left streaks in my vision, but I pushed the power further, forced it to move faster, to burn hotter. When there was nothing else I could do to strengthen the power in my blood and the cloud had gone from crimson to bright light, I released it, leaving it applied to his leg.

And watched.

And waited.

Breaths sawed in and out of my chest.

The cloud didn't dim. No blood rain fell from it. I wasn't sure if it had helped or if Wade had run out of blood to feed into it. I was afraid to remove the Empyrea from him, but knew I'd done all I could.

"Your chest," Crest whispered, his forehead dipping toward me. Water sluiced from his skin, carrying Wade's blood away in rivulets.

I looked down. My scar flared white beneath my skin. The Empyrea I'd conjured for Wade flared in time with the light beneath my skin.

"Take it off him," Magma quietly ordered.

I couldn't bring myself to yet…

"Elira," she said, catching my attention. "Remove it, please."

Slowly and with trembling fingers, I peeled the Empyrea off his skin the way one would carefully strip away a bandage.

The crowd leaned in to see what had become of his leg… and collectively gasped.

Chests were clutched, mouths covered, prayers uttered to Talay.

Crest choked from where he kneeled beside his grandmother.

Even my lips parted.

Wade's wound was closed, the skin sealed with a burn scar that had already healed. Crest's eyes met mine and in them swam wonder.

"The light and heat…It cauterized his skin," Magma marveled. She placed a hand on his chest. "His heart-beat is strong and steady." Then she wiped her brow and relaxed her tense back. "You just saved his life, Elira."

Breaker, who'd just returned from running for more supplies, arms laden with the items his grandmother had asked him to retrieve, asked everyone to move back to give the Mender room to work. But Magma insisted that Wade be moved to her tent. "It's more private there," she said, warily glancing over the sky.

"Are you sure it's safe to move him?" Koa asked, flip-ping his hair out of his face with one jerk of his neck.

"I wouldn't have asked for it to be done if it wasn't," Magma snipped. "But let me look him over again one more time."

Magma checked Wade's pulse at his neck and wrist. She cupped her hand and felt his warm breath.

"How did you know it was safe to remove it?" I asked Magma, kneeling across from her.

"How did *you* know to apply it and surge it with your power?" she volleyed.

I just knew. I don't know how, but I did.

Her head tilted sideways. She pointed to my side. "Elira, could you have healed your own wound?"

My lips parted and I huffed a small laugh. "Maybe so."

Magma watched me as Crest, Breaker, Koa, Frey, North, and Vasa, the tattooist, divided the blanket evenly, picked up their designated section of hem, and carried Wade to the Mender's tent. She leaned in closer. "I wonder what else you're capable of," she quietly said before stiffly standing up and brushing the sand from her skirt.

Crest found me lingering on the shore. Where the waves swept, the brine had diluted Wade's blood and absorbed it into the sea. There were places the tide hadn't touched, though, patches still stained a deep crimson. "Are you okay?" he asked.

I managed a nod, not sure that what happened had sunk in yet. Maybe the weighty truth lingered like a crimson stain in my mind.

The Shark let out a heavy, pent-up breath and stretched his shoulder blades back to ease the tension he carried there. "The Salt wants to talk to you. She'll be waiting at your tent."

While he was at Magma's workshop, I'd heard her shell horn's distinct sound. My heart dropped, worrying that the Empyrea hadn't been enough to save Wade. That in debating whether I should apply it, I'd taken too long.

I started toward the Mender's tent but stopped myself before I reached the trail that would lead there. I couldn't bear the thought of seeing Wade dead.

I wasn't particularly fond of him, nor was he of me, but he'd put that aside and helped Crest build my floor. He'd walked me down from Flat Rock high in the Green Mountains instead of shoving me over the ledge and wiping his hands of The Scourge.

"Is he…?" I couldn't even bring myself to say it.

The knot in Crest's throat rose and fell. "Wade's alive – thanks to you. He was swimming over a trench alone and the beast came up from the deep. Wade didn't even see the shark before it was tearing him apart." He pinched the bridge of his nose. "He knew better than to swim alone that far out, that deep."

The younglings in Empyrean knew not to fly during a storm, but sometimes, people did what they knew they shouldn't and faced consequences no one would wish on another soul.

"My Commander, Sannika was struck by an arrow just before I fell. I saw in her eyes that she thought if only she'd been watching the archers instead of arguing with me, she might have been able to avoid the shot. She was right. She didn't have to die that day. But I didn't tell her that. It would have been cruel. I lied to her instead. I'm pretty sure she knew it, but she was afraid and the words of hope and denial were a comfort, even if they were false."

"What *did* you say to her?" he rasped.

"I told her she'd be okay." The Shark gave me a look of pity. "My point is that Wade is alive. You didn't lie to him when you told him you'd pull him to safety," I told him. "He'll be haunted by his choice for the rest of his breaths.

He won't need you or anyone else to remind him that it was the wrong one."

He nodded, swallowing thickly.

"Well, I don't want to keep The Salt waiting," I said in parting.

"Have dinner with me?" he asked, a tinge of hope in his voice.

I didn't want to draw him too close, but he needed a friend tonight after what happened today. "Okay."

He stared out at the sea, at the task that was now required of him. Most sharks kept away from Talay's kind, he'd once told me. It was almost as if they could sense that they were equals and not prey. But there were always exceptions, and the shark that bit Wade was dangerous and had to be hunted and killed. Crest was duty-bound to slay it.

I jutted my chin toward the deep. "Be careful out there."

"Always am," he promised.

It unsettled me to think that Wade was likely careful, too, and it didn't matter. Sometimes calamity came, even when you did everything in your power to prevent it.

I scanned the sky for any threat to him, any predator perched above. When I found nothing but empty blue, I started toward my home to meet the Seer.

Every step away from Crest felt heavier than the last, even as a gentle wind blew against my back as if nudging me away from him and toward the Seer. I opened my palm and caught as much as my hand could hold, keeping the slight, swirling air trapped for a time. It tickled my skin as it moved, antsy, never able to keep still.

The Great Wind reminded me of Neera's lightning in that respect, but there was no threat in it most days. There was no hatred or pointed malice like her bolts held.

The Empyrean Scholar, Era, claimed that the first soul Neera created lay hidden within me, and the woman who first housed the soul could control the Great Wind. I thought he was grasping, hoping that the first unique spirit and the powers she was blessed with might somehow help our people. Until last night.

I'd rushed to the shore, unable to breathe. Needing to feel the wind and know they weren't really there… even when rational thought told me they *couldn't* be.

Whenever I closed my eyes, all I could see was my father and mother's wide, empty eyes as they bobbed on the sea just beyond the breaking waves, their hands clasped so tightly, not even the waves could pull them apart. Stars reflected in their eyes as they gazed upward, unseeing. The sky had forsaken them, and their vacant stares accused me of the same.

In my dream, the Great Wind slid through my feathers as I soared above them and left them to the sea as I glided toward Empyrean. In my dream, I'd bent that wind and used it to do my bidding. To test the dream, I reached out my hand and caught some. I never thought I'd be able to take hold of it; to warp, bend, or influence the Great Wind. The breath of all things.

And yet I did.

I pried my fingers open and set the bit of wind free. Slipping coolly from my hand, it ruffled the sea oats as it flitted away.

To my people, the name Elira meant freedom. To Talay's it meant sky.

My heart believed both were fitting and both pointed toward my future. I just didn't know if I should free the sky from the tyrants who ruled it, or free myself from the sky kingdom once and for all, as Aderyn had.

Maybe The Salt could see my path more clearly now. She might not be able to see my future, but what if she could see where my feet last pressed into the wet sand? In which direction would my future-self walk?

The soles of my feet led me into the trees where I could hide and disappear for a time. Where I could rest and think and worry without burdening anyone else.

The Salt matched me in height, but she was curvier in the hips and breasts and far prettier than I would ever be. Her long, dark braids were adorned with scalloped shells today, with her signature cowrie necklaces draped over her chest. Her dark skin glowed dewy and fresh. Perfectly put together.

But I'd seen her tear all of that away. I'd seen The Salt cover herself with ash. Watched her claw at her skin and rend her clothes because, like the wisp of wind I'd just grasped, she caught a *feeling* of what awaited me if I returned to the sky. She couldn't see past the clouds with her sight to know what would befall me, but a simple, guttural feeling sent her into a tailspin. Like a seed with a single wing, swirling recklessly to the ground.

Waiting before my tent, she was the picture of steadiness. Her strength made it easier to breathe. Her smile made me want to keep walking, one foot in front of the other. And the warmth in her heart had over time begun to melt the ice in mine.

In the safe crook of her elbow, she cradled the bowl of cowries – one to represent every person alive in Kehlani who belonged to Talay.

He'd claimed me the instant I splashed into the sea, so I had a shell, too. One that once bore a vivid blue impression on its back of splayed wings. That image had faded, and I knew it meant that something would change. Either I would leave Talay's kingdom, or I would leave this life.

The Seer never said when or which either would happen, but the shell was already faded, so I knew it wouldn't be long now.

"Elira," the Seer greeted, wearing a lovely sunset orange top and skirt.

"Crest said you wanted to see me."

She ticked her head toward the door. "It's best that we speak inside."

I was afraid she'd say that. The Seer had been busy lately and I hadn't seen her as often as I had before my father fell. So when Crest said she wanted to see me, I figured it was because she'd spoken to Talay and needed to deliver a message to me from the sea god.

My tent was mostly bare. The only thing in it was a small table with a cup and plate, and in the back, Crest's bed. The one I'd healed upon after shattering upon the sea.

He and Koa had hefted his over to my tent while I was away. I would've refused them if they'd asked beforehand. I *tried* to refuse them when I showed up in the middle of the move unannounced, but Koa griped that the blasted piece of furniture was too heavy to lug back. He even rubbed his back dramatically and groaned – loudly and fakely, I might add.

Crest insisted he'd already hung a fabric hammock in his house and claimed he preferred it to the bed, adding he didn't want the bulky furniture anymore because the hammock made him feel like he was floating in the sea and he slept more soundly in it than he ever had in the bed he'd given me.

I told him that in the hammock, he would look like a fish caught up in a net, which made him laugh instead of encouraging him to be reasonable.

I had little choice but to accept his gift and wave them inside. Koa's backache was instantly forgotten and they took the time to set it up for me.

So, like the goddess in her sanctum, here the bed lurked in the dark corner of my home. Bearing his scent so I had no choice but to close my eyes and breathe him in. I couldn't possibly put him out of my mind even for a moment.

I cleared the table, placing everything stacked upon it on the floor. "I haven't made chairs yet," I told her sheepishly.

"You saved Wade," she noted, dumping her bowl of shells onto the table immediately. "I was hoping you might help *me*."

"Help *you*?" Did she have a wound I couldn't see? No blood trailed her steps.

"Help me understand," she whispered absently as she waited and watched the cowries. I wanted to ask her what she was struggling with, what she didn't know. She was Talay's Seer, after all.

But then the shells began to vibrate as if the table itself shook. Slowly, I crouched down to watch the tabletop at eye level. The wood did not move. I pressed a hand to the floor planks. They weren't trembling, either. The cowries were the only things jumping.

I stood again and searched the patterns until I found Breaker's and Crest's shells. The brothers' cowries were easily recognizable to me now, along with Frey's and Koa's.

"Have you sought her out?" she asked, glancing at me from under her bent brow. I knew she meant Aderyn. The last time The Salt and I spoke, she'd told me I should make amends in case the opportunity to do so passed me by.

"No."

I *had* gone looking. Not to tell her I was thankful she was alive, even though somewhere deep down inside, I was. I'd never admit that to her or anyone else. She didn't deserve it. Just like she didn't deserve my concern anymore. Instead of unburdening her heart to me, she faked her death and left me to mourn her. No... I went searching for Aderyn because I wanted to claw her eyes out.

If I wanted anything, it was for Aderyn to suffer as I suffered. To hurt as I hurt. I just didn't want to harm the hatchlings by causing harm to her.

But as the days and hours passed, I realized she would never hurt as I had. She would never feel what I felt because she didn't love me as I loved her.

Aderyn was like a sister to me my entire life before I knew we were truly siblings, even if only by half. We shared a sire, I now knew. She had known the truth far longer and hadn't told me. She'd kept it hidden away with her duplicity.

If only she'd confided in me with her plans, I would have gladly shared in the risk and reward of protecting our hatchling siblings from the greedy claws of the Elders the same way we shared victories and defeats, worries and questions that came with growing older and into new skin. Entering new seasons of life with her was thrilling because we were close.

Or as close as any pair could be in the sky.

I didn't know the true meaning of the word *sister* until I saw the brotherly bond between Breaker and Crest flex and bend, ebb and flow, never breaking. But Aderyn did not consider me her sibling. She didn't consider me her family and certainly didn't see me as her friend.

Aderyn turned her back on me long before she left that night, so why should I seek her out to make peace between us?

Still, I wanted to see my hatchling siblings and know they were well, even if only from a distance. But I was the sky's primary target. My father's last warning was that I was being hunted. The last thing I wanted was for anyone in Empyrean to find the hatchlings my father gave his life to save, and Aderyn sacrificed her wings to protect.

"The shark attacking Wade was a very bad omen," The Salt confided, still watching the jittery shells. Goosebumps spread over my arms and neck. "But I fear something far worse is coming."

"We know that."

"It's not the war I speak of," she clarified, her dark eyes slicing to mine.

The shells kept vibrating across the table, but never arranged themselves into any particular pattern. Was she asking them a question about me? Was my shell now blank like my father's – The General's?

"Can they no longer sense me?" I asked, voice as raw as my heart.

Before I came here, I feared dying but accepted and faced the inevitability anyway. I'd been struck by lightning and incapacitated while flying, but still rose the next day to fly and fight for the sky. Back then, I was more afraid of losing my standing than anything else.

It reminded me of Aderyn's return to the sea after being rolled by the waves. That wasn't part of the plan she'd carefully hatched behind my back. She must have been terrified to get near the water so soon after the wave almost took her under.

Now I knew it was because her plan to live with the hatchlings had almost drowned along with her.

My thumb ran across the raised line where Magma had sewn up the arrow wound that sent me here. I was terrified of dying now. When they carried me from the water, just as they'd lifted Wade, I was so close to it that even Magma hadn't expected me to live.

The Salt pinched her lip. "There's nothing amiss with the shells. I just don't understand them. They're nervous. Like everyone in Kehlani is afraid all at once and of the same thing."

"But you don't think it's the war?"

She shook her head. "It's not that. I know it's not that…" Slowly, patiently, she collected them back into her bowl.

"Do you think it has to do with me?"

She paused, then shook her head resolutely. "Your shell is among the others."

That meant the shells indicated that I, too, was afraid.

I wondered why she came to me with this. I had no direct connection to Talay. If she wanted to speak with him, she could wade into his sea and spend the day. "Have you asked Talay?"

She picked up the last shell. The faded blue pattern indicated it was mine. "I have, but he hasn't divulged what it means. Sometimes, I'm not meant to know. Not meant to warn. But he showed me something else. That's why I'm here."

I swallowed thickly. "What did he reveal?"

"Talay woke me late last night with a vision. He called me to the sea, so I went. I walked onto the sand and stepped into the surf, and Talay revealed that you were standing in the ocean with me."

Even with a quarter of the Isle between us, she sensed me.

"I was there," I confirmed. The goosebumps pebbling my arms and neck spread down my spine.

"I knew your father, Elira. He came to me first. Unarmed, with a guarded expression. He told me he meant me no harm and Talay told me he was being honest. By the time he touched down upon the shore, his shell was already pinched in my fingers. I was so afraid of him. I'd feared him much of my childhood, remembering the fury on his face and people shouting warnings about the black-winged warrior. He was the best of your kind when he was young. Before he rose to the role of Commander, then General. At one time, *he* was our Scourge. But the night he came to humbly ask for help, he left his fierce reputation in the sky. He was afraid and he told me so. He begged me not to kill him, then begged me for help.

"Last night, I dreamed of him floating on the sea, his eyes fixed on the stars. He held the hand of a woman I did not know. You flew circles above them before flying away, back to the sky kingdom. One minute, I could see and sense you. The next, you were obscured by Empyrean's clouds." She looked down at her shells. "Are you planning to return, Elira?"

I shook my head. "I've made no plans, Salt, but I understand why you'd question me, given the vision. After all, I had the same vision and questioned myself on the matter. The woman you saw holding my father's hand was my mother," I croaked. "She died not long before I fell. I don't know what the dream means, but it's concerning that we shared the same one. Is it pointing me toward Empyrean?"

She sighed. "I can't tell you where it leads, but after last night, I know the weight of the guilt you feel because of their deaths. I just wanted to tell you that I understood, in case you wanted to talk about it with anyone."

I didn't want to talk. What was there to say? Respectfully declining, I said, "Thank you."

"Can I be bold for a moment?" she asked.

"The bold don't ask for permission," I teased.

She gave a sheepish grin. "How is Crest dealing with your rejection of him?"

My brows furrowed. "What do you mean, my rejection of him?"

"As his lacuna," she amended.

I shook my head. "I… He never expected me to be his lacuna. He certainly didn't want me to be. Talay should choose another."

"I think you and Crest need to talk. Talay doesn't *choose* for us; he only reveals what one's heart will ultimately want. Did you and Crest talk about what it means to be lacunas? Did he tell you that Talay *won't* reveal another?"

"Ever?" I asked, my heart panicking for him.

She shook her head.

"He didn't tell me that." Or anything. We hadn't talked because I hadn't given him the chance.

She pressed her eyes closed. "I think it would help if you asked Crest about the tradition."

"I'm not meant to be his lacuna," I told her more adamantly.

She ignored my statement and situated the bowl of shells in the crook of her arm, suddenly staring at the tent wall closest to the sea. "I'm here, Elira. But if you won't speak freely to me, consider Crest. He'll be there to listen when you feel strong enough to let someone in."

"Strong enough? Isn't it weak to reveal your vulnerabilities to others?" If someone knew your weaknesses, they could exploit them and use the knowledge against you.

She shook her head. "It takes far more strength to trust someone with them and let someone into our vulnerable inner thoughts and feelings. Our hearts weren't made to hold an ocean of regret, and yours holds many seas."

CHAPTER FOUR

"Sannika said you're to fight Jorun," Aderyn quietly informed me as our peers gathered in clusters all around the sparring ground.

Jorun was a threat. He was tall, but not lanky like the other boys. And he was fast.

"I can conjure some Empyrea for you," she offered.

I nodded and took the tiny clouds she quickly made and stuffed them into my nose. If he broke it, Aderyn's clouds would absorb my blood. "One for my mouth," I asked, hand waiting at my side so no one else saw.

"Beat him, Elira," she told me, placing the Empyrea in my palm. "If we can make it to the top of the Youngling class, we won't have to spar as often. We won't have as much to prove…"

"Then they'll elevate us, and we'll have to start a much larger ascent," I reminded her. "Who are you fighting?"

"Soraya," she spat.

"When?"

"After you're through wiping the firmament with Jorun's face."

I tried to smile, shaking the nerves from my fingertips before placing her Empyrea in my mouth.

There was no way to guard against a split brow or lip, save the greasy salve I slathered over my face. I just had to hope I was quicker than him, avoid his jabs, and end this match before he exposed my blood.

This never got easier. Every time I sparred, the risk overwhelmed me. But I wouldn't let fear win. I would not be clipped.

Aderyn patted my back as I strode toward my opponent. "Be quick."

It was what we always told one another.

A wish and a prayer wrapped into two short words.

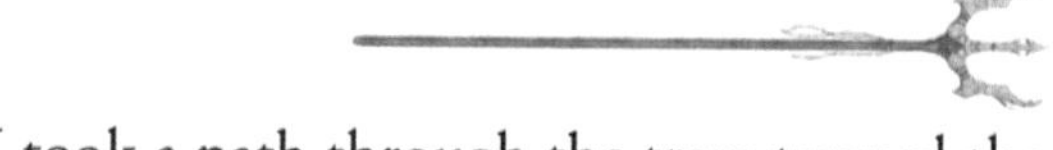

I took a path through the trees toward the grove the next morning, quiver half full of arrows on my back and my bow in hand. I'd never been gladder that Breaker listened when my father insisted he allow me to arm myself than when I crossed paths with North, who'd already tried to kill me once and had threatened me in every way imaginable since I landed on their shores.

His upper lip curled when he saw me, an arrow at the ready. He was alone and carried a sack of fruit on his side, the bag's thick strap slung across his chest. He spat toward my feet as he passed me by, muttering something vile and adding *Scourge* for good measure.

To his chagrin, I quickly stepped out of the path of his phlegm.

I never turned my back to him, but watched as he strode back toward the village wearing an air of confidence like the one I once wore. I thought about planting my arrow in his back. From this nominal distance, I could send it right through his heart.

If it wouldn't upset Crest and Breaker, I would have sent it soaring.

At some point, he and I would have it out and it wouldn't end well for one of us. Before I fell, I would've been certain I would emerge the victor. But such arrogant bravado had failed me. Like thick morning fog, it swelled around me. Soraya had hidden herself within it. When she stabbed me, she poisoned the overinflated opinion I harbored of myself.

I'd become a realist, I supposed.

The edge of the grove loomed before me, the sun's soft light filtering through the leaves to speckle the ground. The sweet scent of ripening fruit filled the air. Most of the trees' bounty was plucked when the fruit was ripe or near enough to it, but some pieces were inevitably missed. They hung too long on the branch and eventually fell to the ground. It was how the grove perpetuated its legacy, the seeds sinking into the rich soil, made richer by the rot. The fallen pieces gave the bees something sweet to turn into honey. It gave game something other than vegetation to enjoy. Something by which to be nourished.

A small, tawny deer went rigid when I stepped off the trail and into the trees, snapping a branch underfoot. Its ears pointed outward, the furry canals facing me; its nose sniffed the air. As we stared at one another, I looked at the creature's large brown eyes and the pale spots adorning its back. Something just beyond it moved. The fawn's mother watched me over the back of her offspring, keeping the youngling in sight.

Then, the animals' heads jerked to the left where a muscled, prowling mountain cat large enough for me to ride with fur the color of wet sand gracefully stalked forward. Crest had warned me of these creatures. He said they mostly kept to the mountains but would sometimes wander as they followed their prey. They were dangerous and deadly.

It targeted the fawn. Planting its large paws, the feline eased back on its haunches and poised to spring forward.

Mother and youngling both recognized the stance. The deer bolted.

Instantly, I drew an arrow, nocked it, and aimed at the cat in case it reevaluated its options and decided to choose me instead.

The beast left before I needed to fire. It gave chase to the graceful, fleet-footed animals, but the great cat was faster still as its sleek form blurred through the maze of tree trunks.

I eased my bowstring back to resting.

A feral, animalistic scream made the hair on my neck rise. The sound came from just a few yards away. Soon the sound was followed by a worse noise: a miserable bleating. Pain and fear flowed in desperate shrieks from the animal the cat had brought down. I slinked forward to see, wondering if I should kill the dying prey so it didn't suffer needlessly.

The beast dug its sharp incisors into the deer's throat and severed its voice along with its life.

It growled when it realized I was near and postured to defend its kill.

Slowly, I backed away, giving it a wide berth.

The strap of the bag on my shoulder slipped down my skin, reminding me of its emptiness. I moved through the varying fruit trees until I was far, far from that cat. It would be busy for a while, but there was no need to test its foul temper.

Climbing was far easier now that my wings could flex and move with me. My balance had gradually improved. And when I came to the grove, often my mood did, too. Though only recently had I been allowed to come alone.

I smiled remembering how intensely I'd resented The Shark's guardianship at first, his stifling, constant presence. That was before I knew and believed him when he said he didn't kill Aderyn. But even when he was as sour as the grapefruit at the bottom of my bag, he was there and I wasn't alone, even when I'd lost all connection to the sky and my position in its bitterly cold hierarchy.

Slowly, the empty space in my bag was filled with sweet apples, juicy mangoes, and tart citrus. The fruits not only nourished, but lent their sweetness and flavor to those brave enough to climb and pluck them.

Life was like that bag… what you filled it with mattered. And what consumed your time, consumed you.

I moved among the branches, feeling lighter with my feet off the ground. Watched the birds flitting to and from their nests. Sat in the treetops and felt the Great Wind brush my feathers. *Soon*… Soon I would be able to fly again.

Two voices drifted through the grove. On the sun-speckled ground, Crest walked with Nori – a female who wanted him more than she cared about whose mark lay on his chest. She was the foul, spitting sister to North. In addition to her brother, she and I had already had one altercation.

My feathers bristled at their volleying voices. *He deserves a new lacuna*, I told myself. But I hoped with everything in my heart that he wouldn't choose *her* to take my place.

Their conversation was light. She inquired about his grandmother and praised Magma's skill in keeping Wade alive. Nori told Crest she had visited him earlier that morning in the Mender's workshop and he remained quiet when she sat beside him, although he'd squeezed her hand when she took hold of his.

They were friends. All of them had grown up together, swimming in the sea between leviathans and kraken, racing each other over the land, climbing the grove trees and Green Mountains. They slipped into adolescence behind the heavy curtains of the falls and splashed barefooted through the streams that bled into the sea.

They were friends, and she worried for him.

"What's bothering you?" she finally asked.

"Nothing. Why do you ask?"

"You say that," she said gently, "but I see otherwise. I've known you my whole life, Crest. I know when something's wrong."

He waved away her concern but stared off into the grove, refusing to meet her eye.

Unhurried, they passed the tree in which I was perched. Quietly, I shifted to watch them.

"Wade knows he will never walk again. I could see it in his eyes. He's giving up. How do we help him?" she asked, sounding choked up.

"He'll have to learn to live without his leg," Crest told her as if there was no question. "It'll take time, but he's up to the task. And we will be there with him. He just needs to know *we* haven't given up on him."

I gripped the branch overhead as a sudden thought came to me...I'd carved a bow. Carved my quiver. A leg could be carved and somehow attached to his form. Perhaps there was a way to even mimic the mechanics of natural movement. Magma could help guide my carving knife.

I looked back to Crest and Nori to find her smallest finger reaching out to brush the side of his hand.

"Don't," he warned her, walking away and placing several feet between them.

"She doesn't want you. Or at least that's what it looks like to everyone watching from the outside," she said, her voice wavering. "She kissed you as part of a *game*, Crest. She didn't expect to hear Talay. None of us imagined he would reveal *her*."

"But he did," he argued, raking a hand through his hair. "He did and I need you to respect it, even if you don't want it to be her."

"I don't want it to be anyone but me," she tearfully admitted, swiping at her cheeks. "How can your heart possibly want your greatest enemy?"

He hesitated for a moment, then opened his arms. "I don't know how to swim through all the converging currents," he admitted softly.

She planted herself against his chest and snaked her hands around his back as he closed his around hers. I wished I was anywhere else in the world. "If anyone can, it's you," she said sadly.

When Crest and Nori finally released one another and continued their walk, I slipped down the branches, my feet smacking the ground too loudly for comfort. I quickly wended through the trees toward the trail that would take me home.

The cat was still there in the orchard feeding, its maw bloody. She possessively crouched over her kill when I slipped by.

At the trailhead, two younglings approached, laughing and shoving one another. The boys' steps stopped when they saw me. Each held their breath for a moment until it forced its way out again. "Scourge," one addressed me, frightened but holding his ground. He puffed his chest out as if that might scare me. His friend wasn't quite as brave and moved back one slow step at a time.

"You shouldn't go into the orchard," I warned. "There's a great cat just within the grove's boundary that just killed a small deer." The boy farthest away looked down at his empty bag. He must need the fruit… "I could collect some for you," I offered.

The loud, puffed-up fellow made a disgusted sound. "Never."

"Very well. Since you won't be deterred, if you must enter the grove, I suggest you keep to its edge," I advised, pointing in the direction they should go.

They eased around me the same way I'd eased around the feeding feline.

Then they ran, not heeding my words *at all.* They rushed straight toward the testy beast. The boys were barely larger than the fawn the creature had just taken down and feasted upon. If they startled her or the cat felt the need to protect her kill from them as she had me…

I raced after them, shouting at them to stop or at least not to run in the direction they were headed. The younglings didn't listen, of course, they just pushed faster. The two boys were impressively fast on the soil.

And then, silence. Small feet pounded the ground no longer. No rushed breaths sawed in and out. No more shrieks or shouts came to urge one another further, faster.

My wings flexed on my back. Hair on the back of my neck stood on edge when a guttural growl rumbled just ahead.

"Help!" one of the boys suddenly yelped.

My feet flew, but I knew, *knew* I couldn't reach them unless *I* did, too.

When I fully extended my wings, my remaining bindings broke and fell to the ground in tatters. I pushed into the air, weaving beneath and between the low-bent branches. I swept in front of the younglings, an arrow drawn back as the cat, who'd been startled, swiped at the one nearest her.

"Don't kill her!" the boy just behind me shouted in defense of the beast who would've gutted them. "The cats are important."

We didn't have time to discuss the balance between Isle predators and prey. The cat wasn't retreating. It growled and swiped the air again as if daring me to let my arrow loose. It would strike her in the eye and end her quickly, but the younglings would call me a monster.

Not that they already didn't.

My wings beat behind me, disturbing the dried leaves caking the ground.

My feet dangled beneath me for the first time in three moon cycles.

Time seemed to slow.

The mountain cat seemed mesmerized by their movement and provided just enough of a distraction to give me time to sling my bow over my shoulder and quickly secure the nearest boy under my right arm. I turned and swooped to grab the second, who willingly reached for me, and took off.

Some would've called him a coward for willingly begging his enemy for help, but he was no more cowardly than I was. He hadn't puffed up and called me a name, daring me to talk back like his friend had. He simply moved away. He was the smarter of the two, preserving himself at all costs. And he was the one who cried out for help when they needed it most.

Both boys screamed as we rose out of the cat's reach and out of the grove. They kicked their feet so hard I thought they might tear out of my arms, so I snarled at them. "Keep still unless you want to splatter onto the earth like a raindrop!"

"You'll kill us!" the one who thought himself brave squealed.

"If I wanted you dead, I wouldn't have saved you from that beast! Now, stay still until I land."

They listened after that, finally taming their panic.

I brought them to the earth at the trailhead where I'd first met the pair. The boy who'd called for help immediately breathed his quick and quiet thanks. His friend didn't have such manners. He took off running, dust and sand kicking up into low clouds behind his swift feet. He pumped his arms and was soon out of sight as the trail bent to the right.

"Wait!" the youngling cried after his friend, trailing a few steps before realizing it was futile to try to catch up to him.

"We should've listened to you," the youngling admitted.

I wasn't sure what to say that wouldn't frighten him. He was obviously shaken from the entire ordeal, so I stowed my words and inclined my head, accepting his apology and hoping he'd learned his lesson and he might see me as something other than a monster now. On quaking legs, the boy plodded down the trail toward the villages, leaving the bounty of the grove behind.

Speaking of bounty, most of the fruit had spilled from my bag during the encounter. Only one lemon, a small red apple, and two bulbous grapefruits remained. They would have to do. I wasn't going back into the trees today. The bees and gnats could find and enjoy what I lost.

My wings were sore, but they'd carried me *and* the boys with their flailing legs. My bones hadn't snapped. I stretched them out wide and sighed at the feeling, relieved. They'd been bound for so long…

"Elira?" Crest's voice reached out to me from the edge of the grove. "We heard a commotion."

Nori stood at his side, looking pretty in a pale-yellow smock with a matching flower tucked behind her ear. Her long, dark hair blew sideways in the wind, brushing over his chest and the lacuna mark as if trying to erase it from his skin, or crawl over it to obscure it like leafy vines over rock.

I pushed into the air, keeping as low as I could as I flew toward home, leaving them to embrace and comfort one another. I refused to acknowledge the errant tear that fell the moment I turned my back on him.

The Great Wind brushed it away.

As if it was the first right thing I'd done. As if it was what I was meant to do.

CHAPTER FIVE

Crest had asked if we could have dinner, but after today's strangeness, I expected him to change his mind or blow me off. Instead, he came to my tent that evening with enough fish for a solid meal, then took the grapefruit from my hand and stole half without asking. I'd planned to eat it *and* the apple for dinner – also intending to dine alone.

The Shark went about his business, working around me. He didn't ignore me, exactly. He acknowledged my presence but didn't make eye contact. I realized he was comfortable in my space and with me, taking part in the end-of-the-day moments that somehow seemed like ours.

Even if he was upset, he was here. Even though today was awful, he wanted to end it with me.

I'd collected a substantial amount of wide, heavy rocks from the bank of a river that emptied nearby from the

Green Mountains, bringing them home one by one, where I fashioned a circle with them right outside my tent. The rocks contained the fires I managed to kindle and allowed to die. I didn't trust a small ring inside, even though Crest offered to build one and promised that if I only added small pieces, I'd be safe.

Neatly stacked beside the porch was a new, solid wall of firewood, courtesy of him, I was sure. Though I wasn't sure how he managed to build it today while I was gone, because he had been, too.

He took several of the split logs and built his signature wooden tower within the rocks, then sat quietly with me on the wooden porch protruding from the front of my tent.

The flames caught and grew from the coal he'd carried over, slowly overtaking the wood. It was humid and still warm, but the sun had gone down. The fire's heat wasn't overbearing in the twilight.

We sat beside one another a very long time without speaking until the bats came down from their mountain cave for their nightly feast. Finally, his silence grated on my patience.

"What are you doing?" I asked, trying to keep my impatience from oozing into my tone.

The corner of his mouth rose just a little. "I thought that much was obvious."

"It's not," I griped, hugging my middle. My thumb grazed the scar Soraya gave me.

His eyes didn't meet mine when he answered, "I'm here to make dinner and eat with you."

I shouldn't have told him we could share this meal. I thoroughly regretted it now. Other than half a grapefruit and half an apple, I had nothing to offer him in return for the fish and fire he'd brought. Not even civil conversation, apparently.

"Your wings are healed," he noted. "Are they strong enough to carry you to Empyrean?"

Was he upset that I'd flown?

I shrugged my shoulders, feeling the comfortable, familiar weight of them on my back. "Likely yes."

"But you still haven't left Kehlani…" he led.

"Are you asking a question, or suggesting that I leave?" I turned to him and waited for him to finally look at me. When he did, I saw what Nori noticed. What I'd seen for weeks and hadn't asked him about because I was a coward. Crest was troubled. Upset.

Emotions too great to be named lingered with sadness in the deeper shades of blue in his eyes and surfaced with the lighter hues.

Sadness– a leviathan in and of itself, weaving a lonely path through life's depths.

He angled his entire body to face me then. "I'd *never* ask you to leave. I'd never want you to. I only ask that you tell me first if you make that decision."

"Of course I would tell you," I croaked. "Unless I had no other choice, I would speak to you first, Crest. I owe you that much at least."

"You don't *owe* me anything, Elira. Are you still considering bartering your blood and future for peace?" he asked with a sharp edge to his words that cut into me.

"Have you considered the number of your people who will die in this battle if nothing is done?"

"You don't truly believe the war will end if you return, do you?"

I didn't and he knew it. "Someone has to do *something*, Crest. Someone has to *try*, even if the attempt fails."

"Why does it have to be you?" he countered. "We can find another way."

And yet, no other way was visible. Not to Breaker, who led his people, and not to Crest, who led the Guardians. Not even to The Salt, Seer of Talay.

"You know why," I rasped.

I had what they wanted. What they coveted more than anything: Power.

We were running out of time. Empyrean had been suspiciously quiet. There had only been a handful of descents to gather fish and fruit. Just enough to keep them *barely* fed. I watched the skies as constantly as possible because when they flew down en masse to gather food for a feast, it meant war was imminent.

I knew it was coming – soon. I could feel it.

"Are the Guardians still spread out, watching the skies?"

He nodded. "We've cast our net."

Neither Crest nor I was naïve enough to believe that Empyrean's leaders would be satisfied with slipping into a peaceful neutral with Talay's kind. They didn't just want access to the sea and grove for food; they wanted to control them both. To avoid being beholden to anyone else. To avoid an even greater war in the future.

Empyrean had been built upon an unquenchable thirst for power, and those vying for power would never be sated until they had it all.

"You saved those boys today." Tension bled from his shoulders. I watched them sink. "Their parents are grateful."

My eyes slid from the fire to him. I watched his lithe movements as he folded his fingers together and leaned forward, forearms on his thighs.

"In one swoop, you saved two children and became a Guardian in the eyes of my people."

I pursed my lips. "Hardly."

"Their parents went to Breaker and asked him to thank you. He'll tell you himself when he has the chance. He's very busy."

A Guardian in the eyes of his people? Yet they were too afraid to thank me personally instead of involving Breaker and Crest and asking them to relay their appreciation. How odd.

Crest intuited my thoughts. "They don't hate you anymore, Elira, but the absence of hate doesn't mean fear has also abated."

"I did what anyone would do if they had the means," I argued, flexing my wings. I sighed. Make no mistake, they *did* hate me. They might be more tolerant of me now, but forbearance was not absolution.

"Our people know you risked breaking the bones in your wings again. They understand the pain you'd suffer and the time you would lose in waiting for them to heal again. Beyond that, they know you put your life before theirs. It seems to be your nature – to protect."

No one in the sky would say that of me. How could it be true of me now just because my feet struck sand instead of cloud?

I winced as I considered the Mender's temperament. "Is Magma upset?"

He grinned. "She's glad you did it, but she fussed over the thought of having to set your wings again."

I offered a closed-lip smile.

"Wings or none, you'd have put yourself between those boys and the mountain lion no matter the cost. You've done it before. It's your instinct. It isn't just to claw your way to the top. It's not selfish. It's protective."

I gave a rueful smile, embarrassed. "You give me far too much credit. You didn't know me in the sky." I was terrible. As harsh and cruel as everyone else wanted to be, yet not nearly as awful as Neera expected me to become.

When Crest peered at me with his sea blue eyes, I couldn't look away. His lips parted. "I know you now, though."

Sometimes Crest saw me the way the Seers did. He saw parts I sometimes wished could be kept hidden. But in the end, I was glad he saw and knew, because I saw and knew him, too. I couldn't say that with anyone else. I couldn't even say it was true of me and Aderyn.

Talay had declared us lacunas, but in doing so, he'd given me my first *true* friend. One who cared about me in ways I wasn't sure I could reciprocate, but desperately wanted to try.

I cleared my throat. "I saw you with Nori in the grove." The wood in the fire popped, spewing sparks and settling again. "I saw you hold her."

I wasn't upset because of their contact. It was what any friend in Kehlani might have done for the other. I was upset because, though we were now friends, I couldn't give him that kind of affection. It wasn't just because I wasn't used to it. It was because it would further encourage the lacuna bond Talay had made. It surged between us, a silent pulse echoing between our hearts.

"She was upset about Wade," he began to explain, so I put up my hand. I didn't bring it up to him because I was jealous.

"She noticed what I've seen for weeks. You seem sad. I wish you'd tell me what's bothering you."

"I'm not *sad* at all," he said, frustration hardening his tone.

"Then what are you?"

He shook his head. "Not in the mood to talk about me."

The wood popped again, punctuating the finality of his words.

The flames had died down into the tower's middle, no longer lapping at the top. He placed the pan and filets over it. We'd shared many meals since I fell, but none that felt as significant as this. I felt connected to him in a way I didn't understand.

"It's shark," he noted, jutting his chin toward the meat.

"The one that attacked Wade, I assume."

"The same. It had a distinctive scar. I saw it when I pulled Wade away from it… It circled just below us, like it was considering rushing back to finish what it started. Most don't do that. They mistake us for prey and when they bite, realize it right away and leave. This one knew what he'd bitten and wanted more." His eyes slid sideways. "So, did The Salt impart any wisdom I should know about?"

"How subtle you are," I teased. I leaned forward and blew out a heavy breath. "She said the cowries are troubled… and she was awakened last night because Talay showed her the nightmare that woke me."

He sat up straighter. "You had another one?"

I brushed off his concern with a shake of my head. "The dreams don't mean anything. I'm no Seer, Crest. I'm more concerned that The Salt and her shells are unsettled."

He scrubbed his face. "Yet you had the same dream as The Salt."

"You look tired," I told him, changing the subject.

"Thanks," he teased. "The Guardians spread out during the day, but there are fewer to keep watch at night. I've been guarding the shore nearest our homes."

It shouldn't be his responsibility to bear alone. "Did Breaker ask you to –"

"No," he answered. "I just want to help. *Everyone's* tired."

"Perhaps that's part of Empyrean's strategy, too. Exhaust us until we can't properly fight. How long have you been doing this?" I asked, angry that I'd been sleeping soundly while he suffered and hadn't even known it.

His eyes flitted away as he focused on our dinner, flipping the sizzling filets before they burned. The cooked side of the pink flesh had turned white with a brown rim around the edges. "Since you moved over here."

That was ridiculous, given the other responsibilities he shouldered as the sun shone.

"I'm taking half the watch," I volunteered.

"That's not necessary."

"I could go back now that my wings are healed. Try to sway them, maybe stop them."

He shook his head, then finally met my eye. "No, you can't." I was about to argue when he leaned forward. "The General isn't there to champion you anymore. Your quad isn't loyal. Your Oracle is beholden to the goddess's whims. The Elders want to use you to further the strength of Empyrean's bloodline. Who in the sky would listen to reason? They'd probably claim that you lived among us so long we'd tainted your mind, but I'm not sure it even matters what they say. If the people of Empyrean ever find out you're alive, they won't give you another chance to descend. And they'll make sure you don't have the opportunity to escape."

"You've spent some time considering all the possible outcomes, haven't you?" I rasped.

"I have. Returning there only leads to a future you don't want. If that life is forced upon you, I think you'd spend the rest of your days longing for the sand and sea, wishing you'd never flown from it. Maybe at some point, if Neera took your feathers, you'd even be grateful for it."

I sucked in a sharp, painful breath.

I would *never* be thankful for the loss of my wings.

He pressed his eyes closed. "I'm sorry," he quickly apologized, rubbing his forehead, scrubbing his fingers over his mouth as if he wished to remove the blunder from his lips. "I didn't mean it like… I don't know what I meant."

"My wings – my feathers – are my freedom, but more than that, they're a part of me the same as my arm. When Wade lost his leg, it forever changed his life. He'll never run or swim the same way he once did. Do you think he will one day be thankful to the beast that bit it off?" I snapped.

"No. It was a stupid and insensitive thing to say, let alone suggest. I just… I want you to have a life you love instead of what the sky wants to force upon you." Crest scooted closer until the outside of our thighs touched and warmth from his skin seeped into mine for just a few heartbeats. "If you truly want to go back, Elira, I won't stop you. I couldn't if I tried. I know that now. I guess I just hoped you wouldn't *want* to leave."

Oh... I looked away from him.

"I don't belong in Empyrean anymore," I told him. It was true. But I stopped short of claiming Kehlani as mine because something in me said that wasn't entirely right, either. Or perhaps it wasn't right *yet*.

A long moment passed between us. Crest seemed to be gathering his thoughts, and mine seemed so jumbled they refused my attempts at collecting them.

"I'm not sad," he finally admitted, throwing a piece of bark into the ring of rocks. "I'm *angry*. So incredibly, indescribably angry. There isn't a way I can see forward that won't hurt you. And I know you've been pushing me away because you want me to find another lacuna, but that's not what I want. The last thing I want you to do is put distance between us right now. I told you I thought we might have to work together to end this war. I still believe that. But we can't work together and be apart."

I *had* been pushing him away – not that it had worked. Evidenced by how closely we sat, a hair's breadth apart.

With a fork, he lifted a slab of shark meat off the pan and slid it onto my plate, then placed the other on his. He'd brought his own plate and fork since I only had one set.

"I know you think lacunas have to be mates or lovers, like Breaker and Katalini, but I think lacunas can be whatever they want. What if a lacuna is nothing more than a close friend? Seems like you could use one." His vulnerability stirred something deep within my heart. "I certainly could."

"You have plenty of friends, Crest."

"None like you, though," he easily replied.

"Would you be *satisfied* with only friendship?"

He took a bite, chewed over it and his answer. "I'd be satisfied having you in my life in whatever capacity you'll allow and be happy with."

I looked to the sky, balancing my plate on my thighs. "And if we're ripped apart by forces beyond our control?"

His countenance darkened and my toes curled at the gravel in his voice. "Then Talay help the one who *tries*." Something crackled between us, a sound like a burning sea. Crest cleared his throat and tried to lighten the mood, but I was almost certain he'd felt and heard the same thing I had. "The Scourge and Shark aren't so easily conquered separately. Imagine us working in tandem."

He nudged my thigh with his and another ripple of warmth slid over my skin. I thought about easing my fingers into his. Allaying his anger and exhaustion with just a touch. But I wasn't sure friends should do such things. Frey never touched him like that. Neither did Koa.

Could we truly be what he said? A pair of friends who traversed life and its trappings together? Would that be enough for Crest?

"What are you thinking?" he asked.

"I'm thinking –" I started, but abruptly stopped.

Over the noise of the flickering fire, beyond the sliding of his fork on his plate as he sat it down to take a sip of water, past the insects singing in the trees and the push and pull of low tide, a familiar sound pricked my ear.

My heart sped, thumping hard against my chest. I pressed a finger to my lips, sat my plate down beside me, and reached behind me just inside the tent. My fingers found a feathered fletching and dragged the arrow toward me. The barbs of its sharp tip dragged across the wooden planks. I reached for my bow, palm curling around the familiar curve in the wooden form.

Overhead, wings flapped.

Overhead, someone *flew*.

Close.

Too close.

Someone was searching; I just wasn't sure if they'd seen us.

I nocked the arrow, trying to decide which one of them it was: Talon or Jorun. The male's silhouette was too broad to be Soraya, unfortunately. I would have taken great pleasure in plucking her from the sky. The moment I pulled the bowstring back, *he* heard, his eyes quickly fastening onto us.

"Elira."

Jorun.

His leathers shone as he swooped close, his dull brown wings adjusting to carry him with precision. His full lips curved into a jubilant smile. "Elira! There you are…"

I kept my aim.

My father said he'd been spying on Soraya and Talon for him, but warned he'd never send him alone.

"How did he get through your Guardians' defenses?" I asked Crest under my breath.

"I have no idea," Crest answered warily. "Is he a friend?"

"No." I had no friends in Empyrean.

I released the bowstring.

My arrow soared into the top of Jorun's shoulder and embedded into the wing behind it, binding the two together.

It was difficult to fly with only one functional wing, he soon learned. I eased toward him, another arrow ready to strike. "I'm not your enemy!" he shouted, cursing me soundly for shooting him. He struggled to stay aloft as Crest let out a shriek, calling for the nearest Guardians to come.

"Land now, or I'll send up another arrow. That was a warning; the next is your death."

With a pained grunt and hiss, Jorun touched down on the sand, clutching his shoulder. Blue fletching stuck out of his skin just below the clavicle. "Please don't kill me," he begged, trying to raise his uninjured arm in supplication. "The General –"

"The General is *dead*," I snapped.

"Yes, but…" He let out a groan. "Elira, help me. I'll explain everything, I swear, but…" His blood held little Empyrea. It didn't burn white like mine, but miniscule veins of Neera's power flinched through what seeped from his wound.

Crest's Guardians rushed the shore and surrounded him with pointed tridents, ready to strike.

"Elira?" Jorun asked, looking as if I had betrayed him. "Tell them I'm not a threat."

I clamped my teeth together, staring him down.

His eyes widened. "You can't possibly think that I mean you harm! The Oracle said she told you I was innocent, that I was trustworthy. She read my feather."

"She read your feather before I fell. It's been a very long time since I spoke with the Oracle about you, Jorun. From what I hear, the sky has suffered great upheavals of late. I have to assume things have changed. Until I know you are a friend, I will treat you as an enemy."

He shifted to look at the wound, still seeping blood. His face paled. He swayed a step.

The Guardians tracked him in case it was a ploy.

Jorun again offered, "I promised your father I would watch over you. I *know* what's at stake." His insinuation caught in the thick, humid air between us, though I wasn't sure *what* he knew.

Did he know about Aderyn? The hatchlings? Was he just as enamored with and protective of my pure blood as the Elders? Or was he searching and hoping I'd reveal something he might use against me? Maybe he'd struck a new bargain now that The General wasn't there to run him through should he fail him. If I found out he was working for the Elders, I'd run him through myself and remind him of the ferocity of the bloodline the kingdom had for so long taken extraordinary measures to conceal.

"Take him to Magma."

The Guardians looked to Crest, who immediately reinforced my order.

"Who is Magma?" Jorun demanded from me as I walked alongside him, keeping a safe distance. Frey kept pace on his left. He took in her silver trident, burgundy hair, and the danger that lurked in her eyes. I'd seen that look in one other creature on the Isle: a solid, bright green viper I'd startled among the roots of a gnarled tree. One wrong move and she wouldn't hesitate to strike. "Elira, please."

Another string of expletives erupted from him as each step tugged the arrow back and forth through his wounds.

"Magma is a healer," I explained.

"I wouldn't *need* healing if you hadn't shot me," he growled, pressing his shoulder again, his mouth opening in a silent, agonizing cry. Sweat beaded on his brow and just above his lip, where the dark shadow of hair lurked just under his fair skin.

"I had no choice," I told him.

His eyes shone with anger. "There's *always* a choice."

"There's never a good one, though, is there?"

CHAPTER SIX

Last night, Magma worked on repairing the damage I'd caused to Jorun. She wagged her finger at me and told me I was impulsive.

To me, impulsivity was a positive trait. In battle, sometimes there was little time to assess, so fast decisions weren't only important, they might save your life.

But it quickly became apparent that she hadn't meant it as a compliment, just as she wasn't complimenting me the first time she called me terrifying.

"Did you even think to let him land and speak his peace?" she asked, harrumphing when I told her no. Harrumphing again when I told her that the moment he saw me, I knew I had to make sure he couldn't fly off to tell someone else – to keep her people safe. When I asked her how many more Empyreans she thought I should 'let land' on Kehlani, she finally stopped shouting.

She grumbled some more but didn't tell me that my argument was nonsense. It wasn't and she knew it. She might not approve of my methods, but she approved of me protecting her people and this Isle.

With a clenched jaw, Jorun watched me move around the tent of our enemy and talk to them as though we weren't only familiar, but friendly. When Magma tried to help him, he gently batted her away, staring at me with so much hatred, I couldn't help but grit my teeth at the silent threat in his eyes. He'd forgotten himself. Forgotten who I was in the sky. If I was still that girl, he wouldn't be here glowering at me.

"Elira, get out," the Mender finally ordered after heaving a heavy sigh.

"Why?"

"Because he's distracted with you and I need to work," she snapped. "Now, go." She shooed me away as though I was a bothersome fly.

"I knew you'd do what it took to survive, Elira. But I never envisioned *this*," he hissed to me as I passed him.

I lunged toward him, making him jerk backward. His pain must have flared with the movement, but he wisely held his tongue. "You would do well to let her heal you, but know that if you cross me, I'll make it so that *no amount* of her ministrations will piece you back together."

"Elira!" Magma snapped, stepping in front of him like a hen before her newly hatched chick.

Jorun looked away, his jaw ticking angrily.

I stalked outside. Crest walked with me back to our tents and paused at mine for a long moment. "Will you go back to see him tonight?"

"Absolutely not," I seethed, dragging my hair over one shoulder. "And *I* will watch the sky until I think I might be able to fall asleep. You need to rest."

He ran a hand through his hair. "Normally I would argue, but I'm too tired."

"Then go and sleep and trust *me* to guard *you* tonight."

He inclined his head and bade me goodnight, walking slowly toward his hammock. "You can sleep in the bed if you'd like," I offered.

His steps paused. Back straightened. For a few beats, he considered it. "My hammock is very comfortable."

I highly doubt it, I replied inwardly, cursing the stubborn male.

Crest wasn't in his hammock when I went to wake him this morning. I hadn't noticed him leave, but his footprints led to the shore, so I waited for him there. Somehow, I knew he would come to meet me.

Strong waves, painted a brilliant cherry hue by the burgeoning sunrise, rushed the shore. They broke against my shins, filling in the space between my bare feet. Grains of cool, wet sand shifted to cradle them until the sea reclaimed its briny water. Clams, swept up by the tide, wriggled to bury themselves. Schools of tiny silver fish chased the water to and from the shore, riding the waves as if that was all they were born to do.

Just beyond the shallows, a pair of gulls flew. They cried out to one another, their wings crooked just enough to catch the Great Wind sweeping beneath them. Content, they teetered and soared together. A feather tore from one of the gull's wings. It rolled, catching on the breeze here and there as it fell before gently landing on the sea. A determined wave capped in white crested and tumbled over it.

Then it was gone.

The bird didn't notice the loss. Didn't care that the feather sank.

I wondered if I would feel the same when Neera demanded the rest of mine. Would I feel grateful at some point, like Crest suggested?

Only two moon cycles remained until Intention Day. Was that what they were waiting on? To reorganize and wait to see who would wager the most in search of power and glory?

Crest emerged from the sea.

The gulls squealed and flapped away, flying southward until they were alone.

He raked a hand through his wet hair to clear his vision, easily walking through water in which I could barely stand. The copper scales lining his legs matched the sun's first wash of brilliant light as it rose from the sea. The orange-yellow seeped into the red until the color was nearly gone.

The black cloth tied at his waist, wet and bunched over his hips, matched his intricate tattoo. Swirling around my mark were rows of shark's teeth to signify his ferocity. I liked to think that perhaps Talay had a sense of humor and also used that pattern to reflect the nickname I'd bestowed on Crest. Beyond the teeth were strings of shields to honor him as a protector of his people, the sharp barbs of his trident, and the powerful waves for which he was named.

He looked as furious as the sea itself this morning, but the dark circles under his eyes had receded.

"What happened?" I asked.

"Jorun told Frey that the Empyreans have been descending, frequenting a part of the sea we rarely watch because the currents there are treacherous. He was telling the truth. They descended right where he said when he told us they'd be there."

"How convenient that he's cooperating so quickly upon landing," I noted, already suspicious. Last night he was disgusted; this morning he offered help?

I knew there was a reason Empyrean's Gatherers had been strangely absent of late. I worried that the Guardians of Kehlani were just missing them, but Crest had a network of people watching the skies. They were stationed in a perimeter of small, wooden towers that skirted the shores of the Isle and spread throughout the ocean. All were armed, thank goodness, but I knew he'd lost several of his people in the battles waged before my fall.

Guilt still sluiced like the seawater from his frame. Leader of the Guardians, his word and strategy led them.

"*To victory or ruin*," my father used to warn the quad leaders. "*You are responsible for those fighting for and beside you.*"

Perhaps I noticed the emotion play over his face because the same haunted me. My orders and actions had affected many. I was subject only to The General and Sannika while she lived and commanded. None other. But being the top quad's leader meant that my word affected the lives and movements of many beneath my rank.

"Did you go alone?" I asked.

He nodded. "Yes, but they didn't see me."

"How many Empyreans were there?"

"I counted thirteen," he answered.

Not a deluge by any means, then. "That number is encouraging. If you see a large group, it's for a feast, and the Empyreans only feast before battles."

He was quiet for a time. "Talon wasn't among them."

I wondered where my second had gone. Had Soraya so quickly managed to remove him from her path as well?

Crest had done exactly as I would have and searched every face for the one responsible for his mother's death. The people of the sea wanted peace, but maybe the kind of peace Crest needed wasn't the kind that drew a line between or a promise from either side. Maybe the only thing that would truly give him peace was to thrust his trident through Talon's chest to be sure he couldn't take the life of another child's mother.

But Talon hadn't acted alone. If Crest's mother died in a battle, it was because I led Talon into the fray. I wasn't defending my former second, but neither would I defend myself when I was also to blame.

"How can you forgive me so easily? I played a part, Crest."

"You didn't," he passionately declared before turning to stare back out at the sea. "My mother didn't die in battle. She was struck by his arrow while swimming alone. Talon was by himself when he attacked her and he didn't simply shoot her; he circled until he was confident no one else had seen and then descended upon her. He tore out her throat with his teeth."

"What?" I breathed, confused. I'd never seen anyone do something so abhorrent or reckless.

"My mother managed to cry out for help just before he ripped her life away. Koa saw her blood on his lips and chin. He said he was crazed and stayed just out of range to watch as we came for her. He didn't try to shoot any of the rest of us, though we were within his range. He was toying with us, just as he did the children he hunted."

Talon's actions had nothing to do with the war. He sought to instill terror.

"I think I saw Soraya at the feeding ground. If it was her, she was leading a quad."

"Pale green armor? Dark hair?" I asked.

He nodded to confirm.

"*Leading* a quad?" I seethed. Maybe she *had* already killed Talon and assumed his role. With the way she attacked me, she proved she didn't have to be stronger, only more devious to get rid of anyone holding her back.

Crest groaned loudly, scrubbing his hands down his face. "Look at us, craving the death of those who've wronged us even as we dream of peace."

"One does not have to wage war to exact justice," I reminded him.

He sighed heavily.

But Crest was right. I wasn't sure how to stop being what I was. The thought of killing Soraya, as would be my right in the sky, was something I couldn't stop thinking about. And disturbingly, it was starting to consume my waking thoughts as much as it soaked into my dreams at night.

"Magma said this would be difficult," I reminded him. She said anything worth doing was. And as hard as it would be to question him… "I need to talk to Jorun."

"Frey stands as his guard," Crest said with a malicious grin. "She battled him most of the night. Apparently, he's stubborn."

"He *is* stubborn, but Jorun is also strong," I warned. "What if he escapes?"

"Frey is stronger. I promise you that. And he'd have to get through her to reach the sky."

I enjoyed imagining the side of Frey we would soon meet. There was no doubt that Jorun now knew her ferocity well.

We ducked inside the Mender's tent as Frey growled a warning that would cow a lesser man. Jorun didn't even blink. Shirtless and with a dark sarong tied at his waist, he shouted back as loudly as she had.

I'd told him he was strong. I gave Crest an I-told-you-so smirk.

Magma sat at her counter grinding herbs, working the pestle so feverishly around the mortar I thought she might make an ember. No smoke rose from the bowl – yet.

Frey held her trident inches from Jorun's chest, her teeth bared. Her burgundy hair was torn from her braid.

"What did we miss?" Crest asked conversationally as we walked farther into the room.

"If you're going to keep him grounded, you'll have to break his wing," Frey gritted.

"Then break it," I allowed.

Jorun's lips parted and for a moment, he looked hurt. "You can't be serious. I came here for *you*, Elira!"

Before he could bellow further, I moved to stand before him and cut him off. "Mind your tone and tongue when you speak to me, Jorun, or I'll cut it out! You will tell me how he died, but before you cite The General as your champion, you should know that he instructed me not to trust anyone. I know of the orders he charged you with and that he did not send you here."

He dipped his head respectfully. "My quad leader," he formally addressed, "you are correct. The General did not send me here. I came of my own accord to offer you my protection. Due to circumstances beyond my control, I can no longer fulfill the duty with which he entrusted me. Talon and Soraya now have separate roles and I am privy to neither."

He cleared his throat. "Your father, upon returning to Empyrean, was met by the Elders and a host of Warriors, who were ordered to immediately bring him to face a tribunal. But before any of them could reach him, The General died by his own hand. He plunged his sword through his middle. A final act of protection for you, I would imagine, though it seemed he was desperate to reach the sea before dying. He just wasn't able to fly fast enough."

Trying to reach the sea?

My heart sank like a heavy stone. Would Talay have saved him?

No one should be forced to make such an unspeakable choice. "I feared he had been caught and tortured," I rasped.

"None of his Warriors would have allowed that to happen and the Elders knew it. Your father had true power in the form of the respect of those he commanded. When they heard the Elders' accusations, every Warrior in Empyrean demanded that he receive a fair trial." Jorun paused and let his eyes search mine. "The General is gone, Elira. I came to keep my promise to him, not expecting I'd ever get close enough to find you. I can't help but wonder if his soul somehow guided me here. And whether you believe me or not, the only allies you have – the only friends you have left – are me and Era, and the Scholar is in no position to assist."

"Is he in danger?" I demanded sharply.

Jorun gave a mirthless laugh. "*Of course* he is. As is the Oracle."

My brows rose and my feathers prickled uncomfortably. "Would the Elders dare harm Neera's conduit?"

"The Elders risk much more than that. When you fell, Empyrean descended into chaos. Fearing they were losing their grip on the power they'd been given, they took even more." He stopped himself before revealing more. "Unfortunately, Era and the Oracle confirmed that you are, indeed, still alive and on the Isle and they're working with the new General to make plans to retrieve you because they think you're being held against your will."

To what lengths will they unravel to drag me back to the sky?

"Who is the new General?" I asked. I needed to know everything that had happened since I fell. Everything he thought or had heard might happen next. Jorun's knowledge could be crucial to preparing a defense against the Warrior quads.

He pointedly glanced at Frey, then down at the barbed tips of her trident. His gaze travelled to Crest, then to Magma, who had stopped working to listen and now held a bowl of medicinal green goop I recognized by scent. My nose wrinkled at the memory of having to wear it pasted on my side, thickly applied to the wound Soraya gave me.

Jorun pursed his full lips and pulled back his wings, wincing when his shoulder moved with them. "I'll tell you everything."

I waited. And waited. And waited for him to speak, but he pressed his lips tight in silent refusal.

"Then speak," I prodded.

Another quick flick of his eyes to the people of the sea surrounding us in the tent, and I knew his mind went where mine had gone when I was in his place: that this was how they surrounded us when we descended. He wouldn't speak in front of them. Jorun wouldn't reveal the sky's secrets to its enemies, even if he still respected me as I stood among them.

"I said I would tell *you* everything."

Koa sauntered into the room with a loud "Hello!", his golden scales on full display and wearing a thin scrap of fabric that barely covered him. He loudly clapped his hands. "I'm here to relieve you of your post, my darling Frey," he announced to her.

"*What* are you wearing?" she laughed.

Koa spun in a circle, his arms extended. "Enjoy the back view as much as you obviously have the front, Frey."

She groaned and turned her attention back to Jorun, whose lips had parted in surprise. His brows were scrunched together, and he looked completely thrown off balance and confused.

"Is there someplace we might speak privately?" he asked.

I looked at Magma, who was boiling. She snapped, "Not before I'm finished with you!"

"I don't need your –" Jorun hissed, crying out in pain as Frey poked the skin above his flayed collar bone with the wicked tip of her trident. Magma had treated his wound last night. It still bore the green stains of her slimy concoction, but he'd mussed his bandage. "That's sharp!" he complained.

Frey grinned. "Yes, she is."

He leaned far away from Frey and her weapon.

"How bad is his shoulder?" I asked Magma, not bothering to lower my voice.

"You split skin, tendon, and bone, Elira. It's not good," she said disapprovingly. "But he will heal, if he'll *keep still and rest.*" I smiled because she'd told me the same thing after having to set me right a second time, too. "The lot of you are stubborn to a fault. I'll tell *you* what I told *her*, boy. You keep fighting me and you'll never be rid of the pain. Never heal up."

"You're *causing* the pain," he fired back insolently.

"You need her help," Frey told him. "Even if you don't want it. You can trust Magma."

He snorted. "Next you'll say I can trust The Shark…" His voice trailed away and he looked wholly uncomfortable. I surprised him by sitting down on the cot beside him, even though I kept a respectable distance. "Have you met *him*?" he whispered.

I looked at Crest, his ocean eyes washing over mine, and gave a small smile. "I have."

Jorun was no fool. He followed my gaze and noticed how Crest crossed his arms over his chest. Then he stared at his copper-scaled legs. "I think I'm going to be sick," my fourth warned, doubling over.

"Move!" Magma barked at me. Her reflexes were wholly impressive for a person her age. Before I could even search for a bucket, she'd found a large wooden bowl and deftly shoved it into Jorun's hands just before he heaved.

The sound and smell of retching filled the tent. Frey and Koa covered their noses and stepped away. The movement drew Magma's attention.

"The lot of you, get out!" Magma fussed, motioning her hands toward the door as if she could sweep us all away like the leaves that tumbled in from outside. "I need space and so does he."

Koa and Frey immediately obeyed, the tent's door flapping behind them.

"What do you need me to do?" Crest asked his grandmother.

She laughed in the way one laughs when they think something isn't funny at all. In a way that said she would certainly and happily give him a task if he wanted one, and he couldn't dare complain about it because he'd asked for it. "I need you to go home. Catch up on some of the chores you've been ignoring and take a nap, for Talay's sake. Don't think I haven't noticed the dark circles rippling beneath your eyes."

I silently bristled. *I thought they looked better.*

Magma was *done*. Done with excuses. Done watching him grow tired and weary. Crest's words of refutation crumbled and caved into a mumble.

"Elira will stay and help. Won't you, Elira?" she asked, her gaze cutting to me and holding. Threatening in a way I hadn't expected. In a way that garnered even more of my respect.

"Of course," I quickly agreed. "It's my duty."

To Jorun, she asked, "Are you finished?"

He nodded and a moment later accepted a damp cloth from her and wiped his head and mouth. She took the bowl from his hands.

Crest shook his head. “You owe no duty to the sky who cast you out, Elira,” he said so slowly, so adamantly, his body so rigid I worried it might snap like Jorun’s bone had when my arrow’s head nicked it.

“He has information we need,” I told him. I *would* have every detail, and from the way he stiffened, Jorun knew I would take it from him by force if necessary.

Crest hesitated, which was the wrong thing to do in the moment.

Magma snapped before either of the men, or I, knew she was about to explode. “Do you have sticky honey on your feet, boy? I said to *get out* and *go home*!”

“One of the Guardians will be posted outside,” he told her. His eyes found mine and he nodded in Jorun’s direction. “I don’t trust him.”

No, that wasn’t it at all. It was true he didn’t trust Jorun, but what he also meant and didn’t say was that he didn’t trust *me* with him.

Did he think I would leave? That I was a skilled liar who had only been ‘doing what I must to survive’, as Jorun accused last night?

When I heard him shout to someone the moment he left her workshop, I realized Koa and Frey were still close by. Crest ordered Frey to get some rest.

Koa popped his back. “Guess *I’m* the lucky one.”

Crest shook his head, a small smile playing on his lips. “I can’t take you seriously while you’re wearing… *that*.”

“Afraid your lacuna will…?” Koa’s voice trailed away at Crest’s warning growl, guttural and full of menace.

Koa's hands rose in surrender. "It was only a joke, bro."

Jorun, who had hung his head, again looking sick, lifted it toward me. He looked suspicious and upset. "What's a lacuna?" he whispered.

"We have a lot to discuss," I answered stonily.

"It certainly seems that way."

Magma inserted herself into our conversation. "After I bandage you *again*, young man."

CHAPTER SEVEN

Under the camouflaging canopy, Crest and I waited outside Magma's workshop as she worked to bandage and splint Jorun's arm – *again*, she reminded him repeatedly. I couldn't help but smile at her righteous irritation.

"Is he a danger to you?" Crest asked, pushing a hand through his still-damp hair.

"Jorun?" I searched my memory for a single moment where I'd felt threatened by him, anything from a look he'd given to something he said, and found nothing. We competed for the top quad, but he'd accepted the status of second graciously, even congratulating me every time my quad was ranked higher than his. Beyond that, Aderyn spoke highly of him. She'd never spoken to me about anyone else, and I didn't hear a lie in her voice when she told me how kind and attentive he was. That she enjoyed spending time with him. "No, he's not a danger to me."

"Who is he to you?" Crest asked. "You said he wasn't a friend before you shot him."

"For the past couple years, he led the quad that was second only to mine. At the last Intention Day, things shifted and he became the lowest ranking member of my quad."

"What caused the shift? His intention?"

"Yes."

The sky burned bright white behind lofty clouds. I couldn't help but think they might conceal *them*. My eyes roamed for aberrations, finding none. My stomach was still unsettled. When the sky was clear we could be sure, but on days like this, it was impossible to be anything but wary.

"What did he intend?" The Shark asked, something dark swimming in the depths of his eyes. It was as if he'd scented Jorun's first intention before I'd spoken it.

"Firstly and most importantly, the Oracle revealed his intent to join my quad, accepting the empty position of fourth. I had already raised Talon to second and Soraya to third that day, so there was a vacancy. Many people spoke that intention, though. It was an honor for so many to vie for the spot, but only one could be awarded it."

"If that was first, what was his second intention?" he prodded, staring skyward just as I was.

"He expressed his desire to pursue me as a mate."

Crest's gaze slowly slid to mine.

"I refused him. He'll lose a feather or two at the next Intention Day because of my rejection, but otherwise he'll be fine."

"I don't like him," he said testily.

"Because he wanted to become my mate?" I scoffed.

"Are you *fond* of Nori, Elira?" he deftly volleyed.

Well-played, Shark.

Chin raised proudly, I refocused my attention on the tent where Magma and Jorun talked quietly. Though my ears strained, I couldn't make out their words. Only that they were calmer now. Perhaps it was that gentleness that set me on edge. I wanted to know what he was telling the Mender and whether it had to do with me.

"Did he know you well enough to mate with you?"

"That isn't how it works in Empyrean. We knew each other because we were pitted against one another in everything, both vying for an honor only one of us could claim. He knew my strength, not my character. I never saw Jorun as a friend. To me, he was an opponent. If he wanted to seek me as a mate, it was because our hatchling would be strong, and maybe, he could use it as a way to unseat me. To steal my position while I was on leave. It's easier to stay on the mountain top than to beat the one standing on it."

He gave a noncommittal hum.

"Aderyn used to be close with him." I looked back at the tent. "I don't know if he knows about her."

"Will you tell him?"

"I want to see what he knows before offering anything," I answered.

The tent flap lifted and Magma's gray hair blew sideways as she approached, salty once more. "He's to keep that arm *still.* It's the only way to mend the bone. He shouldn't lift anything. Shouldn't even try to pick up a section of fruit with that hand. He'll have to learn to use the other."

I nodded. "I'll remind him."

She pursed her lips sourly. "You don't need to worry about that. The pain will be reminder enough, but I leave him in your care, Elira. There's nothing more I can do for him right now."

Jorun ducked out of the tent. His angry brown gaze immediately trained on me.

I sighed and looked at Crest when he nudged my arm. "Dinner?"

I nodded.

Jorun stared at where The Shark had touched me and his eyes flared.

"Jorun!" I snapped as he tracked Crest's movements. The Shark stalked with purpose toward the sea, then took off into a run when someone let out a shriek from somewhere along the shore. My body went rigid at the sound, remembering the emergent shrieks made when they went in search of Wade.

Magma noticed. "That was just Koa telling him to hurry up."

"How do you know their sounds?" I asked her, ignoring Jorun's presence. He was still an annoyance. A fourth and mate I never wanted.

She ran a hand down her pale blue scales. "I don't swim much anymore and I've never been a Guardian. My mother was a Mender, and I grew up knowing in my heart that was my path, too. But I've been around long enough to know the language of the sea." She tugged on the ends of her long, silver hair to punctuate her words.

I wondered if *I* would be around long enough to learn even a fraction of it. Then I pondered if the hatchlings one day would be fluent in sea speak and whether I would ever know my path. Not one shoved at my feet to please someone else, but the one I was destined to tread. Would it be made of sand, sea, or sky?

"You never *wanted* to be a Guardian?" I asked, wondering if she'd changed her mind at some point in her youth.

"Never," she earnestly told me. "To be a Mender, one must appreciate and want to save lives. To be a Guardian, one must be willing to end them. I couldn't stomach the latter, and thus, ran toward the former as fast as my feet could carry me. My mother would shoo me from beneath her feet, I was so intent on learning as soon as they could carry me." She looked toward her workshop. "This was where she worked. The cot you're both *now so familiar with*, though it's been repaired more than a few times, was hers. The mortar and pestle and stool were hers, too."

I could almost imagine her young mother inside, busy at the counter, moving this way and that and tiny Magma getting bowled over a time or two until she learned not to tread too closely while her mother worked.

"My son was a Guardian, as was Crest's mother. Crest took to the sea quicker than any babe I've seen. He could swim before he could walk." Magma dismissed us by saying she had a mess to clean up and walked back into the workshop in which she was raised.

Jorun's pale brown wings, inlaid with a darker hue, flexed on his back.

"Let's go," I told him, finally accepting that I was stuck with and now responsible for him. Was this how Crest felt when The Salt first asked him to guard me?

"Go where?"

"To my new nest."

A towering Kehlani man I didn't know stood outside my tent, his arms as broad as the split lumber he stacked beside my home. With a start, I realized the wall of firewood I'd assumed Crest built had been built by his hands.

He acknowledged me with a nod, his eyes flicking warily over Jorun. I wondered what thoughts ran through his mind. Did he think we'd invaded the Isle? Was he sick of seeing our kind so close?

But I had questions of my own, chief among them being why he was providing me with wood.

His scales stretched to his calves and were the color of the bark on the timber, and like the material, the brownish gray tones varied in unique patterns. "Who are you?" I asked warily.

He paused for only a beat and kept stacking. "One of the boys you saved was my son," he said by way of explanation. "Just wanted to thank you in some small way."

"It's not small to me," I told him, appreciating every piece of wood he'd given me.

"I won't bother you. I'm just finishing up," he said, glancing at Jorun again.

"Which of them was your son? The runner or the wise one?"

The man placed the last piece of firewood and stood up straight, wiping his hands down his sarong before stretching his back. With a proud smile, he told me, "The smarter of the two, for sure."

"He needs a better friend."

The boy's father nodded in agreement. "He told me what happened."

"Was it the whole account?" Younglings would lie to avoid punishment. I should know.

"I believe so. He was pretty shaken up. I forbade him from going anywhere near the other boy again."

People could change. *I* had changed. But it took either a great deal of experience or momentous tragedy to prompt such a drastic alteration of one's views. The boy who ran off would've left his friend behind for the cat to feast upon when he, at the very least, could've tried to help his friend run faster.

I didn't blame this father for preventing his further influence… or injury.

"I'll bring more when I can," he promised, wiping the sweat off his brow.

"You don't have to do that. This is wonderful, and far more than I deserve."

"You saved my *son*," his hearty voice cracked. A tear fell down his cheek and he fought a quivering chin. "You saved my son. There isn't enough firewood on Kehlani to repay you for that." He reached his hand out.

I'd seen some of the Kehlanians clasp hands briefly. I extended mine in return and let him squeeze it once, acutely feeling Jorun's judgment.

"I'm sorry for how I treated you *before*," he added, looking at the ground.

"I'm sorry for how I treated you before, too," I echoed.

"I've told everyone I've come across what you did," he said, meeting my eye again. "I hope – however long your stay – that it'll be easier now." He surprised us both by nodding to Jorun before strolling away. As he walked back down the path, the wind quickly erased his steps from the sand.

A disturbing thought struck me. If I hadn't seen him stacking the wood, I never would've known he was there…

Jorun stood stock still beside me. He didn't understand why I'd just touched the stranger. Why I treated Crest like a friend. Likely didn't understand Magma and her fussing at all.

I started to think about what I wanted to tell him and what I might keep to myself. I wondered what *he* might say about Empyrean.

This would be a very long afternoon, and a tedious conversation.

I walked inside knowing Jorun would follow – he was too upset and curious now not to – then sighed because the only furniture I had was a table and bed. I needed to craft chairs, but before that, I needed to find a sturdy, long piece of wood to shape.

"This is your nest?" Jorun asked in an obvious attempt at civility.

The tension in my chest and shoulders eased a little. "I'm still working to fill it."

"It's nice." I could tell he didn't want to compliment it, but when he did anyway it gave me pause.

"Are you in pain?" I asked.

He took in the table, the small counter with my one plate and cup, the bed Crest had given me, and stared at the sliver of light peeking in through outside. "Some, but it's not unbearable. I wish you hadn't shot me," he said sourly.

"Yet you understand why I felt I had to," I assumed, correctly judging by the way he ran his tongue over his front teeth, his lip swelling and falling with the movement. Jorun was proud, and the proud did not easily admit when they were wrong. "I need to find a large piece of wood from the grove," I told him.

"Is that your way of asking if I'll accompany you?"

I nodded.

"What are you carving?" he asked as we walked back outside. "More arrows now that you've used them all on me?"

Jorun would've shot me if the situation was reversed. At least, I was pretty certain he would have.

"I'm carving a leg, if you must know."

Jorun's head tilted. "A chair leg?"

"No, not for a chair, for a person."

His head ticked back in surprise. "I don't understand. But to be honest, I don't understand *any* of this. I thought that when I found you, you'd be starved and tortured and a million other awful things – *if* you were even still alive."

Jorun still looked pale and slightly sick. His arm was immobilized by a tightly knotted fabric that cradled and kept it mostly still, even as we walked. I knew he didn't feel like taking the trek, but I couldn't stand being confined with him in the tent. I needed to breathe beneath the endless sky. Still, he looked a little green.

"Are you *sure* you feel well enough?"

"I'm fine!" he snipped.

"How did you descend without anyone on the Isle or in the sea noticing?" We walked down the path toward the grove, my senses prickling at every sound. I didn't want to encounter another predator – from land or sky.

"Back when we came to collect the plants for Era and had to come back for soil, we touched down for a while before anyone knew we were there. They only have a few lookout towers in the mountains. Only on the tallest peaks. I just went to the spot where we'd landed and walked down on foot," he offered. "I still *could've* been seen. I guess I just got lucky."

Clever. "I hope no one from Empyrean saw you or realizes the weakness."

"Let me guess. You'll be happy to tell your new friends and forsake your old ones?"

I narrowed my eyes at his insolence, but Jorun was not easily intimidated.

Fury glistened in his brown eyes. "Why would you want to protect *them*? Our whole lives, they've terrorized us!"

My anger rose to meet his. My heart pressed so hard against my chest, straining to allow him to see her. To know who she really was. That she wasn't the monster she used to be, or that people believed her to be.

"And we haven't done the same? Defending the Gatherers is a necessary and perfectly honorable task, but I now know there's far more going on that isn't spoken of in the sky. Our kind hunt their younglings; did you know that? They've made a game of it." I imagined Crest's mother in Talon's grip, his teeth at her throat. "Worse still is that I'm sure there are more atrocities I haven't even learned of yet."

"No one respectable would harm a youngling," he snapped as though it angered him, too. "But I knew of their games. Talon creatively imagined many of them. Are you seriously expecting me to believe you didn't know?"

"I didn't!" I shouted. I was tired of having to constantly prove my character. How did anyone in Empyrean raise a fist to honor me if they felt I was capable of such terrible things? Did they approve of torturing Talay's kind as another form of battle? Were they *all* so vile?

"How could you not? You were his quad leader."

"In battle, yes, but I wasn't aware of what he did in his free time. He always pretended that going near the shore was too dangerous. I never imagined he would approach it to hunt children."

"You seemed close," he observed.

I wasn't near close enough. I would never condone such behavior.

"I could say the same of you. He told me you were friends. Had grown up sparring."

He gave a mirthless laugh. "Oh, we grew up sparring, but not because we were friends. I have always despised Talon."

"I would have *gutted* him if I knew of his recreational activities," I seethed.

Jorun's brows drew in. "You're being truthful."

Of course I was. "Talon's actions have ruined my reputation. That's yet another thing I will set right in time."

They said I was the best quad leader, and perhaps in battle, that was true, but I obviously didn't have my subordinates on a short enough lead. I allowed them the privilege to go and live their lives and didn't pry into areas that didn't apply to our duties as Warriors and as a team.

"How long was he slipping away?" I asked carefully.

"I'm not sure exactly when he started, but he's done unspeakable things since The General bade me watch him."

My back went rigid. How long had Jorun been watching us? "When was that?"

"Since he joined your quad." He cleared his throat. "Your father assumed you knew and were okay with his little expeditions."

"If my father thought I was so wretched, why did he bother asking you to watch over me?"

Jorun stared into my eyes until I began to squirm. "Because you were the monster he made and loved."

A knot formed in my throat at the thought of being loved for so long and not even knowing it. Now, the ones who loved and protected me, even when they thought I was capable of horrific things, were dead. Gone forever. And they died thinking I was just as bad as Talon and whomever he invited into his private life.

"I'm sorry to be the one to tell you all this, Elira."

I just couldn't believe he'd been in my father's confidence so long. Years now. He must have known him like none other. I stopped as the trail bled into the grove of fruit trees. "Why did my father trust you and not me?"

"Because he couldn't risk it. No one but Aderyn was ever close to you, Elira. Your father couldn't take a chance on trusting you with anything that went against the Elders' mandates without knowing where your loyalties lay. With them, or him."

Pain and anger filled my stomach because I knew… I *knew* what she'd done. "Let me guess… Aderyn wouldn't vouch for me."

He shook his head. "She didn't warn him away exactly, but said she simply wasn't sure how you would react. I know about the hatchlings, and that she's here. I assume the two of you have spoken."

"We have not," I bit out.

Jorun's eyes flared in surprise. "She hasn't come to you?"

"She refused when they told her I'd been hurt and was on the Isle. She asked them not to tell me she was here. Only recently did I learn she wasn't dead. My father revealed it when he descended and found me – the night he died."

Jorun muttered a soft curse, so mild compared to those that churned in my mind.

We left the trail and walked quietly into the grove. Jorun marveled at the trees all around us, turning in a circle to take in all the branches and trunks. Scattered among the larger trees were saplings, and while they bore no fruit, the promise of it was there in the vibrant green of their varied leaves.

"It looks very different from the ground," he said. "It's beautiful." He slowed his steps and waited until I turned to face him. "They're never going to stop hunting you. They know you're alive, Elira. You seem to have managed just fine since splashing into the unforgiving sea. You're even friendly with The Shark himself. But if you care for them, and the hatchlings and Aderyn, you should consider what will happen when Empyrean's Warriors learn that they've hidden you."

"My father said the Oracle told the Elders about a vision she had of me on the shore."

"She did. That's why the Elders locked her inside the sanctum. They want her to spend *every minute* searching for you and communicating with Neera to help bring you home."

They trapped the Oracle – the conduit – and the goddess in her own space?

"Are they mad?"

"I think so," he acknowledged with a few shallow nods.

"I was wondering what she saw of me here. Did she know they spared my life? Did she see the treatment and care I've received? I hoped she might persuade them to consider talking to the leader of Kehlani. The war can't rage forever, Jorun."

With his uninjured arm, he reached up and pulled an apple down from a branch that strained beneath its weight, blew a small bug off its scarlet skin, and bit into it. "To our leaders, any compromise, no matter if or how much either side sacrifices, would be akin to losing this war – *especially* in the eyes of our new General."

The Great Wind suddenly gusted, rattling the leaves on every tree in the grove. Wind that my anger and apprehension had stirred.

Did he know, could he feel, that it had responded to my emotion? Jorun looked frightened and his eyes went wide. He gripped the apple so tightly, a fissure formed in its pale yellow flesh.

"Who claimed the title, Jorun?" I demanded. My hair whipped back and forth, swirling in every direction and tangling in the feathers gracing the top of my wings. His lip curled and I knew… I *knew*. "That vulture."

"Talon is an opportunist. He seized it before Soraya could. She had it in her sights, mind you."

"Oh, I'm certain she did," I growled, thumb running over the scar she'd given me.

I wasn't sure if Jorun was right. Was Talon an opportunist or a master strategist? Could he have suggested to Soraya that she remove me from her path because it benefited him and played into his true intention – to surpass me, Sannika, *and* The General?

It wouldn't surprise me if he'd fletched some arrows with Aderyn's feathers, stolen from the cuff I'd given him, just to strike Sannika with them and anger me that day. It certainly made me want to descend and fire at every being whose scales glimmered like jewels in the sea that evening.

Talon was the leader of every quad, every Commander, every Warrior in the sky. The Elders thought they had his ear, his hand. His will. But they were mistaken. Talon hungered for power, and true power answered to no one. It did not bend to anyone else's desires.

"Aderyn and I *were* friends – as much as anyone in the sky could be," he admitted. "I thought for all these months that she was dead, too. Your father told me of their plan just before he descended to try to find you himself."

"I still don't understand," I told him. "If she and my father planned this, why didn't the Oracle see it in her feather? She asked me for one to read and I gave it to her; straight from the greedy pile I tore from the wing I found bobbing on the sea. If *you* knew, why didn't the Oracle see it in yours as well?"

He perked up. "That's easy to explain. Aderyn and your father worked with Scholar Gamut. She could erase things from the barbs and make them look seamless to anyone who would read them."

"Gamut – the Archivist?" I gaped.

He grinned. "Gamut is a very interesting woman. She is of the order of Scholars, specifically an Archivist, by choice, but Gamut was born a Seer. Neera passed her over for another. She knew she wouldn't be chosen in the future, so she asked to follow her passion to the library, where she's made her home among the tomes and scrolls." We walked a few steps in silence before Jorun spoke again.

"Elira, I know I've given you a lot to think about, and there are many questions you probably have that I won't be able to answer. But I *do* know that Aderyn cared – *cares* – for you. She came to see me a few days before she left just to talk. I brought up Intention Day and asked her what her goals were for the upcoming year. I considered asking her if she'd allow me to pursue her as a mate, but she seemed… off. Now I know she was distracted. She told me she wasn't sure what she wanted, but that she was worried for *you*.

"It's clear now that she was asking me to look out for you after she left. That's one reason I asked the Oracle to reveal my intention to pursue you. I also thought you could use a friend, and that being close to you would make it easier for me to watch over Talon and Soraya for your father."

A nice strategy indeed. If any of the pieces of this puzzle had been shared with me, it might have made all the difference, or none. It was difficult to say. But if my path had been anything but what it was, I wouldn't be here now. On Kehlani. Crest's lacuna. Friend of Talay.

Maybe Crest was right when he said I might one day thank Neera for taking my feathers away, because despite all the pain and heartache, I was glad for every moment. They brought me to this point, to this place.

Jorun suddenly winced, pinching his eyes closed as a fresh wave of pain seemed to lance his shoulder. It passed quickly. "Are you okay?" I asked.

He gave me an annoyed look. "I'm alive, at least. I know your aim, so I count myself lucky." He plucked at the sarong Magma had scrounged up for him. "I don't understand *this* at all, but it does seem to make this oppressive heat slightly more bearable."

I fought back a chuckle. "I'm sorry I shot you."

With his good arm, he wiped the sweat from his brow. "Me too. But I'm glad I found you. I suppose in *that* respect it was worth it."

"How did your perspective change so swiftly when only moments ago, you thought I was like Talon?"

He gave a painful smile and took another bite of the apple he'd plucked, ignoring the crack he'd made from squeezing it and the gnats buzzing around its browning flesh. He chewed it carefully as he chose his words. "Beyond the fact that I hear the truth in your voice and believe you when you said you didn't know he was doing atrocious things, I'm positive Talon would've done anything to hide his true nature from you. He knows *your* ambition if not your character, and knew how you'd react if you learned of his recreational ventures. And I never saw you do anything like him and his friends, never saw you with him when it wasn't required or ordered. Beyond that, Aderyn wouldn't have protected you if you were like Talon."

Before she left, there were times she didn't. Times when I felt her pulling away and mistakenly assumed she was caught up in her budding friendship with Jorun. And then there was the fact that she left and withdrew her protection and presence from my life. Perhaps Aderyn felt I was unworthy of it. Maybe she thought I was like Talon, or even worse than him.

"Did she know about him?"

Jorun sighed. "You and she were together most of the time, so if you didn't know, I doubt she did unless your father told her."

He'd given me a lot to think about, and I was anxious to find what I came for and get him back to the tent. Magma said he needed to rest, and Magma was always right. I scanned the grove floor for an appropriately sized branch, drifting further into the trees. The gusting winds had died down once more and the grove was peaceful.

"We claim to value truth, but don't know or trust anyone around us, Jorun. What does that say about us?"

He blew out a long breath, his cheeks puffing with the exhalation. "It says we are gravely misguided."

"I hope you're being sincere when you say that, because it's true about more than just our kind." His eyes sharpened in response. As if he could sense what I was going to tell him next. "*They* aren't like we were told. At all. We were wrong about them."

"That's something I'll have to see and decide for myself," he replied stubbornly.

"You already are," I quietly reminded him.

His eyes flicked down to his bandages.

A cloud of flies buzzed above the ground as we approached the place where the great cat had taken down the fawn yesterday, supping on what remained of the small, docile creature. I watched to make sure we wouldn't be pounced upon from branch or ground and hurried to a large branch lying in the distance.

Jorun rushed to keep up. "I can help you carry it," he offered.

"You can't. Magma's orders."

He scoffed. "She isn't my leader. *You* are."

"Then, as such, I *also* feel it's unwise for you to lift anything right now."

"Would you accept *my* help?" Crest's deep timbre questioned, a second after I heard his footsteps behind us.

"I would," I answered, ignoring the barbed glare Jorun gave The Shark.

Crest pulled a forearm-sized blade from his side and began to cut the smaller limbs away, hacking and sawing until only the bulky core remained.

"Making furniture?" Crest asked conversationally.

Jorun postured in front of me as if to protect me. "Her intentions are her own, Shark."

Crest smiled at me over his shoulder. It wasn't playful. Nor was it full of malice. It was the smile of a friend that said he knew what he was getting into and was willing to dive head-first anyway.

"I'm carving a leg," I told him, moving around Jorun.

"For a chair?" he asked. "This is far too big for –"

"For Wade," I corrected.

Crest's gaze shimmered with appreciation and a thousand things I couldn't name but desperately wanted to know.

"I came to find you because Frey was on patrol far out to sea. She said a terrible gale is moving toward the Isle. We need to secure everything we possibly can and take shelter in the grotto." Crest nodded toward Jorun. "Are you going to fly home before it hits?"

"I'm *not* leaving Elira's side," Jorun blustered.

Crest smiled, this time in challenge. "We'll see."

Jorun growled.

Crest breezily ignored him, picked up the thickest end of the branch, and began to drag it. I caught hold of the smaller end and moved closer to help bear my share of the weight. When Jorun tried to help with his unbroken arm, I barked at him to stop.

"I gave you an order and if you intend to stay, you will obey it. *And* me."

He eased his uninjured arm back down to his side. "I'll be healed soon," he vowed.

We walked from the grove at a fast pace. Crest led the way down the narrow path and Jorun kept step behind me. "When the storm passes, Breaker wants to speak to you, Jorun."

"Who is Breaker?" he demanded.

"The leader of the Isle and Crest's brother," I explained.

The Great Wind began to gust again, only this time, it didn't stop. By the time we reached my tent, it was already bowing sideways. I wondered if it would survive the storm.

"You need to hurry to the falls!" Crest shouted over the howling wind tearing over the Isle. "Do you remember the way?"

I nodded. "What about you?"

"This isn't a normal storm, Elira," Crest declared. "Gales are deadly to anyone caught out in them. The sky will swirl, and the sea will sweep up over the dunes. It's not safe to be without shelter."

"I'll take Jorun to the grotto, but what about you?" I repeated. "Won't you be in danger in the gale?" The way he described it, these storms were monsters in their own right.

"It's my duty to make sure everyone is out of the sea. Some children were diving at the reef on the far side of the Isle. I'm going to make sure they're all out of the water and heading toward safety. Frey and Koa are spreading out to cover the other sides. I'll come to the grotto as soon as I'm sure everyone is safe."

"Safe?" Jorun sneered. "The water is ruled by your god, isn't it?"

"Do you fly during gales, Empyrean?" Crest spat. "Does the Great Wind not threaten your wings and homes at times? Does Neera not control *it*?"

Jorun didn't admit it, but Crest was right. We had no time to discuss the matter further. The sky was darkening by the second, the clouds beginning to bend and sink like sea water into Charybdis's throat.

Crest lingered as if there was something he wanted to say, then glanced over his shoulder, the strange spell broken. "I'll see you soon." Then he ran toward the shore.

I wondered if something beyond the impending gale might be wrong, but I didn't have time to worry.

Second by second, the gray clouds turned a sickening shade of ocher. The yellow-orange hue blanketed us in yet another omen, another warning. Was this gale the cause of The Salt's trembling shells?

CHAPTER EIGHT

"Hey," Aderyn said, startling as I stepped onto the balcony. Moonlit clouds scattered across the midnight sky.

"Where are you going at this hour?"

She gritted her teeth but couldn't hide the stain on her cheeks, ruddy even under the pale, cold light.

"I'm going to visit someone."

My brows rose in question.

"Jorun. I'm meeting Jorun."

My brows did not fall, though my eyes blinked rapidly at her admission.

"He's funny and smart. He's not like most of the other males."

I hoped she was right about that – and him.

"Are you thinking of mating with him?" I asked, hoping she would say no, breathing easier when she did.

"No. It's nothing like that. We're just friends."

I nodded and turned to walk back inside. Over my shoulder, I said, "Goodnight, Aderyn."

She smiled and took off into the darkness. I hoped she knew what she was doing. At dawn, Jorun and I would spar for the honor of being named the highest-ranked Warrior in Empyrean.

The wind blew so hard against us, my wings and Jorun's were forced sideways. As was our hair and clothing. When he cursed the sarong gaping at his hip, showing the pale skin of his leg, I couldn't help but smile.

There was something about a storm that made me feel alive. The sheer power of it invigorated me. Thrilled me. Made me want to challenge the elements at their fiercest just to see how I would fare against them even if I might lose.

I smiled at the sky.

"Did you break your wings?" he shouted over the roaring tree limbs as we entered the Green Mountains.

"Yes. They're healed now – mostly."

"Mostly?" he said loud enough that I could hear it, yet quiet enough I'm not sure he meant for me to. "The Shark. How did the two of you, of all people, become friends?"

How – when I sought to capture and kill him? he meant. *When he'd aimed his trident and arrows at me just as many times?* The answer was simple. The credit or blame lay with Crest.

"He saved my life."

His steps slowed. "He did?"

I stopped, stretching to show him the scar on my side. I needed him to see the evidence and know it was real.

That I wasn't influenced by coercion, but by kindness. "Soraya stole one of the poison-coated arrows Era made for me to use on Crest. When everyone left the battle, knowing there was no one left to witness her actions, she stabbed me. Here." I tapped the healed wound with my finger. "The toxin stunned me, and I slowly lost control and spiraled into the sea. Then… *he* was there, and he kept me from drowning." Kept me from dying.

Jorun was quiet for a moment, but when he spoke again, he voiced the same question that had plagued me for days and weeks afterward. "Why?"

Why did he do it when I was literally hunting him when I fell? Why did he do it when I'd killed so many of his people? Why, when I was the monster their people feared and loathed? When others of my kind did unspeakable things to them when I wasn't paying close enough attention?

"Because he saw my fear," I answered.

Jorun stopped. Despite the wind and rain that splattered nearby trees and headed right for us, he stopped. "Then he saw your true self, because we've been afraid our whole lives."

In that moment I felt seen, but more than that, completely understood. Jorun was unequivocally right. He glanced to the churning sky and I followed his gaze, marveling at how these storm clouds resembled the turbulent sea.

"My fear of the sea people hasn't abated the way yours has, Elira. I can't help but wonder if they're using you now, or ultimately will, to get what they want. It's all I know. The constant posturing, constant moving of pieces in this great game we find ourselves a part of."

I couldn't blame him for not trusting Talay's people implicitly simply based on my word and experience. Some things could only be learned by being felt and seen and heard. We were taught from birth that the people of the sea were nothing but mindless monsters, but mindless beasts were incapable of granting mercy. They didn't form families or love their neighbors or a thousand other things the sky had never held but should.

"I'm afraid to leave," I told him.

"I'm afraid for you as well, but you must know in your heart that you don't belong on land. You are winged for a purpose, Elira. You hold the goddess's blood in your veins for a reason, and it isn't for the sea or sand."

I studied him for a moment. The set of his jaw. The strength of his posture despite his injury. "Why did my father risk trusting you?"

His attention flicked to the sheets of punishing rain racing toward us. "I'll tell you, but let's get out of the gale first."

I acquiesced, quickly leading him up the wending trail to the slippery rocks that lined the bed of the pool of water the falls splashed into, then behind the heavy curtain of water to safety. The wind was severed by the water. Behind the falls, only balmy air dwelled.

Lit torches revealed more faces than I could count. The main room of the grotto was quite full, and Talay's kind spilled into the small cove closest to the roaring water. I began to walk further into the space, but Jorun stopped me. He'd yelled my name and I couldn't hear him, so he bent to collect a rock and tossed it at my back. It thudded against my wing.

"I mean no harm," he offered quickly, holding his hands out peacefully. "I shouted for you but you couldn't hear me, and I didn't want to touch you disrespectfully." A thread of irritation laced his words. I knew he'd seen The Shark do exactly that.

"It's fine," I assured him, shouting above the roar of water. "What did you want?"

"I'd rather remain close to the exit," he told me, his eyes begging me not to fight him on this. In his eyes swam the fear we shared. The desperate need to survive was insurmountable.

"Okay." We retreated toward the entrance and found a boulder large enough for both of us to sit. Its height accommodated Jorun's long wings.

He launched into his explanation as soon as we settled. "I went to The General, concerned about Talon because of some things I'd seen and rumors I'd heard. It was before you elevated him to your quad. Your father was aware of it all and was equally disturbed. He asked me to watch him and report back when I had more information."

"And you did," I surmised. It was a test of loyalty, one that likely spanned a long time. The General's confidence wasn't easily won.

"I did, though Talon was a master at evasion. He preferred to hunt alone, but I saw some of the damage he caused – afterwards." A shiver slid up my spine at the thought that he might have seen Talon attacking Crest's mother. "Your father believed me even though I had no tangible, irrefutable proof of his actions. Even then… he reprimanded and punished him as his General, but that was all he had the power to do. Unless Talon attacked one of *our* people, his actions didn't matter to the Elders. He wouldn't face a tribunal because no one cared if he slew one of the people of the sea."

"Why didn't he trust me with this knowledge, or task me with stopping him?"

Jorun looked wholly uncomfortable. "I think he sought to keep you safe from Talon. Imagine what Talon might have done if he suspected you knew of his deeds and might bring him to justice?"

Truth had a certain ring to it. A tone that undeniably belonged only to it. Jorun wasn't speaking the truth. Perhaps there was a kernel in his words, but I may never know why my father hadn't trusted me with the nature and actions of a member of my own quad when I would have made Talon pay for what he'd done and made sure he never misrepresented me again.

"Did you watch my father die?" Pain flared in my heart at the thought. He'd revealed himself to me just before he died, though I'd known all along he was my sire. But more than our blood relation, he revealed his love for me, admitting he'd done all he could to protect and guard his children to the extent that his distinguished position would allow.

Jorun held my eye. "I was among the Warriors ordered to find and apprehend him and bring him to the Elders. I had no other choice but to go. He'd ordered me to never deviate from playing my part, even if he was in danger. And he protected me to the end. He didn't even glance in my direction when he..." Jorun hung his head. "I'm sorry I didn't stop him. I've regretted my inaction on that day each one I've breathed since."

"Don't waste your time trying to change something you can't. You followed my father's orders – which was what he wanted. If you had implicated yourself in order to defend him, he would've suffered at *their* hands trying to save you," I rasped.

Jorun grew quiet. Pensive.

"I came to find you to – well, I know I can't atone for what I've done, but I thought that if I could get to you before they did..."

The water rushed so quickly in front of us it seemed to blur. The crushing weight of that curtain of water could crush wing bones. Could crush bodies upon the rocks lurking below it. The water here was shallower than it appeared.

"Someone once told me there are never any good choices," Jorun said, shifting to find a more comfortable perch on this rock.

I tried to smile. "It is a sound observation of truth."

I stared at the sliver of space gaping between the mountain and tumbling river water and waited. And waited.

Frey stepped in, burgundy hair soaked and plastered like serpents to her cheeks and back. Her dark trident glinted menacingly in the light from the torch fire. I rose to meet her. Jorun shot to his feet beside me. "Have you seen Breaker or Katalini?" she panted.

I shook my head. "We haven't been here long and haven't ventured into the main room."

She nodded absently, already striding in and searching faces for the two she sought.

A moment later, Frey emerged from the inner room with Breaker on her heel, and Katalini on his.

"What's the matter?" I demanded.

"We can't find Crest or Koa," she noted.

My stomach plummeted. I started toward the exit.

Breaker caught my elbow. "You can't fly in this wind, Elira. It's too dangerous."

"Watch me," I growled, trembling with warning and an iron will that would break *him* if he didn't unhand me. He did exactly that.

"And if you find them in the sea?" he demanded. "*You can't swim.*"

"I can. I'll go with her," Frey offered immediately.

Breaker couldn't swim either, but he wanted to. He would do anything to save his brother. I saw the desperation in his eyes and knew the feeling of helplessness coursing through him. "You need to stay here – for *them.*" I gestured to his people, a sea of worried eyes all fixed on their leader. "*I* can find him, Breaker."

The Salt appeared over Breaker's shoulder. "I'll help Elira." In her palm lay two shells – Crest's and Koa's. "They're both alive and Talay is with us," she told Breaker. "We *will* bring them back."

Jorun stood behind me with a resolute look on his face, ready to serve.

"No, Jorun."

He shook his head. "You can't go out there alone! What if they're—"

Frustrated, I put a hand out, severing his words. "Jorun – I'm not asking. I am ordering you to *stay here.*"

My eyes flicked to Crest's brother and I gave him a meaningful glance. I needed him to distract Jorun. He'd requested to speak to him. Now he had the opportunity, and a conversation would keep both men busy until I returned.

The leader of Kehlani stepped forward and leaned in to speak into my ear so only I could hear his worry. "Talay wouldn't trap my brother in the sea. Something is very wrong." Breaker's eyes burned like Crest's, but not as hot. Not as passionately, despite his fevered plea.

"I'll bring him back, Breaker," I promised before jogging to the exit and stepping into the gale. My bow and quiver blew sideways with my hair and wings. They rattled on my back with every step I took toward Crest.

Frey and The Salt were behind me. The wind was erratic, swirling and shifting in varying directions – none of them predictable. "You can't fly in this!" Frey shouted.

I tucked my wings in tight to my back and looked between her and the Seer. "Crest told me he was heading to a reef because children were swimming there earlier."

Frey confirmed as much. "Koa was going to meet him there."

"Which direction is the reef?" I demanded.

Frey shook her head. "Flying in this will –"

"Do you *want* to save them or not? Trust me, Frey. I'll be of no help if I break my wings while searching for them. I know my limitations and this wind isn't one of them."

She swallowed thickly and pointed. I made mental notes of what I could see from the ground along that path from where I stood. One tree taller than the rest with peeling white bark and more vibrant leaves, and in the distance the sharp peak of a partially hidden lookout tower.

"How fast can you run?" I goaded her.

Frey gave me a feral smile and her grip tightened around the shaft of her trident. The Salt chuckled, already moving down the rocky path. "Go, Elira. Talay will guide your heart to your lacuna. We'll meet you on the shore."

My wings snapped outward. I closed my eyes and imagined the wind smoothing, cutting a sharp path directly to Crest in the direction Frey had indicated. The next second I was flying on that wind, sure and steady and as fast as lightning itself.

The ribbon of wind I could command was thin. It extended just a few feet before and behind me and was barely wide enough to accommodate my wings. When I strayed too close to its edge, I was reminded of the threat lying just beyond the sliver I could control. The rain poured in torrents, washing over my skin and wings, sliding into my eyes.

"Talay!" I shouted, invoking the god of the sea for his help. "Where is he?"

I tilted my head left and right, honing in on a section of sky that was far darker than the rest, a section of sea that seemed more unhinged. The only place where the sky and sea both thundered.

The Green Mountains fell away to flat land where the pitched tents that weren't already broken were bent and looking as if they might give way at any moment. The ocean churned beyond the village. Every wave was capped in white and swelled taller than the grove's trees, the troughs bearing the weight of massive surges. Eager to fight, they crashed upon each other, then together roared onto the shore, pummeling it flat like great fists.

In the place of thunder, two funnels swirled over the ocean, gathering seawater into a menacing, dark cloud.

From somewhere near the dancing twins, I heard his shrill cry.

"Crest!" I yelled, pumping my wings as fast as I could, gathering the wind before and behind me and letting it push me even faster now that I knew he was close, that he was alive.

Frey shrieked to confirm that she was coming to help when she reached the shore behind me. A flash of burgundy along the sand and then she was gone, disappearing beneath the crashing waves.

She was a faster swimmer than she was a runner, but even she had to be careful and stay out of the funnels' paths – paths that changed by the second and were as perfectly unpredictable as they were precise.

The Great Wind only bent like this for Neera. I could feel her vast and terrible presence, her outrage and ire, in the torrid gusts I'd bent around me in protection.

The spouts began to circle one another. If they converged and joined, it wouldn't matter how skilled a swimmer or flyer one was; no one could survive such raw, unbridled power.

From the nearest funnel came a garbled cry. For a moment, my heart stopped. I panicked. "Crest?"

But then his voice came from the sea below.

"Koa!" Crest was just ahead, cutting through the towering waves toward the base of one of the funnels, but he disappeared beneath the surface before I could reach him.

In the tightly swirling water, golden scales shimmered. Koa was trapped.

Crest would reach Koa or die trying. He dove down to approach the waterspout from the deep. He was a Guardian, sworn to protect Talay's sea and the people he'd crafted for it. But if he joined Koa, Neera would have them both in her grasp.

It seemed the goddess's bow was still aimed at the Shark, even though I was no longer her arrow.

Time slowed.

The seconds bled away between thunder and lightning, between breath and heartbeat, indecision rendering me useless.

The wind I'd stolen from Neera had kept me safe thus far, but would the funnels take back the air I used if I got too close? Would the spinning wind snap my wings and render me useless again? If I drowned, Crest and Koa would truly be at her mercy, and the goddess of the sky was incapable of showing charity.

Palms out, I called more wind to me. But in doing so, Neera's attention slid to me. I felt the moment she recognized that I had taken what was hers, and that I hadn't come for her, but for *him*.

The funnels shifted course and crossed nearer and nearer, fed by the waves and bolstered by the wind. That was the problem, for the funnels were made of both. I might have the power of Neera's first soul, but I didn't have enough to stop the goddess's assault, and I had no influence whatsoever over the brine.

"Talay!" I cried. "I need your help to save them."

With perfect timing, The Salt stepped into the raging sea. I felt the reverberation in every droplet of water pouring over me. The air around me recognized her and recoiled.

It turned cold.

My skin prickled with goose flesh.

And like the layers of an onion peeled away from its middle, sound fled. First, the wind in my ears faded away. The booming of the sea beneath my feet was next, followed by the slap of rain against my skin. I couldn't even hear the flap of my wings or my heart beating against the wall of my chest. I couldn't hear my breath saw in and out of my throat.

All I could hear was *her*.

She lifted the cowries she'd brought with her, then chanted and shouted as she called upon Talay. "Deliver Crest and Koa!" her voice demanded. "Keep Frey," she begged, "and guide Elira through."

Through. Not around. Not within. But *through*.

That was my path.

If Neera could bend the Great Wind, then Talay still controlled his sea, even what was being dragged into the sky…

I raced toward the funnel that held Koa and begged Talay to bring him up to meet me. I had one chance, I knew, to dive into the spinning cloud and pluck him from it.

All at once, The Salt went quiet and the gale began to howl, tearing around the cocoon of safety I'd managed to craft. The waves grew taller, smashing harder into one another mercilessly.

The wind that shielded my wings began to tear away the closer I flew toward the spouts moving over the water until I was so close, the brine was all I could taste. The funnel bent and spun into a darker cloud and I could almost hear her voice there. Daring me to come closer, promising she would break me if I crossed the line I'd been only toeing to this point.

But louder than the goddess I knew was one word that reverberated from the mouth of Talay – yet again.

As if I had forgotten.

As if I needed his booming reminder.

Lacuna…

Crest resurfaced far too close to the spinning water, looking at both funnels to see if he could tell which one held Koa. He hadn't found a way into the funnel from beneath, so he swam right for its base on the sea's churning surface. Waves crashed over him, never slowing or deterring him.

"Crest, no!" I shouted.

He stopped in the water and looked up, then shook his head and pointed wildly, back toward safety. Toward shore. "Get back!" I thought he said.

Another scream from the funnel and I knew Talay had answered me. I *knew* where Koa was.

I soared up, daring the funnel and its wicked maker to dance with me instead of its twin. A flash of gold in the rushing, murky gray and I dove toward it, toward Koa, with my wings tucked and Neera's wind cloaked tightly around me.

"Talay, guide me!" I screamed. My outstretched hands found the funnel's edge and I plunged inside where only wind, water, and malice lived.

Koa was there, right where I needed him to be. As if Talay had surged his water to lift him up for me. I barreled into his middle, pushing him out the other side of the mammoth waterspout. We plummeted toward the ground, caught off guard by the sudden loss of the sheer force to which we'd been subjected. The wind I'd used to shroud my body and wings was gone and I grappled for more, struggling to catch hold of anything but fear.

"Koa!" I shouted as I dove for him, though I wasn't sure my wings would work and flare and stop us before we smacked into the surface, or if he'd be too stunned to survive such a fall, even into the arms of his god.

All he could do was gasp, panicked and desperate for air, as he fell with his back to the sea. His dark eyes blinked, wide with fear. He strained toward me with both arms, his teeth gritted. "Elira!"

I clawed toward him. Just before we struck the white curling crest of a wave, we clasped forearms and I let my wings flare out wide, dragging him over the enormous swell. His feet cut into the water, dragging foamy twin trails.

Crest was there, swimming so fast he blurred beneath us.

Koa's grip slipped to my wrist. I gave an anguished cry, clenching my free hand around his and trying to hold on. I could see the shore, but it seemed so far away; the waves seemed to grow all around us. He was too heavy.

"Koa, I'm losing you!"

"Let me go!" he shouted.

I shook my head. "No! I see the shore. Just… hold on."

"The swells are too big!" he yelled, looking all around us. "You can't get rolled by one of these waves. Not these."

I didn't want to let him go.

I knew what it felt like to fall. To feel the stifling weight of the sea.

"Elira, I'm good now. Let me go. I'll swim to the sand and meet you there."

He sounded so sure, but I couldn't bring myself to release him. Koa tried to pry my hands away. He gripped my wrist and shouted my name as if to snap me out of whatever daze I was drowning in.

"I was born to swim, but you were not. You have to fly to shore before one of these waves sweeps over you! I'll meet you there. You can even stay and watch Crest kick my ass." He retracted his fingers so that I was the only one holding on. "Let go," he encouraged again. "I'm good now, I promise."

I searched his face for a lie and found none. He seemed fine. Like normal Koa. Brows raised encouragingly.

My fingers relaxed.

Koa splashed into the middle of a foamy swell.

Seconds later, Crest and Frey were there. Before they dove, the three were swimming a straight line toward The Salt.

I saw her in the distance and still felt her in the brine spraying over every inch of me, though I'd risen above the incessant waves. I paused to make sure the funnels weren't giving chase, but it seemed Neera was gone and had taken her destructive twins away with her. A heavy sigh of relief poured from my chest.

My heart rejoiced to see the sky slowly lighten shade by shade. Cloud by cloud. The swells stopped cresting and toppling, the tide stopped pummeling the shore. Even the wind softened as the gale took its last breaths.

Every storm, like every battle, had an ending.

The Salt's red sarong and shirt were heavy with the rain they'd collected. It sluiced from her skin and the braids and shells falling down her back. From her clothes, droplets splattered onto the dark sand, leaving a pattern of lighter circles in a ring around her feet. She watched as I landed, punctuating the moment my feet touched the Isle with a proud smile. "Well done."

"Thank *you* for revealing how to save him."

The Salt's hand clutched the cowries she'd brought a little tighter. She laid her fist against her chest. "I don't know what you mean."

"You asked Talay to see me *through*."

"Ah," she said appreciatively. "Talay spoke to your heart using my voice and lips, it seems." She looked to the sky. "Watching you dive through the funnel was something I promise you I'll never forget. How did the wind not touch you? It was like you tore a hole through it, like you were immune."

I shook my head. "I'm not sure." I'd used a sliver of the Great Wind, but the goddess had ripped it away when I entered the storm. When Koa and I fell, I couldn't grasp it again in time to help either of us.

Just then, a commotion came from the waves, followed by a guttural roar and an explosion of water. I flinched, startled, and grabbed my bow.

"Oh, no," the Salt said warily, staring toward the foam-laden shallows.

Frey's burgundy hair emerged between Crest and Koa. Both men shouted at one another, seawater and spittle flying from their mouths with the curses they flung.

I moved toward them, but The Salt stopped me. "Put your bow away… They need to get this out of their systems."

"What do you mean?"

"Their anger. They must release it before they can move on. This is their way."

Then it's a foolish way! "But they're friends," I argued.

"Have you ever fought with a friend? Or someone you commanded?" she asked, one brow quirked.

"Many times," I relented.

"There is a time for forbearance and a time for reprisal." She winced as Crest tackled Koa into the waves.

The two rolled around like hulking mountain cats pouncing on one another, claws and fur flying. Like two sea-slickened krakens tangling their suckered limbs, bent on ripping one another apart. Frey soon realized they wouldn't stop and left them to fight, waving off their ridiculous antics and walking to join The Salt and me on the sand.

"Asinine," the Guardian snarled, flinging an angry hand in their direction. "They show one another they're glad they survived by trying to kill each other."

"May I use your trident?" I asked. She gave me a questioning look before handing it over.

I hurled it at both men.

It landed just shy of their heads.

The weapon's barbed tips buried in the sand, a swell of a wave sweeping over the wobbling handle as if to investigate the intrusion before pulling away again.

CHAPTER NINE

The tactic startled Crest and Koa enough to make them finally part, both turning their attention to me instead of one another. Then Koa stormed from the water, cursing Frey soundly.

She doubled over laughing, not phased by his threat in the least. "I only wish *I'd* thought of it."

Their heads swiveled to The Salt, immediately dismissing her as the wielder of the trident. The process of elimination had them gritting their teeth.

If it had been Frey, they would have dragged her into their fight. If it had been The Salt, they might have grumbled, but their respect for her would've ultimately stayed their tongue. But it wasn't their friend or Seer who'd targeted them…

It quickly became obvious that it rankled them they couldn't bark at me for hurling the spear. They didn't owe me a chewing out. They owed me their gratitude. I'd saved Koa, after all. With Talay's, Frey's, and The Salt's help, of course.

And if they dragged me into the fight despite what I'd done, I'd show them how Empyrean warriors sparred when angry. "The two of you were acting like children. Someone had to stop it."

"By hurling a trident at us?" Koa finally chuckled. The tension between the men slowly ebbed.

I shrugged a slender shoulder. "Frey tried to be civil and you ignored her attempts. I assumed the two of you would only respond to violence. After all, that was the language in which you spoke to one another."

Crest's blue eyes darkened to match the sea, and in their depths swam something menacing, something that burned. Something that made my traitorous toes begin to curl yet again. My blood heated at the thought of that anger unleashed in *other* ways…

Koa wiped blood from his split lip. "Hey Elira, want to conjure a cloud to stop this?"

"Not on your life," I quipped.

He groaned but trudged from the sea to stand before the three of us. He looked at me, then away again, pinched his lips together and paused for a moment. Then he turned to Frey and apologized for scaring her, and for any blows he might have accidentally landed when she tried to break them apart.

She waved him off. "I'm just glad you're *alive*."

That set off a wave of emotion. Her words formed the head of an arrow that struck him in the heart. The blustering confidence Koa usually exuded melted away like wax from a wick.

He looked to the sky and knotted his fingers behind his head. But I didn't miss the fact that his chin quivered. "I couldn't breathe in there," he finally said, his voice thick with tears. "There was only wind and water, and I couldn't tell where one ended and the other began, whether to breathe through my mouth or gills. Neither worked, no matter what I tried. It was just confusion and a slow, torturous suffocation." Tears gathered on his lashes.

"How long were you trapped?" I asked.

"I honestly don't know," he answered, then looked to Crest.

The Shark's dark countenance lightened a fraction. A muscle ticked along his jaw. "Too long. If you hadn't come for him, he wouldn't have survived it."

At that, Koa blew out a tense breath and began to cry, attempting to hold his fear and angst at bay, but in the end, crumpling in on himself. He put his hands on his hips, then bent to brace them above his knees, trembling all over. Frey and The Salt comforted him, patting his back and reminding him that he made it through.

It took a few minutes for Koa to calm himself, but when he stood, he met my eye. "Thank you, Elira, for what you did when you didn't have to do it. When it might have…I… there's no way for me to repay you."

"I didn't do it so you'd be indebted to me," I rasped, his emotion catching me up in its net.

"I know," he said. "I know why you did it." Koa glanced toward Crest, who'd moved to stand at his side. He gave a loud, colorful curse. "I'm sure glad she's your lacuna, man," he told Crest. "And I'm sorry I got myself into the situation by not listening to you."

Crest forgave him with a single, staunch nod. The Shark was still angry, but more than that, he was upset. He'd almost lost one of his dearest friends. I knew what that felt like.

Aderyn might be alive, but our friendship died the day she led me to believe she had. After all this time, it still hurt. Mostly because I still loved her for what she'd been to me and hated her for the lengths she went to in order to rid herself of me.

I wasn't certain I could forgive her at all, let alone as easily as Crest had Koa.

Koa cursed again and squeezed his eyes tightly closed, more tears pressing from his lids. "Elira, damn it. I… I know you don't like to touch or be touched, but I'd *really* like to hug you right now if you'd let me."

I thought at first he was just stating a fact, but then I saw the hopeful expression he wore. Brows slightly raised, his arms slightly opened. He waited for an answer of whether I would embrace him or not.

Frozen, I wasn't sure what to do or if it was appropriate to hug him. No one objected. The Salt, Frey, Crest… they waited for my answer, too. So, I slightly opened my arms to match his, figuring I could allow a small embrace to soothe him.

Koa saw my consent and rushed toward me, almost knocking me over. He pulled me so tight to his body, it was hard to breathe deeply. "Thank you," he said again, rocking me back and forth.

"You're welcome," I eeked out, afraid to pat his back and afraid he wouldn't release me until I did. Awkwardly, I tapped him a few times.

Frey laughed as he set me free. "That was the most painful thing I've ever witnessed."

"My hugs are the best," Koa bristled. "Even *you* love them, Frey. Don't pretend." Glittering in his gaze was pure orneriness as he zeroed in on her.

"No," she said with a slight smile on her lips. "You don't deserve a hug after today."

"I do, though. You're glad I'm alive. You even said it. They witnessed it," he insisted, darting left and trying to clobber her with his affection.

"I take it back!" she shouted. Frey deftly slid right and he gave chase. Frey was fast. I'd give her that. Sand flew behind her every step as she raced down the shore, but Koa was faster.

He let her stay ahead until she grew tired and then he tackled her to the sand, hugging her and rolling them both into the water. She laughed and tried to pry him away, but he wouldn't have it.

"Say you love my hugs," he told her. "Say you love my hugs and I'll let you go!"

She gritted, "I hate them! And if you ever pull a stunt like that again, you…" She let out a string of the most insulting words I'd ever heard, followed by threats that amplified my appreciation for her as a warrior and woman.

He chortled with laughter, not the least bit offended. He thought she and her denigration was hilarious. Finally, he told her he loved her back and smacked a loud kiss on her cheek. She quickly wiped it away when he let her go.

He ran back to take The Salt's hand. When she glared, daring him to treat her as he had Frey, Koa respectfully thanked her for helping. He told her he could feel her even when he couldn't see her, that he heard her words in his heart. Then his eyes flicked to mine again. He knew I was there beyond the wind and water. But did he know I hesitated, trying to figure out how to manage it without harming myself or my wings?

He'd indicated he knew why I did it – for Crest. And he was right. Would I have saved Koa if it wasn't for The Shark? I wasn't sure.

The memory of Crest swimming close to Neera's hand made my stomach sour. She had him in her palm, she just hadn't tightened her fingers.

"You two should go and tell Breaker we're okay and the storm is over," Crest told Koa and Frey. "He'll want to assess the damage and begin repairs, and he'll need help from anyone able to give it."

Koa waited, apologizing again as Frey retrieved her trident from the shallows, and they walked together down the shore, heading toward the nearest village.

The Salt began to follow their footsteps. "Salt?" Crest called out.

She slowed, stopped, and turned to look at us over her shoulder.

"Thank you."

She gave him a kind, almost motherly smile. One that made my heart ache. When she made it to the dunes, Crest finally relaxed his shoulders. He must have been holding his breath because he released a long, stress-filled exhalation.

Hands on his hipbones, I waited for him to rage at me, mentally preparing myself to shout right back. There had been no other way for Koa to survive the funnels but for me to charge through them. Talay suggested it, so I knew it was the path I had to take.

It was the *only* way through.

I prepared my defense so well, I was ready to lash back at him when he began to pace back and forth. He seemed to be searing with anger, his hands flexing and relaxing at his side.

I'd had enough of this silent tantrum. "Stop pacing and face me."

"You have no idea …" His words broke off like exposed rock from a mountain, but the look in his eyes was as ardent as it was intense. He scrubbed a hand over the scruff above his lip and down his jaw.

"No idea what?" I demanded. He stayed silent so I pressed on. "No idea how… angry you are? How you want to throttle me the way you did your best friend after his insubordination? Well, allow me to remind you that I am *not* your subordinate. I don't care what your title and position is on the Isle or in the sea. I *do not* answer to you."

He finally stopped and turned to face me. His crystalline eyes locked on mine. Two strides and his chest was a hair's breadth from my own. I tried to keep my breaths shallow to keep my breasts from brushing his stomach as he towered over me, though I stood higher on the shore than he did. The shallow, gentle waves brushed his heels and never touched my toes at all.

"You have *no* idea," he began again, more resolutely, "how terrified I was."

Oh. Of course…

"I was scared for him, too," I admitted.

"Koa was drowning slowly. He kept crying out for me to help him and I was trying my hardest to do exactly that, but I couldn't. I couldn't find a way into the funnel

– not from beneath the sea, not from the surface. I tried to swim directly into it but every time I got close, it shifted. It was like the storm didn't want me."

Didn't want The Shark? I glared at the sky, wondering if the lure Neera had cast wasn't for The Shark at all, but for me all along. If he was in danger, if he was hurt, she knew I would come.

"Elira, Koa was *drowning*," he said again in disbelief.

"I know," I quietly said. "But he's safe now."

He swallowed thickly. "My best friend in this world was drowning. He was dying. But when I saw you flying near the funnels, all I could think of was that you were in danger."

A long pause filled with too many thoughts to capture and name stretched between us.

Until one broke free and asserted itself.

My eyes fixed on the circle of feathers gracing the skin above his heart. "It's because Talay told you to feel protective of me."

His pained stare tore at my heart. "Talay didn't *choose* you for me. He never *told* me to feel any certain way about you."

"But he chooses lacunas… doesn't he?" I asked, trying desperately to understand the ways of his god, of his people.

He held my eyes, passion and emotion swirling in their blue striations. "The only thing that Talay does when one asks for a mark is reveal what, if anything, is already in the person's heart. He doesn't choose mates for us like the Elders in the sky. The decision is ours. He just reveals it. Sometimes before we even recognize it ourselves."

He lifted his hand and ghosted his palm over my arm, never touching me, but drawing forth an ache so deep in my belly I wasn't sure touch mattered anymore. I felt him prickling at my skin, burrowing beneath it.

"We can reject the mark once we hear the pattern."

My breath caught.

He suspected the feather pattern represented me the moment he heard it. And he could've rejected it. Likely regretted not doing so a time or two – or many – since then. Could've rejected me the way The Salt said I had rejected him.

"Why didn't you?" I breathed.

"Because part of me already knew. The other part grappled with it ferociously," he gave me a devastating grin, "but in the end, there was no fighting it. For me, there's no fighting *this*, Elira. And not because I'm powerless, but because I've never wanted something so much."

And yet I still feverishly fought against it because if I caught hold of something like this and was torn from it, I wasn't sure I'd survive it. I wasn't sure I was brave enough to take this path yet.

But what would it feel like if we stopped warring against wanting one another just for a few moments? Even if we knew the battle would resume?

What if we knew it would end with one of our deaths?

"You let Koa embrace you," he rasped.

I wrapped my arms around my middle. "I wasn't sure what else to do. He seemed so upset."

"Do you regret comforting him?"

I shook my head. "No. I don't."

"Then could I ask you to do the same for me?"

In his voice, there was a rawness, a vulnerability I'd never sensed from him. My toes curled, dragging through the soaked sand.

We were already so close. The slightest movement was all it would take for us to touch.

Slowly, I extended my arms as I had with Koa, but wider, never taking my eyes off his. I wanted this and I wanted him to know it. I didn't fear *his* touch. And if comfort was what he needed, *I* wanted to be the one who gave it to him.

He didn't leap forward or nearly knock me down as Koa had.

A muscle ticked in his jaw and I knew… knew he was restraining himself for my benefit. I didn't know until that moment how much I craved abandon instead.

Knowing that this feeling in my chest wasn't caused by a god forcing my feet in a certain direction made my wings flutter at my back. His eyes caught the motion and flared, darkening with desire.

He bent forward.

His strong hands landed upon my waist, then slowly slid around to my back.

Pushing onto the tips of my toes, I threaded my arms around his neck and pulled him so close, not even the fine barbs of a feather could fit between our lips.

Our breath mingled.

As did the brine on our skin where we touched, his flesh to mine, and mine to his.

If I were in Empyrean, I would be told who to touch and when it was allowed. On Kehlani, I was free to make that decision.

I am free…

He held me for several long moments, his hands strong and sure and steady on my back. Crest was a deeply powerful grounding force, but somehow his hands on my skin made me feel like I was flying.

As the sea lapped at our toes, Crest wrapped me tighter and buried his head into the crook of my shoulder. The tension in his body bled away beneath my hands. As he became pliant, my body went taut as a desperate ache flooded every inch of me.

I closed my eyes to just… *feel.*

The strength of his arms.

The warmth of his breath fanning over my neck.

The way our bodies melded so perfectly together.

Our drenched clothes snapped as they were wrung by the steady breeze that blew in off the water. For several long moments, we stayed like that. Until his grip slackened and he let me go, stepping away and giving me the space he thought I wanted.

I couldn't swallow the whimper that rose and escaped my throat as the loss sent a wave of ache through my body. I opened my eyes to find him staring, then felt his hands land upon my hips again. His lips slowly parted, the question flaring in his eyes.

"Elira?" he softly spoke, his brows pinched.

My heart pounded toward him, indignant. She wasn't ready to let go; unsure when she'd get another chance like this.

His fingers flexed against my skin as his oceanic eyes searched me.

"I don't love you," I breathed.

"No?" he asked, an irksome smile lifting the corner of his lips just so…

"No," I confirmed with a slow shake of my head.

"But…?" he led.

"But I need… I don't know what I need." I was frustrated and becoming angrier by the second.

"Tell me, and I'll provide it," he vowed.

This was a bad decision. I couldn't be his lacuna the way that Katalini was Breaker's. And we'd decided – well, he suggested – that we would be friends instead.

But I loved the feel of his touch. I found it hard to look away from his lips.

What would it feel like to kiss him when we weren't playing a game of dares? Was I bold enough to ask it of him? There were consequences to every action, some more dire than others.

What if he, too, thought this was a bad idea and refused me?

What if he doesn't?

I fought an entire war with myself and in the end… abandon won out over restraint, and I finally decided to dive toward the thing I wanted most. Giving in wasn't free-falling. It wasn't a dizzying spiral. It was a sharpened arrow pointed at its target – perfectly aimed.

"I want to kiss you," I said before I lost my nerve.

I wanted to kiss him, but I wasn't sure he wanted the same. This was something I didn't know how to initiate, a sky in which I'd never flown. The kiss I craved wouldn't be a simple pressing of my lips to his. It wouldn't be a meaningless moment of curiosity.

It wouldn't be nothing.

But it couldn't be *more,* either. I couldn't promise him anything beyond this moment, so I didn't.

A kiss… a single kiss was all I wanted.

The Shark didn't agree to my demand with words. His blue eyes caught fire, then turned absolutely molten.

His head tilted as he achingly slowly leaned down and did just as he promised. He provided.

His lips found mine and he showed me how different a kiss could be when it was wanted. When it was *needed.* When it was so powerful it consumed everything, every thought and feeling, sound and smell, until the world spinning around us faded away.

His fingers tightened against my bare skin, his thumb brushing back and forth, pushing a warm heat deep into my belly. And as our mouths and tongues moved in time together, our chests brushing, the roar of the sea was suddenly all I could hear.

All I could feel was truth.

I kissed him until I was dizzy from it. Until he and I blurred, never growing tired of the sensation, but instead craving more…

More…

When we finally peeled away from one another, my lips tingled, swollen. My tongue swept across the bottom. Crest watched every movement but stayed silent. And per usual, his silence was maddening.

Did he not enjoy it? Was I terrible at kissing?

Had he heard Talay?

He must not have been affected by it at all.

Perhaps it was for the best. We could spend the rest of our time as friends, and he could take a lover who knew what she was doing. I could find peace with that.

I could.

Liar.

Finally, I realized that the fire in Crest's eyes had been smothered by a smugness I didn't understand.

"Why are you staring at me like that?" I demanded.

"Because I'm imagining the look on Jorun's face when he sees you."

My brows scrunched together. "I don't understand."

"Your lips are swollen and the skin around them is red."

"That means nothing," I told him, tipping up my chin.

Crest quirked a haughty brow. "It meant everything, and you know it. And soon he will, too."

He was infuriating. Why would it matter if Jorun knew?

What did it matter if anyone did?

CHAPTER TEN

By the time we arrived at my tent, my lips still tingled and felt as raw as my heart. Crest claimed I had no idea how terrified he was to see me in danger, but I didn't tell him that seeing him approach the funnels struck me with fear more powerful than the bolt that had seared through my chest.

He needed to hold me in a different way than Koa's quick but violent and friendly embrace. I needed more than that. To feel him in a way I hadn't before.

I didn't regret one second of what happened between us on the shore. It was the most beautiful, meaningful moment of my life, second only to the one where he saved me. And yet the two moments were similar, weren't they?

Our hearts dancing together like the twin funnels of wind and water.

Jorun watched as a team of four Kehlanians quickly raised my tent where it had buckled during the storm. He apologized to those helping for not being able to assist them. I could tell he hated being injured as much as I had.

Crest and I rushed ahead to help tie the fabric down to the thick wooden pegs driven far into the sand. When it was finished, I walked inside. Nothing was damaged, though some things were overturned. It only took a moment to set them right.

From my small porch, I could see that Crest's home was upright and intact. As he strode toward it, I watched his muscles ripple with every movement.

Those who had come to help Jorun, and me, moved on to find others in need of assistance, to raise more poles and homes so they could stand against future storms.

Jorun shouted a last thank you to them and watched them leave, his wings rigid and his hands perched on his hips.

"Thank you for overseeing the uplifting of my home, Jorun," I told him.

His eyes cut to mine. "This is *not* your home, Elira," he snapped. "Breaker explained many things to me. He told me what the word 'lacuna' means. What the marks mean to them." Then, his gaze fell to my lips. "Are you mating with him?"

I looked away from him, my attention gravitating to the tent pitched nearest the sea where The Shark dwelled. "What I do is none of your concern. You'd do well to remember your place."

"*My* place?" he gritted. "We aren't in Empyrean anymore. This isn't a battle you're leading me into. This..."

He raised his uninjured arm and pinched the bridge of his nose, exasperation evident in every uneasy breath. "What are you doing, Elira? Do you have any idea what might come of this?"

Happiness was the first word that came to mind.

Happiness.

Joy.

Freedom.

And a life I could claim instead of being forced into a cage.

"You're rebelling because you don't want to be clipped," he stated matter-of-factly. "But you haven't thought this through."

"We haven't mated, Jorun," I answered wearily. "Crest took the mark, and he and I have kissed. Once during a game, and…"

"And?" he pushed angrily.

"*And* just now, because I asked him to," I hissed, moving toward him threateningly. Jorun did not cower as I expected.

He was different here. I was different here.

He was right. On the sand of Kehlani, the hierarchy we'd carefully carved in Empyrean had crumbled into dust and was scattered by the wind.

"Have you considered what will happen *to him* if the Elders learn who he is to you?" He took a deep breath. "The Elders are divided in their schools of thought at present. If you return and tell them that the people of Talay showed you mercy and sought an end to the war, I know some of them would listen. There seems to be a sliver of a silent majority who still uphold the duties with which they were charged. *Those* Elders might be swayed right now. They might feel inspired to change. But if the reasonable women and men among their number are made to believe Crest manipulated you into mating with him, or if they think it was forced..."

"It wasn't," I gritted.

"I know that, Elira. But if, Neera forbid, a hatchling is produced, who knows what the Elders would do to Crest or your babe? If they can use either or both to control you, they *will*. You know how ruthless they are."

The vision of my mother falling through the firmament, followed by the echoing sound of her screams resurfaced.

My shoulders deflated along with my anger. He was right, because he knew their nature. Just as he was right to remind me what was at stake.

"You cannot be his lacuna, and he cannot be yours. Not if you want to protect him. Your time on the sand must come to an end. You are the greatest Warrior to ever fly for Empyrean. This... this is your chance to lead. The only opportunity you'll likely ever have to rip the power from Talon's greedy grip and take your rightful place. And if you do that, you *will* be able to end the war, because no Warrior in their right mind would stand against you with the first soul embedded in your flesh, the blood of Neera in your veins, the Scholars behind you, and the Oracle to guide you forward. The Warriors... they look up to you. They have for years. They will follow if you lead. And that doesn't even include the allies you've made among the sea god and his people."

His expression fell, waxing from passionate plea to pity in an instant. "I'm sorry, Elira. I can see that you care for them..." He took a breath and paused. "I think you might have until Intention Day to make a move. Before I found you, Talon hadn't finalized any plans, although it's possible they've changed since I've been here," he warned. "But he wanted to mobilize every Empyrean on that day to descend en masse, with one shared intention."

One intention to end them all.

One fell swoop.

"We don't have long, then," I noted breathlessly, trying to grasp exactly how little time remained until then. Only a few short weeks...

"The people of Kehlani aren't ready for the fight he will bring. He described it as decisive – a battle to end the war. If you want to prepare them, I'll help you, Elira. And when you ascend, I will fight at your side."

"Why?" I asked, looking down at the sand my toes pressed into. I wished I could memorize every grain, that I could know them all the way The Salt knew her cowries.

He scuffed his foot on the damp sand. "Because you're right about these people, and it didn't take long for me to realize it. *We* were wrong. Just as I was wrong about you in many respects."

"How do you know I'm right about them?"

"Breaker offered an unexpectedly warm welcome and even explained that his trust could be earned in time. He said that he'd grown to trust you to an extent, something I never imagined might be possible given all we've done to shred one another. Then when Frey and Koa came to tell us the gale was over and everyone was safe, Breaker and Katalini invited me to stand with them as he spoke to his people, already offering help he knew they would need.

"He's a good man, Elira. He loves everyone on this Isle, knows their names, their families, their difficulties and triumphs. It was eye-opening to see him speak to each and every person who passed us by. But as they did, I lost count of the number of children who cowered at the sight of me because of Talon and his vile followers," he said disgustedly. "Though there were a few who seemed curious and whispered your name. You've charmed many, despite the lingering wariness of others."

I tried to smile. "Did you expect less of me?"

He gave a mirthless laugh. "Long ago, I learned never to underestimate you. I'm not sure Talon ever truly learned that lesson, but I'd love to watch you teach it to him."

My heart was cracking, but I knew it would be torn to ribbons if something happened to Crest and his people. To my siblings still hidden here. Even to Aderyn, despite the fact that I hated her as much as I'd once cared for her.

Even so, I owed her my protection for as long as I could offer it. She'd shielded me for years.

Crest emerged from his tent and walked toward us. "Would you want to go with me to see if anyone else needs help with their homes?" he asked, his eyes flicking between me and Jorun.

Jorun wiggled the fingers of his bound arm. "I won't be of much use, but it would be nice to tag along, if you don't mind."

When I nodded, Crest inclined his head and pinned me with a look I couldn't decipher. Had he heard all that Jorun revealed? Did he already feel the sense of loss seeping in?

"I'd like to check on my grandmother first," The Shark suggested. So, we hurried to Magma's tent.

The Mender's tent was upright, but she wasn't in it. Worried, Crest suggested we go to The Salt. At her tent, we found them both.

The jaw bones of the animal that once hung over her door lay separated on the ground. Some of the sharp teeth were strewn over the sand. "What is that?" Jorun breathed.

"Decorative accent," I explained under my breath as Crest jogged to his grandmother and wrapped her in a hug. She whispered something to him and nodded toward The Salt's tent.

"Wade!" Crest called out, pushing inside to see his friend. The Salt trailed him. The troubled look she wore when she came to show me the trembling shells still rested on her features.

Magma waved Jorun and me over. She looked me over, studying my wings and side. "The Salt told me it was quite a sight to watch you fly," she marveled. "For once, not hurtling to kill us all, but to save my grandson."

I wasn't sure she was complimenting or thanking me, so I held my tongue. She would reveal the meaning, I had no doubt, when she was finished lecturing to make her point.

"Crest wasn't in the funnel, Magma. Koa was."

"And so you saved Koa so Crest didn't do a foolish thing like getting himself stuck in one as well. I know your heart, girl. You can't hide it from me." She pursed her lips together, gathered her long gray hair, and threw it off her shoulders. "What you did could've ruined your wings."

I knew that.

"But you risked it anyway," she continued.

Jorun stood stoically at my side but didn't defend my actions. He likely thought I was a fool, too.

"Interesting that you would risk your life to save Crest's," she pressed, one gray brow raised.

I shrugged a slender shoulder. "He did the same for me."

"He wouldn't have drowned dragging you from the water, dear. So, it's *not* the same at all." She turned to Jorun. "How does your shoulder feel?"

"Awful," he chirped, rocking back on his heels only slightly before the pain righted him once more. "Just as you warned me it would if I moved, or walked, or breathed…" His voice trailed away at the sour look she gave him.

"Yet you did," she tsked, shaking her head.

I almost laughed. Jorun did all three of those things at once and Magma knew it.

She offered me a sly wink while Jorun looked away and cleared his throat.

"The storm made it necessary for me to flee into the mountains. Did you stay here during it?" my fourth asked the Mender. "I didn't see you in the grotto."

"Wade couldn't make the trek. The Salt's tent has never collapsed, so a couple of Guardians helped him over and I stayed to keep him company," she said, giving me a shrug of her own.

"How is he?" I quietly inquired.

She leaned in. "His leg is healed, but his mind has difficulty accepting what happened. Before others, he puts on a brave face, but he's struggling. At times, he even forgets his leg is gone. Especially at night. That's why he's staying here for now."

I thought of the branch I'd pulled from the grove and imagined the leg hidden within it, ready to be carved by my hands. "He'll walk again."

"He has crutches and refuses to use them." She nodded to two limbs propped in the corner.

"Soon enough, he won't need them to move."

Magma's head tilted sideways. "I'm not sure how he would manage that, but he'll learn to adapt and live without his leg."

"Can I see him?" I asked.

"Of course, but don't you dare tell him he doesn't need his crutches," she warned.

I inclined my head. "Very well. I'll keep quiet." *For now.*

She snorted. "I highly doubt that."

Wade was sitting up in the middle of the Mender's cot talking to Crest, who'd pulled a chair over. The Shark straddled it and leaned his arms over the back, his copper leg scales on full display. I couldn't help but appreciate them for a moment.

The two men discussed the storm's intensity. Wade admitted he was surprised The Salt's tent didn't fail, and he'd already heard about Koa and the waterspouts.

The Salt moved toward me, the rows of shells on her chest clacking against each other with every step. She carried her bowl of cowries. "Have they settled?" I asked, anticipating her answer.

"No," she answered. "They tremble still."

She brought the bowl closer to my ear. I could hear their gentle clatter.

"Talay has not revealed what distresses them."

I had an idea now that Jorun told me what Talon had been planning – assuming his plans hadn't changed.

"The omens lately have been ill ones. Wade being attacked by a shark. The unsettling dreams. The boys you saved from death. I even consider the fact that your friend slipped through our defenses a dire warning. Then there was the ruddy sky and the storm. Koa…" She shook her head. "But this string of bad things only leads to something greater, if the shells are right. They have never been wrong, and they've never shaken for me or any of my predecessors." Her fingers trailed the necklaces draped concentrically from her throat to her chest. The cowries of her forbearers.

Wade and Crest spoke quietly with one another as I conversed with The Salt. I missed their words. But now with Crest on one side and Jorun on the other, Wade gripped their hands and stood. "Elira," he said. "Would you come here for a moment?"

Lips parted in surprise, I moved across the room, stopping before him.

Beads of sweat dotted his forehead and upper lip. "Two of my friends carried me here on the Mender's cot because everyone thinks I'm broken. And for the last few days, I thought I was, too. But when I heard that you'd healed and the moment you thought your wings would carry you, you saved two boys, then flew into a waterspout's funnel to push Koa out of it… Well, I knew that if you could fly again without fear, I can learn to make the most of what I have left. I… uh. I'm glad you came. I wanted you to be here the first time I stood. I know it's with help and everything, but –"

"But nothing!" I interrupted. "It's a step forward, Wade." Emotion washed over me.

"I wanted Crest to see," he continued. "I wouldn't be here if it weren't for the two of you and I want you to know how…" His voice cracked. "How grateful I am for what you did." His chin quivered like the shells in The Salt's bowl. "I knew you would come that day, Crest. You're always there when someone needs you. The greatest Guardian of Talay's sea." Wade smiled wistfully. "But I didn't expect you to help me as I lay on the shore dying, Elira. Especially given the way I treated you. I wanted to apologize to you for that."

My eyes sharpened. "If you truly want to thank me, you'll accept my gift and learn to use it well."

"What gift?" he asked, his head tilting.

"It's not ready yet."

He nodded. "Right. Well, whatever it is, I give you my word to put it to good use."

"No matter how difficult or frustrating the process. You don't quit, Wade," I pressed.

"I won't give up," he vowed. "I might not be whole, but –"

"None of us are whole. We all lack something. And you're right; it's what we do with what's left that matters."

He took a deep, shuddering breath. "Thank you."

Magma moved around me to reach Wade. "Sit back down. You're going pale." Crest and Jorun supported him as he lowered himself back down to the cot. "But do that several times a day with help, and soon you'll be able to do it on your own. You have to strengthen your back and legs and arms to accommodate and balance you."

"I will, Magma. Thank you," he said, winded.

The Salt showed us out. I leaned in to ask, "Does Wade still hum?"

She shook her head, and I knew she'd noticed. The loss of his joy was as significant as the loss of his leg. "He hasn't since he woke up and realized his leg was gone."

"He will," I told her.

I envisioned Wade whistling as he walked through the grove on a sunny day. Bees buzzing here and there between flowering trees. The sun warming his bronze shoulders.

Frey came to fetch Crest for Breaker and the two jogged toward the Guardian's Hall, but not before he promised to catch up to me when he could. We both knew he was needed elsewhere right now. He knew this land and the people on it. He knew how to make right what the storm had upset, and that doing so meant far more than raising and securing blown-over tents.

Jorun and I walked the island after that and I thought of every impression my foot made upon the Isle, and how Wade would soon make new ones. We saw families working all around their yards and homes to set things right. The wind had scattered and spread anything that wasn't secured. Rags and clothes, cups and plates littered the yards. We helped those who would allow it.

Jorun enjoyed watching the families orbit together, as curious as I was when I first arrived. He saw their trust and love, their loyalty and steadfastness. In the sky, we had no comparison, but if *anything* came close, it was the quads we formed. You had to trust those fighting before, beside, and behind you. But there was no love in the quads, which was why it was so easy for Soraya to cut me down. We trusted one another in battle, but not out of it.

The only time we banded together was when our lives depended on it. And when it didn't, we were pitted against one another in a never-ending clamoring for clout and power. Like the plants we brought to Empyrean couldn't survive the frigid air, love couldn't grow on poisoned soil.

Strands of rounded clouds like violet-tinted pearls spread over the darkening sky as the last light of day wrung from the setting sun and the warmth gave way to cool night.

Jorun and I stood together near the trees lining the sacred shore before Talay's temple.

A tree's roots had peeled up from the sand and the heavy trunk toppled over onto a tent where one gentleman lived. He'd refused to leave his home for the safety of the grotto, saying he'd seen storms aplenty in his lifetime and no longer feared the sky. He made a mistake in losing that fear.

Pushed over by the thunderous wind, the tree crushed him as he slept.

Magma said he hadn't suffered, but his daughter was now that he was being returned to the sea. Her lacuna tried to soothe her but there was little solace to be found when one lost someone they loved. The couple had two children, a boy and a girl, one toddling and keeping himself upright with the help of his tiny fist twisted into the girl's sarong. The older one stood beside her mother and cried as they brought the man's body down from the dunes. It was covered in a sapphire shroud sewn closed on all sides. Crest and Breaker waited in the water as the Guardians brought the dead into the shallows.

At the edge of the shore standing apart from all the others, whispering to the god of the sea, was The Salt. She held a cowrie in her outstretched hand as she spoke to Talay, then curled her fingers around it when she finished speaking to the sea god. I could almost hear him reply to his Seer, telling her he was ready to accept the body that housed the soul he'd formed of bravery, breath, and brine.

Together, the brothers ushered him into deeper water until Breaker could go no further.

Then the task fell to Crest alone.

He faced the vast ocean and guided the man past the waves, into the deep where Talay waited to welcome him home.

Salted tears bled into my lips, the same as everyone else's as his head sank beneath the breaking waves.

I couldn't help but imagine how many times in the past years Crest had to do this. Had he taken his own mother into the depths because the duty was his? Was he able to let her go when he came to the trench in which Talay would keep her? Or had someone shown mercy and volunteered to shoulder the task so he didn't have to?

I hoped it was the latter.

I took a deep breath and watched as The Salt left her people to walk with Talay in the shallows, watching the sea as if she could see past the mirrored facets to Crest.

Frey came to us when the crowd left the shore and the man's daughter, her lacuna, and their children peeled away from the water that now cradled their loved one. "It'll be a while before Crest returns," she told me. "In case you were worried or thinking of waiting."

"Is there anything else we can help with?"

She shook her head. "Not tonight."

There was a heaviness in the faint lines on her face. Even her bright hair seemed duller. "Did you know him?"

She tried to smile. "Very well. My family lived close enough when I was a child that I could've thrown a stone and struck that tent. I still remember his quiet presence. His watchfulness. He cared for everyone around him." She gave a sad smile. "When we got into mischief, he noticed, and we stopped because we didn't want to disappoint him."

"I'm sorry," I told her.

She nodded her thanks, gripped her trident tighter, and bid us goodnight, trailing behind the ebbing crowd with sunken shoulders.

I turned to Jorun. "Would you mind if we walked home along the shore instead of taking the trails? If it wasn't lost in the upheaval of my tent, I should have some fruit we can split between us."

"This isn't your home, Elira," he softly chided.

"It is right now," I argued, some overwhelming emotion welling inside my chest that I couldn't put into words. "Just… right now, let me have this."

"As long as you know the truth from the lie you tell yourself," he said pointedly, but quietly.

Together, we walked down the sand, watching the sky for movement. Perches at this time of night would flicker and glow with Neera's power. There were none of those. Nothing but a tiny, bumbling bat.

Jorun hissed and ducked when it swooped over our heads. "A fowl of the night?"

I couldn't help but laugh. I caught a piece of wind and blew it at the creature, sending it careening back toward land and a mass of gnats that might fill its belly.

Jorun's feet went still in a small tide pool, almost making our heights equal as I stood above him outside the divot. "Did you just…?"

"I can control small amounts of it," I told him. "That's how I saved Koa."

He choked. "The first soul could do that and much more. Era told me all about her before the Elders sequestered the Scholars."

My interest piqued. "What else was she capable of?"

"The better question is what *wasn't* she capable of?" he corrected. "Aren't you glad I descended when I did?" he teased. "And aren't you glad your father trusted me, and that the Oracle bade you allow me onto your quad even though you wanted nothing more than to cut my throat with your glorious sword?"

"Back then, I thought it was warranted." Then I sighed because my sword *was* glorious, and it was lost to the depths.

"You were hurt because Aderyn was gone and you wanted someone to blame," he said. "I knew that."

"She was wrong about many things, Jorun, but not about your character."

He gave a slight smile and started walking again. His wings dragged the wet sand when he stepped out of the tide pool.

Like gifts from the deep, the storm tide had delivered several large shells onto the beach. I collected them as we walked, then positioned them all around my porch like spiked, beautiful sentinels.

Mimicking Crest's technique, I built a firewood tower. At its base, I piled some wood shavings, then ducked into The Shark's tent to steal a few embers and the sharp knife I knew he kept hidden beneath the floorboard where he'd once concealed my weaponry.

The space smelled like him.

Despite the smoke, despite the sea that doused everything with salt, it smelled like Crest. I realized that though he wouldn't be gone long and he was safe, I missed him.

Jorun split the fruit he found beneath the bed. As I stripped the bark from the branch that would become Wade's new leg, Jorun told me everything he knew about the first soul.

She was endowed with nearly all of Neera's powers. The goddess wanted her to be strong so she could bear her presence.

"It was like," he lowered his voice as if Neera could hear us, "either she was lonely and needed a friend, or she needed an ally when she had none. When she made the first soul, she did so with the balance she always strived to find," he said. "The first soul could control the Great Wind – from the fiercest gust to the gentlest breeze. She could harness the power of lightning and tear it from the heavens, wielding it as a fiery blade. She could fly and never tire. Never need a perch. The Empyrea she produced never weakened. She made our firmament. That's why it's so strong; it never erodes or weakens. The first soul was very much Neera's equal in might – but perhaps not in thought or heart…" his voice trailed away. He sat with bent knees, his forearms perched upon them. More at ease than I'd ever seen him.

"What aren't you telling me?" I asked.

He hesitated. "Era found a fragment of a scroll. He couldn't verify its accuracy or determine where it came from, only that it's very old."

"What did it say?"

He leaned in ever so slightly. "It said the first soul used the powers Neera endowed her with to trap the goddess in a cage with bars made from none other than the Great Wind. It claimed Neera cannot escape it."

My brows pinched. "That's nonsense."

He shook his head. "Era doesn't think so. He said the goddess and first soul she created were absolute equals, and that fact damned Neera in the end. She poured all her power into the first soul, which meant she couldn't best her or destroy anything she made."

I watched the fire spark, tiny embers bursting and then going cold. I shook my head. "If that's true, then how do you explain her scale and the intentions and feathers she demands? I felt her presence in the sanctum. I heard her voice. She sent a bolt to threaten me here…"

I hadn't mentioned that before.

For a moment, he was quiet, studying the fire before us, stretching his hands toward the warmth. "Like the storms she brews, her demands seem to come from afar, though. Think about it." He twisted to face me. "You felt her presence in the sanctum, but you didn't see *her*. She once *walked with* the first soul, Elira. She demands feathers and takes them from those who displease her, but with a distant power, not with her hand." He leaned in further. "You and the new Oracle are the only ones who've ever heard her voice."

"No one else? Not even the Seers who came before her?"

He shook his head. "This Oracle is different. She is the goddess's conduit. The line of communication between them is unprecedented, but Era doesn't think it's a coincidence that she was born or elevated now – when the first soul rose to the top of her army."

He flung a piece of bark into the popping fire, which took immediate interest. Seconds later, its edges began to glow orange, then flame flickered over its rough surface.

"We were always taught that Neera had pulled the soil from the bottom of the sea for us, but the scroll claimed that there were once *three* gods. Neera of the sky, Talay of the sea, and Tella of the earth."

I glanced at the glistening sand around us, wondering if it could truly be the grainy flesh of a sleeping goddess.

"Talay and Tella were as close and as interdependent as their kingdoms, while Neera was alone in the sky. The scroll said that Neera was jealous of their familiarity and felt slighted by their affection for one another. She felt the three were imbalanced, so she sought an equilibrium."

"That was why she made the first soul…" I surmised. To instill the symmetry and balance she coveted.

Jorun nodded. "Neera and the first soul descended under the guise of friendship. Neera called down from the sky a great bolt of lightning, then slew Tella where she stood upon the sea. The goddess fell into the water, but Talay caught her and held her up. He refused to let her sink. He doused Neera's hot blade and with monstrous waves, called forth the monsters that thrive in the depths. Neera was pushed back into the sky.

"This Isle is lush because of Tella's sacrifice; Kehlani is all that is left of her. To honor her, Talay gave his souls the ability to live above the surface, as well as complete dominion beneath it."

Tella. What would the earth look like if Neera hadn't slain her? Would there be plenty of orchards and crops for everyone to plant and sow and pluck, with no need for war?

Jorun sat back upright. "The first soul was not as much like Neera as the goddess thought. She saw Neera's jealousy, her rage, her hatred, and didn't think she deserved to strip Tella away from Talay. She did not believe Neera deserved to rule the sky after that, so she sought a way to rid the world of the cruel goddess. She learned how to harness every power she was given and built the sky kingdom as the goddess made lesser souls to fill it – in an effort to match Talay's equally fervent efforts to populate the sea and sand.

"Neera began watching Talay, searching him for weakness so she could strike him down, too. When she thought she'd found it, the first soul plucked from the sky a lightning sword and placed herself between the goddess who made her and the god of the sea she felt deserved to live and rule beneath the waves. Though the scroll does not say how, she managed to seal the goddess behind the wind. Her boundary stands, just as the firmament she built stands. And it will hold strong as long as you don't release Neera from her cage of wind."

This was a lot to take in – if it was even true.

"Neera has been waiting a very long time for your soul to resurface, and she has, from afar, molded a ruthless kingdom whose solitary goal is to destroy Talay and his kind. Era thinks the goddess believes you will set her free in the end."

Because I was the fiercest of her warriors, an arrow she carved and fitted with a sharp point, one she aimed at the sea and The Shark. And because I was afraid of failure, and was selfish and desperate to keep my wings…

On Intention Day, before she demanded my feathers, she would have made a deal with me when I failed to capture Crest. *Remove the wind that binds me.*

Jorun cleared his throat. "Era thinks she'll try to force your hand this time. She knows the stubborn will of your soul."

I swallowed thickly as a chill seeped into the tropical breeze, pebbling my skin.

Jorun's spine straightened. His eyes snapped to mine.

Air *this* cold did not belong over Kehlani. It belonged in Empyrean.

"The scroll was penned by the first soul?" I guessed.

Jorun nodded. "That's what Era thinks."

"Did he tell the Elders this?"

Firelight flickered over Jorun's features. "He hid the scroll – I don't know where. But he didn't want them to know. I don't know if they've found it since I descended."

They could torture Era for information and the Scholar, in a profession unfamiliar with pain, would likely give them anything they wanted to make it end. The Oracle would see it in his feather if one was plucked and given for her to read. I wondered if she could choose a side other than Neera's, or if the goddess would strike her down and choose another to take her place just as quickly.

What would the Elders do if they knew the goddess was trapped and I alone could free her? Would they ask me to, or would they kill me to prevent me from doing it?

I followed the wild swoops of a pale moth flitting in circles around the fire and thought of all Jorun had divulged since landing on the Isle.

"Wait… you said before that the Oracle *and Era* told the Elders that I'm alive. How does Era know?"

"The first soul's Empyrea is unique," he led.

The power in my blood glowed brighter, the power of Neera flashing through it more intensely. That was why I didn't build Aderyn's and my nest. She did. It was why I hid my blood. I didn't know when I was younger that I was the first soul, but it was obviously different than the blood of my peers.

She'd cut me in a sparring session when we were younglings and had just joined the Warrior ranks. I remembered our eyes widening at the same time. Aderyn flew to me and clamped her hand over the wound, quickly cutting into her palm to use her blood to form a cloud to dilute mine as much as it could. Then she tucked the cloud that she knew would damn me into her leathers and flew fast with me, rushing away to hide until the bleeding stopped. She threw it into the sea that day and we watched as the glowing cloud was swallowed by the ocean.

She never cut me again. Never punched me in the face to split my lip or break my nose. And I, in fairness, did the same for her.

Jorun continued, "When the first soul dies, her Empyrea remains strong, but its light fades little by little until she is reborn again. Yours has not faded. In fact, after you fell, it brightened."

"The cloud in the sanctum," I said.

He nodded. "Your blood overwhelmed all others and it still lights the space, like lightning sparking over a dark sky. The Oracle said the goddess amplified its light because she wanted everyone to know your soul still breathed. She claimed it was your indication that you wanted us to save you… A cry for help."

Of course she did, because I was the only one who could set her free. If I died, she'd have to wait for my soul to be reborn again, which might not be for a very long time.

A cry for help. "Why did no one come sooner, then?"

"Because Talon stopped them. I'm not sure why or what he knows, Elira. Only that he's dangerous."

There was a large pile of bark and shavings beneath the branch. While we talked, I whittled furiously, trying to find a way out of the predicament I was in. I hoped the Oracle might at some point stop seeing visions of me on the sand, giving me a chance to escape the Elders and stay here. When given the chance, I didn't want to leave.

"The Elders are hungry for power, Elira, and they know you're the first soul. They know the strength that sings through your blood. But if they knew the goddess wanted you… what would they do then?"

An insane laugh bubbled from my chest. "Everything makes much more sense now. The goddess protected me until she needed me to move on her behalf. She *let* me use Aderyn's blood to hide mine from the Elders all these years. I bet she even ordered the old Oracle to look the other way."

The young new Oracle knew right away that the blood I added to the Empyrea cloud wasn't mine.

The conduit was elevated at the exact moment Neera thought I was strong enough to free her. I wondered if she'd killed the former Oracle just to see her plan take shape.

I glanced at my fourth and suddenly noticed how wretched he looked. Exhausted didn't begin to describe what weighed down his features. "You should get some sleep." I ticked my chin toward the tent.

"I'm fine," he tried to lie, brushing my comment off like lint.

"You're not."

"And you are?" he challenged.

"I'm not either, but I don't look as haggard as you," I snipped. "You need to rest. Magma said so."

"She's altogether frightening," he admitted with a slight grin. "We should pit her against the Elders and see how far and fast they fly."

"We'd never see them again," I teased.

Jorun looked back toward the tent, then scrubbed a hand down his face. "Maybe just a nap. Will you give me your word you'll wake me if anything happens?"

"Of course. Though I hope tonight will be calm for us all."

He bid me goodnight and ducked inside. The planks creaked under his weight as he made his way to my bed. In minutes, soft snoring poured from the tent's flap.

CHAPTER ELEVEN

The fire burned on, whittling the wood it hadn't yet turned to ash as I did the same to the branch that would become Wade's leg. I wasn't sure how long the leg should be, so a simple stripping away was all I could do for now. I would need some reference or measurements of his other leg in order to match it. I hoped either Magma or Crest could help with that without giving away his gift.

Crest resurfaced hours after Jorun laid down to sleep. When I saw him walking from the dunes toward his home, I sat up straighter. The sky glittered with a blanket of stars and pale moonlight silhouetted his form as he strode with his back to the great light of the night.

His gait faltered when he saw the fire, then saw me sitting before it.

He passed his tent to come to mine, crouching before me with his side to the fire. "Hey," he softly said.

I was so glad he'd emerged from the deep unscathed. That he was here…

"Hey."

"The sky is clear, and there are plenty of Guardians watching tonight if you want to get some rest. My hammock is free."

"I've already taken your bed, Crest. I'll hardly take your hammock, too. *You* need sleep."

He ticked his head toward his tent. "Then come and lay with me."

My ribs tightened. Heart beat faster…

Faster.

"I can't –"

"Can't? Or won't?" he challenged. He made it sound like a question, and a simple one at that. But nothing with Crest was simple. The sharp glint of a dare lay in his tone.

"I'm not sure how we'd manage it. The hammock is made for one," I argued weakly.

His eyes shimmered in the firelight. "Let me show you."

I hesitated. "I'm not sure how my wings…"

He pressed a finger close to my lips but didn't touch them. "Just trust me."

Lacuna… was all I could think. All I could feel and hear. I wanted to be surrounded by him, enveloped in his warmth, drenched in his scent and drowned in his arms, his touch.

Like the moth buzzing lazily around the fire, I drew closer, my lips brushing his finger. A ghost of a touch.

A whisper of a smile and fire caught in his eyes. He held his hand out for me to take or refuse.

I took it, and this opportunity, this time, while I had it.

His cool hand enveloped mine and my warmth leached into his palm. I let him pull me upright and walked with him to his tent with my wings fluttering at my back, leaving Jorun to snore, and the fire to die, and the moth to lose interest when it lost the light.

My feet fell into the impressions of his heavy steps. When we reached his tent, he held the flap up and ushered me in. Firelight doused the room in its warm glow. He tossed a log in the pit and slowly, the coals lent their heat to the wood. Smoke rose and filtered out the vents cut into the top.

The hammock was strung between two beams. He brushed the sand off his feet with a cloth, then knelt and reached for one of mine. "May I?"

I swallowed thickly as I raised it. He cupped my heel and I nearly whimpered at his touch. He gently cleaned the sand away from one foot, then the other.

My hand hovered just over his hair. His eyes caught sight of it and rose to mine, questioning. He leaned over to brush against my fingers, watching to make sure it was okay. It was so much more than that.

My nails raked into his still-damp hair and Crest closed his eyes. His breathing was so careful, so deliberate, I wondered whether he had control of it, or *I* had control of him.

"Elira," he exhaled quietly.

I extended a hand to him, and he took it and rose when I indicated.

"What do you need?" he rasped.

Need. Not want. What did I need?

I needed many things. None of which I wanted to think about while Crest stood before me tonight. I walked him to the hammock and released his hand.

He stretched the fabric and sat in the center, then kicked his legs up and laid back, the muscles in his stomach tightening into knots. I wondered what it would feel like to rake my fingernails down them – slowly. Would it be The Shark who whimpered at *my* touch if I did?

My wings flared slightly at the thought. A shiver ran up my spine and I ruffled them behind me.

"What was that for?" he asked quietly.

I shook my head, then before I could talk myself out of it or tell myself a thousand reasons why I shouldn't, I put one knee across his lap, held tight to the top of the hammock, and raised the other so that I straddled him.

His hands hovered at my sides, ready to clamp onto my hips the moment I gave him permission. "Tell me I can touch you," he begged. Beneath me, I could feel the vibration of his need, the restraint rippling through him. His skin, so cool from ocean and wind, now burned like the log being consumed by the flames in his fire pit.

"We're already touching," I teased, a smile tugging at one of the corners of my lips.

"Elira," he growled, his tone sharpening.

I dove in, clasping the scruff on his jaw, and kissed him. The hammock gently rocked from the sudden motion. If he'd been standing on the ground, I would have knocked him to it and we would've landed just like this.

The sounds that tore from his throat were a symphony composed just for me. To hear. To enjoy. To memorize so I could replay it in my mind again and again…

Our mouths moved together, our tongues dancing wildly.

My chest pressed against his and I slithered my hands up his chest and arms to take hold of his wrists. I held them captive, pinning him to the makeshift bed he'd offered to share with me tonight.

His wide pupils drank me in.

Lacuna…

My wings flared, making us sway, first to one side, then the other.

He saw them over my shoulder and muttered, "Beautiful."

I silenced him with another kiss.

Beneath me, he swelled. I marveled at how well our bodies were fitted together while still clothed, then imagined we weren't.

Something stirred deep in my belly. A looming, dark presence I *knew* rivaled Neera's, one I knew was powerful and capable of anything and everything all at once. And the beast that lived at the core of who I was reared her head and claimed The Shark as hers. She promised to protect him with her very existence, declaring to the heavens and the deepest sea trenches that if anyone tried to harm or take him away, she vowed to make them beg for death a thousand times before she let them have what they craved.

The Shark flipped his hands to grip *my* wrists and dragged them around to the small of my back, to the base of my wings. They writhed like the beast in my belly, wanting more. Wanting him.

Crest sat upright and ghosted kisses from my lips, to my jaw, to my chest, craning me backward so he could reach the skin between my breasts and below my tied-on shirt, to my stomach, which was as far as he could reach.

He left me wanting.

"What's the matter, Elira?" he said with a dangerous grin.

I growled at him in response. He knew what was wrong.

This feeling consumed me and I reveled in it. In him. "*My lacuna…*" I whispered.

Crest went still. His fingers, still a vice on my wrists, tightened.

"Say it again," he demanded.

He needed to hear it, I realized. He needed it and I was the only one who could provide this for him. The power that knowledge gave me was heady and unequivocally addictive.

My skin thrummed at the utter force of his tone. "My lacuna," I rasped louder, my lips stinging from his kisses.

He set my hands free and ghosted his fingers over my wings, making me shudder atop him. In return, I raked my nails over the scales on his legs, dragging them up and letting them catch on every ripple. They were so fine and soft to the touch… A satisfied rumble came from his chest so deep and delicious, I wanted to taste it again and again.

I realized Crest liked it when his scales were toyed with. His eyes fluttered closed and he sucked in a breath as I raked over them again.

The second I moved to smooth my hands over the muscles tensing across his stomach, he pinned me with a stare. His hand gripped my bicep, but his thumb grazed my taut nipple beneath the knitted shirt I suddenly, desperately wanted to unravel and tear off.

I wasn't sure what sound I made, but Crest enjoyed it. Suddenly his lips were on mine, peppering them with more kisses and in between, telling me how he loved how I tasted, how I sounded, how I felt. I let him taste and hear and feel and look his fill while I drank him in, too. Until he finally stopped me.

"Elira," he quietly said, pulling away. "We need to slow down."

My heart dropped at the thought of slowing at all. Or that he'd want to. It was like I was flying as fast as I could only to flare my wings, my body flinging to a halt.

"Why?" I choked.

"Because I want you to be sure this is what you want before we go any further."

I blinked rapidly, trying to understand. "What do you mean?"

"I mean," he started, "that if we become true lacunas privately, I don't want to hide it publicly. Are you ready for that?"

I swallowed thickly.

No. I wasn't.

We couldn't be true lacunas, not like Breaker and Katalini. He *knew* that. He'd offered me friendship – to wade only where I was comfortable – and tonight, I'd thrown caution to the wind and dove into deep water headfirst without thinking what it might mean for him when the dawn broke.

Embarrassed, I placed one foot on the ground. If humiliation was a sea, I would have drowned in it, and even The Shark couldn't have saved me.

"Don't," he chided softly. My eyes flicked back to his. "Don't leave. Just… lay with me. Sleep here, with me. Nothing more than that."

My toes raked across the floorboard as I hovered above him, wondering if such a simple act was a terrible idea, one that might further ruin me. Because the more time I spent with him, the stronger this pull seemed to get. The more I wanted to feel free, to feel him, before I couldn't anymore.

With a hand, he stretched the hammock out wide. "See? There's plenty of room."

I settled beside him, still greedy for what I could have. My wings were a little cramped at first, but they quickly became used to the gentle pressure of the cradling hammock. I laid tucked against his side, enjoying his warmth.

He stretched his arm around my shoulders. "Is this okay?"

I nodded, my cheek brushing against his chest. My fingers lay over his heart where my feathers circled.

His heartbeat was a song in my ear; a comfort to hear and feel that he was alive and well.

"Goodnight, Elira," he softly told me, closing his eyes.

A moment passed and his breathing evened out. He wasn't asleep, but he would be soon.

"I don't love you," I said, my heart still galloping.

I heard him smile. "I don't love you, either."

Where Skies Fall

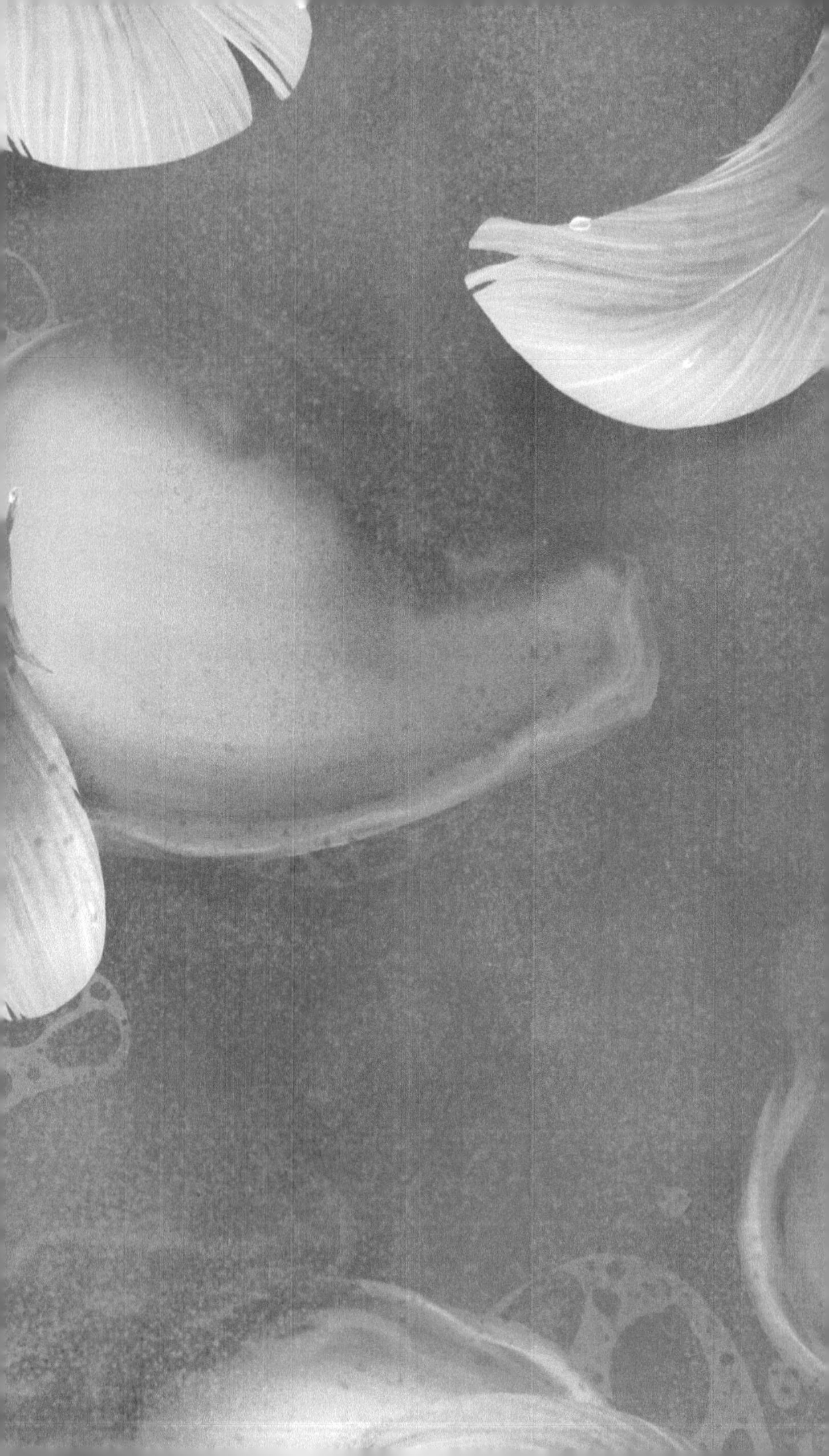

II

BREATH

CHAPTER TWELVE

The sun rose in a violent flash of gold, drenching the people of Kehlani who reverently gathered at the shore, clad in blue, dark and light. Jorun hovered beside me near the trees to give them the privacy required for such times as these. Breaker and Crest stood together where the small waves rolled up to brush over the smooth sand. Breaker patted Crest's back and bent to speak so only he could hear as The Shark doubled over, his hands on his knees.

Crest heaved, bile spilling into the sea.

I took a few steps forward, stopping when the Guardians, led by Koa and Frey, appeared atop the swell of dunes, carrying a sewn-shut shroud comprised of the same startling shades held in my wings. A shade between blue and gray.

The Salt trailed them. Her forehead and eyes were smeared with ash. Unlike the last time, she stopped near Breaker and remained close to the brothers instead of wending away to speak privately with Talay.

"Who died?" I asked Jorun.

He shook his head and wiped tears from his face only for more to spill onto it again, unable to speak the name.

I trailed closer when Crest let out a groan filled with pure agony.

My heart dropped. Magma?

I skirted the crowd and rushed toward Crest, but he didn't notice me. His head was buried in his hands. He heaved a powerful sob and I watched as his entire body shook with sorrow.

I wanted to comfort him. I reached out to touch him but couldn't. Something kept me from reaching him. The wind. A powerful wall of it separated us.

No… the shore was devoid of a breeze and the Great Wind swirled around me, as if binding me.

"Crest?" I called.

He didn't, couldn't, hear my voice.

Breaker stood with his brother in the shallows, in the brine and bile, until Crest could straighten once more. Then he guided The Shark into the sea until the swells swept up to graze his waist. The Guardians brought the body to them and laid it upon the somber water. As the ocean rose and fell again, the dead rose and fell with it.

"I can't!" Crest cried out. "I can't do this." His voice broke and so did my heart.

His eyes were bloodshot, a constant stream of tears pouring from them. Breaker looked at his brother and nodded. "It's okay, Crest. It doesn't have to be you."

"It should *be me," he cried, saliva and misery webbing between his lips.*

"Koa and Frey?" Breaker called, gesturing for them to come.

The two stepped forward.

Koa broke down for a moment when he looked at Crest, sobbing for his friend because he hurt, because he grieved, while Frey's silent but steady tears fell back into the sea.

"Would the two of you take her to Talay?" Breaker rasped.

"No!" Crest wailed, splashing toward them.

Breaker stepped in front of his brother and placed a hand on his chest to hold him back. "We owe her this honor, brother. She's gone."

Crest shook his head, tore the hair at his scalp, and paced in the knee-deep waves, bereft but also crazed.

"Crest!" I called out.

He let out a cry, then pressed the heels of his hands to his temples. "I can hear her. I swear I just heard her voice!"

Dread coiled inside my stomach.

"Crest, you have to let her go," Magma said as she approached.

"How?" he hoarsely cried.

And I knew…

I'd known before, but now I knew I lay in that shroud. It was me he mourned. He was falling apart at the seams because I was, too. My heart sank when he dropped to his knees the same way he had when he told me what – who – I was to him. Waves swept over his shoulders as if Talay himself sought to soothe him. "She's my lacuna. My missing part."

Breaker nodded to Koa and Frey, who each grabbed a corner of the bobbing bag with one hand, tridents clasped in the other.

Crest struggled to his feet and pushed Breaker when he blocked him from stopping their procession. "No," he gritted. Breaker held his position and shouted for Koa and Frey to go.

"Don't do this!" Crest begged, running through the water. A large wave knocked him down. He thrashed to right himself. "Please, Breaker. I beg you. Don't take her… Don't… Please."

He reached out to his best friends as Breaker held him back, asking them not to go, not with her.

He said losing her was worse than dying. He said he'd rather be dead.

And then… the sand under everyone's feet began to tremble like the cowries The Salt kept in her bowl.

I blinked awake, so shaken from the dream, it felt as though the sand still vibrated underfoot. I raised my head from his chest.

Blearily, he blinked awake, then went still. Did he feel it, too? Had he dreamt the same nightmare?

"Earthquake," he breathed.

Quickly, he lifted me out of the hammock, taking care with my wings. My feet struck the floor and headed for my bow and quiver as he strode to get his trident. "Outside," he ordered.

I followed him out the door to see Jorun stumbling out of my tent. "What's happening?" he shouted.

"The earth is quaking," I replied.

Like me, he wanted to look down and study what was happening, but we knew not to turn our backs to the sky.

"We need to go to The Salt," I told Crest, remembering her shells and all the ill omens of late.

Jorun hurried after us. The Seer stood atop a dune just outside her tent, staring – not out at the sea or sky – but at the Green Mountains nestled in the heart of the Isle.

"Is it coming from the mountains?" Crest asked, panting after our run.

Grains of sand displaced from the top of the dune and slid down its side like tears falling down a cheek.

"I can't tell," The Salt lamented. At one point, she'd told me she couldn't see beyond the clouds to know what was happening in Empyrean, the kingdom perched in the midst of them. But now, she couldn't see beyond the present. The future was unclear. Blocked from her view. Perhaps it was still malleable.

"Why does the origination point matter?" Jorun asked.

"An earthquake on the Isle may cause rockslides and the like, but one born from beneath the sea can heave an enormous wave toward the shore. They're deadly, vicious things," The Salt explained, still watching.

Jorun's eyes fastened, not to the mountains, but upon the water. "Do you see an anomaly?" he leaned in to ask me.

I searched the horizon and saw nothing but that ever-present, solid divide. But I wondered if what I was seeing was true. The Salt was frightened of this wave. Maybe it was as long and great as the horizon itself and all I was seeing was its massive head raised as it charged forward.

"My eyes are no keener than yours," I told him.

"I highly doubt that, given your other attributes," he pointedly replied.

The earth stopped quaking almost as quickly as it began. I waited, watching the sand dunes to see if the shaking might begin anew, but it seemed to have settled. No more grains cascaded from the dune's peak.

Breaker and Katalini's feet pounded down the trail. "Salt, has Talay spoken to you? Are we safe?"

She shook her head. "Talay remains silent."

Breaker took a deep, frustrated breath. He didn't understand why Talay had suddenly stopped guiding his Seer. "Then would you please sound the shell?" he asked. "People need to take cover."

"Has any Guardian at the shore noted the sea receding?" she asked.

Breaker looked to Crest. Beneath the waves, echoes of shrill cries bellowed. "They're saying the sea is all clear," The Shark told his brother.

Breaker pursed his lips. The decision was his, but it wasn't an easy one without Talay's guidance. "I'd rather our people be safe and inconvenienced than crushed and killed. Please, Salt. The conch horn."

She hurried into her tent and brought out her shell. Her breath forced out the distinct sound. I had no doubt people would heed her warning.

"High ground is safest. You should start toward the mountains," Breaker advised me and Jorun.

Katalini waited a few steps away while Breaker spoke with his brother. Jorun obeyed and began to walk inland. "Elira?" He paused for me.

But I wasn't leaving without Crest. I stood at his side as Breaker confided in him.

"I need you to go out there," Breaker told him, clapping him on the shoulder.

Crest stretched his neck and back and smiled. "You didn't even have to ask."

"No!" I seethed, startling both brothers. "You just said it isn't safe."

Crest gave a smug grin. "It isn't – for anyone who's *not* me."

I narrowed my eyes at him. "If only you were as indestructible as you were conceited. The safest thing for everyone is for me to fly out and look," I offered.

Breaker braced his hands on his hips. "And when someone from Empyrean sees your wings?"

Then let them come for me and learn what sort of warrior I've become…

"I'm going," Crest told Breaker, even though he stared at me while saying it. "Worried for your Shark, Scourge?" he teased, handing his trident to me.

My fingers curled around its shaft as if it was his neck they wrung.

At our exchange, Breaker choked on his laughter, brows raised as he glanced between us, annoyingly entertained.

Katalini was just as bad as he was, with her grin that showed she assumed far too much.

"Take care of that trident. It's very important to me," The Shark told me. "It's my favorite." He punctuated his infuriating sentence, packed with insinuations that would cause Breaker and Katalini to crow for days, with a wink just to provoke me.

How quickly he'd forgotten me hurling Frey's trident at his head and Koa's…

Crest sprinted toward the sea and dove into the foam-laced water. Breaker turned to me, but I refused to look at him. Refused to look anywhere but the spot Crest left behind. Until the waves erased it like I knew they would.

"*Your* Shark?"

I scowled at him, at which he chuckled. "Take time to laugh now, Breaker. When this emergency has passed, you and your Guardians have your work cut out for you."

"Doing what exactly?" he asked, folding his arms over his chest.

"Jorun explained how he managed to infiltrate the Isle under your very noses. Don't you think that's something you should make sure can't happen again?"

He relaxed his posture. "I definitely do."

"And I'd like to see your archers. They need to improve significantly."

"They strike their marks – most of the time."

"Striking isn't enough," I argued with a defiant tilt. "To win this war, they need to be able to sink their arrow into hearts and heads."

He scrubbed a hand over his mouth.

"The battle that's coming is one in which you can't simply fend your enemy off. You'll have to eviscerate them, or you will lose."

Katalini, who along with Jorun had been listening to our conversation, walked over to Breaker with one hand clutching her womb.

My brows soared and my mouth gaped. For a moment, I was too stunned to speak.

She saw my expression and her feet went still. She glanced at Breaker for help.

Breaker's lips parted. "How did you…?"

I pointed toward her cradling hand.

"*No one* knows yet," she blurted. "We haven't told anyone. Not even Magma or Crest."

I nodded slowly. "I won't ruin the surprise for them."

Katalini exhaled loudly. "Thank you. It's been a difficult secret to keep. Especially from Magma, but there is a reason for it."

She didn't elaborate, but I couldn't help but wonder if the sadness in her eyes was left there by a child she'd lost before bringing it into the world.

The leader of the Isle held his lacuna, pressed a kiss to her forehead, and ran his hand lovingly over her stomach. It was only slightly rounded. I wasn't sure how long it would be until she gave birth, but I worried for the couple and their budding family.

Breaker said he dreamed that any children the couple were blessed with would be born into a peaceful world. Certainly not one in which his youngling might be stalked and hunted for sport. Not one in which throats were torn out by sharp, greedy teeth. Not ones where my people descended, not only to gather food but to sow terror.

And now, Katalini was pregnant and would bring forth the child for which they'd hoped – and as of yet, there was no peace, nor any promise of it.

Breaker quietly spoke to Katalini and though they were aware that Jorun and I could hear, it felt as though we were trespassing on a moment far too intimate for prying ears. This was not Breaker, the leader of Kehlani. This was Breaker, the lacuna. The future father. His tone was tender instead of commanding, worried instead of steady.

"Higher ground is safest right now. Do you feel up to hiking the nearest hill?"

"I'm *fine*, Breaker. I feel perfectly normal. You don't have to treat me like I'm fragile," she said. Her tone was not tender, but raw. An opened and abraded wound.

He whispered his apology and told her he worried for her, and she replied that he did so unnecessarily. That she'd had no trouble *this time.*

He kissed her again, then took her hand and they waved for us to come with them. We did so, but I kept watch behind me. If a wave came, I could lift and fly Katalini to safety. Jorun, even though his shoulder was still bound and healing, would save Breaker.

We wended around The Salt's tent, taking a path that led toward the foothills.

"Can your people not swim through the great wave if it comes?" Jorun asked out of the blue. He'd been watching the sea for a shift in its depth, his mind obviously still preoccupied with the prospect.

Breaker, it seemed, wasn't the only one concerned.

"The water isn't the problem," the leader explained. "It's the force of it. The crash is so heavy, we might not survive it. Even if we do, the water quickly fills with debris that proves just as deadly. Waves like that can uproot trees and toss boulders around in the waters. They can wipe away tents and all the contents in them, including the ropes that hold them to the soil. I could see how you might assume it would be something we could weather, but as soon as it breaks upon the shore, it fills with things from the land and becomes a different sort of danger. It's not something anyone should take lightly."

Fury tore through me and I flung my hand toward the water. "Yet you sent Crest out into it!"

Breaker looked taken aback. "He's the most capable swimmer Talay has ever made, Elira. And he'll be able to tell if there's a disturbance and return here to warn us if there is."

"It's safest in the deep if a tidal wave is pressed toward the Isle," Katalini further soothed.

"Crest is the most capable ever?" Jorun asked, carefully studying me. I could almost see him comparing and contrasting me with The Shark and aligning all the things I already had. The conduit of Neera and The Salt of Talay.

Sky. Sea. Land.

The things that were unbalanced and had balanced once more. The things that still weren't even but could, in theory, be.

"Ever," Breaker solidified. "Crest is the only one who's survived the strongest currents of the sea. The only one brave enough to even attempt to swim them. And he's incredibly fast, as you likely have seen from above."

Jorun and I both acknowledged his words.

Breaker turned to me. "I know he's your lacuna, Elira, but he's my brother. I love him. *I'd* sooner die than send my brother to his death."

The Salt had left us behind and none of us realized it until she sounded her shell horn again from farther up the trail.

"Does she think it's imminent?" I asked anxiously.

Breaker shook his head. "There's no urgency in her steps. She's only doing as I asked, warning people to get to higher ground. She doesn't know if the wave will come, which is more troubling than the earth quaking or any push of water..." He trailed off as he considered the implications of Talay's silence.

Katalini threaded her arm through his and told him she wanted to go – just in case. He let her guide him up the path. "Elira," he called over his shoulder. "Are you coming?"

I didn't want to. I wanted to fly over the sea searching for Crest and anything that might cause him harm.

"What about Magma?" I asked. "Will she retreat into the mountains?"

Absently, Breaker answered over his shoulder, "She'll hear The Salt's warning. She'll go."

I planted my feet. "She didn't leave Wade during the gale." She wouldn't leave him now.

Realization spread over his face like sunlight over the sea. In the tumult and the preoccupation with his pregnant lacuna, he'd forgotten about Wade.

My face hardened with resolve. "You and Katalini get to higher ground. Jorun and I will go to them. If the crushing wave comes, we can fly them to safety."

Jorun nodded his readiness.

Breaker thanked us and offered an apology that wasn't necessary before leaving to take the trail from which The Salt still sounded her shell. She was a beacon, their Seer. Ready to shepherd them in any way the sea god deemed important. And where she walked, they followed. As Jorun and I broke away and walked toward Magma's, people in vibrant colors streamed into the hills behind her.

"Their clothing is like our feathers," Jorun observed. "Every color and shade nature offers."

I nodded. "In our hearts, we aren't so different from them, either."

Surprisingly, he didn't scoff or argue.

Breaker once told me he wanted to prove that our people had much more in common than the things that separated us. He'd accomplished his goal, because daily Crest proved it to me. With her steadfast guidance, The Salt demonstrated it. By the care she showed her people, as well as Jorun and me, Magma embodied it. Breaker and Katalini, Koa and Frey, they confirmed he was right.

He was so, so right.

CHAPTER THIRTEEN

No humming came from Magma's tent, but life stirred within its walls, as evidenced by the clattering of a pan and a frustrated curse escaping the mouth of the wise healer inside. The deeper tone of Wade's voice rumbled just after.

Jorun motioned for me to go first. I smiled, understanding his trepidation. Magma would demand to see his shoulder, I had no doubt.

She shouted and threw her hands up when I quietly stepped in. She turned to find me standing before her, sucked in a startled breath, clutched her chest, and gave me a cross look. "You scared me to death."

I grinned. Sitting up on the cot across the room, so did Wade.

She wagged her finger at me. "You're sly."

My grin stretched. "Thank you."

She narrowed her eyes. There was no point in her telling me she hadn't meant it as a compliment. I loved it and she knew it.

"And *you* – how's your shoulder, hmm?" she asked, stretching to see Jorun, who literally stood so close behind me that he couldn't deny hiding from her. Coward.

I stepped to the right to expose him, enjoying the sound of his gritting teeth.

"Still woefully miserable, Mender," he answered with a bright, fake smile. I didn't miss his glance at the door or her muttered, half-hearted, hateful response.

"The Salt's horn was a warning, not a beckoning," she told us. "I take it Crest was sent out to sea?" It was obvious Magma did not approve. Her lips pursed at the thought of her grandson in harm's way.

"I offered to fly and surveil the sea instead, but Breaker sent him anyway."

"Because he trusts Crest's abilities and wants to keep you hidden the way he promised your father he would," she added. "The two of you should head into the mountains like everyone else."

We were effectively dismissed in Magma's eyes. She turned her back to us and busied her hands with things on her counter. She picked up bottles, only to move them a few inches, straightened cloths she had ready for wounds yet to be tended, moved her mortar and pestle to the other side of the workspace…

Magma looked out the window to the sea, then slowly turned, leaning her ample hips against the counter and folding her arms over her chest.

Jorun whispered a curse.

"Let me guess," she started. "Breaker sent you here to fly us away if the wave he's so worried about comes to wash us away."

The smile Wade had greeted us with might have faltered, but it didn't disappear. He smirked at the exchange. "Magma, you should lead the Guardians in the war to come," he teased. "Even the sky goddess would shrink under your attention."

She waved him off. "I won't be carried from my home."

"If there is a wave, you will," I told her.

She dug in her heels. "I will *not*."

She didn't intimidate me anymore. I grabbed a small apple out of a bowl of them and tossed it in the air before taking a bite, chewing and swallowing it. "Magma, I give you my word that if the wave comes, I will pluck you off this soil and deposit you on the mountain top. And Jorun will carry Wade, even if he tries to be as stubborn as you."

"No one is as stubborn as Magma," Wade chirped. She swatted the back of his head with a towel.

Jorun glanced at the door again. "I'm going outside to keep watch."

"Wait a minute, you!" Magma crowed, chasing after him. "Since you're here, I want to see your shoulder. I need to clean it and mix more salve."

"Thank you, but it's not necessary."

"I insist," Magma pressed.

"Mender, I want that smelly salve applied to my wound as much as you want to be flown to the mountain top," he told her.

"Any sign of trouble?" Wade shouted outside.

"No!" both Jorun and Magma snapped back simultaneously.

"The quake came from the caldera, same as before. That volcano just went to sleep after the last eruption. It didn't die," the Mender grumped.

"Does the quaking mean it's waking up?" I asked curiously.

The Mender was too busy arguing with Jorun to lend her attention to my question.

Magma, of course, won her argument with sheer will and the knowledge and persuasion only a seasoned, intelligent woman possessed.

I laughed under my breath.

And she called *me* sly…

Jorun hovered near the door so he could watch the ocean for any threat it might thrust toward us. He let her examine his wound and bones, crying out when she applied pressure. As the two squabbled, I turned to Wade. Sitting here with Magma, while entertaining at times, had to be quite boring. I wondered if he felt up to coordinating a defensive maneuver against the Empyrean.

I eyeballed the injured Guardian. "How well do you know the Green Mountains?"

"Almost as well as I know the sea." He leaned forward, suddenly interested. "Why do you ask?"

"Because they aren't guarded well enough, and I need the help of someone who knows the mountains to plan strategic lookout points."

"Crest won't help you?" he asked, testing me.

"I'm sure he would if I asked, but I happen to be of the mind that Crest is too busy with other things to worry about guarding uninhabited hills. The problem with ignoring those mountains is that they spill into your villages. I thought they were guarded more completely, but Jorun came through them with no trouble."

"So *that's* how he did it!" Wade said as if it all made sense. "I wondered."

"We descended within the green heart a few times to steal soil and plants before we were caught," I confided. "It never took long for someone to notice, but we did have time to at least take some of what we'd come for."

"Where was this? Do you remember any landmarks?"

I nodded. "A waterfall far broader and taller than those that conceal the grotto."

Wade smiled. "The falls are beautiful. We don't visit them near enough." He frowned and looked down at his missing leg, probably thinking he'd never be able to climb those hills again.

"So, about the trees," I hinted, shifting the conversation back to the point of it.

"How many more towers do you think need to be built and how far apart would you like them?" he asked, back to business.

I shook my head. "Towers are too easy to spot. I want the Guardians spread through the range to go unseen."

He smiled appreciatively. "Clever. Besides the fact that on the shore, there isn't much natural cover, Breaker thought that by making them visible, they might serve as a deterrent."

"Removing branches here and there won't harm the trees and will still hide plenty of archers. We can blanket the Isle with them. Assign everyone a position to take. Even younglings can be taught to shoot."

"I know the tallest trees and many broader ones that would work," he said, his mind already fixed on his new task. "And I can call on my brother to train the younglings in the West Village. He's a Guardian, and he has better aim than Crest."

"Do you have any estimation of how many people in all Kehlani can take up a bow? Also… are they all as large as Crest's?" The Shark didn't favor the weapon over his tridents. He rarely used it, but at least he could. And though he wasn't as accurate as I was, he could easily improve with a few tweaks…

He ticked his head back. "Is there something wrong with the design of our bows?"

"Yes," I answered. "There is. Smaller individuals and those who aren't built like they can wrestle kraken need smaller bows and shorter arrows. Given the right tools, they'll shoot more precisely."

"Bows like yours, then," he asked, nodding to the one hanging on my back.

I smiled. "Exactly like it. We can alter them to fit the archer. I can show you how."

He was quiet for a long moment. "Why are you involving *me*? No one else seems to think I'm capable of anything anymore."

"That's nonsense. I'm asking for your help because I need it, and because it doesn't look like you have anything better to do." I hoped he knew I was teasing.

For a moment, his expression was stony and I was worried I'd hurt his feelings. Then he began to chuckle, the chuckles quickly turning to laughter.

"I'm definitely not busy, and I'll gladly help, Elira. Anything you want, consider it done."

After Magma finished cleaning Jorun's wound, much to his chagrin, she set about making more of her green goop concoction to smear into it once he'd bathed. She had me hang a couple of broad blankets using a tree branch and one of the ropes tethering the tent to its ground stake to allow him the privacy without which he refused to wash up. And he did exactly that as quickly and as best he could with a large basin of water, a square of her scented soap, and a cloth. Then he moved indoors where the goop was waiting and ready.

Secretly, I was sure he welcomed it. Despite its pungency, there was something in the medicine that not only healed, but eased pain. And I knew that though he was healing, he still hurt. Judging by how he held his arm in the position she'd insisted it stay in for the past days, Jorun was ready for her to tie the splint at his nape.

"While I'm tending him, empty that water and collect more from the stream, would you, Elira?" Magma asked.

The stream wasn't far. Trickling pleasantly off the nearest hill, it made its way to the sea, passing Magma's workshop on its way.

I completed the task quickly and wondered if she would ask Jorun to help Wade over to bathe once she finished mending his shoulder. But as soon as I returned with a fresh basin of water, she told *me* to wash up. Unlike Jorun, I took her up on the offer without complaint. Afterward, I planned to wander to the lagoon, though I would be well-armed. I needed my weapons at the ready at all times – just in case North found me again and tried to make good on what he promised to do to me before ending my life.

Magma didn't approve of Crest going out to sea – in case she'd been wrong. But deep in her heart, she knew the feel of the quake. She'd lived through the last eruption. Over the strung blankets, I watched the mountains for any leaking smoke and ash, but there was nothing but blue sky overhead.

I scrubbed and rinsed my hair, then scoured the sand and salt from my skin, feeling like I'd removed a layer of it as well. Refreshed, I stepped back inside the tent.

Jorun was patched up, his arm cradled in a new sling. Magma saw me looking him over. "He won't need it much longer. He doesn't heal as fast as *you*, but his injury isn't as severe as yours was. He's mending well," she said approvingly. "It seems you *listened* when I told you to rest and not lift things," she pointedly told Jorun. Like a child, he glowed under the praise given to him, but Magma watched to see if I was bothered by her needling.

She sighed when I simply shrugged.

Then her eyes unexpectedly lit up. "Do you want to see what I've been working on, Elira?"

"Sure…" I said, suddenly suspicious.

I wasn't sure what Magma 'worked on' other than people – their injuries and infirmities. She waved me over and scooted a sizeable wooden box out from beneath her counter. "You can't tell a soul," she whispered, her tone so serious, I wondered for a moment whether peeking into the cube was wise.

She unclasped a copper latch and gently eased the lid open. Inside was a woven blanket dyed the softest pale yellow, a shade only found in delicate lilies and the morning sky on its most serene days.

"It's beautiful," I told her, gingerly taking hold of her handiwork and marveling at how soft the blanket was.

"It's for Breaker and Katalini's baby."

My lips sprang open.

She put a finger up to her lips. "No one is supposed to know yet. They haven't told a soul. Not even me." Magma grinned.

Not true, but I didn't dare tell her Jorun and I already knew. I cut a look to Jorun that said I'd end him if he blabbed.

"Wow," was all I could manage. "If they haven't told anyone, how did *you* know?"

"She's showing. Just a little," she confided. "She hides it, but I've seen more than my fair share of expectant mothers and have helped bring many a babe into this world. I delivered Breaker and Crest."

"And me," Wade reminded her.

"And Wade," Magma parroted.

"They'll love this, Magma." I held the blanket out for her and she gently folded it and tucked it back into its hiding place, then pushed the box back into the shadows.

Magma snickered. "Katalini's been feeling poorly in the mornings, not that they've come to me for help. I had to sneak over there to watch a few times, but that was all it took to confirm she needed something to help settle her stomach. I told Breaker I was experimenting with new teas and insisted she try it. She loves tea," she added with a conspiratorial grin. "It has ginger root and..." she listed a handful of other things I didn't recognize. "She's been glowing ever since and sends Breaker to ask for more of my new tea every few days."

Jorun and I passed the time in relative quiet and waited with them. My fourth hovered at the door with his eyes focused on the sea, just in case, until we heard The Salt's horn sound. Then we heard it again. Startled, I turned to

Magma, who explained that the second blare indicated that all was clear and it was safe to return home.

Jorun was ready to go. He started up the path, stopping when I lingered at the doorway.

"I'll be right there," I promised.

He didn't know that Magma had stopped me. Her hand rested on my arm, my name whispered from her lips as I was getting ready to leave. Jorun finally nodded and set off toward home. I turned to Magma.

So low that Wade couldn't hear, she whispered, "Do you remember the evening of the ceremony?"

It was a moment I would never forget. It was the night I realized how much pain I'd caused these people and how many lives – loved ones – I'd taken from them. The people of Talay, unlike Neera's, loved fiercely and I'd stripped it away. Fathers. Mothers. Brothers. Sisters. Friends. I'd only considered what I was gaining, not the loss I perpetuated.

Magma leaned closer. "You have that look about you again."

"What look?" I rasped.

"Like you might take to the skies at any moment. I see flight in your eyes again."

I brushed off her comment, hating how it flayed me. "My wings are mended now, thanks to you. Of course I'll fly."

She narrowed her eyes. "Don't condescend to me, girl. Are you planning to leave?"

I straightened my back and flexed my wings, sharpening my resolve so she could hear it. "That evening, I gave you my word, Magma. I will not rescind it. If it means taking flight, I'll do so. If it means planting my feet, you can be assured they will be planted."

"I know you want to honor your word, but I was wrong, Elira. That's not something I say or admit often enough, but it's true. You're meant to fight *with* us, not for us." Magma silently pleaded for me to stay and keep my feet on the ground. But she forgot who I was and that I was meant to fly. That I was taught to fight before I knew why I needed to. That I would fight with them no matter where I waged the battle.

"I'm not leaving." *Yet.* "I spoke with Breaker earlier about how we can quickly improve your archers' aim."

"*Our* archers?" she questioned, immediately detecting my slip of the tongue.

"The archers of Kehlani." I looked down at my bare feet, now hardened enough to withstand the pebbles, sand, and even the tiny briars that somehow took root where nothing else would. "Don't read too much into my verbiage. I've lived on the sand a fraction of the time I dwelled in the sky."

She tried to smile, but it didn't reach her eyes. "Alright. Then you also remember the other half of the promise you made, I assume."

That I would come to her, or tell Crest, before I left.

I swallowed thickly, nodding once. "I remember."

"Good," she said, worry deepening the wrinkles cut into the skin on either side of her mouth.

"Magma," I started, "I need to know the measurements of every part of Wade's remaining leg. Lengths and circumferences..."

She narrowed her eyes. "I'll see what I can do."

I winked at her. "You're *clever*. I'm sure you'll come up with something."

"Are you insulting me?" she asked without flinching.

"It's a compliment, Magma."

She shook her head and smiled. "Go on. Get out of here."

I took a few steps. "You shoo me away like a common fly. Like an annoyance."

"Yep." She cocked her head and hip and waited until I began moving like she'd ordered.

Jorun, impatient when I lingered with Magma, left me behind and walked home. When I caught up with him, he was standing outside my tent with none other than Nori. I warily approached as they laughed at something shared between them. He was immediately charmed, the smile on his face genuine and open. He heard my footsteps. "Elira," he greeted. "I assume you know Nori."

"Yes," I answered coolly, slowing before I walked too close. My fingers flinched, eager to wrap around her throat again.

Her hand drifted there. I wondered if she was aware of the fear she silently displayed. The thought made the corner of my lips curl.

"She came to check on Crest, but he's not back yet," Jorun explained, hooking a thumb toward The Shark's tent.

"How nice of you," I remarked, trying and failing to keep the edge from my voice.

Nori turned away to bat her eyes at Jorun. "It's just that… I know how hard it is for him to be responsible for the entire sea. He feels the weight of it on his shoulders, especially in times of danger."

I imagined striding up to her wearing the crazed smile I could feel straining to dominate my lips and leaning in to tell her that if she touched my lacuna again, I would break each and every bone in the hands that offended *me* by roaming *him*.

They had been friends since childhood, but she knew whose feathers adorned his chest. He'd been clear about his lack of romantic feelings for her, yet she pushed at the boundary using the trust they'd built to shield her true intentions.

I didn't act on my inner impulses, but Nori seemed to intuit them. She swallowed thickly and offered Jorun mindless conversation.

A flash of movement caught my eye, not from the dunes beyond Crest's tent where I hoped he would at any second appear, but in the sky.

I quietly ordered Jorun to *get inside*, pushing Nori along with him into the shelter. He recognized the urgency in my tone. Before ducking in, he peeked to see *her* soaring out over the sea.

I was immediately taken back to the dream I'd had in which she circled over my cleaved wings, acutely aware of the feeling of satisfaction and joy that came from ending the dream version of her, and then watching Crest drag her into the sea.

Jorun and I watched every flap of Soraya's wings. How she gracefully moved her arrow, searching for a target.

"Call to the Guardians," I ordered Nori.

She bristled. "What's out there?"

"An Empyrean Warrior is hunting above us."

Her breaths went shallow. She wrung her hands as if she didn't know what to do with them. "Crest keeps weapons in his tent," she whispered.

"Nori," I said sternly, "I need you to calm down and call out to warn the Guardians before someone gets hurt."

"Anyone in the open is at risk," Jorun gently explained. "She's flying just out of range of your people's arrows, but our arrows can reach the soil from her altitude," Jorun told her. "And Soraya is not one to be trifled with. She's the one who betrayed Elira and cut her down."

Nori's eyes widened. She moved back the flap and let out a series of shrieks that made my ears ring. Her message was quickly received and answered by several voices, some in the sea, some on land.

"You did it," I told her. "Thank you."

"I didn't do it for you," she told me haughtily.

"Believe me, I'm aware." For an instant, I considered tossing her out of my home and letting Soraya rid me of her.

"We need a greater cache of weapons in here, Elira," Jorun mused, oblivious to the tension building between me and the woman who would have Crest if only she could.

"I have a knife and fork, if wielding them would make you feel better," I replied sweetly.

He scoffed. "A lot of good a fork will do us."

"It's better than nothing, which is all you brought with you. I don't know what you were thinking, descending without your bow or sword or… *something*," I told him – again – like I had a hundred times before. He was foolish.

"I descended *peacefully* only with the intention of finding and rescuing you, Elira. If I came armed to the teeth and one of Talay's people saw me, they would have shot me down."

I knew it was coming… My eyes pressed shut as I waited for it.

"Like *you* saw fit to do anyway," he chided.

I refused to discuss this again. I didn't feel the need to apologize for defending myself. How was I to know he came to help me?

If I didn't have a powerful feeling in my gut that he was being truthful about his motives, he wouldn't be breathing to argue with me right now.

He turned to Nori. "What did your call mean – exactly?"

"I told them there was danger in the sky and gave the location of the nearest guard tower. The Guardian assigned to it today is the one who answered. He will relay to all where she is, what weapons she has, and what she's doing… unless she moves beyond his sight."

"Crest doesn't know she's out there," I hissed. "He'll come here first."

Nori's lip curled. "Of course he will. *You're* here."

I started out the door. "What are you doing?" Jorun grabbed my arm. "You can't go out there!"

I shook him off. "Don't *touch* me," I warned.

He raised his hands. "I meant nothing of it and you know it! You can't go out there, Elira. Listen to reason."

"I can and I will," I told him. Reason be damned.

"Soraya knows your wings," he pressed.

"And my rage, Jorun." I reminded him. "She won't get too close if she knows I aim back."

He tossed up his uninjured arm. "And when she runs back to tell Talon you're here, fighting for *them*? Then what?"

"You already said they were coming! What does it matter when?"

He loomed over me, trying to intimidate me with his height the way most males did in the sky kingdom. It made me want to take up the fork and show him what it was capable of when driven by anger and imagination.

"I *also* said they needed time to prepare. If you're seen and they come for you now, Kehlani's loss would be catastrophic," he reasoned.

Nori interjected. "Not true. We've lost many, but never the war."

I cut her with a glare. "You've never faced *every* Warrior in Empyrean at once, and never on the shore. Talon won't keep to the sky. He'll push until every grain of sand is slick with Kehlanian blood."

Nori blinked rapidly as if she couldn't imagine the sheer number, or perhaps the carnage that might come from such a battle. She quickly scanned my tent. Rushing to the bed, she grabbed the thin, sand-colored blanket and returned, holding it out for me. "What if you used this to cover your wings?"

I dropped my bow and quiver, tossing the fabric over my shoulders and gripping it at my neck. "Why are you helping me all of the sudden?"

Nori inhaled loudly, then let it out again. "Because you're going to protect *him*. I won't lie and tell you I don't have feelings for him."

"He's *my* lacuna," I told her, watching closely to make sure she understood.

"I can see that *now*," she replied sheepishly. "Before, it didn't seem like you cared about him at all, but I can see that much has changed."

"Good!" I snapped. I would deal with her later if she didn't understand exactly what I meant when I called him mine.

When Soraya flew with her back toward me, I took off running.

Jorun's deep voice melded with Nori's soft tone as I ran toward a copse of palms on the seaward side of The Shark's tent.

Soraya soared lower, but she didn't see me enter the trees. Didn't notice me shrug the blanket off, pluck up an arrow, and raise my bow. Didn't see me look at her with both eyes as I aimed the arrow's sharp tip at her throat.

Several Guardians shot at her, but their bows wouldn't carry their arrows as far as mine would…

I aimed, made sure it would strike, and released the string. My arrow cut through the palm fronds and soared through the sky with a telltale whistle. Soraya heard it and dodged left a split second before it hit her.

She cried out, but the injury didn't impede her ability to fly.

Instead of her throat, the arrow – fletched with Aderyn's feather – lodged in her side. Inwardly, I cursed for missing her heart, even if I appreciated that she would now have a scar to match mine.

She flew higher, flying out of *my* range, too.

When it was clear that she was returning to Empyrean, the Guardians shrieked to let everyone know. They called out again when she was out of sight.

My eyes slid to the sea just a jog through the sand away from the palms that hid me. From it, Crest emerged. I didn't know how I sensed him, but I did. Didn't know how his eyes cut straight to mine, but they did.

Water dripped off every inch of him as he prowled toward me. My heart beat faster.

"It was *your* arrow, wasn't it?" he asked, wiping water from his eyes.

I nodded.

"How?"

"Your bows are good for use on the land, where you hunt from shorter distances, but if you want them to soar, they must be lighter, as do your arrows. There's still time to alter what you already have."

"Time?" he asked warily. Jorun's footfalls came just before he and Nori appeared from around his tent.

"I wanted to tell you my plan last night, but you distracted me."

The Shark's brows jumped. "I distracted you?"

"Yes."

"*I* distracted *you*?" he said again, as if he couldn't believe I'd accused him of exactly what he did.

I put my hands on my hips. "How many more times will you find it necessary to repeat the words? Yes, you distracted me, and I didn't think to tell you until this morning, but then the entire Isle shivered, there was the looming threat of the wave, which you never should've swam toward…"

"There *was* no wave. False alarm," he said breezily, a curious smile hanging on his lips.

I continued as if he hadn't spoken. "And then there was Soraya, who could've shot you from above if you weren't careful…" I plowed forward with my thoughts, my feelings bleeding into them.

"But she didn't," he argued.

"She could have. She's very good with a bow," I told him.

His smile grew. "You were worried about me."

My mouth gaped. "I tell you that you could've died and all you got from that is that I was worried about you?"

"Yes," he said, every shade of blue in his eyes sparkling. "Do you need a hug?"

Jorun and Nori slowly inched closer, both watching our rant of a conversation with morbid fascination.

"Of course not!" I bit, grabbing my blanket off the ground and shaking it so the sand trickled out.

The Shark slowly extended his arms as if waiting for me to fall into them.

I scoffed. He was being ridiculous. I was fine.

"Elira…" he pressed, slowly walking forward. He should've lowered his voice. Jorun was listening, likely judging. And Nori… well, I didn't mind if she heard him address me as his. "There isn't a place in sky or sea where you'll find more *comfort* than in the arms of your lacuna."

His arms began to sink. I bit my lip. I knew he was right. I liked that we were worried about one another. Because I *did* want the hug he offered.

I rushed forward and threaded my arms around his waist. A deep rumble of a laugh resonated throughout his chest when I pressed my cheek against it.

"Don't pretend you didn't covet *my* embrace, too, Shark," I told him, closing my eyes for a moment just to hear his heart beat and to listen to the sound of his breath pouring in and out of his lungs.

"I'd never lie to you," he told me softly, his chin resting on my head. "I craved it long before you allowed it."

My arms tightened around him.

"I absolutely do *not* love you, though," he whispered into my ear.

I smiled. I didn't love him either. "Good." Letting go of him, I remembered our small audience.

Nori looked away from us and stared toward the sea, while Jorun's disapproval was as palpable as the sand stinging our bare legs, thanks to a gust of irritated wind.

CHAPTER FOURTEEN

The wail from The Salt's horn was different than it was when she warned her people away from the sea they loved, and different from when she rescinded that warning. Yet, I recognized this call because I'd heard it before – from the time when I first spoke to the Seer after Crest saved me and brought me to Magma for mending.

If a tone was made of angst and mingled with sorrow, it would be the one she used for The Shark. "She only calls on me when she *has* to," Crest paused. "Come with me?"

I tossed the blanket on the ground and announced I would collect it later, then repositioned my quiver and slung my bow over a shoulder.

Jorun refused to leave my side and Nori followed Crest, walking beside my fourth on the path to The Salt's tent.

The sun-blanched bones of the beast that used to adorn the Seer's tent still lay scattered on the ground, though the sand had swept up and begun to cover them the way the green of the mountains slowly swallowed the rock to which its roots were affixed.

In The Salt's tent, I immediately stopped to stare at the strands of cowries overhead, one shell for each of her people who had passed away. From the sheer number, the tradition had begun long before she was born. But that wasn't what gave me pause. The cowries overhead thumped with a steady beat. And when I pressed a hand over my heart, I realized that the sound perfectly matched its cadence.

Their low, steady vibrato chased a shiver up my spine.

Beside me, Crest turned a slow circle. Jorun slowly stepped around the space, examining the sound and movement. He even reached up to touch one, wiping his fingers on his sarong afterward. As if the feeling resonating from them was something that could be so easily removed.

"What's happening to them? What does this mean?" Nori asked The Salt, who sat with her bowl, raking her hands through the cowries that represented the living souls who still dwelled on Kehlani.

The Salt's dark braided hair was bound with a charcoal gray cloth that twisted around and around her head, reminiscent of the funnel cloud Koa had barely survived. Her clothes matched the steely swath that bound her hair. Her cowrie necklace, made from the shells of Seers who came before her lay on the table beside the bowl she worried over.

"Salt?" Crest asked when she didn't answer Nori.

"Talay bade me call you, Crest."

"What would he have me do?" The Shark asked, ready for whatever task the sea god required him to undertake.

"He hasn't revealed it yet, but he will very soon," she answered. "I can feel him moving… in the water…" Her eyes glazed over as if she could see Talay beyond the shore in some deep, blue, cold place among the leviathans and kraken. Among the sharks…

She snapped out of her daze and gestured to her bowl of cowrie shells. Her eyes fixed on mine.

"They stopped trembling," she rasped. "On the mountain, they finally stopped. Talay spoke to me there. He said they shook because Tella is shaken."

I met Jorun's knowing stare. From what the first soul wrote, if the scrap of a scroll Era found was truly her account, Tella was slain by Neera and Talay kept her from sinking into the sea. She became this land when she died. "How could Tella be shaken?" I asked carefully.

Was Neera behind it?

The Seer studied me for a long minute. "Empyreans believe that Neera only made a finite number of souls and that they live on far past the bodies that first house them, later taking on other bodies to dwell in the sky again and again. Do you not?"

Jorun and I nodded.

"*Why* do you believe it?" she asked.

I wasn't sure how to answer. I suppose we believed it because we were taught it was so.

"When you are young, you believe what you're told. But when you grow and mature, you believe because of experience. Because you've seen it or felt it – here." She patted her chest, just over her heart. "Do you know of Tella?" The Salt asked carefully.

"We've only recently learned of her existence, but what we were told was that Tella was slain by Neera," Jorun advised, a question in his tone.

"That is the truth," the Seer said adamantly.

Jorun tried to smile as he gently replied, "Few Empyreans know the truth."

The Salt's bottom lip began to quiver. Not as if she mourned, but like she felt Tella's indignant anger within her bones. "In a fit of jealousy and rage, Neera killed the body of the earth goddess."

I stepped closer. "The body? Are you implying that gods and goddesses have souls?"

The Salt sat her bowl down and pinned me with a stern look. "Of course they do. The souls of gods and goddesses live on, too, Elira. This island and all the life on it would not exist or flourish from nothingness. Tella's soul lives beneath this rock and sand, and she is *upset*. The tremors were her way of warning us."

"Against what?" Jorun asked.

"That's the question," she answered. The Salt stared at the shells in the bowl, plucking mine out. The blue wing pattern was even more faded than it was the last time I saw it. It was like my cowrie showed my truth: that day by day, little by little, I was slipping away.

The Salt suddenly stood. Her brows furrowed. Crest moved toward her because his task had been defined. I wondered if he tasted the brine more strongly on his tongue when the sea god spoke through his Seer.

"In the wake of the earthquake, there's been a tragedy. You must escort the dead into the depths."

"How many?" he breathed.

"Three as of now," she answered. "Rocks broke away from the bluffs and tumbled into the hollow," she somberly added.

"The hollow?" I asked, panic and fear flooding my bones. I clutched my stomach. Her words struck me and knocked away my breath. My wings stretched, ready to fly. I blinked away tears that pricked my eyes and stumbled toward the door. Only The Salt's voice stopped me.

"I don't know who survived, Elira, or what you might find. The few Guardians Breaker could spare are still sifting through the rubble."

Jorun's brows cinched in confusion as he strode toward me, demanding, "What is *the hollow*?"

The hollow was a narrow valley cut between the craggy hills that jutted between the Hall of Guardians and West Village. My feet had dared the rocky pathways several times, but my conscience always steered me away.

"It's where Aderyn and our siblings live," I choked, jogging across The Salt's sandy floor and pushing outside. Jorun was on my heels, deftly snapping back into the position of my fourth.

A tear slipped from my eye. My teeth chattered. I was trying to hold it together but completely falling apart – like the mountain had just done.

"Don't assume the worst," Jorun said, trying to calm me. His wings flared in time with mine as we prepared to leave.

"You'll hurt your shoulder," I cried as I lifted from the ground to see him flying across from me.

Jorun held his injured arm, still in the fresh sling Magma had applied, close to his stomach. "I don't care."

I nodded my thanks, unable to speak.

It meant so much to have him with me. To have more than a fourth, to have a friend. And not only to fly with me to the hollow, but the fact that he came for me, that he promised to return with me, to fight at my side, not because I ordered it but because it was the right thing to do.

"I would carry you if I could," I told The Shark.

He shook his head. "I'll swim. I'll be there," Crest promised. I could only nod to him, fighting the ache of tears forming a tight knot in my throat. Fighting the cry my heart pumped out with every contraction.

We flew swiftly over the land and soared past the towers. Like oysters, each held its pearl of a Guardian, poised and ready to shoot until they saw the blue of my wings and lowered their weapons.

All that mattered was whether they were alive. And if they weren't… I didn't know what I would do.

My heart sank at the possibility. Worried tears rained onto Kehlani. When we finally passed the Hall of Guardians and rushed toward the rocky bluffs, a keening wail flew from my chest.

Incredibly tall, harsh ledges of rock, craggy and cold and devoid of the green that draped the rest of the Isle flanked the valley they towered over; a hollow carved by patient, persistent water flowing down the side of the nearest mountain.

The Salt warned that some of the rock had broken away and tumbled into the hollow, but she hadn't revealed that half the face had broken away and large slabs had crushed everything beneath it. Even from our perspective, which wasn't high above the canopy, the Guardians working around them looked as small as younglings.

I dove, my wings flaring to catch me just before my feet touched the ground, already striding into the rock pile.

"Aderyn!" I yelled, walking toward those helping clear the rubble. Amidst the dust and broken rock were impossibly thick timbers that looked as though a god had taken and broken them over his knee. "Aderyn!" I shouted louder.

Jorun's presence flanked me. Hope bled away when I looked at the rocks and the empty, shadowed crevices in the cliff faces that weren't large enough to hold one person, let alone three.

"Have you seen an Empyrean with hatchlings?" I asked the two closest males searching the spaces between rocks to see if anyone or anything possibly survived them.

"Everyone in the hollow came from Empyrean," one answered. "You'll have to be more specific."

"How many lived here?" Jorun asked carefully, as taken aback as I felt.

"There *were* eight homes, shared amongst their number," the Guardian replied.

I turned a slow circle, scouring for something, anything… desperate to cling to a hope I worried might have died when the rocks crushed everything that lay beneath them.

"Are the survivors gathered elsewhere?" Jorun questioned, walking up to the men while they took a break to wipe the mixture of pale, white rock dust and sweat from their foreheads.

The man nodded. "We pitched a tent for them. If you take the path toward West Village, it's the first one you'll see." He pointed beyond the destruction to where a trodden pathway, paler than the stone around it, emerged from the flats at the base of the bluffs.

Jorun and I flew over it and reached the tent a moment later without difficulty. Striding toward it, I stopped, paced, worried… "What if they aren't inside?" I cried, pressing a hand against my stomach.

"Then we'll go back and help find them."

I angrily flung a hand back in the direction we'd just flown. "They wouldn't be *alive*. You saw the rock that –"

"I know," Jorun interrupted, his voice breaking. He looked away to hide the emotion overwhelming him because that was what Warriors were supposed to do. They weren't supposed to care about anyone else or show emotion, but Jorun had. He'd loved Aderyn, too. I could see it in the way he pressed his eyes closed as though he might at any minute wake from a nightmare, and in the way he cleared his throat and pressed on. He came for Aderyn – however he might find her. He would be strong – for her. "I know, Elira, and if the rock took them, we will find them nonetheless."

I couldn't see through my tears. It felt like the sky was crushing us slowly. How could this happen among all the other terrible things lately? How?

"Breathe, Elira," Jorun commanded as though he were my quad leader. My lungs desperately tried to obey. "You have to calm down so we can go inside."

I shook my head and braced my hands atop weak knees, trying to stop the dark spots swimming in my vision. "How many more must fall before this is all over?" I breathed with difficulty. "What else must we endure?"

Jorun pursed his lips together. "We endure what we must, Elira. There is no way to plan for the battles that catch us off guard. Sometimes, we just have to act and react as best we can and hope it's enough." He pointed toward the tent. "I'll go in."

He started that way.

My heart constricted. My ribs cinched. I forced my back ramrod straight and did what he said; I acted and reacted as best I could, hoping it was enough to carry me inside and guide my eyes and heart on what to do if they were there and safe, and if they weren't. "No. We go together."

He paused just outside the door and waited for me to take the steps I had no other choice but to take.

The tent's interior was dark and my eyes took a moment to adjust after entering the space. The scent of wood smoke filled the air. At the far end of the vast structure, a fire thrashed in its pit. There weren't many souls inside, but the Guardian was right. Every pale face was Empyrean. And all of them were staring at Jorun and me.

"Aderyn?" I sharply called out.

Near the fire pit, someone slowly stood.

Someone holding a swaddled hatchling.

An elderly woman beside her rocked another.

Through the haze, I locked eyes with my former best friend. Though the panic and worry of finding them dead had abated, a new feeling washed over me.

My fists curled. Tightened.

Instinctually, I reached for the sword I'd always carried on my belt – a belt I no longer wore. A sword I'd lost to the depths. A blade that drowned with the girl I used to be.

The Empyrean survivors took note of us and moved to conceal my sister – *from me.*

Jorun muttered a soft curse.

I turned on my heel, accidentally bumping into his injured shoulder before stalking back outside. He followed me.

Aderyn foolishly gave chase. I could feel her before I heard her footsteps. "What do you think you're doing here?" she demanded.

I wheeled. "What do you *think*?"

She was no longer skin and bones. Her skin glowed, tanned by the sun, and her dark hair shone. She wore Empyrean clothes, loose but comfortable, as did everyone spilling from the tent behind her.

Her eyes narrowed. "You've put the hatchlings in danger by coming here. Did you fly?" she demanded.

"I am *one second* away from finishing what the quaking mountain started," I warned, removing the bow from over my shoulder.

She drew a hidden knife in response and took up her favorite fighting stance, legs parted, the left slightly positioned before the right to guard the hand she favored.

Those behind her weren't Warriors. They shrank away from the threat of violence, some returning to the false safety of their flimsy tent. It wasn't even tied down properly, I noticed.

"You told them I couldn't be trusted," I accused, my voice hoarse, raw.

"You couldn't!" she retorted. "You were the champion of Empyrean. Do you know what that indicated besides your strength in battle, Elira?"

I bared my teeth.

Aderyn's eyes blazed angrily. "It meant you were the best at taking orders. At falling in line and doing *exactly* what your superiors ordered. It never troubled me when you followed Sannika's or The General's mandates, but you also upheld the Elders' whims. You never noticed what they did to others, did you? The injustices that demanded far more than Neera's horrible scale ever could. Did you know of the punishments they doled out for the most menial of crimes? Or did your eyes only open when their wrath was turned upon you?"

I remembered our father and his mace facing off against the youngling who hid behind Era.

She continued her rant. "You didn't see how they treated the Clipped because you were too afraid to know, too afraid to look too closely at a future you knew was yours. You added Talon to our ranks simply because of his reputation in battle. Did you ever ask anyone else about his character? You certainly never consulted me!" she spat. "I would've told you what I knew. I would have offered it freely if I'd known you were even considering him."

I hadn't asked for her opinion. It was a mistake. I knew that now. But… "You must have known he was in contention. Why didn't you speak up?"

Guilt washed over her face before she continued berating me, taking the opportunity to spew a lifetime's worth of venom at the person she used to call friend. "You didn't *listen*. You didn't *look*. You didn't *care*. You were too worried about yourself, too worried you might fall off your lofty, golden perch to see they already had you in their cage. Why should I have bothered telling you anything?"

"Because you were my second! If I was trapped in a cage and powerless to see its bars, let alone escape, you never *once* revealed it to me, despite apparently seeing it so clearly!" I spat with equal venom.

She cut sideways at the air. "And what would you have done differently, Elira, when all you could focus on was hiding? You couldn't risk raising eyebrows. Couldn't risk scrutiny, and neither could I. I hid you for *years.* I kept you safe. But I couldn't keep doing it anymore. Just because of your position, your life was already worth more than mine. But your blood was priceless. If they found out about it, you would've been clipped. You would have been housed and fed well, but at least you would've lived. If I'd been caught concealing your blood from them, do you have *any* idea what they would have done to me?" Her voice caught on the final word.

My mother's shrill screams as she tumbled toward the sea filled my head.

I knew what Aderyn had sacrificed, the risks she took, as well as the potential consequences. And yet when she looked in my eyes and told me she wanted to help, insisting she was happy to because she couldn't stomach me being clipped, claiming she did it because we were a team and that was what friends did for one another – they helped – I believed her.

Perhaps *that* was the greatest lie she ever told. Maybe she was angrier about the fact that I hadn't seen through *it.*

I stared at my sister, wondering how we were of the same blood.

Once, I thought she and I were like Breaker and Crest, with an unbreakable bond – until she severed it.

She thought I was selfish climbing to the top, but she left out the fact that she didn't hesitate to climb that mountain beside me.

I'd trusted her with a secret that could've ruined me, but she didn't think I would be willing to shield *her* given the chance. Then she just left… she cut ties without saying goodbye, even though she knew how it would break me.

Now, I stood before her shattered and she was upset by the shards.

I narrowed my eyes at her. "You're a coward, Aderyn. I never saw *that* before now, either."

"A coward?" She gave a harsh laugh. "A coward doesn't defy every rule that's ever been set before her. A coward," she hissed, slithering forward, "doesn't take responsibility for hatchlings that aren't hers. A coward doesn't ask her enemy to cleave her wings and let her live amongst them." She smirked. "I've heard how *close* you've become with Crest." She cruelly smiled, dangling his name in front of me like sweet pomegranate arils.

It would be the last time his name would ever fall from her lips.

I removed my quiver and dropped it on the ground. The arrows jostled and some slid out. I had no knife to meet hers, but I needed no weapon and she knew it.

My wings flared as I closed the distance between us.

Her eyes lit with dare and fury. "Did he tell you he was the one to cut my wings away, or that it was *his* idea to float them atop the sea for you to find?"

What?

My chest felt like it was crumbling, the pieces falling like the rocks had from the bluff. As if I lay in the hollow, crushed and dying, I heard him call my name.

"Elira!"

Crest told me he would be there as soon as he could, and here he was. His feet pounded the path Jorun and I had just flown over.

A tear trickled from my eye as I turned to look at him.

Suddenly, a commotion erupted behind me.

"No!" Jorun shouted, struggling to stop Aderyn before she reached me with her dagger. She took advantage of his injury, lightly striking his shoulder before pushing him to the ground. She used restraint, but any pressure was too much on the fragile wound. Agony rippled over his face.

"You said you'd come *with* me," she heaved at him. "But you didn't. You came for *her*!"

My eyes bulged. He failed to mention that part.

"I told you I had matters to finish before I *could*," he gritted, pushing himself up onto his knees and getting back to his feet slowly. "And you haven't exactly been reasonable enough to let me explain!"

"You didn't bring her!" Aderyn shrieked, ignoring his accusation. "Do you know how hard it's been? They need her. I'm not enough."

"Her *who*?" I asked him.

A muscle in Jorun's jaw jumped angrily as he glared at Aderyn, the two silently cursing one another with equally heated glares.

"Who were you supposed to bring to Kehlani, Jorun?" I demanded.

His gaze cut to me. "I was supposed to deliver your mother here. The General couldn't be involved, so…"

So Jorun volunteered to do what my father couldn't. And after he brought my mother to her hatchling babes, he planned to remain here with Aderyn.

I would wager my father didn't know about that specific portion of his plan. The death of a Clipped was often explained away as suicide – claiming they jumped to their death, or perhaps an accidental stumble that sent them hurtling off the firmament's edge – but if a Warrior didn't fall in battle, their disappearance was harder to explain and too great a coincidence to brush under the rug. If Jorun had gone through with it, someone would have investigated.

The evening of the feast surfaced, and I remembered how they accused my mother of harming her twin hatchlings…

But that wasn't what happened at all.

After Aderyn escaped, she hid them here.

Aderyn had gone pale, her face as still as death itself. "You were *supposed* to deliver her, Jorun. What happened?" she asked, her dark brows cinched.

Her stare found mine, so I gave her the answer I already knew prickled at her skin.

"My mother is dead and so is our father," I told her.

Her chest caved. She pressed a hand to her brow, her lashes fluttering in disbelief. "No."

I stared at her and let it soak in, watching the truth drench her. I could almost see it inching up like fast-rising water. In silence, I watched her raise her head to the sky as if the flood was up to her neck and creeping higher. And then, Aderyn began to silently cry. She lost her grip on the knife's handle, only to reposition it in her palm when she remembered I was near.

Did she really think it would be so easy for Father to smuggle one of the Clipped from the sky after he'd managed to whisk the hatchlings to safety? Didn't she realize there was a chance that her care of them wouldn't be temporary?

Crest caught up with us, his steps slowing when he saw her knife and my weapons on the ground. He saw how close we'd come to ripping one another to shreds.

"Why didn't *you* tell me?" Aderyn demanded of him, tears building and blurring her vision before they fell. "You should have come and told me."

The Shark looked at me, worry creasing his brow. "Because I didn't know… I didn't know about your mother."

A tear fell from my eye, slid down my cheek, and splashed onto my chest. I shook my head. "It wouldn't have been fair to burden you with the story of my mother's death when you'd so recently lost yours."

"Don't hold back with me," he chided softly, moving closer. "I want to know everything, Elira. The good and the bad. The joy, sorrow, and everything in between." He raised his hand and let it hover near my cheek, waiting, offering comfort. I leaned into his touch and allowed him to draw me into his arms, wrapping me in his warmth. "I want to know your heart as well as I know mine."

Aderyn choked.

I pulled away from Crest at the sound.

She studied the two of us, then her gaze caught on the dark patterns splayed over his chest and arm, dragging on my feathers… She dropped her knife, only to point her skinny finger at his heart. "Is that… Does that marking represent *you*, Elira?"

I flayed her with a glare. "My life is no longer your concern. You left it behind because you hated it *and* me."

She shook her head. "I didn't hate you. I don't…"

"*Yes*, Aderyn. You did, and you do."

CHAPTER FIFTEEN

The parchment's edge crumpled under the grip of my tightening fingers. I'd heard her moving around the nest but didn't know she would leave or do something as foolish as this. The sea had just rolled her, nearly drowning her.

Her writing was so fresh, some of the ink smudged beneath the pad of my thumb.

> *E-*
>
> *Don't be angry, but I have to descend and I have to do it now. It can't wait until morning. It can't wait another minute. Someone is going with me to keep watch. Someone I trust and who is more than capable of keeping me safe from them. I promise I won't be long.*
>
> *-A*

I tugged my leathers on over my shift and hastily buckled them, shoved my feet into my boots and quickly laced them, grabbed my weapons, and waited to see if she would return as fast as she claimed. But the sour feeling in the pit of my stomach intensified, and the seconds ticked by painfully slowly until I thought both may drive me mad. I had to know she was okay.

Striding to the balcony, I took to the sky and flew toward the sea, terrified. Something wasn't right.

At Jorun's plea, Aderyn let me see my hatchling siblings. She stood between two men who brought them out into the open so I could look upon them at least once.

She watched me carefully as I took them in.

They were held at a distance, but I could make out their features. I covered my mouth when one of the boys opened his eyes. They were our father's eyes, and they were mine. They weren't newborns. They'd grown, but their wings were still fleshy, covered in delicate, pale fuzz. When they grew old enough to walk, the follicles for their feathers would appear. Soon thereafter, they would fill and stretch until the flesh and fuzz was covered.

I studied their delicate features. Their fingers, curled into fists as though they were born ready to fight. The curves of their tiny ears. The hair on their heads wasn't as pale as mine. It was honeyed.

I wondered what color their wings might one day hold. Clipped wings that would never catch the wind and lift them in flight.

I didn't thank her before turning to leave. Didn't care when Jorun told me he wanted to stay with her for a time. Didn't look back.

Crest fell into step beside me. If my sister hadn't been right with her claim that I'd put the hatchlings at risk by flying, I would've pierced the sky. I might never have touched the land again.

We strode over the pale rock path until the sand usurped it and then trailed close to the sea, taking advantage of the cover provided by the palms' shadows.

"Elira," Crest pleaded for the fourth time.

I finally stopped and turned to him, pressing against the base of my diaphragm. I couldn't breathe through the ache in my chest. "She said you cleaved her wings, Crest. She said it was your idea to float them on the sea so I would find them."

He nodded. "It was."

"I'm not even upset about that," I told him, tears pushing from my eyes. "That was before."

Before he saved me, before he gave me the chance Breaker saw and begged him to take, before the mark, and the kiss, and a thousand other moments we'd managed to steal from the greedy goddess who would crush and crumble the thought of us if she could.

"I just loved her so much. She was my sister before I even knew it was true, and…"

"And she hurt you," he interjected softly.

I nodded, turning away and hugging my middle because I didn't know what else to do with my hands. Then another truth rose and I wanted him to know it. He said he wanted all of me. The good and bad.

I took a shuddering breath. "Before the Oracle declares our intentions, we privately meet with her in the sanctum, which is a sacred space where Neera is said to dwell. She's never there, but I could always sense her. On the last

Intention Day, I *felt* her there in that far too small a space. I heard her speak. She told me the war would end where oceans burn."

He nodded.

"Each person cuts their palm and adds their blood to an Empyrea cloud that floats within the sacred space. Aderyn had always given me a conjured cloud of Empyrea to wear, concealing her blood within it. Everyone assumed it was mine. With Aderyn gone this past Intention Day, I was forced to make a new arrangement."

His eyes glinted. "With whom?"

"Talon agreed to help me because Aderyn was gone."

The muscles in his shoulders tensed at the mention of Talon's name. He rose to his full height, looking far more dangerous and barbed than any trident his Guardians brandished.

"The former Oracle died before anyone spoke their intentions that morning, and the goddess swiftly chose and installed a new Oracle. The new Oracle realized immediately that Talon's blood wasn't mine and demanded that I add mine while she watched. I had to cut my palm in front of her to spill my blood."

I swallowed thickly, remembering that day.

"Outside, she announced my intention and Neera's great scale weighed and made known what the goddess demanded if I should fail."

"All your feathers," he rasped.

"All my feathers," I confirmed. "After the demand was declared, the wound on my hand began leaking. Everyone saw my blood and knew I was a first soul."

Crest scrubbed his hand over the back of his head. "What did they do?"

"The Elders postured, and the Oracle moved to protect me from them, but she knew what they wanted. They decided to pretend like they were throwing their support behind me and gave a feast in my honor. I'd asked for command over the quads to achieve my intention, which was to capture you. Before we began, the quads had to be fed."

He nodded. "I remember the day so many of you descended on the fishing grounds."

"It was to supply the meat for that feast," I confirmed. "But the Elders hadn't just planned to nourish us. They also provided a vile form of entertainment. They… began the event with an execution."

Crest went still.

"They brought forth, among the tables of Warriors readying to eat and potentially die for my intention, a Clipped woman. They often were made to serve the Elders and Scholars, and I recognized her from among their number. The Elders seized the opportunity of having a captive audience to hold a mock trial. She fought against them, proclaiming her innocence for all to hear, but it wasn't enough."

"What crime was she accused of committing?" he hesitantly asked.

"Harming two hatchlings who had gone missing."

Fury lit his blue eyes. As did recognition.

"As they disintegrated the Empyrea at her feet, I was seized with a sense of protectiveness and leapt to my feet and *went* to her. But I didn't stop them before they pushed her through the firmament. They knew she couldn't fly. That she would die the moment she hit the sea. And her screams…" I pressed the heels of my palms to my ears as if that could silence them when nothing else would. "Her screams are all I can hear sometimes."

"You didn't know she was your mother," he gently reminded me.

"I didn't know here," I tapped my head, then tapped my heart, "but I knew here."

Crest looked to the sea, always drawn to its steady wisdom and the secrets the water held. He cleared his throat and put his hands on the cut of his hips. "We made arrangements with your father for Aderyn to descend, but we didn't know she was coming until that night. She found me on the shore and was so panicked, I called for Breaker. He'd been visiting our grandmother and The Salt was with them, so they all came. Aderyn kept staring at the sky as if Neera herself might swoop down to collect her. She said we had little time, then begged us to cut off her wings and hide her. She claimed that *you,* not Neera, would come for her."

"You thought she was afraid of me..." The first twist of her knife in the wound that was my reputation.

"She said that if you dragged her back and anyone saw, she'd be given a traitor's death. She didn't go into detail about what that might entail, and Breaker didn't press. The look in her eyes was enough." He paused. "Grandmother refused to cut off her wings. She chided her and told her she hadn't thought it through and would regret her hasty decision later, but Aderyn was insistent. Grandmother told me how and where to cut to try to minimize her pain and the damage to her back. In the end, it didn't matter. The pain was overwhelming, and Aderyn passed out. Grandmother stepped in to treat her wounds."

"Then you swam out into the sea and waited for me there," I surmised.

"She said you were fast, but I never imagined we only had a moment, maybe two to spare before you swooped down. And when you saw her wings and tried to save her…" He stared at the ground beneath our feet guiltily.

I'd tried to save the one who didn't want to be saved. How pathetic I must have seemed to them. How predictable I was to Aderyn.

"The look on your face when you realized…" He pressed his eyes closed. "Maybe *that* was the first time I knew you weren't just capable of killing, when I saw that your grief stemmed from love."

How ironic, because in that moment, I thought he was a monster. That was the moment, in my heart, I vowed to kill him.

The remainder of the day, Crest and the Guardians who weren't cast over the land to keep watch ushered the bodies of the few who were crushed into the sea. There were three, and while the loss of even one was great, I shuddered to think how many it could have been and that my siblings might have been among the dead. Aderyn wisely fled the moment the mountain began to shift and brought the hatchlings to safety before the rocks broke and fell.

The Kehlani people didn't typically gather to bear witness to the sea burials, and this time was no different. This was aided by the fact the former Empyreans sequestered themselves, choosing distance even though Talay's people had granted them a life of freedom on their Isle. My father had helped each one escape the sky, though not often directly. He couldn't risk his position or his life.

I wondered whether they were grateful for the risks he took, or for the mercy they were shown because he was brave enough to ask for it. I wondered if they even cared enough to carry the dead to the shore for Crest, let alone linger to honor those who fell.

I didn't stay, because being near Aderyn made me want to kill her and add her to Crest's duties. I'd been living on the opposite side of the Isle from her, and even that distance was too close.

That evening, Jorun did not come back to the tent. He was likely fully under Aderyn's thrall now that the two had reconnected. She'd probably already convinced him that I was as terrible as she believed.

Seated beside a crackling fire in front of my tent, I worked on whittling Wade's leg without stopping, except to flex my hand when it cramped. The wood gradually gave way to my frustrations. I forced the sharp blade through it again and again until there was a pile of shavings beneath the limb that would become Wade's leg.

Crest was working with Wade on his plan to thickly spread archers over the land like the green vines that slinked and crawled over the mountaintops. He planned to speak to his Guardians about altering their bows – and fast. I'd told him what Jorun overheard from the new General as he discussed his plans to decisively end this war. Then I told him who the new General was.

To say he was livid was an understatement, but it was necessary to rile him.

Time, too, was being whittled away.

Time and opportunity.

Tomorrow, he wanted me to climb the mountains with him – for Wade. The Guardians would start their task, then assign the posts from which they would defend themselves.

Tomorrow, Frey would undertake to teach the younglings that were ready how to shoot the bows once they were carved and arched for them.

Just when I wondered what task he'd been assigned, Koa broke through the dark night and made himself comfortable, slouching beside my fire with a groan. He hooked his arm over his eyes dramatically. "You just *had* to give Wade the task…"

I waited for him to remove the arm that blocked me from sight so he could see me smile. "Yes, I did."

He answered with a heavy sigh, then reached into his bag and pulled out a pouch, extending it for me to take.

Inside were several pieces of smoked fish. "Dinner," he explained. "For you and Jorun." He looked over my shoulder at the tent but didn't ask whether he was inside.

"Thank you."

"Thank Crest," he corrected. He looked over my handiwork and whistled at the pile of curled wood shavings. "What did that branch ever do to you?" he asked with a light laugh.

"Sat at my fire and complained," I teased.

Koa smirked. "Who would've thought The Scourge would have a decent sense of humor?"

I gave him an annoyed look as I laid the food down beside me and returned to my carving. "Don't you have someplace else to be?"

He smiled broadly. "Nope."

Wonderful.

Koa sat up and leaned forward, his gold scales made even brighter by the shimmering firelight. He braced his forearms on his bent knees and looked to the dancing flames. "Actually, I wanted to talk to you about something."

The knife my hand held went still. I readjusted the leg to thin the ankle area further, then waited for him to continue.

The fire rapped and roared, hissed and guttered. For a long moment, it was the only sound save for the loud, constant insect song.

A vine that grew nearby gave off a sweet scent day and night. It seemed especially aromatic tonight.

"Crest sees you as his lacuna," he began.

I blinked.

"And he and Talay have this intense bond. I don't completely understand it and I'm with him more than anyone. Well, I *was* before you splashed into his life." He was proud of the pun, grinning to see if I'd gotten it. I had. Unfortunately.

"Is there a point to this drivel?"

"Yeah." He smiled as if I was teasing. "I just wanted you to know that he's serious. About it… about *you*." He pressed his eyes closed and gave a frustrated growl. "I'm not good at saying this sort of thing delicately, and I probably shouldn't say it at all because you saved my life and he's my best friend and everything."

I stuck my knife in the sand beside me and placed the carved appendage on the sand so I could give him my full attention. "Koa."

"Hmm?" He glanced my way.

"For the love of the sea, say what you came to say and feel free to be indelicate and direct, because *I'm not good* at listening to you fumble for words."

Koa looked sheepish for the slightest of moments. Gave a groan. Scrubbed his face. Scratched at the dark hair gathered into a knot at the crown of his head. Then, as if he'd won the war his conscience waged, he met my eye and said one thing: "Don't break his heart."

I wasn't sure what to say.

I'd have to *have* his heart in order to break it. We didn't love each other. We'd told each other exactly that – more than once.

But I wondered why he'd come here this evening, why he felt the urge to tell me what he saw in his friends, and what he saw in me.

Could he see the flight in my eyes that Magma noticed?

"I would never purposely hurt him, Koa."

He nodded, staring at the sparks flying from the firewood. "It's just that… you're his first thought, you know? 'Is Elira safe? Is she happy?'" He nodded at the bag of smoked fish lying beside me. "'Do you think she's eaten?'" He laughed. "Even right after The Salt asked him to guard you, back when he still hated you, he worried over you. He would ask, 'Do you think it's normal for her to sleep so much? Did she swallow too much water? Do you think the bed is big enough for her wings? I didn't think she could look peaceful…innocent. Do you think she's sad?' " Koa shook his head. "He never asked all at once like that; he just peppered his concerns into our conversations here and there." He sat up straighter. "He didn't love you *then*."

My eyes cut to him. *Then*… implied there was a *now*.

"Come on, Elira. Don't give me that look. You have to know it. See it. He took your mark. Even when I told him he was crazy and should refuse it… That enemies didn't become lovers, let alone lacunas. Do you know what he said to that?"

I shook my head.

"He said they weren't supposed to become friends, either, and yet it happened. Crest was lost after losing his mom. He closed himself off, even to me and Breaker. But with you… It's so crazy, because I know he saved you from drowning, but you saved him, too. You saved him from drowning in a different way, I guess."

I swallowed thickly.

"You watch the sky," Koa said when I glanced upward. "Is it because you miss it?"

"No."

"Because you're afraid?" he guessed.

"I was taught to be very aware of my surroundings," I rasped.

He nodded.

"Are you planning to fight with us?" he asked pointedly.

"Yes," I told him.

Koa ran his teeth over his lip. "From Kehlani?"

My teeth clenched. "From wherever I can best defend you."

He nodded. "I happened to be walking past Magma's tent when she was talking to The Salt. She thinks you're planning to bring the fight to Empyrean now that your wings are healed. She said that if you left, you'd try to keep the island safe if you can."

I heaved a sigh, thinking I should teach Magma to be more aware of *her* surroundings. "Do you ever get bored with rumors and drama?" I asked, exhausted.

He thought about it for a moment. "Not really. No." He smiled, and like the click of a finger, breezy Koa was back. "She was very convincing."

"Magma can be very persuasive." I smiled, hoping he would drop the insinuation and stop suspecting what Magma had inadvertently revealed. I changed the subject. "How is The Salt?"

"Worried," he answered, scooping up some of the wood shavings nearest him and tossing them into the fire. "*Our* cowries stopped shaking, but those of our ancestors still drum. The Salt is frustrated. She feels like she's failing us because she doesn't know what the drumming means, and she's frantic to figure it out before something else happens. She said she should've known what the shaking was, but I don't see how. She wasn't made by Tella. She can't be expected to know the feelings her soul projects, even when they affect Talay's people."

"She's not failing anyone," I told him, bristling on her behalf. "Foresight must be much more difficult to decipher than hindsight."

"I know. We all do. And we've told her that again and again."

I tossed another handful of shavings into the fire to feed it and rid my sand of the mess. "Keep telling her."

"I will," he said. He stretched his back and then slowly stood. "I should get home."

"Thanks for the fish."

"Thanks for saving my life," he immediately chirped.

"You've already thanked me for that," I reminded him. He'd even punctuated it with tears and an incredibly awkward hug.

He grinned. "And I shall continue to do so until I forget about the entire ordeal."

"Which will be…?"

"Never," he happily informed me.

CHAPTER SIXTEEN

All of Empyrean is gathered on the piazza. Warriors and the general populace stare up at the sanctum. It is Intention Day.

The Oracle's jade wings snap angrily as she is wrested from the holy structure and brought before the trio of Elders standing between her and Neera's weighty scale. There is silken-tongued Tanu, owlish Idris, and foul Grieg.

The rest of their ilk waits below. Several pairs of pale eyes writhe with anger as they bear witness to the travesty unfolding before them. The balance of power between the factions within their number has somehow shifted, and the cruel now control the wise.

"You will give our shared intention to Neera," Tanu purrs, haughtily waving the Seer toward the scale.

She grits her teeth against the very notion. "This is not our tradition! Neera sees one *of her people at a time. Not amassed. And first, those who survived from last year to this must have their prior intention weighed. They must pay the goddess her due."*

"She may take as she sees fit, but you will *go to her on our behalf," Tanu hisses slyly, circling her and the Warriors who hold her wrists.*

Tanu bends the knee to the Seer, and I'm not sure why, but I don't like whatever it is he's doing. When the Elder stands again, the Oracle is released.

She angrily rubs her wrists.

I wonder if she will fly away. Escape them. Go to Neera, still trapped behind the wall of her wind.

But when the Seer takes a step, there's a distinct clinking noise coming from her leg. She tugs at a thick brass chain affixed to a matching, heavy ball behind her. Those around me don't know how to respond, or what to do to stop this, but they're as shocked and appalled as I am.

"The Oracle is Neera's. Hurting her will bring nothing upon us but the goddess's wrath," the woman beside me breathes. She's frightened, but so is everyone else. So afraid, that no one acts. No one is brave enough to even raise their voice, so I know none will raise their hands.

Our Oracle drags the brass ball weighing her down. She maneuvers closer until she stands before the scale, and then… with righteous fury in her tone, she invokes the goddess.

To weigh us all.

To take away what wasn't earned.

To see the scale balanced once again.

And the goddess does exactly that, violently. Shocked screams erupt as feathers don't just fall from wings, but are ripped from them. The plucked plumage falls all at once, flooding over the feet of her people.

I glance over my shoulder. I felt no pain, and my feathers are still seated in my wings.

The younglings cry desperately. Murmurs and whispers ripple from fearful, wary mouths.

"Perhaps this is a mistake," many say.

Perhaps the Elders are wrong.

Perhaps our tradition should be upheld.

But whispers and murmurs do not incite. They don't rally. They fizzle and burn out as quickly as they spark. The wisps of their smoke disappear in the blink of an eye.

"Tell her!" Elder Tanu demands. "Give the goddess our intention. After all, we are one people. We rise and fall as one."

"We are not a people unto ourselves. We are hers,*" the Seer reminds him.*

Tanu only smiles. And waits. He ignores the worry and fear of the people who elected him and uses the power they trusted him with against them.

The ponderous brass scale's pans lay still and empty.

The Oracle soon remedies that. She cups her hands and speaks directly to the goddess, her eyes darkening from angry amethyst to nearly black before she sets the intention of all Empyrean before Neera. "Your people have spoken as one and offer you a single intention. Empyrean will end the war raging against Talay's kind and will – in your honor – reclaim the Isle."

The chains that hold the pans begin to rattle. They quake like Kehlani did when the mountain woke.

The shaking builds until the entire scale is jarred back and forth, side to side. As if it cannot, or will not, hold the intention of everyone at once.

Gasps and cries erupt as the scale struggles against the goddess to whom it belongs. Now, not only is their intention shared, but so is their terror and fate.

A cloud of purest Empyrea forms within the still-rocking right pan. From it, feather after feather peels away, landing in the pan's bottom.

The copper quickly sinks beneath the weight.

The chain links holding the pan strain,

bend,

break…

The pan clatters upon the sanctum stone and rolls down its steps. Its tinny sound seems amplified because the kingdom is devoid of all others. The wind is dead like the will of the citizens. Not a soul dares speak.

Neera's people silently behold the goddess's acceptance of their intention – their demand – in horror.

The scale's pan may have broken, but the goddess is not finished.

Her Empyrea cloud did not move. Nor did it stop pouring Neera's demand. So many feathers. Not the mere one or two per person the Elders were expecting.

Intentions of this magnitude require all effort, and therefore, she demands all their feathers should they fail.

Without the ability to fly and with no way to descend, the goddess has issued the greatest demand of her people – their victory, or their deaths.

The gushing of feathers begins to slow.

The final ones to fall are stark white. I begin to laugh because I know to whom they belong.

The Elect are no longer exempt.

I drink in the moment they realize their mistake in tempting the goddess.

Tanu's lips part. Idris clutches her thin chest. Grieg chokes, taking several steps backward, as if he could run from Neera or her bargain.

Tanu hears my laughter as the last white feathers peel from the cloud and it evaporates entirely. His eyes find me across the piazza, an archer sighting his target.

"Bring her forward," Tanu instructs, waving to those holding me. He begins down the staircase, his white robes billowing.

"No!" The Oracle tugs at her chain, dragging the brass weight behind her. It gouges at the Empyrea forming the sanctum's platform and blinding white light shines from the wound. Grieg shields his eyes from it.

Hands fall on my shoulders, but I shrug them off. "Do not *touch me," I warn. "I go to my fate willingly."*

I know all four of their names, faces, ranks, and worries. The Warriors flanking me allow me this final act of respect and I walk forward freely with my head held high.

"You cannot harm her. She is the first soul!" The Oracle fights and begs, trying to free her arms from the meaty hands that hold them at the base of her wings.

The crowd parts for me. From the other side of the piazza, it parts for Elder Tanu as well, and we meet face-to-face in the middle of the square.

The blanched winged who followed Elder Tanu surround me, and the Warriors who once looked to me to lead them fall away.

Tanu leans in so that his warm breath puffs onto my ear. "I know what you did, first soul. And I want to be sure you cannot, in this lifetime, undo it."

I cry out as a shock of liquid pain cuts across the base of my wings. Warm, wet, Empyrea-rich blood flows freely down my back for all to see. I can barely breathe.

He couldn't... Did he cleave them off? I can feel the weight of them, but they drape to the ground, useless.

The power in my blood sets fire to the rope binding my wrists, but the flame does not burn my skin. I catch hold of that power and urge it to burn hotter, faster.

The Elders press their hands to the firmament at my feet. I watch it disintegrate. They grab my arms and try to drag me toward the hole. I plant my feet and resist them.

Grieg calls for the Warriors to help. I lock eyes with one. He knows what they're doing is wrong.

"Don't!" I beg. If they force me through the firmament, I'm as good as dead.

The sharp pain reminds me that my wings won't work. Won't help. Won't save me.

Tanu barks at the Warriors. "Do as you're told!"

Still, they refuse.

Then Talon is there, lurking behind the four he appointed to guard me. He steps between his quad leaders, copper hair and leathers lit by a shaft of sunlight, the top curve of his gray wings towering over them all, with a silent grin on his face.

"Behold," he quietly says. "How the mighty are conquered, and the patient persevere."

I meet his eyes unflinchingly. "If you consider yourself the mighty now, who patiently waits to conquer you?"

Someone will do to him what he intends to do to me. It is the way of things; a natural, feral order in Empyrean, where expectation meets reality with a knife.

He shoves me through the hole.

The wind is sucked from my lungs and my scream is swallowed by the hungry, hollow air. My wings are useless. They don't tear away, but my feathers begin to.

Neera always collects her due...

I tumble, and as I fall, The Elders stare through the firmament to watch me die.

Between them and me, life and death, my feathers litter the sky.

I sat straight up, gasping for air, my wings flinching on my back as I woke. I felt behind me to be sure they were still there, relieved when I found I wasn't cut and wasn't bleeding from a wound that could be felt but not seen.

It was as dark as the depths outside the tent. The insects screamed, but the thunderous whoosh of blood through my ears drowned them out. My mouth was dry. My skin was cool and drenched in sweat. Even my hair was damp.

I tore the sandy blanket off and paced the wood floor. When my tent wasn't large enough to contain me or the feelings erupting, I left it.

I went in search of water, but water wasn't what I needed.

Crest's tent lay dark and quiet. I couldn't even make out the faint orange glow that usually brightened the seams.

Barefoot, I pushed toward the stream, trying to catch my breath but more than that, grounding myself. How ironic that I sought such a feeling since I was a creature of flight, but feeling the sand and grass underfoot, even the pinches of the sand briars, was a comfort.

I wasn't clipped.

Wasn't pushed.

Wasn't dead.

A sound escaped my chest. One full of frustration and fear that refused to be tamped down. A fire that would not be easily stomped out.

My hands trembled. I shook them violently to remind them they were mine.

Was this how the goddess felt, knowing that her people sought to shirk her control and claim it as their own?

In the distance, lightning flashed a moment before its sound reached me. Light danced through the branches of my scar in reply.

I heard the stream before I saw it in the dark. When I reached it and fell to my knees, the water looked more like starlit silk than liquid. Cupping my hand, I lifted gulp after gulp to my lips, then splashed cool droplets across my throat.

When I could drink no more, I sat by the water and waited for my soul and flustered heart to calm.

Was the dream a warning from Neera? Was that why she tossed her power over the sky like a shroud, to claim the vision she'd sent? To let me know she would let them cast me from the firmament if I refused to be obedient?

A salty taste coated my tongue. I drank from the stream one more time. Every other time I'd drank from it, the water was clean and perfect, but tonight it tasted like I'd been drinking from the sea itself…

A gentle clacking sound came from behind me, cutting through the still darkness. Following the footsteps I'd just laid walked The Salt. I stood to greet her, wondering why she was here.

"I now know the rhythm to which our ancestors beat." She drew nearer. "But so do you, don't you, Elira?"

I gave a nod. I could feel it the moment I stepped into her home and stood beneath the strands of beads representing each and every one of Talay's passed souls.

"Do you know that the beating has slowed? The rhythm no longer matches your living heart, but echoes the sound your heart will make as it dies… Like a war song of sorrow and desperation, its melody rises and falls with your last moments, thoughts, breaths, and heartbeats."

I pressed a hand to my chest, hoping she was wrong, but realizing she seemed very confident about the sound now.

"Talay said you were here." The air seemed to crackle, charged and alive. "He has asked me to reveal something to you that I've never told another soul. Not Breaker, nor anyone who led Kehlani before him. And when *he* is ushered into the deep, his successor will not know this truth, either."

I waited, my ribs cinching tightly. "Why?" *Why would he do that? Why would Talay trust me with something so secret?*

"Because you and I are similar, Elira," she answered. "Walk with me to the shore?"

Every step closer made me wonder if I would regret having the knowledge passed to me. The stream quietly spilled out onto the sand. Its fresh mountain water joined the brine with a relieved sigh. The flow wrinkled the shore the salted waves had worked smooth.

The Salt stared out at the water as the wind toyed with the fringe on her sarong and whipped mine against my bare skin.

"You're not alone," she said finally, waiting to see how I might respond.

Was that Talay's message? What did it matter to the god of the sea whether I was, or felt, alone? And why did the Seer look so upset to have to reveal something so simple?

"When we last spoke, Crest mused that Talay does not reincarnate souls, and that is true of every soul that is his – save one."

The moisture in her eyes shone with every burst of lightning that flared over the midnight sky. "He leaves *one* soul to be reborn, again and again… so that her wisdom is never lost. She forgets nothing. Every lifetime is as vivid as the one she currently lives." She stroked the draped layers of cowries on her chest. "He trusts her and speaks to her like none other."

A deep layer of silted sorrow settled into the bottom of my heart for her. My brows kissed. I couldn't believe none of her people knew or suspected…

"How long… how many lives have you lived?" I asked softly.

"I was there when you battled her, just before you sealed her away," she admitted.

I shook my head. "*I* didn't do it, though."

"Yes, you did. In the beginning, after you imprisoned her, you were born again and again – like me. One life just after the last. But then your rebirths became less frequent, many years passing between your appearances. Decades came and went. Then centuries… It was like you found a way to resist her attempts at reincarnating you. Like you hid from her somehow. Or perhaps she wanted to give you time to forget your previous refusals."

She worried her hands. "In your prior lives, Elira, at some point, memories would surface for you until the past was clear and every battle engrained. And once your soul and skin fused and you refused her again, a tragedy would swiftly befall you and the body you wore would die. This time, though, you haven't remembered anything. Have you?"

I shook my head. It was a fluke that made me realize I could control a sliver of wind, and desperation that fueled me to take enough to save Koa from the funnel. A few times a day, I wondered what it would have been like to be caught inside one of them. Neera laid a trap for me that day and I didn't get caught. She would try again with something far worse, I knew.

"Maybe you've been gone so long, you've truly forgotten."

"Did I know you in any of my lives?" I asked her.

She stared out at the sea. "Not as a friend. In each, you ultimately rose to lead Neera's war." The Salt turned to me and softly explained, "Even from afar, Neera has always instilled fear in her people, always demanded their loyalty and obedience. She told them the Isle was rightfully theirs, although it was only a blanket of lies to cover what she'd done to Tella. The Empyreans felt entitled to its fruits. Beyond that, they needed them. With Tella gone, there will be no more islands born."

If Neera hadn't slain the goddess of land, we might have requested an isle for our people to tend and reap, but Neera severed all hope of that peaceful existence.

"When they descended to claim what they thought was theirs, they came with arrows pointed at our hearts. Talay ordered us to defend ourselves and refused the Empyreans access to everything Tella provided, and to the sea's great bounty in penance for what Neera had done."

It was a bitter thing to know we were all punished and starved for Neera's offense. I cleared my throat. "You told me you were his only Seer, but I never imagined what you truly meant."

"I've worn many skins," she acknowledged. "Walked through many lives. Seen you live and die more times than I care to remember. Just when I began to wonder if you would *ever* return, a girl rises through the ranks faster than anyone before her. A girl with blue gray wings – a shade that only ever belonged to you. She flies faster than the rest. She's fearless. Where her arrow aims, she strikes true. And behind all her efforts is an energy, a vibration I've only felt when your soul reclaimed the sky as her own."

Her eyes dragged over the water, the sand, and then fastened back on mine. "If you don't stop her this time, Elira, the war *will* end in the place where skies fall. Not at the tip of your arrow, buried in Empyrean bone. Blood will be wrung from the heavens, but it will not be our hands that twist the clouds. It will be Neera's, and the blood will be yours." A tear fell from each of her eyes. "If you don't defeat her, this *will* be your final battle."

My lashes fluttered as I struggled to grasp what she'd said.

"What do you mean by final?" Did that mean if I lost, I wouldn't be reborn?

"Neera seeks to kill your *soul*."

My brows furrowed, my heart drumming again. "Can a soul die? You… you said that even Tella's still lives."

The Salt lamented, "I can't see how it's accomplished. I can't see through the clouds. But Talay says that Neera believes your soul is like Empyrea. She made you and formed you, and therefore, if she touches you with the same hands, she can unmake you."

"But she's trapped…" The Salt stared at the clouds as though she would burn through them if she could. The hair on the back of my neck rose. "Isn't she?"

Still, The Salt remained quiet. "I can't be sure, but I believe so."

I breathed a little easier, until I considered her prophetic words. The Seer thought the goddess would soon be unbound. If she broke free and came here for me – what would happen to Talay's people then? I couldn't bring that sort of destruction upon them.

"How long do I have?" I asked carefully.

Neera had destroyed my body every time my soul refused to let her loose. She was done asking for my compliance, done demanding it to no avail, and now sought to destroy me. I was all that stood in her way.

"I can't say for certain," she hedged, "but given Tella's response and Talay's warning, I would imagine you don't have long."

"Salt… has Talay ever given me a cowrie before this lifetime?"

"No," she answered. "You were never worthy of one."

"Does the fading pattern on my shell mean the death of my soul?"

She pinched her lips together and stared at the sky for a long moment. "With most, it indicates the death of the body. You saw your father's fade with his last breaths. But I've never seen or experienced the death of a soul. I don't know how its cowrie would react. It might fade, or it might crumble into dust."

She kept saying she couldn't be sure, didn't know for certain. Couldn't see beyond the clouds. I needed to know not what she saw or knew, but what she felt. "Can you feel the truth?"

Her eyes slid to me, and in them… it was there. She thought the death of my soul was exactly why my cowrie faded, and there was nothing either of us could do about it.

"You won't only face the Empyrean Warriors you once commanded in this battle, Elira. You will face the goddess who made you."

The goddess who, more than anything else, wanted every part she'd created of me dead. Who, despite craving balance, had learned her lesson and would never elevate another. With no one to stand against her, she would fight Talay for dominion of both sky and sea. If she succeeded as she had with Tella and Talay perished, so would his people.

As unsettling as it was, I could see how much she and I were alike.

The clamoring for power. The desperation to conquer. The thirst for freedom. The fear bracing it all.

Standing in the dark, facing the storm, the scar she'd given me lit with Empyrea and writhed in time with the sky, as if Neera wanted me to know that the power in me was hers. As if the sky was her flesh and the lightning was the power trapped in her veins beneath its surface. As if the horizon was nothing but a mirror.

I walked in stride with The Salt until the top of Crest's tent could be seen over the dunes. Hovering by the trail leading to him, I fought with myself over whether to ask her what I should do regarding him.

"I would appreciate it if you didn't repeat what I shared with you tonight, to anyone," she said pointedly. The wind tugged our skirts toward The Shark. "If you tell him he will interfere, and interfering will get him hurt, if not killed, Elira."

A knot formed in my throat. "I know that. I don't want to tell him any of it. I just… don't want to hurt him worse than it will if…" I couldn't say it. Couldn't bear the weight of the words on my tongue.

Koa had *just* asked me not to hurt him, but he didn't need to. It was the last thing I wanted to do. I just had a feeling it was already too late for that. My chin began to quiver as I fought back tears.

She gave me a motherly smile and brushed a pale strand of hair from where it caught on my lashes. "Go to Crest while you can, but spare him the knowing."

The wind rattled every feather's barb, even the down. Sorrow wracked me to the core.

"Pushing him away didn't work, Elira. You are his lacuna. That means his heart has already chosen. Hearts don't easily un-choose."

A terrible flaw in their great design.

The Salt continued, "But the beautiful thing about hearts is that they don't often forget the things that matter most. I want you to know that I'll do anything in my power to prevent the vision I've had from coming to fruition, but if it does and the two of you are parted, perhaps the greatest thing you can do for Crest is to leave him with good memories."

The Salt was right. I knew I didn't have long to give him that.

It was just so difficult to accept what she'd so surely felt.

When the shells trembled, it wasn't because of Talay, but Tella. That was why her vision wasn't stirred. The god of the sea wasn't responsible for disturbing them.

Talay marked the last beats of my heart as though the goddess and I stood before one another and I swayed, wounded and dying before her.

"If I remember how to fight her and learn what my soul can do, is there hope?" I asked.

She nodded once. "While your heart beats and your soul clings to life, there's always hope."

"Thank you," I told her.

She inclined her head and opened her palm to reveal my faded cowrie. "I'm sorry you have to face this."

Alone.

She had assured me I wasn't alone because she was like me, even though I didn't remember my prior existences. But she couldn't face the goddess or Empyrean with me. The path before my feet was only wide enough for one. Even so, it was a comfort to know that someone waited and wished for me to somehow overcome my fate.

I couldn't fathom going back to Empyrean any more than I could imagine falling on my own sword to sever my life before Neera could unmake my very essence or harm my lacuna, like my father had done for me. Maybe I couldn't envision such desperation because I wasn't in a position that called for it. Maybe I could be as brave as The General I never realized loved me.

Love.

Koa implied that Crest loved me. Could I prove how much I cared for him? Merely thinking of parting with him caused a deep ache in my chest, but it also stirred something visceral and primal. Something that would rather destroy the sky and everything in it before it would see him harmed.

"Promise me something?" I asked her.

"Of course."

"When I leave, will you tell him that I loved him with every sharp shard of my soul? And that I know I never deserved him, but had to try anyway."

A tear slipped down her cheek, capturing a sliver of moonlight. "You are The Scourge of the Sky, my dear. And when you return to it, prove it to each and every one of them. Neera included."

She squeezed my arm and turned to walk the shore.

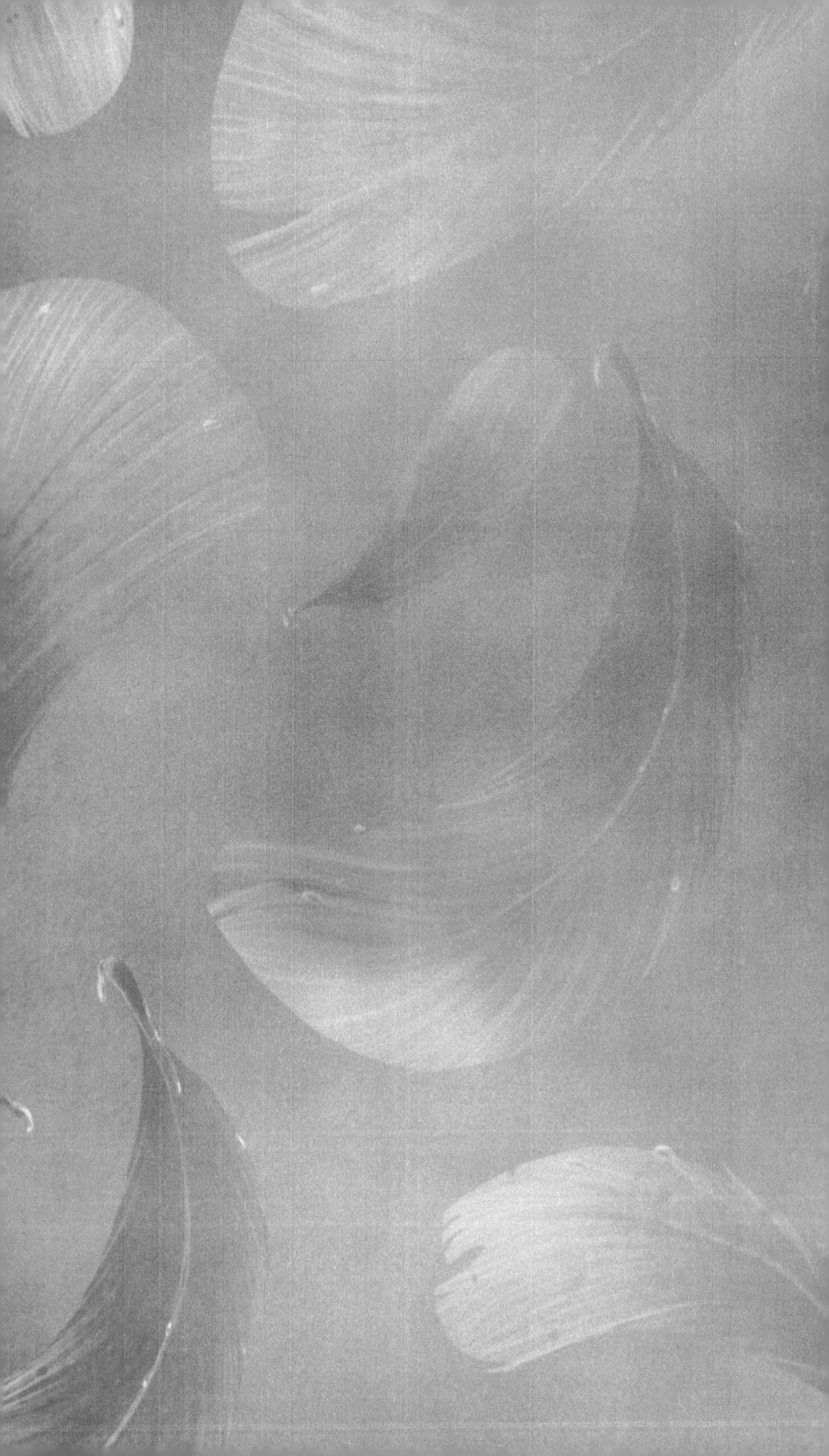

CHAPTER SEVENTEEN

I ducked into Crest's tent and padded across the floor, leaving a trail of sandy footprints on the planks that glistened in the dim firelight. My wings were restless on my back, the need to be near him almost too much to bear.

Crest slept in the hammock, his chest slowly, peacefully rising and falling. His brow was smooth and relaxed.

Another step closer.

The board beneath my foot creaked.

I went rigid, hoping I hadn't startled him, but he didn't even flinch.

Stretching the fabric of the hammock out wide, I climbed in beside him. The rocking and unfamiliar feel of me at his side woke him. He lifted his head and shifted to give me more room, even though I wanted none.

"Elira?"

"Shhh." I cuddled closer, relishing his warmth, the feel of his skin, his scent – like the shore on a sunny, beautiful day. I laid my ear on the mark Talay had given him, the mark he accepted – for me, and listened to his heart beating as we gently swayed back and forth.

"You couldn't sleep?" he asked, still bleary. He ran a hand over my head, smoothing my hair, brushing the feathers at the bend of my wing.

"I thought laying with you might help," I told him honestly, trying my damnedest not to cry on his chest, knowing my tears would rouse him to the point that he wouldn't be able to rest again. "It did last night."

The hand stroking my hair went still. "Did you have another upsetting dream?"

"No," I lied, lifting my head to see him. "I just… wanted to be here."

He smiled and his blue eyes studied mine. I wanted to know and see them in every light. To watch them sparkle and darken. I wanted to know everything that made his pupils flare. I knew a few things already.

"I'm glad you came," he said.

My toes curled, brushing against the soft fabric of the hammock. He shifted onto his side a little, his leg bending to fit between mine. His arm curled around my shoulders, careful of my wings. For a few moments, he dragged his fingers up and down my upper arm. Back and forth in a soothing rhythm I drank in greedily.

"It's hard to think of sleeping when you're here," he softly told me.

"But we need it," I reminded him. He needed rest as much as I needed him.

Another smile.

"I don't love you, Scourge," he quietly said. It had been a while since he called me that. But I felt the echo of The Salt's last bit of advice.

I repositioned my head on his chest so he couldn't see my face, using my hand to brush my tear away before it fell onto his skin and the dampness gave me away. "Good. I don't love you, either."

He hugged me closer and pressed a tender kiss on the top of my head.

Before long, his eyes drifted closed. His fingers stopped brushing up and down my arm, but his chest rose and fell calmly, his heart kept thrumming on, and then… only then, did I hug him tighter and angle my head so my tears slid into my hair instead of onto Crest.

There were no words strong enough to carry the worry and fear I felt for him. No words for how my heart ached knowing these stolen moments might be all we would have.

For the briefest moment, I'd thought I could escape the sky and fall completely into a life with him.

I hadn't realized my heart had already found what she wanted most, or that I'd irrevocably fallen for him. My lacuna. Until The Salt told me that such a future was one I would never have.

Who would've thought that The Scourge of the Sky would meet The Shark of the Sea and see the world the way it should be? That the two would set aside their pasts to build a future and world they could both exist in together. And then to be informed that the future they imagined was only a mirage. An oasis they would never find.

I pressed my eyes closed.

The Salt was right. If this was all we had, I wanted to make it the best moments of our lives so that if he survived me, he would have this piece of me to cling to and remember. These days would become a string that would lay on his chest, threaded with my cowrie and the memories we made when the sky met the sea and slowly fell in love.

So as golden light crept through the seam of his tent's door and he began to stir, I craned my neck to press my lips to his. And when he fastened his blue eyes on me, cupped my face and deepened the kiss, I didn't hold back. I raked my fingers into his hair and hooked an arm around his neck while he pulled my legs over his so that I was sitting sideways on his lap.

The motion was so natural. So smooth. Like a wave brushes the sand, the sand welcoming it again and again.

My sarong left my hip and leg bare for him.

"Is this okay?" he asked when I pulled away from his mouth. "Are you comfortable with this?"

I didn't answer with words. Instead, I put my hand on top of his and guided it from the back of my knee, upward. His callouses raked over my soft skin, creating a delicious friction. He paused on my hip and squeezed it as though anchoring it there as we continued learning one another with our mouths and tongues and teeth, but I shifted to encourage him. Inch by inch, his fingers crept lower until he fully cupped my backside and pressed my body against his.

"Lacuna," he breathed against my neck.

A quiet moan escaped my lips. He moved my hair over before kissing his way down its length, nipping the tender spot where it met my shoulder. I shifted to straddle his hips, the hammock swinging from the movement.

Crest stared at me as if he couldn't believe I was there. The knot in his throat rose and fell as his eyes dropped to comb over the rest of my body. He lifted a hand and with the back of a knuckle, delicately traced the strap of my gray knitted top where it tied at the nape of my neck. His knuckle followed the edge of the garment as it drifted down the swell of my breast and dipped into the valley between them before climbing the other side.

My breaths became ragged. My body tensed as he roamed. And when he paused as if to ask what I wanted next, what I needed, I captured his lips and freed the knot at my neck, then tugged at the one at my back.

The scrap of knitted fabric fell to the floor.

All I could think was that I wanted to know it all. The feel of my bare chest against his and his lips on every inch of me. And I wanted him to know it all, too. To have and keep it and me. The scars on my skin that my clothing always hid, the feel of my hair and mouth dragging over his flesh, and what my eyes looked like in every kind of light. I wanted him to know what would make my pupils flare just for him. When Crest closed his eyes, I wanted the light and form of my scar to glow behind his lids.

Heart pounding, I sat up, our lips peeling apart.

For a moment, he didn't move. Didn't breathe.

His eyes raked over me and I could swear I felt them as solidly as his hands on my skin. Crest's fingers sank deeper into my skin, holding me so tightly, I wondered if he thought I was in danger of drifting away.

Maybe I was.

Or maybe he anchored himself.

The flame in his eyes burned away the calm blue so all that was left was the deep sapphire shade that could only be described as desire.

The hair on my arms rose. Goosebumps flared.

I was acutely aware of every place our bodies touched, of the texture of his scales beneath me, of the restraint he grappled with.

Slowly, he sat up. The muscles of his stomach contracted as he closed the distance between us. He scooted backward so he was fully sitting upright, his long legs stretching to the wooden planks laid under us. He hooked his hands beneath my knees and dragged me onto him. My core settled over his and I could feel how much he wanted me.

It was a heady, powerful feeling to capture The Shark.

One of his hands slid to my lower back and his arm braced me there, holding me close and pressing my belly to his.

My nipples tightened.

Fingers threaded into my hair.

And when he kissed me, it wasn't just with his lips.

Our bodies melded; our scars raked as we moved, desperate to devour one another.

Our hearts were separated only by insignificant sheets of skin and bone. And I swore I felt his soul brush mine.

The ocean in my ears roared as he tugged on my hair so that my neck bent backward, my back bowing like I was the weapon in his hand, his arm the string. I was at his mercy once again, drowning with something far more crushing than the salted sea.

As he teased my breasts with his mouth, raking his teeth over a nipple and dragging it toward him, a pressure coiled in my belly, undoing me entirely. Until I couldn't help but writhe over him.

He slipped a hand beneath my sarong and reverently touched me where no one else had ever dared. Coaxing, until stars were all I could see despite the tent's ceiling; his strong hands were the only thing keeping me from taking flight.

His grip on my hair relaxed and he waited for my breathing to calm. Watched to see what I would do next.

My eyes sharpened and cut straight to his in reply.

I would own him.

I was his lacuna, and he was mine. And nothing could take that away.

I raised up to move the fabric separating us to the side and seated myself on him fully. A gasp tore from my chest as I claimed him. As I became his sheath.

We languished in the feel of each other as minutes unfolded into hours. I could have spent days if only I had the time. Until we came together panting, sweat slickening our skin as I collapsed forward, laying on top of him for a long moment.

His breathing still wild, it disturbed wisps of my hair when he whispered, "Scourge, how am I going to go about my duties when I'll be thinking of nothing but this for the rest of the day?"

"Your pining is pathetic," I teased playfully, raking my nails down his abdomen. My wings tingled upon my back. "I expected more of the mighty Shark."

His eyes already writhed with desire. With passion. With fury.

Mine rose to match it.

"I'm *already* disgusted with you," I told him, a grin tugging at my lips. "And I certainly don't love you."

Koa thought The Shark might love me, though… I wondered if my lie was transparent.

"Is that so?" He flipped the hammock and a startled cry spilled from my lips. Crest had somehow managed to cradle my back before it hit the floor. My wings splayed and he took them in.

"Yes, it's so. Are you repulsed yet?" I teased.

Grinning, he kissed me. "Not even a little."

With his, he nudged my knees apart, settled between them, and showed me just how little The Scourge of the Sky sickened him. With every kiss, every touch, and every scrape of my back on the floor, I felt myself falling.

CHAPTER EIGHTEEN

Walking beside Frey, Koa glared at me. I narrowed my eyes at him. He purposefully darted his eyes toward Crest and back. So, I purposefully ignored him. The four of us had walked into the Green Mountains to see what Wade had devised and to offer our help in case it was needed.

Throughout the forest, Guardians had removed limbs here and there to make hidden perches where they could hide. Wade constructed a crude map to the trees he'd indicated would best cover their archers. Thus far, the work had already been done, the divots made and waiting for archers to fill them.

My rough soles no longer bled on this soil or the flora it bore. My body no longer ached with every step. Such a drastic improvement from the last time I'd trudged to this point. Flat rock stretched out over a cliff's steep drop off. In the darkness of night, I'd walked out onto it and collapsed to rest, unaware of the danger of falling or dying from its ledge. My wings were broken, and Wade was right when he said they wouldn't save me from such a fate before ushering me down the mountain again.

It was hot. The sun beat down upon our backs. Sweat beaded on their brows and dripped from mine. I desperately needed water. When we came to the stream, the three of them laughed while I all but submerged myself in its cold, clean water.

Frey sat beside me on the rocky bank, watching with interest as Koa rekindled his animated inferences – darting glances between me and Crest. She turned and raised a brow as if to ask what Koa meant by all of it.

I ignored her too, of course. Just as I'd turned my chin from Koa.

Crest was determined to commit every Guardian position to memory. Between focusing on that task and me, he thankfully hadn't noticed Koa.

Frey's attention caught on something behind The Shark. She grabbed her trident and rose to her feet, crouching low and deftly maneuvering past him. Crest and Koa, with formidable bodies and deadly tridents flanked her in an instant. My arrow drawn, I covered the three of them from behind, watching overhead.

Voices came from the side of the mountain down a path that, thanks to the Guardians working to fulfill Wade's plan, had recently been trampled down again. "Guardians?" I whispered to Crest.

"I don't think so," he answered. Until we were certain, we would not lower our guards or weapons.

The voices came closer and I recognized one, then the other. "Jorun?" I called out.

"Elira?" he answered, pushing through plants taller than him.

Frey waved me forward and I walked ahead to meet him.

The sling Magma had insisted he wear was gone and his arm was tucked awkwardly, perhaps painfully, over the back of one of the hatchlings, who was bound to his chest with a long stretch of pale gray fabric.

With his small head laying on Jorun, the babe gnawed on his tiny fist as if it was a piece of freshly plucked fruit. Behind him, Aderyn appeared, the second hatchling affixed to and sleeping on her chest.

She placed a protective hand on the babe's back as if I might hurt him. I wondered if the act was purposeful or instinctual and realized it didn't matter. Both bothered me.

"What are the four of *you* doing up here?" Jorun asked, looking us over.

"Taking a little hike," Frey chirped.

He gave her an irritated look. "Well, word to the wise. Don't go down *that* path," he warned, pointing behind them. "To say it's overgrown is a kind understatement."

Frey jutted her chin toward the tangled hills from which they'd freed themselves. "We call those hills 'The Vines'. They'll swallow you whole if you aren't careful."

"I believe it," he muttered.

"Where are you two going?" I asked.

"We need a tent," Aderyn answered sharply.

"You just left one."

"Communal living with two hatchlings has proven… difficult," Jorun replied smoothly. "Their nursemaid was killed by the falling rock. They're hungry. When they aren't sleeping, they cry incessantly. We need to find someone else who can nurse them."

"When can they eat as we do?" I asked.

"They've started to, but fruit isn't enough. They need milk," Aderyn answered.

"I know of a woman who might be willing to help," Frey offered, glancing at Crest. He gave her a nod. "I can take you to her."

Jorun thanked Crest and Frey, but not Aderyn. No, she wiped her brow with the back of her hand and fanned her face. "Why is it so *hot* here?"

She, Jorun, and I were obviously more affected by the heat, but the others weren't immune this close to the sun. The humidity that nourished the peaks and shores stifled those who weren't used to it. Unlike the soles of my feet, just when I thought I'd acclimated to the immense heat, the sun and air efficiently proved how very wrong I was.

"You can take my tent," I told Jorun.

Aderyn's lips parted as if she couldn't believe I'd offer it to them.

"It would be an imposition for us to stay with you," Jorun argued.

But Aderyn didn't care. Her eyes sharpened. She was willing to take the tent, along with anything else that would help her.

I shook my head. "I won't be staying there. Better for you to occupy it than for it to lay empty, especially when the hatchlings need cover from the blistering sun." I scowled at the offending fiery orb, then glanced at my lacuna. He knew where I would be found when it sank into the depths and left nothing but pieces of her to sparkle over the sky.

Crest smirked proudly, but behind the bemused grin was a promise of more. He wanted to toss a log on the smoldering coals of the fire we'd kindled and built and never let it burn out. And I wanted him to.

Koa cleared his throat. "You... uh.... You just got your tent, Elira. You *sure* you want to give up your space?"

I speared him with a gaze that – if it had been a trident – would have pierced his gut and left him wriggling on its tips.

"Guess you're sure, then," he muttered, scratching at the knot of dark hair coiled on the crown of his head.

I stared at my sister as she patted our infant brother's back to soothe him when he began to wake and wail. I knew the sound of hunger and it hurt me to know he was in pain. "There's a large bed and a table, although I only have one chair. There's only one plate, but there's plenty of wood for a fire stacked just outside, and a rock firepit in front of it."

Aderyn nodded once. "We need shelter, so we'll borrow it until we can make or earn our own. We won't disturb your things."

"My *things* are on my back, Aderyn. As always."

She looked me over. Bow. A quiver full of arrows. That was it. "What of your leathers?"

"Gone."

Magma treated me after I fell. Either they were ruined, or she'd discarded them.

Crest scrubbed a hand over his mouth as if he knew where they were and didn't want to tell me.

Interesting. Perhaps Magma kept them. Perhaps she kept Jorun's, too.

Over Aderyn's shoulder a small, cinched bag hung.

"Did you keep yours?" I asked her.

She shook her head.

"That's too bad. You'll wish you had them when the sky falls," I told her.

She looked skyward. When she saw the blue was empty of any threat, her eyes found the cuts in the trees surrounding us. "Jorun told me everything."

I didn't respond, because I would've said it was a shame. She didn't deserve his loyalty or his trust.

"Well," Frey said, pointing the tips of her trident in the direction we'd just come, "I suppose we should get moving."

Aderyn didn't complain or groan again. She placed one foot in front of the last as she trailed Jorun and the burgundy-haired Guardian, keeping a few steps back to avoid stepping on Jorun's long wings. They dragged the ground on the way back down the mountainside.

An ornery grin spread across Koa's lips an instant before something on the ground a few feet away caught his eye. He walked over and snapped a woody stem and brought it back, holding it in front of me. "Hungry? Miss the teal stain in your mouth?"

Between his thumb and forefinger, Koa pinched a piece of the sky fire plant.

"Koa!" I smacked his arm as I'd seen Frey do a thousand times.

"Ow, what was *that* for?" he complained, rubbing the reddening spot on his skin.

"You're brilliant and you don't even know it!" I crowed.

"I am?" he asked, puffing his chest a little and looking to Crest for an explanation.

The Shark already knew what I was thinking. "It's deadly to Empyreans," he told Koa in a dark tone I barely recognized.

Koa choked out a laugh. "Why didn't I think of this sooner? We could poison them with the same plant Elira tried to kill you with, Crest."

I winced. He was right, but it stung hearing it now that things were different.

Koa was proud that he'd reminded us, but his ploy to drive a wedge between us didn't work. To his chagrin, Crest just beamed proudly at me.

I was busy thinking of how many arrows the Kehlanians had, how many more they were fashioning, and how much of the plant they might need. Magma would know. "We need your grandmother's help," I told Crest. "And wax as well. I assume you know where the bees are."

Both men answered, "The Grove."

Koa's golden scales reflected the sun the entire way down the last hill that led to the coast. The trees on it had been cleared, and while it was green like the mountains that towered over it, there was no shade or cover to be found.

"You need to wear longer sarongs," I growled at him.

Koa stopped and flashed me a grin brighter than the white light his scales kept flitting into my eyes. "Why would I cover this…?" His brows lifted as he gestured to his legs.

"Because if it's a sunny day when Empyrean brings the war, they'll see and target you first," I told him sweetly, patting him on the back as I passed him to join Crest.

The Shark laughed at his friend. "She has a point."

Koa looked down at his legs and cursed.

Just then, a shrill call came from the beach. It didn't sound urgent, but I stopped to see how Crest reacted. He and Koa both answered the call. If a tone could hold delight, it would sound like the one they used.

The Shark turned to me with an excited smile on his face. It was so bright, I wondered if it, too, might make Koa's scales glint. "Do you want to see something you might never see again?"

Koa's head ticked back. "He's not that close. Do you want her to risk flying?"

Crest raked his teeth over his bottom lip and I saw the dare squint his eyes. "Too afraid to draw him in?"

Koa's mouth gaped, brows popped. "Are you serious?"

Crest shrugged a broad shoulder. "I can do it alone."

"You remember what happened last time we got too close," Koa reminded him.

"Too close to what? Or whom?" I asked.

"Colossus," both answered in tandem.

"The kraken that nearly killed you?" I hissed. "Are you insane?"

Crest's eyes locked onto the ocean, glimmering beyond the sandy shore. "We won't get *that* close again. Will we, Koa? We'll just rile him up a bit and see if he takes the bait."

"The bait being *you*!" I sputtered. "This isn't the wisest of ideas."

"We aren't known for being sensible *all* the time," Koa said, his words seeming to solidify with his resolve. He turned to Crest, rolling his shoulders. "I'm not one to back down from a challenge or let you take all the glory." He cracked his knuckles, stretched his arms behind his back and waved them in great circles, and bent his neck this way and that as if getting ready for a fight.

"I don't need to see him," I told Crest.

"You do," he argued.

I shook my head. "I saw his tentacle once. That was enough."

"They say it can stick to the clouds, or split them in two," Koa noted, looking to me to confirm whether the rumor was truth or lie.

"I wasn't *that* close, but I can tell you it was terrifying, even from afar seeing something that large and powerful in the sea."

Koa laughed. "Did you used to say the same thing of Crest before you fell?"

I looked at my lacuna when he waved off Koa's question. "I did, actually. Everyone marveled at your speed and feared you. I've seen you pull many a Gatherer into the sea. And you did it so fast, I could never train my arrow on you."

"You tried, though. I remembered you hovering over me..."

The insinuation took me back to last night, *and* this morning, quickening my pulse and making me think of what it might mean when we were finally alone again.

Crest said he'd be distracted all day, and now I knew I was just as affected because one little sentence had me wanting to refuse his offer of drawing in Colossus in favor of *hovering over* my lacuna again.

Koa nudged Crest's arm, breaking the tension mounting between us. "Well, let's go and tempt the monster before he moves too far away."

Crest smiled at Koa, and I realized I'd seen him smile more randomly today than I ever had. He seemed happy.

I followed the friends to the shore. Before entering the water, Crest and Koa glanced back over their shoulders with their tridents in hand. Koa shot me a look of warning and maybe something that said *look what you've gotten me into*. I wiggled my fingers at them. Crest smiled – again – then rushed back to claim a quick, passion-filled kiss. Then he winked and told me he'd be right back.

Koa was *not* happy about that display of affection. Not at all. If his lips pressed any tighter together, they might fuse in this heat.

They were gone a long time. Too long. So long that I began to worry, the worry transferring to my feet. I paced the shore, wearing a deep track in it. If they weren't back soon, I would fly and find them. I would help them if I could.

I worried I couldn't.

Then a shrill call came from the waves beyond the breakers and an ensuing commotion rose as people poured onto the shore. Magma rushed to stand with me as everyone gathered. She carried no mending supplies, which calmed my heart. When I looked her over, she wore an eager expression.

"Colossus is near!" she told me, pointing to the shore. "Watch."

Crest and Koa's arms appeared, cutting through the swelling waves. "Where are their tridents?" I asked worriedly.

"Sometimes, when speed and not force is what will save them, they leave their tridents and go back for them later." Her silver hair whipped against her shoulders as she cast an appraising eye over my body. "You need to stop by. Your skin is burnt."

"It doesn't hurt."

"It will," she told me. "Once the sun sinks, the sting sets in to remind you of the one who marked you. Kind of like the bite on your neck." She smiled, pointing to her own where it met her shoulder.

My ribs shrank in embarrassment. *Crest marked my skin?* With his teeth, no doubt. The Shark did enjoy biting.

No wonder Koa was riled this morning.

"You blush even when you're sunburnt," she teased.

Koa and Crest's feet hit the sand and they trudged from the water just as Colossus appeared. Talay's people gasped, but behind their fear was a current of wonder. I floated on it with them as if it was a stream of air.

The beast never reared its head, but several of its suckered tentacles flailed dangerously close. One landed on the surface with a deafening slap. Bubbles and foam erupted all around the creature every time it lashed out, having no idea that The Shark and Koa watched, laughing from the shore.

Magma turned to speak to the person beside her and I glanced over to lock eyes with The Salt. "It's a good omen," the Seer told the Mender.

Magma didn't notice that The Salt's smile didn't reach her eyes. "A *very* good omen," Magma agreed. Her next words faded as she watched the gigantic beast. "It's about time we had a turn of luck."

I never trusted or put faith in luck. As a Warrior fighting uphill toward the top rank, you could only rely on what you could control. Luck was not one of those things.

Colossus slapped the water closer to shore, startling me. Its appendages were enormous. And if the Great Wind shepherded clouds low enough, the beast truly *might* be able to reach them.

Magma turned to me. "Frey said that Aderyn reached an agreement with a Kehlani woman for the hatchlings to be fed."

That made sense. People like Magma, who gave instead of demanding something in return, were rare. She healed because her heart said she must. Most people's hearts were not so pure. "What sort of arrangement did they make with her?"

Crest's grandmother forgot my question when my lacuna jogged over to us, wrapping her in a hug even as she swatted his back for drenching her.

"If I wanted to swim, I would've dived in and chased that beast with you!" Her fussing and his refusal to release her made everyone laugh – even Magma.

A moment later, Koa called for The Shark and Crest reluctantly jogged back to his friend. I didn't miss the triumphant and very satisfied look Koa aimed at me. I knew he'd be doing everything in his power to stop what he knew was happening, even though he was powerless to stop what we'd begun.

The gathered crowd began to disperse, revealing Breaker standing with Katalini, whose pallor was a sickly shade of green.

I leaned close to Magma. "She looks like she could use some tea…" I hinted.

"Yes, she does," she agreed. Absently, she reminded me to stop by her workshop before walking over to see about Breaker's lacuna.

The Salt moved closer. "Frey has enlisted a small army to alter the bows of our archers. They're making quick work of it and are already firing farther – and higher – than ever before. She and some of the more skilled Guardians are teaching the young to shoot. I wonder, though, what will happen if the arrows aren't enough? What happens if Empyrean's Warriors reach the sand?"

I didn't tell her about the plan to use sky fire toxin against them. The sky fire wouldn't make a difference if the archer couldn't bury the arrow's head in their enemy.

"If the Empyreans reach the shore, the Guardians will have to fight them hand-to-hand," I answered. There would be no other choice. Then I realized why she was leading me to that conclusion. "Did you have a vision?"

A nod. "Our people are used to fighting within the sea. The war has never been brought to our shores."

I hadn't thought their defenses completely through. Too much was happening too fast. But the Kehlani Guardians could fight. I'd seen Crest and Koa come to blows…

The Salt looked thoughtful. "The deal your sister made – I wonder if you would extend it to *all* who would take advantage of it."

"Wait… *Me?* What exactly did she bargain?" I asked, wary but curious.

"The woman who will nurse the hatchlings agreed to do so, *if* Aderyn teaches her daughters to fight the way Empyrean women fight. Aderyn agreed, and she volunteered you to assist her in keeping her word. The two of you will fight tomorrow at sunrise, on the shore just beyond my home."

Aderyn wanted to spar? I'd love nothing more. My lip twitched angrily. "I look forward to it."

Who better to teach them than Empyrean's two top-ranked Warriors?

Talon might now command the entire army of the sky, but if he faced me in battle, he would lose. I would end him. I would plunge a sword through his dark heart and then chop him into so many pieces, the younglings of Empyrean could feast on him for weeks.

And I would gladly use this opportunity to encourage Aderyn to never speak on my behalf, or even breathe my name again.

"Be careful of your anger, Elira," The Salt noted. "Anger tunnels the vision, and I've heard tell that it's wiser to aim using both eyes."

I turned to her. "Would you go to Talay on my behalf?"

She nodded slowly.

"Can you please ask him if there's anything I can do to help myself remember my former lives?"

She shifted uncomfortably. "I will ask him, but you should know that once memories surface, there is no unknowing them. You will be changed from the wisdom you gain, for better or worse."

Her fingers absently combed the cowries on her neck. I wondered if each shell held in its small curves the memories of each of her lifetimes. I wondered how much she had witnessed that she now wished to unknow.

"If what we spoke of last night occurs, I want *him* to have my cowrie," I told the Seer. "I know your custom, but I want an exception to be made."

She looked to where The Shark stood, still laughing with Koa and some of his other Guardian friends. "I'll see that it's done."

Down the shore, Nori lingered with her vile brother, North. His beady stare was fixed on me with undisguised malice.

"Be careful of him, Elira," The Salt warned. He shrank under her knowing glare and turned away.

"Why? Do you think he might kill me before my goddess gets the chance?" I tried to tease.

"When Talay speaks of him lately, all I see is rot. The smallest bad spot on the skin of an apple softens the entire supple fruit before eating to its core."

"Does he hate me because of Nori?" I asked.

"No," she said, plucking at one of her braids. "Two years ago, you killed his cousin. They were inseparable until then."

Until my arrow severed them.

I thought back to the ceremony I'd witnessed. Before Talay's temple, North had stabbed an arrow fletched with blue feathers into the sand to honor his cousin. He'd spoken his loved one's name and cursed mine. Now the bitter taste of vengeance lingered in his mouth like the teal of the sky fire plant, just as toxic to him as it was to his target – *me*.

"But North, too, should be cautious of how he proceeds against any whom Talay champions..." the Seer warned.

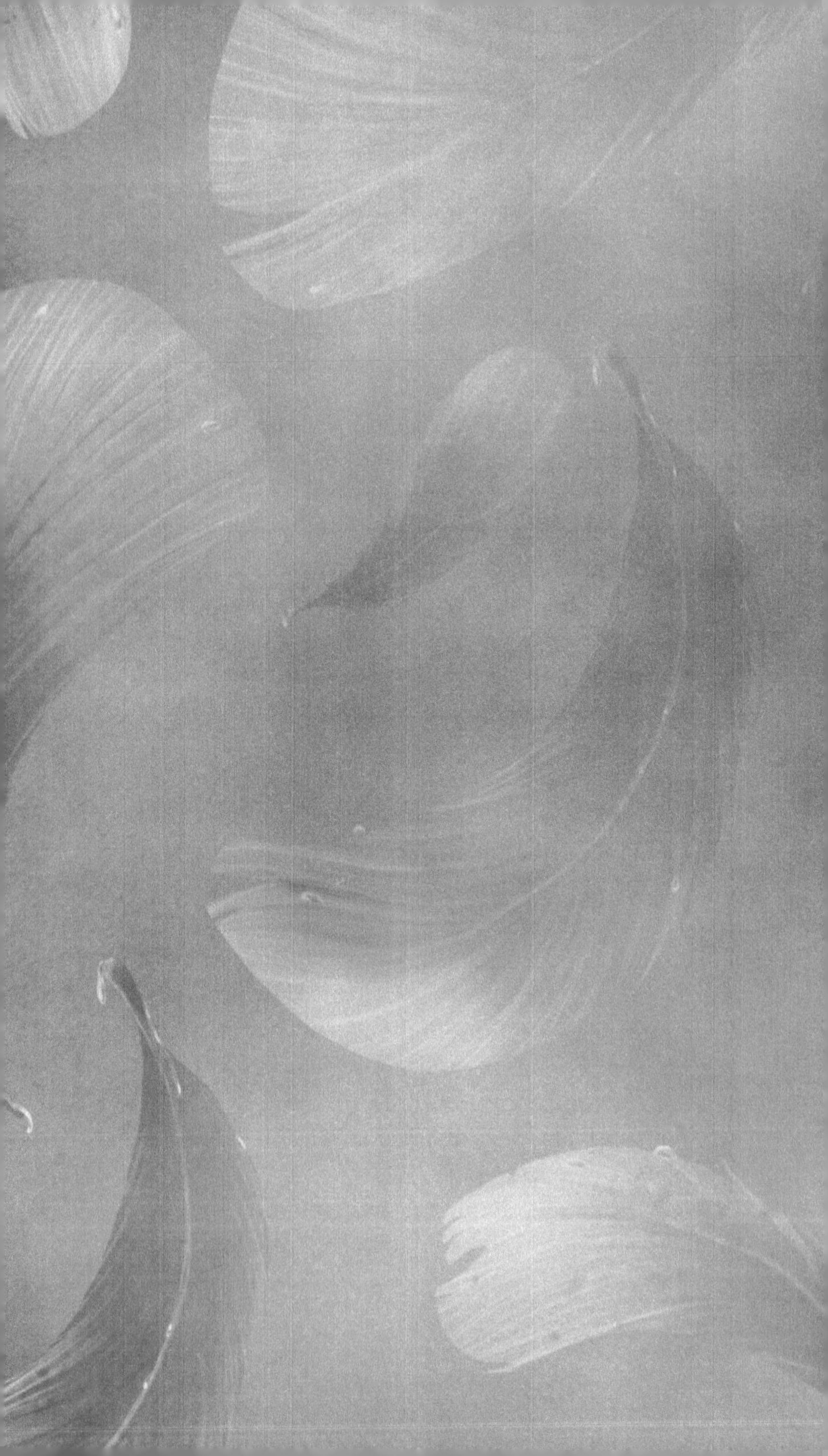

CHAPTER NINETEEN

The Salt seized the opportunity to tell those who had gathered to see Colossus that Aderyn and I would fight at dawn. She invited them to the shore just beyond her home and urged them to watch and learn. To use it as a teachable moment and see what to expect if the feet of the people of the sky hit the ground and they dropped their bows, raising their swords instead.

I watched for a moment as many sets of eyes flitted from the Seer to me, becoming more unsettled by the moment. By the time she reached Crest and Koa, I was gone.

On the sandy path, I caught up and fell into step beside Magma halfway to her workshop. Her skirt was the color of my mouth after the sky fire toxin had spread through my body, which was ironic, really, considering what I intended to ask her.

She twisted to see who was beside her. "Come and get some aloe to coat your sunburn before you scurry home."

"Did you get the measurements I asked for?"

Magma narrowed her eyes. "Is there a rush?"

"Yes."

Her silver brows peaked. "What's so urgent?"

"I want him to walk." *As soon as possible, in case my time here is shorter than I think,* I didn't add.

Wade was a Guardian, an asset and a Warrior in his own right. He could take down as many Empyreans now as he could before the shark incident. The beast may have altered his body, but it would not take Wade's worth. I also needed time to make adjustments if I didn't get things right the first time.

Magma pursed her lips the moment I answered. She didn't believe he would stroll the sand again, but I would enjoy proving her wrong. "You're almost finished with it already?"

"I can whittle no further without those measurements, Magma. But I will work diligently to complete it quickly when I get them. Wade is a Guardian. If no longer of the sea, then of the Isle. He shouldn't be bound to tent and cot."

He was also a young man whom I was certain had no intention of forever living with Magma, and who would appreciate his privacy again. The more freedom Wade reclaimed the more he would crave, and the more he would stop ruminating about what he'd lost and focus on what he still had.

"He's not bound. I'm just helping him adjust," Magma refuted. "He's already taken on more chores and responsibilities than I ever expected him to."

Which further proved my point. Wade was ready for more. He hadn't given up or given in to the despair that normally accompanied such loss. He was finding his way back. Persevering.

Wade would master his situation, not just adjust to it.

One day, he would make his way back into the water. I could almost see him on the shore, staring out at the sea. I bet being so close he could hear it was both a comfort and a certain kind of torture. The ocean probably felt as unreachable for him as the clouds right now, but it wouldn't for long. He would walk. Beyond that, he would fight for his isle and god. And he would swim again one day when his fear was snuffed out by the need to return to the sea.

After the bolt of lightning struck my chest, I was terrified to re-enter the sky again. Storms could be unpredictable, but lightning… Lightning came from Neera and could fork unpredictably. In good weather and bad. In gray skies and blue. But what scared me worse than the bolt was the thought of never flying again. Never feeling the wind in my feathers. My greatest fear was of being caged, and I refused to build my own prison, crafted of fear and worry. So, the same evening I was struck, I took back to the sky in the middle of a thunderstorm.

It was why I believed Aderyn when she wrote that she needed to get close to the sea again after being rolled by the wave. She was with me when I was hit and with me when I coasted back into and through the storm that night. She knew that fear's gentle lies could restrain a person as easily as a soldered bronze skeleton.

When he regained the ability to walk, Wade would see that other things were possible. Like swimming. He needed to realize that he hadn't died in the shark's mouth. When it dawned on him, Wade would hum again and his life would resume. The teeth of a monster had only interrupted it for a time.

"Breaker is coming to get some tea for Katalini." She grinned contently. "I thought you were him, at first."

"Sorry to disappoint."

She gave me a wry look.

Best to get this over with while she was in a relatively decent mood.

"Magma, Koa is going to instruct the Guardians working in the Green Mountains to collect sky fire tomorrow."

She stopped and turned to face me, so I followed suit. "What for?"

"To taint the Kehlanian arrows."

Her face hardened, the fierce urge to help and not harm conflicting her. "How exactly does one encourage the poison to hold on rock or copper and not be washed or wear away?"

"One dips the arrowhead into poison, and once it's dry, into wax to seal it."

Her lip curled. "Devious." She had so many descriptors of me, none of them good in her eyes. "You're asking me to do something completely against my nature. My instinct is to help. To… to heal," she stammered angrily, gesturing toward her tent, now in sight. "Not kill, Elira. Never to kill."

"Magma," I offered sternly, "the Warriors from Empyrean are coming. If you don't *help* stop them, there won't be anyone on the Isle left for you to *heal*." I waited for my words to strike her, as sure as my hand would have on her cheek. They flushed with anger, nearly as brightly. "I wouldn't ask you or burden you with this if there was anyone else I trusted to do it."

"But they're *your* people! How could you do this to them?" she lamented.

I knew what she must think of me. Far worse than naming me terrifying or devious, sly or impulsive…all things she'd called me before. But I would see them poisoned to save hers.

Magma didn't know that Empyrean was now ruled by people who wanted to annihilate them entirely. But Talon and the Elders didn't yet know that they'd severely underestimated both Talay's people and me. It would be their undoing.

The Salt and her shells told the story of my impending death, but my heart had not stopped beating yet. I refused to surrender, and I refused to lose.

The Mender's chest heaved. She didn't like it, but she knew I was right. Her grandsons. Her great-grandchild still in Katalini's womb. Friends and neighbors. The Salt. Wade…

"I'll do it," she angrily agreed. "But I'll need a lot of the leaves. Tell them to leave the root so the plant will live. Then I need your word that *you* will stay away from the plant entirely. You won't come anywhere near me as I work. Won't touch – no, you won't even *look* at anything I take from that plant to give our people a chance. Do you understand?" Her brows arched as she waited for an answer.

Empyreans weren't affected by the plant's outer skin – smooth and thick, not unlike the aloe plant, actually. But if I wanted her help, I had to concede this much. She was only doing it to keep me safe, from a place of love, even though I knew she hated me in this moment.

"I agree to your terms."

She shook a finger at me and pointed to the sky. "Now, you sound like *her*. Always making bargains to benefit herself, never considering how her punishments slowly eat away at those she made, those she should love. Neera is rot," Magma hissed.

Rot… The same word The Salt had used earlier when she spoke of North. An image of a bruised apple flitted through my mind.

I glanced at the outer walls of her tent… noting that still, no humming came from the one seated within it.

She pushed inside her workshop. From outside, I heard Wade ask her what was wrong. She hadn't spoken a word and he already knew her mood.

"Get in here, Elira!" she barked.

I took a cleansing breath before entering her space. Wade pushed up to stand on his leg, holding a cane fashioned from copper streaked with green patina. "Hey, Elira," he greeted.

"You look well," I told him encouragingly.

"Thank you. I'm almost ready to go home."

Magma made a dismissive grunt and muttered something under her breath.

"She's angry with *me*, not you," I whispered rather loudly. That made her turn from her aloe plant to face me. She crossed the small space and reluctantly held out her offering. "Thank you, Magma." Into those three words, I infused my heartfelt gratitude for all she'd done for me and all she'd agreed to do for her people. Even though both pained her, she held true to who she was. A Mender.

A Mender who would never forgive me for making her into a killer, even though she had never and would never draw a bow.

Magma scowled at me and refused to reply. Propriety be damned.

"You did well with the trees," I told Wade, turning to focus on him.

He scratched the back of his shorn head. His icy eyes assessed my shoulders. "Bad burn."

"I'll be fine."

He laughed. "I have no doubt."

"I need to measure your leg," Magma interrupted, pushing between us with a handful of various colored threads.

Wade's mouth gaped, but he let her do what she wanted. With every thread she stretched, then angrily clipped, she called out what part of him it correlated to. I quickly committed each color and position to memory.

"Foot width. Length. Shin just below the knee to ankle, ankle circumference, over the kneecap, just above the knee, knee to hip, waist to ground...."

When I had a handful of colorful string in lengths that ranged from short to long and everything in between, Magma paused and asked if there were any other measurements I needed.

I tapped my left leg in the area of what was left of Wade's limb. I had to fit the wood to it. I needed to know its length and circumference, too. She quickly measured it while Wade, mouth aghast, stood and let her.

"What's this all about?" he finally asked.

"Nothing!" Magma snapped, standing upright and stunning him back into silence. She turned to me. "Don't you have somewhere to be?"

Wade's brows rose. His ice chip eyes widened as if to ask, *What did you do?*

"Wade, I'm sparring tomorrow morning if you'd like to come and watch."

He perked at that. "Sparring? Like… fighting?"

I gave a nod.

"Why are you fighting? Better yet, *who* are you fighting?" he eagerly asked.

"I'm fighting Aderyn, my second, because she invited the beating upon herself. We meet at dawn on the sand just beyond The Salt's tent."

"Are you angry with her?" he surmised.

I nodded.

He smiled. "I wouldn't miss it."

"Good."

Magma grumbled about pointless violence and something about how the other girl wouldn't stand a chance if she was anything like Nori. "She's not," I told her. "She's like me."

Magma went still. I could tell she was curious. That she might want to see us battle one another. She called *me* terrifying, but seeing two Empyrean Warriors fight was something no one in Kehlani had witnessed and likely never would again.

"You should come, Magma."

Her eyes narrowed in reply.

I bid them farewell, smiling to myself as I left her workshop. Magma would come to the shore in the morning.

In her arms, Aderyn had collected wood from the pile the boy's father made for me, placing an armful in the small pit in front of my tent. She already had a small pile of dried grasses and leaves bundled and ready beside the ring of rocks. She heard me approaching and quickly assessed my mood. "You heard, then?"

"Yep."

I moved around her to collect the limb that would be Wade's new leg and my carving knife, then walked past her toward Crest's tent. I was glad I'd come home before she burned away all I'd worked to whittle for him.

"We fight at dawn!" she shouted after me.

My steps slowed.

Stopped.

My shoulders tensed at the challenge in her tone. Did the second finally wish to conquer her first? In her eyes glinted challenge, yes, but also prudence. She knew I would not be so easily unseated.

I glanced back at her and let the corners of my mouth raise with delight. "I know. I can't wait."

I was reminded of how close Crest's tent was to mine when I considered going outside to carve now that I had Wade's colorful measurements in hand. I didn't want to look at Aderyn until morning when the promise of violence would finally bring us together face-to-face for a long overdue conversation. Crest arrived just before sunset to find me in his home sitting amid a pile of wood shavings on his floor. He paused at the door, taking in the sight and smiling at the mess I'd created.

"I'll clean it up," I told him, refusing to stop whittling now that I had the foot and ankle finished. Now for the shin and calf…

He tied the flaps back to let in the last light of day. Golden and warm, it slid across my heated skin and the wood beneath my fingers.

I looked up to catch his ocean-blue stare and noted the way the sun caught on each of his scales as if she didn't want to be dragged away from them. I watched every slow, determined footstep. Every wet print he left behind for the sun to hurry and erase.

My breath caught in my chest. I pushed it out by force.

He slowly crouched down before me, propping his forearms on his sculpted thighs. I tried not to look at the way the fabric tied at his hip moved to accommodate his position. How the sunlight didn't just catch on his scales, but caressed every dip and valley of the muscles hidden just beneath his skin. I remembered how powerful they felt when we came together…

It wasn't mating, what we'd done. It was something far, far more powerful. Something for which I had no words sufficient to describe.

He wet his lips. "I don't care about the mess, Elira. We can throw it in the fire." He tilted his head. "Are you hungry?"

Thirsty better described the way I felt. Thirsty and more than ready to drink him in. The time we were stealing was bleeding away so quickly, not even my Empyrea could stanch it or cauterize the wound the goddess had already begun to tear through us.

"I brought fish," he said.

"Thank you." I cleared my parched throat and looked back at my handiwork. I needed to finish this, but he made it difficult to concentrate on anything.

"I brought enough for Jorun and Aderyn as well."

I lifted my eyes, wondering why he'd caught and brought any for them. The sunset glow crashed over his back and spilled over his shoulders, highlighting every errant strand of his dark hair. It laid a golden carpet at his feet as if he were a king and not a shark at all.

"It *is* your tradition to feast before a great battle, is it not?" he asked. "I have no doubt that's what I'll witness when the sun rises again."

Being reminded of what the dawn would bring, I went back to taking my frustration out on the wood. I wasn't afraid of Aderyn or worried I would lose. She and I had always been ferocious, yet fairly evenly matched.

It was just that every time I saw her now, it tied my stomach in knots. She wasn't who I thought she was. She was a liar. If I'd been the one living in that hollow, she wouldn't have come to see if I'd been crushed. She might have hoped I was.

"Elira…"

I didn't wish she was dead, necessarily, but I now wished my father had never revealed she was alive, and that Breaker and Crest had honored her request to keep her new existence secret.

"Do you not want me to feed her?" he asked carefully. "I just thought that they're caring for the hatchlings and might need help."

I knew if I told him I didn't, he wouldn't even leave the small bones outside for them to pick over. But I wanted a fair fight. If Aderyn wanted to use me to her advantage, I wanted to crush her into the soil while doing it. Maybe the mountains and cowries would rattle again. Not because Tella was upset, but because I was furious. And maybe fighting her would jar loose the pent-up memories and the shells would cease their beating.

"Feed them," I rasped.

He didn't respond. Didn't agree. Just waited. Until inevitably, my eyes trailed to him. The sun beneath him slipped away, abruptly deferring to shadow. Somehow it, too, looked like it was made for him. And when I saw him cast in the low light, I remembered what he looked like rising from the depths the night he pulled me from the water, and how he looked last night in contrast.

His fingers brushed over my carving, emotions warring over his face. "This looks amazing, Elira. I can't tell you how much I appreciate it. I know Wade will."

"I can't figure out how to make the knee joint work naturally," I admitted, finally dropping my knife to wipe the sweat from beneath my eyes. "It'll have to be stiff until someone can come up with something better."

"How did you know how to proportion it?" he asked, curious.

"Your grandmother helped me today." I gestured to the colorful piles of string on either side of me. On the right, the few measurements I'd finished carving. On the left, the work I had left to do.

That was the problem, wasn't it?

I wasn't finished.

Not with this leg. Not with this life.

"I'll be right back," he promised. He slowly rose and left me to carry meat to Aderyn and Jorun.

I listened as Jorun thanked him and noted when Aderyn, again, didn't. Overheard Crest inquire about our siblings…learning they were with the nursemaid for the night. She wanted to keep them close because they would get hungry. The woman said they were malnourished. The Empyrean woman who'd been trying to feed them had great difficulty doing so for two, when she would have struggled with one. Her breasts had started to dry of milk far before the younglings arrived and she never managed to increase the amount she produced, despite trying various methods.

Aderyn did speak then, but only to say it was for the best that the hatchlings were with their new nursemaid.

Reluctant relief swam through her voice when she admitted it, but I also heard the shame of failure lurking in her tone. Aderyn had been counting the days until Father could send Jorun to her – Jorun and my mother. When she could hand the hatchlings over to someone who could give them what they needed.

She'd given up her wings for them, lived among her enemy, and found a way to keep them alive without their mother's milk. She'd run with them the moment the mountain rumbled; she protected them. And I knew she would honor her word to our father to do exactly that, even though she knew my mother was dead and no one was coming to take them off her hands.

The moment she saw me, she was angry. Not because I'd come, but because I had flown and potentially drawn eyes from above. I'd put the hatchlings in danger.

Now that the light was scant, it was harder to see the cuts I was making. When carving, one had to be cautious. Once a piece of wood was cut away, it could not be put back. I laid Wade's leg aside, along with the strings needed to finish it, then fed the chips into Crest's fire pit. They lent a sweet aroma to the air. I sat on the floor and stretched my fingers. They'd been in the same cramped position for too long and were stiff.

Crest returned and moved around just outside the tent, occasionally casting glances my way. I watched as he used a knife to prepare our fish for the fire, thrusting a copper rod through their middles and bringing them in to hang atop the fiery chips of wood. He rinsed his hands in a basin of water, then dried them off. He crossed the room to let the tent flaps down again, sealing us in as effectively as the sanctum's great doors.

I was aware of his every movement.

And *he* was aware that I tracked him.

"Why do I once again feel like your prey, Elira?"

"Because you are."

In one way or another, he always had been. But I was also his…

As I stood, he watched my body unfold and stretch to its full height, much slighter than his broad-shouldered frame. My wings released a shiver when he slowly approached.

"Do you hear that?" he asked, bending to put his mouth next to my ear. Not touching me.

It was what I'd been groomed to want. That lack of touch. And now I knew why they withheld it from us all. Because it was something we would crave more than the blood of our enemies. More than glory.

Because instead of the recognition of many, we would seek praise from the one who mattered most. We would want to please them above all others. Above everything.

What did he hear that I couldn't, or hadn't?

I raised my head a fraction and sought the sound to which he alluded. It was difficult to find over the beating of my heart and the crackling of the fire, but in the distance, there was music.

A soft, slow melody emanated from the nearby village.

Crest stepped closer, still not touching me even in the slightest of ways, even accidentally. His blue eyes heated. "Did you want to dance with me that night in the grotto?"

"I wouldn't have known how," I breathed as he bent closer…

Closer…

"That's not what I asked." His lips curled just a fraction as they hovered over mine. Yet, he didn't reach out for me.

I straightened my spine, fingers flinching at my side. "Then, yes."

"Will you dance with me now?"

There it was. The offer of touch.

My wings began to lightly flutter. My toes curled over the planks as though they might hold onto it while the world spun away. "I face the same predicament, Crest. In the time that has passed between then and now, I haven't learned to dance."

"Then, as your lacuna, it would be my honor to teach you." His brows arched in question.

I nodded once, waiting for the sensation of the pads of his silken fingers tracing my arms, trailing over my back… *something.*

He was teasing me and in doing so, playing a dangerous game.

He touched a strand of my hair and rubbed it between his thumb and forefinger, still not so much as grazing my heated skin.

"It's not unlike the waves, the way we will move," he breathed against the crook of my neck where he'd bitten and marked me.

"I thought dancing required the partners to touch."

His teasing smile answered me. "It does, Elira. In fact, learning to dance is a test in patience."

I wanted to lunge for him, to tackle him to the floor and growl at him never to tease me again.

And then, as if he could see that the limit of my patience was hanging by a thread and I was nearly undone with need, his hands softly skimmed my hips. Where the sarong was knotted, his pinky slipped underneath the fabric and over my skin. His hands traced to my lower back. My wings thrummed at his barely-there touch. "Thread your arms around my neck…"

I did as he said, but did not tease. I took.

I raked my fingers into the hair at his nape and tugged him closer.

He fit my hips against his. Together, slowly, step by step, we began to sway back and forth. It was hard for me to relax enough to feel comfortable at first, but Crest was far more patient. He gently pressed down on one hip, then the other. Soon, we were moving as fluidly as the sea.

"Close your eyes," he coaxed, planting soft kisses along my jawline.

My nails bit into the back of his neck.

"Relax," he whispered.

I wasn't sure how I could possibly accomplish that when everything in me crackled like the lightning forking through my blood. When I was a storm, electric and wild and fed not by Neera, but by my insatiable need of him.

I didn't know how to swim, only how to thrash against and fight the waves for the air I needed, but I knew what it was to lose that battle, to be submerged and at the mighty ocean's mercy. And now, day by day, Crest was teaching me what it was to be caught in the deadly current that was The Shark.

He bent me backward as we moved back and forth, my spine curving for him. His hand gently squeezed my throat before drifting down the middle of my chest.

He captured my lips with his… nipping and licking, until his soft groans and barely-there touches were no longer enough. I grasped his shoulders, gave my wings a small flap, and deftly wrapped my legs around his waist. His arms clamped around my back at the same time my hands gripped his face and tilted his head where I wanted it.

I barely registered it when the wind gusted, blowing the tent doors open and holding them there. But Crest heard something beyond the wind and song. "Elira," he gasped, sitting me down. My feet struck the wood floor one by one.

I was dazed, still trapped in that unrelenting current, my entire body abuzz.

"Koa is here," he quietly informed me.

I nearly growled.

Crest was still holding onto my waist when Koa flounced inside.

"Looks like I'm just in time for dinner." He gave a wicked smile, eagerly rubbing his hands together. He shot me a look that said he knew dinner was *not* what he'd interrupted.

"There's plenty," I surprised him, welcoming him to join us. It caught him off guard.

"Great," he sputtered, removing a bag from over his head. "I brought some fruit – fresh from the grove."

As we divided the fish and fruit, Koa told Crest he'd just visited Wade and had spoken to Magma about the sky fire. He'd made his rounds and instructed certain Guardians to spread over the mountains to collect cuttings from plants. Per the Mender's request, they didn't completely harvest them. This would all commence after those not assigned to lookout duty watched my fight with Aderyn tomorrow at dawn.

Crest was pleased. "How is Frey? Are the younglings progressing?" he asked.

"Frey is cranky," Koa answered. "The children are making great progress, though a few stand out from the rest."

Crest turned to me. "Would you watch them and offer advice?"

"Of course," I answered him, then looked at Koa. "Did Wade tell you he wanted to attend the fight?"

Koa grinned. "He said you personally invited him."

Crest gestured behind me to the leg I was carving. "Don't tell him, but she's making that for him."

Koa's brows furrowed before he leapt up from where he was seated cross-legged on the floor to get a better look at the carving. He gave an incredulous laugh. "I never thought of doing anything like this!"

"If you want to make up for your lack of ingenuity, you can use this as a guide to carve a new one when this one is worn brittle," I teased.

"Going somewhere, Scourge? Couldn't *you* just carve a replacement?" he asked lightly.

"Of course I could," I breezily replied, trying to smother the panic in my chest at my inadvertent admission. "But I'm sure it would mean more to him coming from you, Koa."

Crest gave me an uneasy look.

Koa noticed. While he hadn't considered fashioning a leg for Wade, he recognized that Crest was about to veer toward something dangerous, something best left tucked away and unspoken.

"What weapons will you and Aderyn fight with tomorrow?" Koa asked, deftly changing the subject and shattering the tension now laying over us as thick and heavy as the humid air.

I shrugged as I chewed and swallowed a piece of crisped fish. It had cooked a little longer than it should have while Crest was teaching me to dance. "The choice lies with Aderyn since she called the match."

"Are you scared of her?" Koa asked, popping a piece of mango in his mouth and grinning as he chewed.

"Not in the least." I sipped from my cup of water. "You know, Koa, in Empyrean, the victor is rewarded with the choice to spar in a second fight. They get to choose their next opponent."

"That doesn't sound like a reward at all," he said, his forced laughter dying.

"It's actually a great honor because it's seen as another chance to further solidify their position. If you want to see how we truly train, we should add that element. The top-ranked Warrior must be able to fight, and win, without tiring. Perhaps I should challenge *you*."

Crest looked away for a moment, using his hand to smother a chuckle. Koa, on the other hand, sat up straighter. His eyes flicked to The Shark's as if to ask if he thought I was serious.

"What would the other Guardians say if you were bested by *The Scourge*?" I asked him.

He sobered, clearing his throat. "If I can't win a fight against you, I'm pretty sure they'd lose heart about what's coming."

"Then we need to make sure you're able to before they come."

"We don't have long," Koa noted. "Intention Day isn't far off, according to Jorun."

"No, it isn't." My eyes clashed with Crest's before I looked away. The weight of his stare made me want to tell him everything, even though it would be the cruelest thing I'd ever done. "I need to rest," I told them both, standing and moving across the room. I grabbed a rag and dunked it into the cool water in the basin, then scrubbed my plate.

"I should let the two of you get some *sleep*," Koa replied to Crest, emphasizing the word sleep. He came over and took up the cloth I'd just used, scrubbing his plate beside me. His brows slowly rose and he whispered, "Elira… are you… uh… Are you *serious* about challenging me?"

Crest chuckled under his breath from across the room. Koa couldn't speak quietly if his life depended on it. I hoped it never did.

"Are you *seriously* scared?" I whispered so Crest could still hear.

"Not at all. Just want to prepare. Plan my outfit and such. That's all."

I waited until he met my stare. "You should always be prepared to fight, Koa." I moved toward the hammock as he straightened.

"Seriously, though…" he pressed.

Smiling, I sat on the woven fabric, spreading it to accommodate my wings. "We'll just have to see what tomorrow brings."

"That's not an answer," he grumbled petulantly.

Crest walked with him from the tent, making plans to help Wade to the shore in the morning. The Salt had paid a visit to Wade at Magma's and offered to carry chairs down from her tent. She wanted to sit with Wade and watch. I knew that Talay's people would gather behind the two of them to see me and Aderyn try to tear one another apart.

I laid there remembering every sparring match Aderyn and I had ever fought, reminding myself of her tells, her favorite stances and offensive maneuvers, how lithe and nimble she was, and her grip on various weapons. As if I could forget any of it, or her.

Sisters…

We'd been sisters all along.

What would life have been like if Empyrean honored the bonds found in blood?

I'd seen how tightly knitted the Kehlani families were. Neither the goddess nor the Elders could afford to give us something we would defend – even against them.

Love was the one thing worth fighting for, worth going to war for, against *any* who would see it squashed.

They couldn't allow any of us to be loyal to anyone but them, the goddess, and her war. If we were, they would lose hold of the rope of control with which they leashed us.

That was why the moment an Empyrean began showing signs of attachment, they were torn away from the source.

A Clipped mother's hatchlings were taken the moment they were weaned.

Warriors who mated were thrust together only long enough to conceive, then their intention and duty was fulfilled and they were expected to resume their lives – lives that belonged to their superiors who ordered them to keep clawing toward the top. Who kept them too busy training, guarding, and warring to have energy for anything beyond those things. They even barred them from being ranked similarly or placed in the same quad to keep them separate.

Hatchlings who became of age to train were taken from their house and any friends they might have made and thrust into another with older children who'd been wielding wooden swords far longer than they had. Their beatings would teach them to be worse than their predecessors.

Younglings who graduated to Warrior squared off against adults who vowed to do whatever they could to make them stronger – all in the name of protection from a faceless, sea-bound enemy. No wonder we hated them so early.

Our leaders led us to believe it was all because of them. Every lash. Every strike of the mace. Every blow and kick and curse. Because at the edge of the sea they guarded, if we didn't fight like beasts, we would be drowned by them.

Time robbed seasoned Warriors of their strength and reflexes. Once they lost their edge and usefulness, they were added to the general populace and forced to live among people who watched them with fear and distrust in spite of all they'd done, never appreciating that they'd done it for *them*.

Seers were collected the moment they saw something beyond the ordinary and told to simply wait for a goddess who likely would never choose them to become close to her, never imagining that being in the goddess's confidence was the worst position imaginable and by far one of the most dangerous.

Anyone who showed exceptional intelligence, even if they were strong enough to join the Warriors in their illustrious quarter, was shoved into the clutch of Scholars who sharpened and trained them in a different way than the Warriors were honed.

The Elders were the only ones who *vied* for the opportunity to be separated, once again, from all the rest. Perhaps they were the only ones who could stomach more of it. Likely because they were drawn from the people of the general populace.

Gentle Gatherers risked their lives to provide, but had never been asked to embed an arrow's head in the heart or head of their foe, had never drawn a sword on a friend knowing that the cut they made would make them both bleed.

Those charged with ensuring that Empyrean sparkled. Those charged with serving the Elders, the Scholars, the Commanders. Those who taught children special skills and who instructed them how to fly. There were many thankless jobs in the sky. Too many to name or count. More I didn't even know. Had never given my attention to.

I scrubbed a hand down my face. I'd craved the praise of them all. I fought and cut through everyone, even Aderyn, my friend and sister, to take and keep the top position.

Still awake when Crest returned, I watched him scrub his plate and set it aside to dry. Watched him add a small log to the embers, gazing at the smoke that curled up to the top of the tent where it slid out the flaps like water through a gill.

He settled beside me and wrapped his arm around my shoulder. I couldn't help but wonder how easy life with Crest might be if the sky wasn't falling.

He kissed my forehead. "I sleep better when you're next to me."

"I dance better when you're my partner," I volleyed.

"Your lacuna," he happily reminded me.

I grazed a hand down his gills and he closed his eyes, slowly inhaling. "I didn't realize it until you compared dancing to the movement of the ocean, but there's a sensuality about the sea I never appreciated."

"Not in the sky?" he asked.

I shook my head, drifting my hand to the circle of feathers tattooed beside my cheek. "The sky is so cold, even the sun moving through it can't warm the blue."

He hadn't opened his eyes. I let mine fall closed to match. Crest murmured, "She doesn't warm the sea, either. Just us – caught on the land between two cold kingdoms."

CHAPTER TWENTY

Thrumming with the familiar energy I always had before a sparring match, I woke long before dawn and eased out of the hammock, somehow managing to avoid waking Crest.

Outside, the air was cool. Thin strands of fog stretched between mountain and sea like a spindly spider's delicate web. The grass was damp with dew as I started toward the shore.

In the sky above the fog, there was no movement. It was clear, save for a few lingering stars. There were no clouds. No perches flickered near or afar.

Jorun told me that Talon's plan was to wait until Intention Day, when all of Empyrean could band together to share a final, mighty goal as a united people. All would do their part – great or small – to end the war for good. Talon wanted the glory, to be recorded in our histories as the only General powerful enough to win the war between our people.

The dream in which my wings had been cut and I was pushed through the firmament to share in my mother's fate, if it was a vision, had given me a valuable piece of information. The goddess was incensed at the thought of a shared intention, that her people might band together and shirk the rules with which she had yoked them.

She would come for me first if she broke free, to stop me from using my equal power to imprison her again. But then she would come for the Elders. I had no doubt Talon wasn't the only one misguiding the people.

If they stood against a limitless Neera and lost – and they would lose – they would pay dearly.

I remembered her tearing away the feathers her souls owed, flooding the square to their calves, all while her weighty scale demanded far more than they'd ever been willing to pay, a veritable ocean of feathers and penance.

I took a deep breath to clear my mind of her. The goddess would only distract me this morning and I couldn't allow it. Instead, I focused on what I could see and hear, taste and feel. Focused on the here and now, not what might lie ahead.

An iguana's tail protruded from the base of a thick grass plant, its bowed leaves providing the creature cover as I passed by. Insects that screamed all night were still loudly singing, but the ocean seemed quieter than usual.

The scent of the ocean's brine calmed my racing heart.

The sand felt cool on my bare feet as I crossed the divide of dunes and traversed the thicker, powdery sand to the tide line where it hardened and was easier to walk.

My feet left distinct prints here, unlike the powdery holes the wind would blow across and soon fill in.

This bout was different than all the others Aderyn and I had fought. Never had we gone toe-to-toe on the shore or battled one another before our enemies. Neither of us ever dreamed we'd be doing it so they could learn from our tactics. Beyond that, we'd never sparred when there was so much animosity between us.

Every time I saw her now, all I could imagine was roaring in her face and drawing blood for every feather she let me find.

Raking my hair back from my face, I tried to push Aderyn from my thoughts. The Salt claimed anger blinded and she was right. Neera wasn't the only one in my head today, which wasn't good.

I missed the scent of my leathers, I realized, musky and sweet from the oil I carefully applied to keep them supple. I missed the weight of my sword on my belt.

If she was awake, Aderyn was likely thinking the same things. Did she remember the harmony of our blades drawn across whetstones the evening before a battle?

In the early morning before we were to face off, we would split and eat what we had saved to fuel us in those long moments, then dressed together from bracers to boots. We plaited one another's hair and pinned it back so it wouldn't impede our vision. And when it was time, we flew side-by-side to the Warrior's Quarter.

In the sparring ring, we fought like mountain cats to cover the fact that we were holding back so I wouldn't be cut.

Fists or blades, the choice was ours; we never fell into patterns, never wanted to give anyone a reason to doubt that we were truly fighting. We knew how to make our blades clash and sing convincingly *without* drawing blood, and we used our wings to our advantage as leverage, because if one of Talay's people caught hold of you at the sea's edge, you had to be able to break free.

We fought until sweat dripped into our eyelids, trickling down the hollows of our backs and the valley between our breasts, until even our legs were slick.

Our fights were real, even if they were carefully fought.

Aderyn didn't *let* me win. I had to earn it. I knew she would take it if I didn't deserve it, even when she often told me I did.

There were times when my paranoia flared and I wondered if one day she would grow tired of the constant threat overshadowing our lies, and my truth. I wondered if she ever considered slitting my throat to expose my secret and show the world what she'd kept hidden for me. To remove me from her quad and life, but she never faltered.

Aderyn was loyal.

Until she wasn't.

That was why I never questioned the truth of her death. Never thought her capable of faking it and leaving her wings for me to find – even if the idea wasn't hers.

When we faced one another on the sand this morning, we wouldn't need to be careful. We didn't have to convince anyone we were gnashing at one another, because we really would be. She could cut me and I could bleed, then I would make her regret it by drawing her blood in return.

How would Aderyn fight now that we no longer had to temper our anger or motions?

Now that there were no secrets to be kept or lies to tell in order to keep them?

Nothing but the two of us and the bitter enmity we felt for one another?

In the distance, the moon lit the sliver of sand on which we would fight, and on it, The Salt waited as the sky slipped from raven black to deepest azure. As I got close, I noticed something was folded over her arms.

"Did Talay send you?" I chanced a guess when I drew close enough that she could easily hear me.

"Not this time," she replied, and I breathed a sigh of relief. While I appreciated the sea god's insight, his revelations were heavy to bear. "Magma asked me to give you something for this morning. I hope you won't be angry when you see what she's done. Her heart meant well. What she did, she did in an effort to help."

The Salt was trying to soothe me while she cradled the bundle against her stomach, both arms blocking it from my sight.

What could Magma have done that would anger me?

She moved her arms and I caught a glimpse of familiar blue leather. I couldn't help but smile. Magma had given my leathers back? How would this possibly upset me…?

Then, she held out the *now-mutilated* garment.

I held in a tight breath.

The neckline that used to stretch to my jaw and cover most of my scar had been cut away, as had both sleeves. The protective portion of the breastplate, thankfully, was intact.

The Salt winced at my crestfallen expression. "She thought it would be far too hot for you to wear as it was."

"Did she keep the pieces she removed?" I rasped.

The Salt nodded and apologized again on Magma's behalf. "I collected them and can re-affix them, Elira."

I nodded my thanks, taking what was left of the garment from her. It would never be the same as it was, and for a moment I mourned what had been. Then again, I wasn't what I used to be, either. Perhaps the change better suited who I was now.

Gently stroking the soft leather, I asked the Seer, "What's a few more scars among dozens?"

"She altered Aderyn's as well." The Salt nodded to a rich brown bundle laying on a cloth in the deeper sand.

Would Aderyn care? Would she even want to wear hers?

Was the back stained with the blood from when her wings were cleaved, or had she removed it beforehand?

"Why didn't she bring them herself?" I asked of Magma.

The Salt gently answered, "She isn't sure she wants to watch."

"She should," I told her, then began unfastening the buckles at one shoulder and at the waist beneath it. I slid my arm through, fastening it snugly onto my body as the Seer watched my deft motions. "Salt?" Her eyes rose to meet mine. "Has the shells' cadence changed?"

She slowly shook her head.

I swallowed thickly, wondering if I should ask my next question and deciding it was best if I knew, even if her answer wasn't what I wanted to hear. Maybe the threat would jar something in my memory.

"If what you saw comes to pass, what happens to your people?"

She pressed her lips together as if trying to seal the truth inside.

"Salt?" I pressed.

She walked to the surf where gentle waves tumbled ashore and stood there as foamy edge after foamy edge swept over her bare feet. Shells were scattered all along the shore, none of them cowries. "If what I saw comes to pass, these people, this place, will no longer be your worry."

"That's not an answer."

"Some questions are better left unanswered." She stayed in the water but turned to face me. "You *need* to remember, Elira. I feel hope stir when I think it; that if you just align with your prior lives, there might be something in them that could guide you to victory over her."

Over a goddess? I might be magically balanced with her in many respects, but I wasn't Neera's equal in the ways that mattered. She made souls, and now she sought to unmake one of them. I had no doubt she'd finally figured out how to tip the scale to her advantage.

"You think I haven't tried?" I asked in frustration, unknotting the sarong at my hip. It was too long, so I folded the fabric and quickly tied it again to cover myself, jerking the knot to make sure it was secure.

"I'm sure you have, but don't give up," she answered smoothly. "Never stop trying, no matter how bleak it seems."

I nodded a shallow promise.

"Would Talay have saved my father if he'd reached the sea before dying? He thrust his sword through his stomach, according to Jorun."

She shook her head. "The blade entered his abdomen, but he thrust it upward, Elira."

Piercing his heart and lungs, no doubt. He died plummeting toward the sea, knowing he likely wouldn't make it to Talay, yet knowing my whereabouts would be kept safe, at least for a time.

As the Seer and I spoke, the sky leached from deepest azure into the cold blue I knew too well. The sun hovered just under the water's surface at the horizon. Her brilliant light would soon usher in a new day.

I felt Crest before I saw him, then watched his powerful body move down the shoreline toward us carrying the thick fold of leather, blade, and barb under his arm. The tridents' sharp tips protruded, pointing at me like condemning fingers.

He took in my altered leathers and shortened skirt. His eyes touched my bare legs and slid over the sarong that was as short as Koa had worn when everyone laughed at him for doing so.

My blood heated.

The Shark did not laugh at me as he had his friend. And despite the fact he'd seen my body devoid of all clothing, it was like he was seeing me for the first time, as if he'd scented a droplet of blood in the water and knew exactly where it seeped into the sea.

The Salt broke the delicious tension building between us by politely greeting him. "Crest."

He inclined his head to her briefly. "Salt." His hand unfurled before me to reveal a long, thin piece of torn white linen. "To tie back your hair."

I took it from his palm.

Crest watched me plait and bind the long, pale strands, studying my breast plate; its scars and the feathers I'd painstakingly pressed into the leather. He'd seen me in them the night he dragged me from the sea, but not before or since. I could only imagine how many times he'd seen them from above, my bow string drawn, arrow pointed – likely at him.

"Koa and I will be right back with Wade," he told us.

At that, the Salt perked. "I'll walk with you as far as my tent and bring back chairs."

"I can help you," I offered.

"No. You settle your mind, Elira. I can carry them." She walked alongside Crest for a few steps, then glanced back over her shoulder. "Don't start without us."

I gave her my word that we wouldn't.

Before they disappeared over the dunes, Crest laid his weapon-laden roll upon The Salt's outspread blanket. The woven blue and white fabric cradled Aderyn's filleted leather, a soft buffer from the gritty sand that would rake and ruin it.

For a long moment, I felt alone. Even as the sound of many voices poured from just over the dunes right before a large group of Talay's people spilled onto the shore.

They kept coming, ten at a time, two, four, nearly twenty, until the sand was covered with a myriad of colored fabric and looks of anticipation and perhaps trepidation.

Their expressions matched those they wore when they watched Crest and Koa tempt Colossus close to the shore. I wondered where my eager opponent was just before she appeared in the distance walking beside Jorun with a determined gait.

She'd folded her sarong into quarters, too, and had bound her long, dark hair.

The Salt greeted many of her people as she resurfaced, carrying both her wooden chairs – one for Wade and one for her. She settled one, then the other, before the dunes. Soon, the throng fanned out from it.

The Seer waved me over.

Inadvertently, I fell into step with Aderyn. She stared at my breastplate, her eyes haunted as though it was a terrible sight she didn't think she'd see again and perhaps had begged not to. Jorun followed us to The Salt as she sat before the sea, waiting for Wade and for us to honor our words and help her people.

The Seer pointed Aderyn to her altered leathers and gestured to the weaponry provided to us. Aderyn moved to examine it all.

Jorun stopped beside me. His gaze met mine, worry curving around the brown striations in his eyes. They weren't unlike one of the hues that had been trapped in Aderyn's wings…

The Salt greeted Jorun. He inclined his head to her out of a respect he hadn't yet shown me. He might be Aderyn's… whatever he was. Mate? But he'd descended to keep a promise to my father – a vow that passed to me when The General took his own life to try to save me, not knowing there was nothing anyone could do to preserve me now.

"I'm surprised she loosened your lead enough to allow you to visit," I snarled.

The Salt looked wholly uncomfortable at the turn this greeting had taken, but I couldn't focus on her. For a long moment, Jorun stared at me. Then, he spoke his truth and it struck like a fallen Warrior against the sea.

"I love her." His voice held a steadiness I wasn't sure I'd ever had the luxury of feeling within myself. There was no question. No faltering. No possibility that the feeling might be ripped away like a feather from a wing or dissolve like salt in water. No fear or worry. He simply did and it simply was. "I couldn't above, but I can here. And I will. I won't apologize for it, even to you, Elira."

I found myself respecting him more than I'd recently grown to, which surprised me because he'd more than earned that respect and trust since finding me. His intelligence had been invaluable, and I stood before him being petty.

Jorun let out a low growl of a laugh. "Of course *he* came."

The Salt and I tracked his stare… Behind the mass of people hovered a wingless Empyrean. If his pale skin hadn't announced him, his posture would have, as would have the anticipation in his eyes. He wanted to witness the fight. Was hungry for it.

I didn't recognize him. Didn't know how long he'd lived on the sand, or how long it had been since he touched the sky. What I *did* know was that this stranger's attention was unabashedly fixed on Aderyn – the woman Jorun just professed to love.

"Does *he* have a name?" I asked, tipping my chin toward the stranger, loosening my shoulders by flinging my arms back and forth.

"Bellen," he quietly snapped.

I looked at the Seer. "How did he come to live on Kehlani?"

She gathered her dark braids and twisted them over her shoulder. "Bellen was born wingless. He was the reason your father descended and chanced reaching out to me at all, and he was the first Empyrean he brought to us.

He said that everyone above assumed he fell from the firmament."

"So, he was raised here?"

The Salt nodded. "He lived with a family who had lost their son to illness many years before. Magma could not save their son, but they saw a new hope in Bellen. They spent their days teaching him about life on the Isle. As he grew, he noticed the differences in himself and everyone else and decided he would rather live on the outskirts than within the villages. Bellen claimed the hollow as his own. When others came later, he took them in, to acclimate them. He taught them what he'd been shown and thought they would leave and join the villages and assimilate to our kind. None did, though. They wanted to stay with him, so they built homes between the bluffs alongside his. During the years your father held the position of General, he managed to save less than a dozen Empyreans. It was a great risk, for himself *and* for each one he smuggled away to the sand."

That number included Aderyn and the hatchlings. It would have been thirteen if the Elders had not killed my mother. Fourteen if Jorun's plan to forsake the sky had come to fruition.

"I never knew him as a humble man," I admitted. "I only knew him as the fierce General, his rigid directives, and the consequences of failing him."

I couldn't imagine the immense stress he must have been under with the weight of the secrets he bore from this hidden aspect of his life.

The Salt stared at Bellen, then looked at my sister. "All of those he sent to the shore after Bellen were wingless or Clipped, save Aderyn."

Aderyn, who had surrendered her wings for a life here.

"Was it a stipulation? Her severing her wings?"

The Salt sighed, "Breaker was reticent to allow her to stay because of them. She suggested severing them. She claimed that if she gave up her wings, it would prove she was being truthful and ensure she would stay on the soil and guard our secrets as fervently as we guarded hers."

"It balanced things…" In my mind, the great scale teetered, then its pans evened.

"She didn't have to do it the moment she arrived, but she insisted it be done right away. She was panicked that night," The Salt mentioned, digging her heel into the wet sand.

"She did it so she wouldn't have the chance to change her mind," I told her.

Jorun scrubbed his jaw and stared daggers at Bellen, who just grinned in response. He was going to be a problem – for Jorun.

"Bellen and Aderyn became friends while she was waiting for you?" I guessed.

"So it seems," he said, aggravated.

"She left the hollow and crossed the mountains with you, though, didn't she?" I asked.

"Because the hatchlings needed shelter."

"You had shelter. It may not have been ideal, but it was sufficient. She left with *you*, Jorun. Her heart followed the subject of its affection."

I left Jorun to consider my observation and walked to Aderyn, who made herself busy admiring the weapons.

She wouldn't choose the hatchets or the tridents, even though they were a new thrilling option to consider. Aderyn loved knives the way I loved my bow. If she was ever to best me, it would be while gripping a blade.

Her fingers curled around the scarred, wooden handles of a set of twin knives. She tested her grip on each, chose one for herself, then handed the blade she'd discarded to me. She looked all around at the crowd and blew out a deep breath. "There are so many of them."

"They want to learn."

"I offered to teach *two girls*, not the entire Isle."

I grinned with malice. "Then you should be more specific when striking future bargains. I would think you would already know exactly how horribly that can end for the bargainer."

Her chin jutted to my wings. "You'll miss them when they're bare and serve no more purpose. You'll beg someone to cut the wing bones from your back so they don't constantly remind you of your loss," she said cruelly.

"Do yours still linger in your mind's periphery?"

"Of course not," she bit. "I wanted them gone."

I smirked in response. Her words were a lie I knew she must often tell herself, hoping one day she'd believe it, but the truth lingered in the downturned corners of her lips and eyes.

Aderyn regretted severing her wings. Perhaps she didn't love the sea as much as she thought. Or maybe the forbidden allure of the ocean faded when it became hers to swim in, to wade through daily.

Did she now see the ocean she'd once loved as nothing but her own deep, watery cage? It surrounded the sand well enough to act as one.

Could she see my truth as well? That I might not live long enough to know the feeling of my feathers being stripped away because the goddess had turned her attention from my wings and focused upon killing my very soul?

"I won't use them against you today. To keep it fair," I told her.

"Do whatever you'd like, but you should mind the edge of my blade. Everyone knows what your blood holds now."

Her pinched lips fell open at the sight of my genuine smile. "Yes, they do."

I was free. And so was she…

This fight would be our last. It wouldn't end in death, but in the burial of the ties that bound us.

III

BRINE

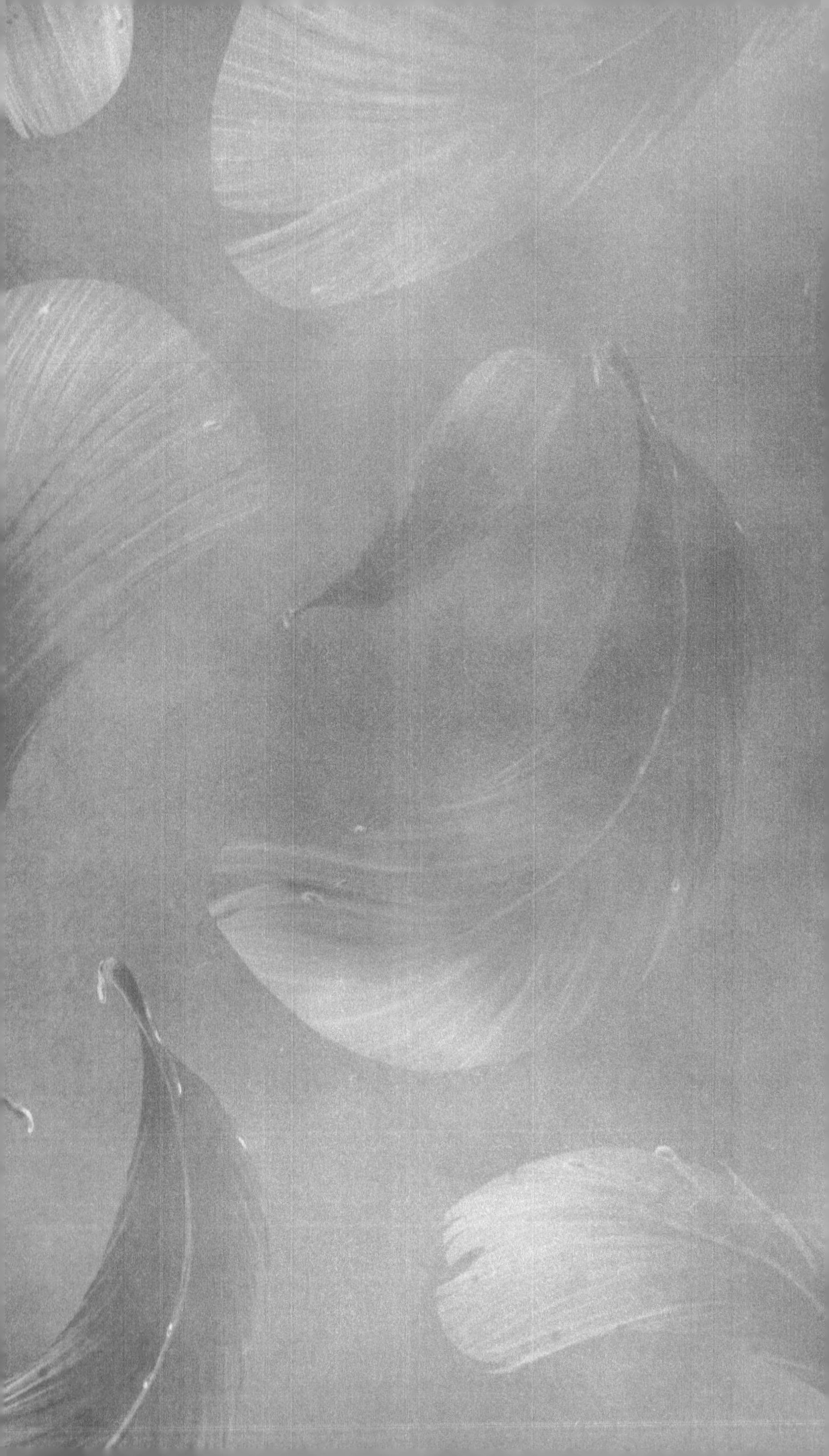

CHAPTER TWENTY-ONE

Jorun stood straighter when he saw Aderyn approaching. Again, she clearly chose him over Bellen, though I doubted the haughty-looking wingless male realized she'd already made her decision.

Jorun held her knife while she quickly donned and tightened her leather breastplate. The armor covered the scars on her back where her wings used to lay, but I couldn't help but wonder what they looked like.

Magma likely did what she could to help her heal, but wounds that left scars couldn't easily be forgotten.

I threw my knife to the sand and it sank to the hilt. I shook out my hands, then lunged from side to side to limber up. Everyone turned to the dunes when Wade appeared. He used Crest's and Koa's shoulders as crutches, pushing off the sand with his foot and wearing a tired, but determined grin.

Cheers and claps erupted for him.

He made it to The Salt's proffered chair and sank into it gratefully, his chest heaving. It was quite a walk, but he had done it instead of being carried. He was regaining his power moment by moment, step by stubborn step and I was glad of it.

When the crowd of Kehlanians settled, he shouted across the sand to me. "Hey, Scourge! Come here."

I walked to him, noting the sweat on his brow and the way his chest rose and fell, puffing with each breath.

"You look well," I told him.

Koa nudged Crest and whispered something into his ear.

"As do you," he said, nodding to my apparel. "Do me a favor?"

"Certainly."

"Don't lose," he said. "If you win, Magma cooks dinner tonight. If you lose, the task is mine, and I hate cooking."

I smiled. "Magma bet against me?"

"She didn't bet against you, per se. But she refused to encourage you by wagering you'd win."

I laughed. "Of course not." Over his shoulder, a shadow fell. I looked up to see North standing behind Wade's chair.

"It's a waste of time to place wagers on the Empyreans," he snarled. "Just let them tear one another apart so we don't have to dirty our hands."

A low growl tore from Crest's chest. He started forward, stopped by the hand of the Seer I hadn't seen approach. "North… Talay has warned you. If you insist that he repeat himself, he will make sure you won't forget it again."

North wisely closed his mouth, raised his hands in supplication, and walked to find Nori amidst the crowd.

I needed this fight to free the knowledge trapped in the confines of my mind.

I needed Aderyn to hit me, cut me. If I had to bleed to find more truth, so be it.

And I was tired of waiting. The sun had risen…

Aderyn was speaking to two girls a couple years younger than we were who stood on the seam of the crowd that formed a broad circle around us.

I met Crest's eyes before jerking the blade from the sand beside my foot and making my way to the middle of the circle of sand, framed in by sea-filled souls. I wondered if he knew how much I wanted and hated this fight.

Aderyn caught my movement and left the girls to meet me.

We wasted no time.

The crowd hushed as we took our first steps, carefully circling one another, neither of us blinking. One second of inattention was one too many.

The goal was to limit your opponent's opportunities to strike, while recognizing when they would falter and cutting when they did exactly that.

The sea that was so serene earlier now roared for us. Wade's wooden chair creaked as he leaned forward. The brine and sunshine clung to my skin. But none of it mattered. All that mattered was the girl standing before me and the edge of her blade.

Aderyn slashed toward me.

I stepped out of the arc of her blade.

She swung out again and my knife's edge met hers with a sharp clang.

The two sang apart.

I quickly twisted behind her and flayed a wide swath of her leather. She turned. Stabbed downward at my shoulder as I deflected, then danced away, smirking. *That* maneuver was for Jorun.

"You shot him," she growled low, indignant on his behalf.

Light glinted from her knife just before it whistled through the air. I waited until it was clear then kicked the outside of her thigh, hard. Her knee buckled, but only for a moment. Sharp gasps echoed from all around us, but Aderyn never lost her footing.

Even wingless, she was well-balanced. Graceful. But she was easily riled and right now she seemed to be on the verge of losing control of her temper. Which was exactly what I wanted, because anger was predictable.

"You're defending Jorun? I thought you'd moved on to Bellen."

"He's a *friend*," she bit.

"Does *he* know that?" I laughed.

Her eyes flicked to something – or someone – over my shoulder. I zipped my blade across her forearm. She hissed as blood quickly overflowed the cut. She put a few steps between us to assess the wound.

Magma's loud disapproval erupted from somewhere behind me. She'd probably come armed with mending supplies – which, in fairness, we'd soon enough need – but she came.

Aderyn's blood oozed from the wound. It was crimson, but every drop twitched with pale Empyrea. And, like that fidgeting, frenetic power, she was incensed. She crossed the distance between us and ripped her blade toward me, cutting upward from chest to chin as tears collected in her eyes.

I moved to avoid her, but I didn't understand why *she* was crying. I shouldn't have questioned it. Seeing her tears caught me off guard. The next time she swiped, I misjudged the distance. I gritted my teeth and inhaled sharply as searing pain flared across my jaw.

At the sight of my blood, Aderyn began to laugh hysterically, despite the tears still flowing down her cheeks. "There it is!" she said in a half-sob. "The blood of Neera, the very power of the sky."

Warm and sticky, blood slid down my throat, bright white splashing onto my blue breast plate and spattering my arms. I tightened my grasp, holding the knife out so I didn't bleed on the handle and impede my grip.

Going on the offensive was my favorite part. I thrust the blade toward her ribs. She didn't move fast enough to get out of the way, so I pulled back so my blade wouldn't slide between them. These edges were sharp, the tips pointed and thin. Perfect for filleting fish – or former friends.

Aderyn's brown eyes darkened. She knew I stopped myself. She roared, offended because I held back. Angry I hadn't taken the victory that was mine. In Empyrea, we'd both broken a few of each other's more fragile bones – the smallest toes and fingers, the wing bones every youngling Warrior broke at least once. We'd bruised and battered one another. Tore at wings and hair and gouged at eyes, but we never crossed the line that starkly divided life from death.

Our knives' blades met again and held as she pushed forward, surprising me with a punch to the mouth. A magnificent flare of pain came a second before the taste of fire burst across my lips. I swung for her nose before my injury weakened me and a sickening crunch filled the air, eliciting a gasp from the crowd. Blood filled my mouth, my bottom lip split and already swelling. I spat upon the sand.

Both of Aderyn's eyes were turning purple in the inner corners and a bump began to rise on the bridge of her nose. She bled from one nostril, wiping and smearing it over her cheek.

Her breaths sawed in and out and she gripped her side as though the muscle there was catching the way it did when we were younglings.

Aderyn was out of shape.

I bent low and kicked my heel backward, sweeping her feet out from under her. She gasped for air that the blow knocked away. Before she could regain her strength, I deftly straddled her hips. I pinned the hand she held her blade with to the sand and pressed my blade to the tender veins inside her wrist. One quick rip and she'd bleed to death… and she knew it.

Would she be angry *now* if I held back? Or did she long for me to let my blade sink into her to free her from this life?

For a moment, there was only her, me, the victory she knew was now mine, and our estranged souls.

Murmurs came. The people of Kehlani declared the battle over and it seemed that way for a moment, but Aderyn could no longer be trusted in a fight.

She relaxed her grip on the knife's handle. I grabbed it quickly and tossed it away, but the moment I flung it and lifted my eyes to see where it landed, Aderyn brought her knee up into my gut and reversed our positions.

The blow hit my formerly – possibly newly – broken ribs. I cried out and curled into a ball while Aderyn pried the knife from my fingers and threw it into the shallows.

This is where lives end and victors are made, The General would say. In the decisive seconds that crept between accepting and refusing defeat.

He didn't want me to lose, not because I showed potential, but because I was of his blood and he wanted nothing but the best for me. Even if it made me the worst to my enemy. The top position was safest for me, despite the cost of my empathy.

A deep breath, two… a mustering of strength and dogged determination.

She sat back on her haunches and clutched her side again, wincing.

I grabbed her hair and yanked her hard into the sand. Hands bracing the shore, she raised her head, coughing. Grains flew from her mouth and rained from her cheek. She blinked to clear them from her eyes. Then I leapt up and delivered a swift kick to her side. She sprawled out onto her back, arms and legs splayed. I towered over her, poised to kick again. She raised a hand to concede. Croaked at me to stop.

But I couldn't.

I didn't kick her. Didn't grab her hair or drag her into the shallows where our knives had sunken to finish this. Because even if one of us died, this agony would not be ended.

Instead, I paced a tight circle around her as every emotion pent-up in my chest burst out until I was powerless against the overwhelming flood.

"You left!" I screamed at her, tearing at my hair until it was half out of the tie Crest had given me, snarled and haggard.

Every soul on the shore was quiet. Stunned.

Spittle flew from my lips when I shouted, my voice raw and ragged like my heart. Like how she looked, still trying to recover from our match.

"You *left* me up there. How could you? How could you do that?" I couldn't keep still.

And at the same time my hurt spilled out, it crushed me from within. I held the space beneath my ribs the same way she did. Both aching from a blow we'd taken from the other, my injury an old one that hadn't – wouldn't – heal, and hers so fresh she could taste it.

"Because you didn't need me!" she finally wheezed. Aderyn fixed her tear-filled gaze on the sky.

"Coward," I hissed, knowing it was the word she hated most.

She got onto all fours, then pushed to standing, swaying on her feet. "The hatchlings needed me, Elira. *You* didn't. You were the best at *everything*," her voice broke. "And not just because you were born with Neera's power or blood, not because of your soul, and certainly not because you naturally have a competitive spirit. Not even because you simply wanted to rise above them all. You were the best because you couldn't stomach anything less. We rose because you would've rather died than accept mediocrity. You were determined to be ranked *first. First Warrior* of the *first quad. Best* archer. *Fastest* flyer. *Deadly* in battle. *Fearsome* in the sparring ring. And you worked until all of it was yours. And I... I spent *every second* of my life trying to keep up with you so they didn't separate us, so I could help until you reached the pinnacle. And when you did and you settled into it like your rank was a stony throne cut into the steep pitch of a mountaintop, cut specifically for you, I knew you were safe. I knew that leaving meant someone might learn your secret, but it *wouldn't matter*. You were untouchable."

A tear splashed onto my cheek. "You were wrong. You didn't know *anything*."

She looked at Jorun.

He'd no doubt filled her in on everything she thought she knew but hadn't, and he didn't know the half of what The Salt had recently revealed. And unfortunately, the sparring match hadn't jarred loose any memory from the soul writhing inside my skin.

"You *don't* know anything," I slowly spoke before I could consider my words.

Aderyn froze. Her brows furrowed and her dark stare sharpened. She searched me for secrets I would never trust her with again. "What *don't* I know?" she asked.

"Don't pretend you care. I came to make sure you weren't dead, crushed by a mountain's fury, and you screeched at me for worrying." I flung my hand out toward Breaker and Crest. "You told them all I was a monster that couldn't be trusted."

"Because you were! You. *Were.* Elira. You aren't *now*," she said softly. "I can see that, and I admit that in all this, I've made too many mistakes to number." Her chest heaved with emotion. She glanced around as if just remembering we had an audience, then looked back at me for a long moment. "I can't do this."

Aderyn did what she did best: she left. She strode straight to Jorun and together, they walked away from the circle of Kehlanians.

She paused at the sound of my voice but didn't turn to look at me.

"Like your wings, you cut me completely out of your life, Aderyn. Don't pull me unwillingly back into it again. The next time you drag me into a fight, I won't curb my anger or pull my blade."

Busying myself before I fell apart at the seams, I went to collect the knives, finding *one*, but not seeing the other Aderyn had flung in the surf. I felt an overwhelming urge to run after her and dig it into her back, lodging the tip and blade right between the bones in her vertebrae.

I wanted to scream into the heavens, chest open and arms wide, and cry until every tear was wrung from me and Talay had more brine than his sea could absorb.

All eyes volleyed between me and my sister, awkwardly waiting to see what would happen next.

Crest waded into the water with me.

I raised a hand. "I don't want to talk."

"Then fight!" North called out from the crowd.

My head slowly swiveled toward his voice.

"North!" The Salt snapped.

He ignored her and fixed his smarmy grin on me.

North was a head taller and a foot broader than most everyone here but Breaker and Crest. He pushed through to the middle of the sandy circle Aderyn and I had scarred.

"I overheard Koa say you could choose an opponent for a second sparring match. So I can't help but wonder, would the great Scourge choose *me* as her opponent, or would she be too scared?" North challenged.

"He's gone too far," The Salt solemnly intoned, but I wasn't sure what she meant or if I cared.

I smiled, that dark thing in the core of me raising its head and snapping its bloodthirsty maw, ready to be sated. "I accept your challenge, North," I growled. "And vow to make you regret it."

Murmurs rippled throughout the crowd.

Crest grabbed my arm as I started toward the challenger. I didn't want him to intervene and weaken me before his people. How would they ever follow my instruction if I didn't deserve to teach them?

But my lacuna didn't offer to fight him on my behalf or tell me I shouldn't face the behemoth. He placed an encouraging kiss on my lips, and when he pulled away, a dangerous glint gleamed in his blues. "I'll enjoy watching you keep your promise to him, lacuna." Then he walked to the other side of the circle to stand with Breaker, crossing his arms over his chest.

Magma fussed. Loudly. Telling Breaker and everyone around her how ridiculous and epically foolish this was – on *my* part, of course. She cited the differences in our sizes as the primary reason this match shouldn't be allowed, but she held out a wet cloth for me to wipe the blood away from my jaw and throat. "It won't help much. You need it stitched."

"Magma." I tugged down my breastplate and accepted the cloth she offered. She narrowed her eyes at me. "I fought men much larger than him to get to the top rank. They each fell at my feet and so will North."

My opponent chuckled, confident I'd never be able to accomplish such a feat. I wanted to not only win, but make him pay for every vile word he'd uttered to me. Besides that, I wanted to do it so quickly he wouldn't know what happened until he was on his back, staring at the sky. I vowed to claim victory decisively so he couldn't claim I hadn't earned it.

Wade cupped his hands. "Elira!" I looked at him, wondering what he might want. "Don't lose! Magma and I just made a new bet since she lost the last one. She's a glutton for punishment, it seems."

The Salt began to walk a slow circle just inside the ring of Kehlanians poised to quietly watch the second sparring match.

I nodded to acknowledge Wade's request as North shook his head, still smiling menacingly. I looked at the giant. "The challenger chooses the weapon – if you *need* one."

"You want to go fist to fist with me?" he scoffed.

I shrugged a shoulder. "The choice is yours."

North's gills flared. He clapped his hands. "Let's do it."

He tied his long, sable hair at his nape, the twin tattooed bands around his biceps distorting with the flexion of his muscles. His indigo scales seemed to absorb the light as he approached. The deep green sarong at his hip flapped in the breeze that swirled protectively around me though I had never called for it to…

My wings flared and he marked them as targets.

He began to circle, his steps pressing heavily into the wet sand. "Crest saved you before our last fight could begin, but he won't step into this ring for you, lacuna or not."

"Things are different now," I answered with a steely glare. "And I don't need my lacuna to preserve me. I'm healed and whole."

"For now," he mused.

Then he did what all behemoths do in battle. He threw the weight of his massive body behind the first punch, leaning into it. And I moved like lightning and struck him just as fast, planting one foot on his thigh and grabbing his beard, using my momentum to swing onto his back. My arm locked around his throat and I held tight.

North tried to gasp.

Began to choke.

I tightened my hold further and watched as the skin of his temples and cheeks mottled.

His meaty fingers turned white, digging at my forearms.

Nails dragged burning gouges through my skin.

He tried to pry my fist away, but I held it with the other in a grip I wasn't sure would hold. North was stronger than anyone I'd faced. I would give him that much.

North began to look for another way out. He tried to throw himself backward, but I unwrapped my legs from around his waist and braced against the ground so he couldn't. He scrambled, spun, flailed, and bucked, trying to free himself until all his energy – like his oxygen – was gone. His hands slowly fell to dangle at his side and he swayed on his knees, then fell sideways. Still, I held on.

"She's killing him!" Nori yelled. "Someone stop her!"

A few Guardians surged forward to help their fallen friend but Crest interceded, looking at me to be sure.

"I'm not," I gritted. "I'm not killing him." When North finally sank into unconsciousness, I released his neck and pushed his body over to free the leg and feathers he'd trapped beneath his weight. Then I stood. "He'll wake soon," I told the crowd, my chest swelling and crashing. *With a massive headache...* I didn't add.

Magma rushed to his side, cursing me soundly for depriving him of air.

"You'd rather he chose weapons? The short-handled tridents, perhaps?" I joked.

She skewered me with a glare. "That cut on your jaw needs mending. It's still leaking. And if we don't cover all your spilled blood, it'll serve as a.... a formal invitation for your kind to descend to drag you out of our clutches and back into the sky where you belong."

Ouch. I tried not to let her see how her words cut me but apparently, I didn't school my arched brows fast enough.

Magma sighed. "Elira –"

I looked away.

"I didn't mean –"

Yes, she did. She meant every word. If anger had one trait that could be counted on, it was its tendency to be brutally honest.

"It's fine," I told her. "And so is my jaw." To everyone gathered, I announced, "If Empyrean Warriors' feet touch the shore, don't hold back. Nothing is off-limits. Kick their most sensitive parts. Blind them with a handful of sand. Cut the tendons on the backs of their heels. Slice their wrists. Jab into the sides of their necks. Sever the place where their wings attach to their backs. Screech into their ears. Bite and claw. Do whatever you must to win, because you cannot afford to lose. If you're not the victor, you're dead."

The Salt stopped before North, staring down at him with a strangely intense expression on her lovely face. The hair on my arms stood on end. I slowly gravitated toward them, my back severing the crowd's view of their fallen friend.

North roused, blinking heavily. "What happened?" he asked groggily, lifting his head off the sand.

I glanced over him to see what she was looking at so intently. My lips parted as I crouched beside him, furrowing my brow. "Magma… what's wrong with his neck?"

Magma knelt beside him. Her delicate fingers tracked a broad purple bruise already deepening, in the exact shape of my forearm. "Courtesy of you," she snipped.

I shook my head. "I've never left a mark like that after a hold of submission."

"I don't feel so well, Magma," North muttered through dry, blanched lips.

"This isn't from the match," I told her, looking up at The Salt.

The Seer met North's eyes and quietly spoke. "I warned you. Talay warned you. And you refused to listen. You brought this upon yourself."

What had he done to invoke such anger from Talay and The Salt, whom I'd never witnessed be anything but kind and fair?

As North's mind cleared and they saw that he would survive the skirmish, Breaker reminded everyone of the many things to be done today. People began to trickle – either back inland, or into the sea – to their posts, relieving others who required rest.

Koa sauntered up, jutting his chin at North who finally sat up. Despite his beard, I could see that the hue of the bruise on North's throat had deepened even further.

"Would you have done that to me?" Koa asked.

"I would have done far worse," I answered with a straight face because I enjoyed watching him squirm. And he did.

His head ticked back, brows kissing. "What would you have done, Elira?"

I just shook my head and smirked at him.

"Elira?" he prodded.

Wade whistled and waved me over. "Well done!" he chirped.

"Thanks." I kept my eye on North. I didn't trust him not to let out a roar and try to tackle me to the ground to resume what he'd started and I clearly finished. But I wasn't sure he was in any shape to come at me again. Something was wrong with his pallor. Like his lips, the rest of his skin was far too pale. He was clammy and kept wiping the sweat from his brow with the back of his arm.

"What's wrong with him?" Wade asked, pushing himself up to stand beside me.

Inwardly, I applauded. He was already far stronger. I studied North. I'd never seen anyone fall so suddenly ill. "The bigger they are, the harder they fall," I mused. "I'm sure he'll be fine. Magma is already tending to him."

"You didn't poison him or anything, right?" Wade asked with a laugh I wasn't sure was genuine.

"Poison and I have a sordid history. I would be far more likely to accidentally poison myself in the process."

"But you didn't poison yourself, right? Someone stabbed you," he asked, now suspicious.

I met his eyes unflinchingly. "Koa, my fourth thrust a sky fire-laced arrow into my side because she failed me in the last mission and knew I would remove her from my quad when we returned. She stood to lose her ranking and reputation in one fell swoop and knew I would deliver the cutting blow."

Wade winced. "That's quite a motive for murder."

Nori helped North stand while Magma insisted he go to her tent right away.

Wade twisted around me to look at Breaker hovering nearby with The Shark. "Where's Katalini?" Wade asked, craning his neck to peer over the ebbing crowd. "Did I miss her?"

Breaker's brows rose and he scratched his head. "No, she wasn't feeling well, so she walked home."

"She's not bruising like North, is she?" I casually asked, although I already knew the cause of her queasiness.

He shifted his weight uncomfortably. "No, nothing like that. Her stomach is just upset."

I smiled. "Magma has a tea for that. It's wonderful."

"Thank you," he gritted. "I'll have to stop and get some on my way back to my lacuna." Breaker looked at Crest. "I want you to go with Grandmother and North. Something's not right."

I didn't miss the way his eyes flicked to me, his expression guarded.

"I didn't cause this, Breaker, and if you want to know what did, I suggest you consult your Seer instead of your mender."

His mouth gaped. "What do you know?"

I shook my head. "Talk to The Salt. I'm not qualified to speak on her behalf, or Talay's."

Crest looked uneasily at the sky. "He's one of our strongest. We can't afford to lose him now."

Breaker asked Crest to go with him to speak to The Salt. Crest was about to press a kiss to my temple when North's strength failed him and he collapsed into the dunes. The brothers ran to help him, then guided him up the path that threaded through the dunes toward Magma's workshop.

Frey waited for me on the shore. I hadn't seen her unique hair color among the throng because it was braided tightly to her head. "You fought well," she said. "And your friend, your sister – whatever she is – is a fool."

I tried to laugh. "Thanks."

She looked away, pinching her lips.

"Do you want to ask me something?"

She sighed. "I hate to bother you, but I need help with the younglings. Many are progressing, but I want to know they can defend themselves or their younger siblings and right now, I'm not confident they can."

I nodded. "Of course I'll help them."

"You should change and clean the blood off your skin or you'll scare them," she gently suggested.

I looked down at the bright blood swirled with sandy grit. She was right. I nodded. "Right. I'll meet you as soon as I bathe."

CHAPTER TWENTY-TWO

After the sparring match, time seemed to freefall.

Over the next few days, each one passing faster than the last, North's bruising faded from the deepest plum to a tangle of mottled yellow and green. His pallor remained ashen, and he oscillated between chilled and uncomfortably hot. Magma managed his symptoms as best she could, but she now knew that North's malady was inflicted not by me, but by the god of the sea. Whenever he caught sight of me, the hatred he held flared into an inferno… and his condition worsened.

I stayed away as much as I could. Not for his sake, but for Magma's.

My days were spent with Frey teaching younglings to shoot, then working to finish Wade's wooden leg and trying to do anything and everything I could think of to jog my soul's memory. If there was an advantage to be had, any means of defending myself against Neera or a way to keep her from touching or unmaking my soul, I needed to find it – quickly.

Time wasn't the only thing fading like the mark upon the back of my cowrie. My hope faded, too. I still remembered nothing. I'd tried and couldn't recall even a simple, single memory from a previous life I'd led.

Dread and desperation permeated my thoughts.

But there were also moments of pure joy.

I found it in the darkest hours when the stars and moon cast the softest, pale light over Kehlani. Where the busyness of the day faded, and laughter emanated from the families living and loving one another in the nearest tents that sat along the edge of the village. Where sometimes, the Great Wind carried the sound of song to me and Crest.

We held one another and swayed back and forth, discussing our days and the progress being made at a pace neither of us thought possible. Discussing what to do next, always looking forward, but not too far… I pushed the future only The Salt and I knew of away from him and made sure that like Neera, it was trapped. At least for now.

My nights were spent with Crest. Wrapped in his arms, lying in his hammock, and in his confidence as much as I could allow. As we prepared for the onslaught The Salt had foreseen, our duties took us in different directions like delicate, floating seeds scattered in the Great Wind's turbulent air. He stayed busy, working to guide the Guardians, helping Magma draw toxin from the sky fire plant, and gathering honeycombs with Koa to render into wax. Not to mention the times when he entered the sea to do as Talay commanded beneath its sapphire surface.

Crest had left at daybreak to find Breaker and brief him on the Guardians' progress. On his way, he was doing a favor for me in asking The Salt to meet me at Magma's tent, North be damned. She'd crafted something for Wade's now-finished leg. It was time to give it to him and hold him to his word to use it. To strengthen himself and never stop.

In the vow Wade made to me, that on its surface seemed so simple at the time, he'd promised to walk again. I hoped I had time to witness his first steps like I did the first time he stood with help, then on his own.

I'd imagined him using his carved leg to walk along the shore, humming as he stepped. Even if his gait was altered and stiff, the lilt of his voice would flow fluidly, maybe even happily.

I didn't know why I felt so strongly about helping Wade, given our difficult introduction. Maybe it was simple atonement. Given all I'd done to hurt Talay's people, carving this for Wade was the least I could do. Or perhaps the truth was more complicated and in him, I saw my own strengths and weaknesses, the struggles of the will of the soul and the ability that lay in the hope of overcoming them.

In Wade's chest, the heart of a Warrior beat, even if he'd forgotten it. He just needed something to remind him who he was and what he could do if he put his will into every effort.

I hesitated outside Magma's tent, adjusting the bow on my shoulder. After the fight, she'd made her feelings about me very clear. According to her, I didn't belong among her people or on this land.

Beyond the hurt she'd caused, I didn't look forward to seeing North.

Pushing inside with the leg hidden behind my back, I was surprised to see Wade sitting alone at the counter, pressing the succulent leaves of a sky fire plant between two rollers. The pressure pushed the deadly liquid into a small bowl beneath the press.

"Elira!" he said, equally surprised to see me.

"Where are Magma and North?"

"North is at his home and Magma will be back any time now."

I took the leg out from behind me.

He looked at what I held and his eyes narrowed. The leg suddenly felt heavier. "What's this? Some sort of joke?" he said shortly.

"Hardly," I scoffed. "I wouldn't have spent my time carving such an intricate trick, Wade. It's your new leg."

He cleared his throat and stared at the wooden appendage in my hands. "I don't understand."

The Salt ducked inside. She greeted both of us and moved toward Wade with what was effectively part tourniquet, part sturdy leather corset for his leg. Where the wood met his skin, he could wrap and lace the leather, tightly binding it to keep the two together. It was the best we could do for now.

I hoped in time, he or someone else might find a better way.

The Salt asked Wade to wash his hands and to refrain from touching me even after he'd done so. He hesitantly scrubbed over a basin, using a small bar of Magma's coconut soap. The fresh scent filled the humid air.

He seemed upset. Quiet. His back muscles were tense as he washed, but he did as she asked.

Maybe I should've told him what I was doing instead of surprising him with it, but if I'd spoiled the surprise, he might have asked me to stop carving it and denied the possibility of walking again, clinging to the lies weakness would gladly whisper in his ear.

Wade thoroughly dried his hands on a cloth and turned on the stool to face us.

The Salt's eyes met mine and her lips tipped up encouragingly.

I brought the leg to Wade.

He held it to the place where his thigh now ended. "It… how?"

"Magma measured your leg for me," I told him.

"I never imagined it was for something like this…" he said awkwardly.

The Salt brought her offering. She instructed Wade to hold the leather in place behind as she laced it, making it as tight as she possibly could. The wood was stiff and straight, but if he could learn to use the other men as crutches, he could learn to stand with this, then learn to step.

I offered him a hand.

He started to take it when The Salt hissed, "No! Don't touch her after handling sky fire."

Wade winced, pulling away while apologizing.

"I doubt it would hurt me now that you've washed your hands," I argued.

The Salt chided, "Poison can linger. It's not wise to take the risk." She held out her hand to help him up, but he shook his head.

"Let me try to do it on my own."

And he did.

Wade stood, bearing weight on only his natural leg at first. Then, he found a balance with the other and smiled. He took a tentative step, smiling broader when The Salt's stiff thigh corset held.

He took another, then another. And while he moved gingerly and cautiously, his eyes caught with purpose and I knew he wouldn't stop now. If something happened to this leg, he would make another.

He would walk.

He would live again. Not the simple repetition of inhaling and exhaling, of steady heartbeats and drifting streams of thought and consciousness, but of action. Of doing what he'd dreamed of, what he dared.

Wade stared at the wooden leg and compared it with his natural one. It wasn't a perfect match, but it was close enough that the flaws didn't matter. He pinched the corners of his eyes. His shoulders shook as he silently cried.

Magma came home then, of course. She took one look and asked Wade what was wrong. When he took a step, two, three toward her, she cried out in awe and caught the hug he wrapped her in.

"You did it!" she said to me over his shoulder, her eyes shining.

"I can't believe you didn't tell me what she was up to!" he scolded Magma. She smiled and told him she was just helping me. He stood up straighter. "Thank you, Elira. This… this makes me feel a lot less broken."

I inclined my head, choking on the emotion clogging my throat. Magma met my eye, an apology lingering there. I wasn't about to stay around to hear her speak words she didn't feel or mean. Instead, I hooked a thumb toward the door. "I should go."

The Salt ducked outside with me and both of us stopped short. The sky that had rippled with gentle clouds earlier had turned dark. In the distance there was a small cloud, constantly flickering.

"Empyrea," I breathed. I watched to see if the flashing moved. When it didn't, despite the clouds pushing in front of, behind and around it, I knew what it was. "It's a perch. Someone is watching." I scanned the sky for other perches and found none.

Whomever watched the Isle had come alone. I couldn't help but wonder if it was Soraya, back to scour the sand for us again. Or maybe it was Talon, playing one of his sick games.

I hurried back inside Magma's tent and grabbed a folded blanket from the foot of Wade's cot. Magma hurried outside as I wrapped the blanket around my shoulders, tugging it up and over my pale hair. With my chin, I pointed out the perch to her.

The Salt tapped her throat when Wade limped out and joined us. He let out an ear-gouging screech of warning.

Soon, others echoed the sound. They now saw it, too.

"Is this it?" Wade asked. "Have they finally come?"

I shook my head. "No. But they're getting ready."

When I'd been tasked with capturing The Shark, I commanded all the quads to assist with surveillance. Things since I fell had shifted and changed so drastically between our people and theirs, the information gathered then was no longer good.

"You'll have to be very careful to cover your wings from now on, Elira," The Salt said absently. She turned to face me. "Will you come to my tent? I'd like to consult the shells."

"Of course."

It was morbidly painful to step inside The Salt's tent; the shells still mimicked the reverberation of my dying heart. Clack...........click

Clack............click

My grip tightened on Magma's blanket at the sound. The Seer noticed.

"Why won't Talay make them stop?" I asked. How could she stand to step inside her own tent right now? How did she sleep?

"The cadence is a gift to me, from him. I requested it because I cannot see beyond the clouds," she said, her lashes fluttering as if upset. "Your shell has faded, so I begged him for a way to know whether you were alive."

"The pattern is completely gone?"

She nodded and my heart sank. The threaded shells mocked my very alive, healthily beating heart. If my past was recorded in the barbs of my feather, my future now echoed through the cowries of Talay's dead.

It didn't make sense. I wasn't gone from her sight – yet. Did this mean the time had nearly come for me to rise and fight? "I'm not above the clouds, though. You can see that I live."

She threw her heavy braids over her shoulder and moved across the room to her table. The impending storm ushered in stronger currents of wind that pulled and pushed against her tent wall, making it seem like the lung of a gargantuan beast that swelled with breath, only to contract and force it away.

"Will you sit with me?"

I blinked from my tumultuous thoughts and moved toward her.

With Magma's blanket folded over my lap, I settled, once more, across from The Salt. This time felt as ominous as the first time I'd been invited to watch her read the shells. I wondered if it would be my last.

She upended the bowl of cowries. They clattered against the wood and each other, but the shells didn't move. Didn't scrape across the tabletop to form any specific pattern. It was as if they were dead. Then, like the cowries of Talay's souls strung above us, they began to thump.

"Why?" was all I could croak. This was maddening. It was cruel. Something Neera would do to torture someone who'd angered her. Was Talay as terrible as she? Was I just now seeing his true nature, not hidden in the depths, but evident on land where the sun could illuminate its gilded form? "Is this about North?" I demanded.

"Of course not," the Seer breathed. "North's punishment has nothing to do with this. This is a gift, like I told you."

"It doesn't feel like one," I snapped. It felt terrible.

Just then, The Salt slumped in her chair with her chin on her chest, her arms limp against her sides. She began to fall sideways and I rushed to her, catching her halfway to the ground and guiding her back into the chair, wondering what had happened and how I could help her.

The Seer suddenly gasped and sat up straight. Wide-eyed, she looked around the room as if she'd never seen it. Her eyes snagged on the table, the strung, thumping shells suspended in the tent's top, at me still holding her upright…

With her forearm, she angrily swiped all the shells from the table.

I slowly stood up the moment I felt *her*. The very air began to writhe and crackle. A familiar scent filled the air. My stomach tightened, my wings flaring instinctively.

In Neera's sanctum on Intention Day, a small bundle of sage was lit and burnt until the entire wad of bound leaves was reduced to ash. Beyond the grove, nearest to West Village, the rich soil that gave life to the fruit-bearing trees abruptly surrendered to thin rock and gritty sand. There was a single knoll with scrubby grasses and white sage bushes. That was where the fastest flyer among the Gatherers dove to collect a handful of the aromatic leaves.

The Salt's dark eyes had been transformed. A deep hue of angry amethyst seeped into her pupils.

"Oracle?" I gave a sharp inhale as I sensed her presence beneath the suffocating blanket of the goddess. "How are you here?"

Her eyes narrowed.

"How are you here?" I slowly repeated.

No answer. Only a skin-crawling stare.

"What do you want?" I challenged. She wasn't welcome here. Not in The Salt's body, and certainly not in her home.

"Return to Empyrean." The voice speaking to me did not belong to The Salt. Nor did it belong to the newly installed Oracle. But I recognized it all the same.

It was the voice of the goddess. Neera was speaking to me through her conduit, using the power she could cast like a fishing line through the airy strips that bound her to try to intimidate me. Assuming she was still bound…

The shells overhead began clacking together so violently they chipped, the broken pieces raining down on our heads. If The Salt was aware of what was happening, she didn't indicate it. Didn't bellow out for the loss of what represented so much to her. She knew each of those souls and had been a part of every life.

The shadows in the room grew and shifted. The Great Wind gusted punishingly against the tent. Its flaps rapped like pennants. The strands of shells clattered and tangled as the drafts threatened to tear them apart and scatter the shells of the dead among those of the living now littering the floor.

"Get out," I told her.

"Return to Empyrean and face me."

I glowered. "You're not *in* Empyrean. You're stuck in the cage I built for you."

She smiled far wider than The Salt ever had. Unnaturally so. "Am I?"

Could she be free? Had she managed to escape? I never knew she could use her conduit this way. She'd never spoken through her or taken over Talay's Seer like this. Now that I thought about it, she felt closer, her power more vital, than ever before.

"If you do not come to me, I will come to you and when I reach the Isle, I will rend that wretched swath of rock and sand and kill every soul on it!" Neera seethed.

Every *soul.* Not every*one.*

I couldn't let her know how my ribs tightened as if bracing against the blow of her threat.

"Get out," I slowly and deliberately repeated.

She hissed through The Salt's teeth. "And so you've made your choice."

The Salt's body went slack and she collapsed in a heap, her momentum carrying her off the chair's bottom. I caught her head before it struck the sandy floor. "Salt?"

Her eyes were still purple when they blinked up at me but no longer amethyst; they were the lavender shade I knew. "They're coming, Elira," the Oracle croaked.

"When?"

The Salt's face screwed up like she was in pain, followed by a deep sigh from the Seer's chest.

"Magma!" I shrilled. I didn't know where she was or if she could hear me from here. Her tent wasn't far, but I couldn't leave The Salt like this. Not like this. "Magma!" I cried louder. No one came. No one heard me. "*Magma!*" I yelled.

Then I saw The Salt's conch shell and scrambled across floor and cowrie to reach it where it sat on the wooden chest. The sound I produced wasn't as smooth as The Salt's, but it *was* loud. Not only did Magma come, but Crest also answered, recognizing the falter of her call.

"What happened, girl?" Magma cried, rushing across the floor to help The Salt.

"She fainted, I think," I told her.

Breaker and Katalini entered the tent, then stopped short. Koa and Frey bumped into their backs when they rushed inside.

"The shells…" Katalini whispered. She knelt and began to pick them up, tenderly gathering them into her sarong. Frey, her chest heaving from where she'd no doubt just run here, began to help her, watching me closely.

With the pads of her thumbs, Magma gently eased open The Salt's eyelids. I was terrified at what she might see, but the Seer's pupils were deep brown again.

I pressed a palm to my chest, willing my heart to calm.

Magma barked at Crest to get the sweet wood. He ran out, returning just as quickly with a smoking stick of split wood no longer than his finger. He handed it to his grandmother, who waved it under the unconscious Seer's nose.

A few breaths and The Salt began to blink, groggily waking. The first thing she noticed were the snarled strands of shattered cowries tightly clinging to her ceiling. She lifted her hands and stared at the shards of broken shells clinging to her palms. Watched as a few fell away.

She noticed Magma, Crest, Breaker…While The Salt took in the cowries of the living scattered over her sandy floor, Frey and Katalini paused their cleaning.

The Seer's breaths turned ragged and panicked as she clutched the shells draped over her chest. Her bewildered stare sharpened, then snapped to me.

CHAPTER TWENTY-THREE

The hair on the back of my neck rose when I felt the staticky buzz of lightning in the distance, followed by a deep rumble of thunder that rippled over the sky. Another bolt. Another rumble, this time closer.

Closer…

The charge in the air felt different. Deadly.

After using The Salt's horn to call for Magma, I should have run outside and flown straight to Empyrean like the goddess demanded. Was it truly a storm I felt, or had the goddess somehow broken free and charged forth to honor the vow of rending Kehlani and every soul on it?

My chest began to burn, then ache. With the heel of my palm, I rubbed the scar she'd given me, knowing that like the shells overhead echoing my heart's every throb despite their brokenness, my mark reflected the goddess's fiery temper.

Every fork and flicker flashed across the intricate mark, lighting my lacuna's face and the space in which we stood, which darkened more and more as the oncoming storm drew nearer.

With each flash, Neera was punctuating her threat. She would burn The Salt's home down trying to lash me with her fire.

"Elira?" Crest questioned, his thumbs lovingly rubbing up and down my biceps.

He couldn't help me now, but I could keep him safe… I'd done it before by drawing the goddess's bolt away from him.

Time slowed and the noises surrounding me amplified tenfold in my ears. From the snarled lines of the shells' frantic clacks to the tiny pieces breaking away to litter The Salt's sand floor. From the wind that threatened to rip the structure from the soil to the harried breaths rushing from every chest in this tent.

"Stay inside the tent, no matter what you see or hear," I told them. "Do *not* follow me."

I tore myself from him, but Crest's blue gaze tracked me as I fled.

He didn't heed my warning. He left the others – his family – and followed me to the shore where he was most vulnerable. The wind roared between us, pushing against him so hard he strained to keep his footing.

"You have to go back!" I shouted, pointing to the barely visible tip of The Salt's tent.

He held my stare unwaveringly. "No."

Sand stung our skin. I noticed the Empyrea perch was gone. None of my people could withstand this wind. Whoever had been watching now sought shelter.

Gusts tore at our hair, clothes, our souls.

Despite me tucking them tightly against my back, the weakest of my wing feathers were being tugged from where they were attached to bone and skin alike. They scattered in the ribbons of wind tightening around us. Lightning cracked offshore a moment before thunder shook the ground beneath our feet.

"It's not safe for you here!" I tried, hoping he would see reason.

The first splatters of rain pelted our skin and soaked into our hair. We welcomed the sting.

"It's not safe for you either," he countered.

A torrent unleashed atop us. Rain doused our hair and clothes. Water sluiced from my lips.

"You don't understand –" I tried to explain.

"I do!" he barked. "I know the risk, but I *will not* leave you to face her alone, Elira."

"And *I* won't let you die!" I screamed.

The deluge faded as suddenly as it began, but the air turned unseasonably cold. My teeth chattered so violently, I wondered if they might chip like the Seer's shells. Dark clouds that rippled with energy and expended it in bolts settled over us and began to rotate.

The muscle in Crest's jaw ticked as he watched the sky goddess's power unfurl. And it did. I felt her anger in the looming bolt. Felt it start downward, its sizzling, forked tongue darting toward us.

The hair on my arms rose. The burst of power harbored Neera's intention, and though she didn't breathe it to life with words and place it into the pans of her bronze scale, I *felt* her malicious goal all the way to my marrow.

She wouldn't target *me* this time… She wanted to be rid of *him*.

He tethered me here. Without him in the way, she thought I would comply with her demands. But did she know that if she took him, I would destroy her?

Crest read the sky and looked at me, his eyes flicking down to my glowing scar. The muscle in his jaw feathered with resolve and bravery and a thousand other things I admired but hated in that moment, because I knew what he planned to do. His tattoo stared back at me – the circle of feathers, braced by a pattern of shields and teeth. He planned to shield me and take the strike so I didn't have to again.

Crest was willing to die for me.

But I couldn't let him.

I wheeled around quickly so my back was to his chest, my wings flaring protectively. As light burst around us, I thrust backward, knocking him to the ground and planting my feet solidly on his chest. And when Neera's bolt was within reach, I curled my fingers around its thick pulse and ripped it from the sky.

My heart, not the lightning, thundered.

I'd torn away a sword of *true* sky fire, not some noxious plant pushed from the soil by the bitter goddess mine had slain. This sword was an inferno of raging energy just as deadly as those she forced from the clouds – but not to me.

I smiled when I felt her appalled worry in the twitching sword I held. Jorun had told me what the first soul was capable of, but I'd taken the bolt not because I wondered if I could, but because I *knew* it.

Finally, something in my soul remembered what it was like to battle Neera face-to-face.

Standing between the sky and sea with my feet planted on the chest of my lacuna, a memory finally, finally surfaced.

I flew through a gale, pushing through torrents of frigid, driving rain. Feathers and delicate wing bones snapped from the wind swelling and crashing over me, as heavy as a thunderous wave and just as unpredictable. But I couldn't stop. Didn't dare falter.

My arm, encased in stained-blue leather, stretched out before me. My hand gripped a sword of lightning.

Teeth bared, I raised it, luxuriating in the familiar burn of my shoulder muscles as I brought it down in an arc to cut down the one before me…

Neera.

The mighty goddess, with thrashing strands of hair that were the deep indigo of midnight. They reminded me of the ponderously suckered arms of Colossus and the lesser kraken over which he lorded.

"You choose to defend him?" she said of Talay, her thunderous voice raw with emotion.

I gritted my teeth as she thrust another powerful stream of wind toward me, bent on tearing me apart with the very thing I planned to cage her with. But I couldn't afford to use even a sliver to form a shield with which to defend myself. I needed every wisp of energy, or this would not work.

Half of the wind was hers to command; the other half was mine.

Bequeathed by the scale she always sought to please, to level our might the way she had intended when she formed my soul to equal hers…

Neera had crafted the rules to her own game without realizing she would lose her power over me when they were applied. She was a fool to use the apparatus to balance us. Now, she was beholden to its appraisal and its demands.

Always even. Always equal. Always true.

She couldn't kill me in her goddess form. When she attempted it, the scale intervened on my behalf, observing the obvious unfairness in such a match. It did not elevate me to her enormity, but instead diminished her, abasing Neera so that she was proportionate and the battle waged would be an honorable one.

She was no larger than I was in the flesh into which the weighty scale forced her soul, but her natural attributes lingered, even if lessened. Her broad, golden wings flapped heavily behind her, fanning out in a glorious display of dominance and aggression.

Like her wings, her pupils and armor were gilded in a shade the exact warm yellow of the last rays of a brilliant sunset. They gleamed despite the gloom.

"You belong to me!" she asserted. "I made you."

"Yes, you did." My meaning was not lost on her. She did this to herself. Her ruthless hatred had honed me into a weapon that wouldn't be used to further her goals, but rather to destroy them.

She'd crafted me from nothing, then assumed that my heart would reflect hers. That her greed would become my goal. That her intentions would become my vows to fulfill. That her commands would become my duties. And that her enemies would fall at the end of my sword.

She never thought I would defy her or attempt to defend what was right. She never imagined I would defend her enemy instead. Or that I would become one of them.

Talay didn't deserve to be butchered like Tella had been. And Neera did not deserve dominion over the entirety of the earth.

Neera, too, brandished a lightning sword, twirling it like it was nothing but a youngling's carved baton. But she did not wield it like a toy. She brought it down with such force, the blow rattled my teeth. The ensuing sound of the two bolts clashing drove all sound from the world except for a high-pitched, incessant squeal.

Something warm and wet slid from both my ringing ears when we broke apart and I circled around, pretending to take up a better position.

She grew more confident every time I retreated to regain some footing against her. Not that I'd lost it to begin with. I only wanted her to think I was questioning my ability to reign victorious.

The scale, I'd finally realized after too many battles, would never let either *of us win.*

So, I shifted my focus. I didn't need *to kill Neera or exhaust myself trying. I only had to balance the pans – to draw her away from Empyrean, and then use my portion of the wind to keep her there…*

Above the woeful, worried waves, with broken, bone-tired wings, I drew her into the far reaches of her kingdom to a place where she could do the least harm. Then, I gathered my half of the wind and with it, formed a wall.

As she fought to break free, I left her there, vowing never to use the power of the wind again. Even drawing a gust from the streams of air that held her might weaken the transparent welds of her cage. A tiny fissure could allow her to break free – in one way or another.

The pans were made to serve their creator, even if she regretted tasking them with finding true impartiality. They honored their purpose and so did I. Neither of us would help Neera ruin everything in and under the sky.

Pressure on my ankle.

I looked down to see The Shark's hands gripping the joint. I stood on Crest's chest, the only thing separating our skin was the wet grains of sand my bare feet pressed between us.

"Elira…" he breathed. Wide-eyed, he stared at my hand – or rather, at the lightning bolt I gripped in it.

Flapping my wings, I flew backward, holding it up and away from him so I didn't accidentally touch his skin with it.

He sat up, his abs rippling as he stood. Crusted, damp sand fell in clumps from his skin.

Breaker rushed from the dunes to make sure his brother was unharmed. Koa and Frey jogged down next. This was The Shark's quad, ready to protect him and the people of the Isle at all costs. The four regarded me warily, as speechless as I felt.

The thunderbolt twitched with power, shifting with sharp angles.

What should I do with it? Hurl it into the sea? Lob it back into the sky?

"Elira!"

Aderyn raced up the shore, her soles swiftly devouring the distance between us. Jorun was on her heels, his arm unbound. She was the last person I wanted to see. I couldn't understand why she was running to me like she would fly if wings still graced her back.

The two ground to a stop a few feet away. She coughed, wiped the sweat from her brow, and dragged an errant strand of dark hair off her cheek. White light from the thunderbolt reflected in her dark eyes.

"Why are you here?" I demanded.

"Because I've seen you do this once before."

I ticked my head back, shocked.

"Do you remember the strike?"

The strike. The moment that changed my life.

"Of course I do."

Fateful moments were impossible to forget, as was the crippling fear that settled in immediately after they passed and refused to leave even though it lessened.

More numerous than the grains of sand under my feet were the times I'd flown terrified of the sky after that, as well as the countless instances I had to pretend to be unaffected and unafraid for fear of someone taking advantage of that emotion and usurping me.

She looked up as if she could see the memory embedded in the blue. "We were flying and everything was so serene, and then I saw this incredible flash. I was blinded for a moment, but when my vision returned, I saw you. The bolt stretched from the sky and pierced your chest, stabbing completely through you and darting into the sea. The lightning should have stopped when it hit you, but instead, Neera ran you through."

Aderyn added shakily, "Time stopped, Elira. You were inexplicably suspended. You didn't fall and your wings didn't flap for many heartbeats. I flew fast to reach you, wondering what I could possibly do to help, knowing I would barrel into that fire if it meant freeing you from it."

I swallowed, remembering what it was like to save Koa in the same way.

"When I got close enough, I could see your hands. They – *you* – were what held the bolt in place, Elira. Not the goddess. She struck you, but the bolt didn't hurt you at all. You gripped the lightning like it was nothing more than the hilt of your sword, then you released it and Neera retracted her power. That's when you plummeted. Your wings, arms, legs, and even your head hung limply from your body…I thought you were dead."

A remnant of the terror she felt haunted her expression.

I looked at the power that burned in my fist. "I remember the flash of white light, the feeling of the energy coursing through me, the malice that fed it, and… I remember falling afterward. But I don't recall touching it, let alone taking hold of it."

"You did, though," Aderyn insisted. "You studied it the way you did a target."

"Because it *was* a target. I just didn't realize it yet." But my soul knew.

She took a calmer, steadying breath. "I reached you just as your wings woke."

I remembered her being there, diving and reaching out to grab me, almost close enough to. She pointed to my brilliant scar. "Your mark glowed like it is right now – so bright, the forked streaks were all I could see for hours."

I nodded, remembering. "You gave me your leather coat and flew home in your undershirt. You were nearly frozen by the time we reached the nest. You needed the healers and refused them."

Aderyn swallowed thickly. "As if I could have explained my condition. Sannika would've lashed us both if she learned I'd flown without leathers. We argued until I thawed out and your scar's light faded, leaving only the impression on your skin."

"Shocking that the two of *you* bickered like that," Koa quietly quipped.

I gave him an annoyed look, then turned back to Aderyn. "We were nearly lashed anyway for not telling her I'd been struck. The only thing that kept her anger at bay was the mark itself. She feared angering Neera."

The Salt graced the shore, walking through thick sand to the tide line where her footprints' impressions formed a small trail that led straight to me and Aderyn.

"You wonder what you should do with the bolt? Neera's fire can't hurt you. The scale won't allow it. Do with the bolt as you will," the Seer encouraged.

I tipped the jerking bolt and pushed its fiery point into my chest, trusting Aderyn and my instinct and ignoring Crest's concerned hiss. I fed it into the scar inch by inch, sheathing it in my heart.

Aderyn and Jorun, Breaker and Crest, and Koa and Frey watched, horrified as my scar went cold.

But the bolt seated inside me was the least of my worries. Pressing a hand to my ribs, I fought to keep calm even as a cold breeze ruffled my hair tauntingly, reminding me of the critical error I now knew I'd made.

When Koa was caught up in the funnel and I was trying to save him and protect my wings, I'd dragged part of the wind away from Neera's restraints, weakening the bands that surrounded her.

"I remember something," I quietly whispered to the Seer of the Sea.

Her dark eyes widened, and she ordered everyone on the sand to leave it.

When Crest protested, she wheeled to face him. Whatever he saw there made him go quiet. Still, he refused to leave me. I saw the dogged determination set on his brow.

"Crest, I need just a few moments with her."

The mark – my sigil – on his chest heaved. He didn't want to go.

Did he see what his grandmother had already noticed? The flight in my eyes?

"You can wait for her in my tent," The Salt told him.

Breaker patted his back and tried to steer him toward the pathway slithering between the dunes. Just as Crest didn't want to leave me, Koa and Frey hovered, waiting for The Shark. Jorun tried to coax Aderyn away, too, but like Crest, her feet were planted and would not budge.

Koa cursed as birds in every size and color flapped frantically into the sky, pouring from the Green Mountains just before the range began to rumble.

"Get my shell horn!" The Salt shouted to the Guardians. Breaker, Crest, Koa, and Frey raced ahead, desperate to help the Seer and warn their people. I flanked The Salt as she raced to her tent.

The reverberation slowly spread over the range until the foothills trembled. This was different than the quake before. There was no question where this one originated.

The timbers of the Seer's tent groaned as Crest exited, loudly blowing on the shell horn. The sand under our feet jolted. He blew another long note before racing toward the nearest village, sounding the alarm again and again.

The quake intensified until we were jerked from side to side, struggling to stay balanced. My wings spread wide, the instinct to flee flaring with them.

"Jorun, can you fly?" The Salt asked over my shoulder.

He nodded quickly. "I can."

"Will you fly north to offer help to those who need it?"

"I'll run and meet you," Aderyn insisted.

The Salt turned to me. "Elira, would you fly to help Crest?"

"Of course." With one thunderous flap, I was soaring toward my lacuna. I caught sight of his copper scales between a thin copse of trees as he sounded the horn again. Diving, I flew low and close to his side.

Suddenly, the top of the tallest peak within the Green Mountains, the one whose caldera had once spewed smoke and fire, exploded with a resounding boom. Despite the distance between it and us, the shock wave that rocketed from the eruption knocked me sideways.

My hip cracked against a tree and I almost crashed to the ground. My feet skimmed the sand until my wings could right me. Crest paused, ready to help, but I waved him on. "I'm fine, Crest. Go!"

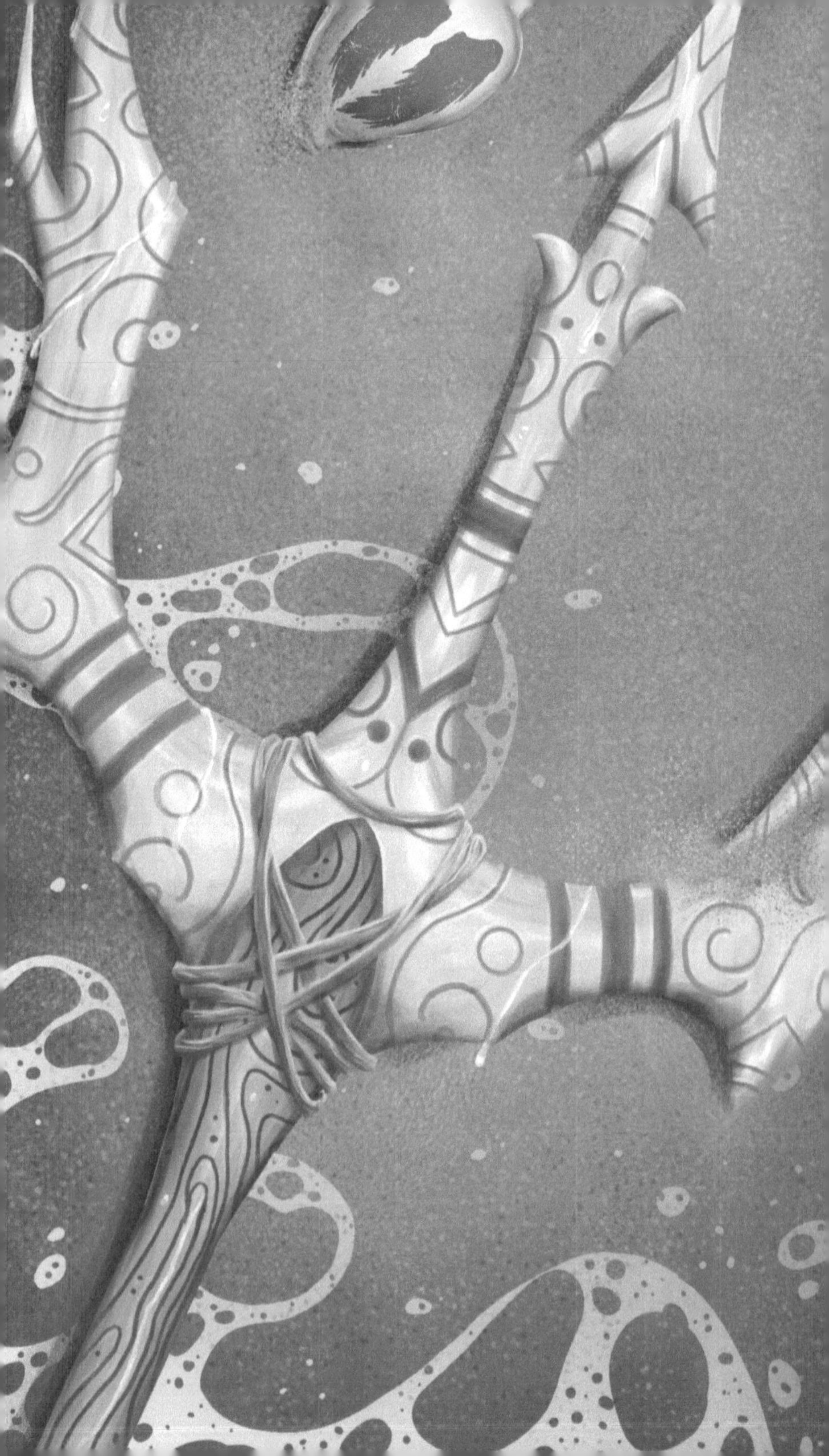

CHAPTER TWENTY-FOUR

The volcano belched smoke and ash into the sky. The scent was akin to the steam we'd encountered just days ago when we were scouting the trees Wade suggested to be altered to conceal their bowmen, but it was a thousand-fold stronger. The plume built until I was sure Empyrean would be buried by it. Perhaps that would solve all our problems…

The explosion was so loud that the shell horn was forgotten in Crest's hand. The citizens of Kehlani helped one another to the shore, needing little encouragement from Crest now that the mountain had blown its top.

The Salt claimed that the shells and earth had shaken before because Tella was shaken. If that was the case, then she was incited and furious now. Lava sparked and spewed from the volcano's top, flowing in thick red rivers down the mountainside, burning lush vegetation and rock alike.

Perhaps Neera wasn't lying when she said she was free and threatened to come to Kehlani if I didn't return to Empyrean. Perhaps the eruption was Tella's way of warning her away from her land and the people who dwelt upon it.

Tella would rather see it all ruined and burned away than to see her Isle in Neera's greedy hands.

When the sun set, the glowing orange-red streams of lava could be seen from every part of the Isle.

I had flown to get a closer look and watched as the molten rivers overtook several tents, the fabric going up in a rush of flame and fury as it made its way, unimpeded, to the shore. Near the surf, the red-hot rock cooled and began to crust black. Still, the flow kept rolling forward, moving adamantly beneath the crusted skin as it pushed into the sea like Tella's scorched fingers, desperate to clutch the soothing sea water once again.

Steam billowed from the salted waves. Until it reached deeper water, the lava kept pressing forward, plunging into the water like it had no other choice.

I landed on the shore near the flow and watched, my heart in my stomach.

Crest found me there. Sweat, sand, and soot tried and failed to mar his handsomeness. He said nothing as he regarded the same thing I did. He just stabbed the handle of his trident into the wet sand and scrubbed his mouth. "You see it, too."

"Yes."

The ocean… looked like it was burning.

We were standing at the place where oceans burned, the very place where Neera said the war would end.

He pointed toward the deep water beyond that which burned. "That's where you splashed into the water. The place where the sky fell…"

Crest turned to me and I to him. He studied my eyes, and I wondered if sometimes – like now – he saw the beast he thought he'd find in the water the evening he saved me – a monster more eagle than girl. More evil than she could ever be good. I wondered if he regretted rescuing me now that my presence in his life had caused so much upheaval and strife.

"We'll fight together, Elira. And we will win," he promised. "Then you'll be free."

"Then *we* will be free."

He answered me by cupping my face and lowering his, then pressing his lips to mine in a simple act of reassurance and an offering of comfort in the moment I needed it most.

I was a selfish, heartless wretch, because I wrapped my arms around his back and memorized the feel and taste of Crest when he loved… knowing I would soon leave behind a bitter taste in his mouth and an ache in his heart that little would assuage.

If he survived this war, years from now he would think back on this moment and know that as I kissed him on the scorched shores of Kehlani, in the place where oceans burned, I was making plans to leave it, and him.

I just hoped he would try to understand why, and one day forgive me for it.

We met Breaker and Katalini at Magma's. Wade, Koa, Frey, and The Salt were already there, along with some

Kehlanians I didn't know. They'd suffered injury fleeing the exploding mountains. One woman's ankle was purple and swollen. A gentleman's head was cut and bleeding. He pressed a cloth to it, pushing against the wound like Magma instructed. Another coughed incessantly. He lived in the mountains and had to cross through the cloying tendrils of smoke. It singed his lungs, according to Magma. Of the three of him, she seemed most worried over him, but when she told him he would heal, I believed her. There was truth in her tone.

Magma walked to me. "Crest said you were thrown into a tree."

"I'm fine," I told her, waving her off.

But the silver-haired Mender would not be so easily dismissed. "Let me see your hip, Elira."

I lifted the knot of my sarong. The broad bruise was sore and already mottled in shades of deep plum.

"I have a paste for that," she assured me, sauntering over to her countertop to sift through her jars. She was keeping herself busy. Mending. Helping.

The discarded sky fire clippings Wade had been pressing for poison lay collected in a small box. A reminder of the thing I'd asked her. When I was gone, she would remember me as a monster, too. But maybe she would also remember the mass of arrows in the corner, coated with the toxin and already dipped in wax to seal it on the metal. Once it bit into Empyrean flesh, the offending Warrior would fade and fall quickly.

She returned with a small, stoppered jar of white paste. "Rub a portion onto the bruise day and night. It'll fade it."

I fought a guilty swallow, knowing I wouldn't be here to use it. "Thank you, Magma."

She gave a rueful smile and held up two fingers. "My entire life, I've loved my name save for two occasions. Twice, I've wished my mother had given me another name."

"It wouldn't have fit you," I told her.

Hand on her cocked hip, she asked, "And how would you know that?"

I smiled. "Because it wouldn't be fiery enough."

She clucked her tongue and went to check the man holding the cloth to a laceration on his scalp.

Katalini pressed a hand to her mouth a moment before she ran outside and emptied her stomach. Breaker hurried after her. He stood and patted her back as Crest held the door open to ask if she was okay. He was so worried.

"She hasn't been feeling well for weeks. What does Grandmother say about it?" he asked Breaker.

Katalini rose and accepted a cloth from her lacuna. She wiped her mouth and glanced at Breaker, who offered a nod, letting her know it was up to her if she wanted to tell them.

Her eye met mine and she tried to smile. "I'm pregnant."

The muscles in Crest's back went rigid. "What?" he breathed.

Katalini nodded rapidly, then smoothed a hand over her gently rounded belly so he could see the confirming shape.

"Magma, did you hear?" Katalini asked.

The Mender's eyes twinkled. "I've known for a while, child. How do you think I knew to make the tea for you?"

Katalini's pretty jaw dropped. "You *knew*?" She turned to Breaker. "Did you tell her?"

"No!" he promised. "She said she had a tea and wanted you to try it, then it helped you some, so you kept sending me over for it."

Crest pulled his older brother in for a hug. "Congratulations, Break. You'll be an incredible father."

Every voice in the room echoed the sentiment.

Tears welled in Breaker's eyes as he thanked them and said he truly hoped so. I wasn't sure if he was worried he might not be what his child needed, or if he wasn't sure he'd live to get the chance to parent his youngling.

Magma, having finished bandaging the man's head, quickly and tightly wrapped the ankle of the woman who'd twisted it, then asked Wade to get the surprise she'd made for the expectant parents.

He stood and got his balance. The foot of his wooden leg struck the floor and everyone smiled as he walked to the chest and opened it. He withdrew the blanket Magma had knitted and walked it over to her. A couple times his balance teetered, but he didn't fall. He was getting stronger already. He stood beside me as she presented the gift to the parents-to-be.

"You're walking well," I told him.

"I made you a promise."

"I appreciate you keeping it. Many don't."

He glanced at me from the corner of his eye. "I fear your wrath should I fail to live up to my end of our bargain."

The thought soured my stomach. That was how my people felt about Neera. "Good," I rasped, trying to smile.

Crest was so happy for his brother it made my heart ache. This was what he one day wanted. A family. Children. A woman he loved more than he loved himself.

Koa called Wade over to him and Frey, asking Wade to settle an argument between them. The two argued so frequently I wasn't sure what it could possibly be over, not surprised at all when Koa dramatically paused to ask him which fruit tasted better: mango or orange.

The Salt came to stand with me. My ribs tightened when she quietly spoke. "The sea burns."

"I know."

"Talay says that though the goddess is not free, part of her essence is, Elira."

I tilted toward her. "Part of her is within the Oracle. She spoke to me through you."

"I remember now." Her eyes sharpened with anger. "Though I'm not sure how she managed to even partially break free after so long."

I winced. "That would be my fault."

The Salt turned to face me now. "What?"

In a hushed whisper, I explained, "I had to save Koa. I didn't know I needed every sliver of wind to restrain her. When I drew from my half to get him out of the funnel and her grip..."

Her lips slowly parted as realization dawned. "It weakened her bond for only a moment."

I hung my head. "That's all she needed. She has a foothold now."

The Seer leaned in. "Then we must keep her from making a stronghold out of it."

"I need to talk to you," I whispered.

"It's getting late. Will you see me home, Elira?" she asked, loudly enough that all could hear it.

"Of course," I agreed.

Crest was beaming with his brother when we passed by. I promised to come right back.

"Keep your bow ready, just in case," he warned.

I patted it on my shoulder. "I'm always ready."

The Salt and I waited until we reached her tent and stepped inside to speak. It was dark inside, no candles lit. But the tent's flaps were open and moonlight poured into the space, cool and pale. And overhead, despite their brokenness, her ancestors' shells still thumped.

Clack….. click.

Clack….. click.

My eyes adjusted. "Their rhythm has slowed."

Her eyes lifted to them. "Every heart slows and weakens when death is near. Will you tell me what you remembered?"

I told her every detail I could recall.

"I have to go to her, Salt, before she comes here for me. Some parasitic part of Neera's essence has taken over the Oracle, but I think I can stop her if I…" I pressed my lips closed, not even wanting to speak it, especially to her.

"If you kill the Seer," she quietly finished for me.

"Can you think of another way?"

She shook her head. A tear fell from her eye.

"I'm sorry, Salt. I wouldn't do it if there was another way to stop her. It's not fair to the Oracle. She's innocent in all this."

"I do not cry for her," The Salt admitted.

Instead of reacting to her comment, I plowed ahead. "Remember what you promised. My shell goes to him – if he wants it."

I wished the pattern representing my wings on the cowrie's smooth back hadn't faded. I wanted Crest to have that much. I wanted him to remember the mark on the cowrie the way he remembered the ink on his chest. Maybe the shell would feel like me – like my soul – to him.

"Please tell him..."

"Every sharp shard," she confirmed, repeating my earlier words to me.

My throat ached with unshed tears because she remembered. She would tell him and comfort him when he needed it.

"Were you able to mend my leathers?"

She nodded and went to her trunk to pull out the top of my uniform. Holding the supple blue leather in her hands, she told me, "Magma still has the bottoms. They're tucked away in the bottom of the chest that held the babe's blanket."

"That's fine." I had to talk to Magma anyway.

She held out my armor.

I raised my trembling chin. "Tell him I wanted to prove I was more girl than eagle, okay? That I had to go and try to save my lacuna. I had a chance to stop it all and I took it. Tell him not to be mad. He would've done the same." Tears spilled down my cheeks and carved warm paths down them, going cold before I wiped them away.

"You're breaking my heart, Elira!" she cried, smoothing her hands over the shell necklace she always wore.

I listened to the slow thump of the shells and decided they were wrong. I could do this. I could grab this chance to stop Neera. A sliver of her essence was free, but the goddess remained trapped. Neera hated the feeling of being limited in flesh and it had been a long time since she'd been confined in it. That distaste gave me an opportunity to win. And now was the time to strike, to sneak home before she came here.

"You know, before I left, the Oracle of Empyrean read my feather and she said that the hope of my victory was imprinted in the barbs. I have to believe it still is. My feathers haven't changed and they're still part of me."

"When will you leave?" she asked, already knowing the answer.

"I need to surprise them if I hope to claim that victory, Salt."

She moved to her table, where she picked up a small cup and returned to me. She dipped her thumb into the water. I could smell the salt as she brought her hand to the skin beneath my eyes and swiped saltwater beneath each of them.

"Talay keep you, *Guardian* Elira."

The roar of the sea filled my ears as Talay accepted the title she gave me. My chin began to quiver.

She stepped back, holding the cup as though it were a fragile thing, worry and hope warring on her brow.

I didn't tell her goodbye as I slipped into the night. Those words were far too final a parting farewell that, in our cases, was too vague. It could mean I'd see her tomorrow, or in a few days or weeks, or in another century or lifetime.

I felt the teetering of the ponderous scale begin… weighing my intention to kill the goddess against her ambition to end my soul.

I hid my jacket beneath the overturned washtub outside Magma's tent as Breaker and Katalini's voices emerged from just inside Magma's door. I hurried to meet them as they stepped outside before they realized I wasn't coming from the direction of The Salt's tent.

Koa, Frey, and Wade were gone, they said. Wade had a new tent nearby so he could have both help and privacy when he needed them.

The lacunas, despite today's eruption, seemed relieved to no longer have to keep their secret from those they loved. "Elira," Breaker began, "thank you for your discretion."

I waved off his gratitude. "No thanks are necessary."

Breaker sighed and ran a hand over his pulled-back hair. "The Salt said that the lava flowing into the sea makes it look like the ocean is burning."

I nodded once.

His blue eyes shone in the moonlight. Not nearly as lovely as his brother's, but so similarly I felt guilt for deceiving him. "It won't be long now, then."

"No, it won't," I agreed. "Breaker, you need to make sure everyone is ready. Tell them to carry their weapons at all times. Make new plans that align with the paths along the archers' posts. Hand out all the poison arrows you have and be prepared to distribute another batch when they're ready."

"They've all been made and divided," he confirmed. "We're ready."

I glanced over my shoulder at the tent door. "But I saw some inside."

"Those are yours and Crest's," he said. "Everyone else has theirs. They've been firing much better and farther with your bow redesign."

I nodded. "Good. Look – the Empyreans won't know of the changes, which you can use to your advantage. Let them come in as close as they usually do, thinking they're out of your range, and then strike at them all at once."

"Aren't you fighting with us?" Breaker asked, ticking his head back. "You speak like you won't be taking aim alongside us."

I had to think fast. "Of course I am, but I have my assigned task and position and you have yours. We won't be close, and the people around you need to be led. Especially the younglings who are newly learned."

He nodded and gave a small smile, pinching the corners of his eyes. "Of course. I'm sorry I jumped to the wrong conclusion. I'm… I'm exhausted, to be honest. I've gotten very little sleep lately."

Katalini yawned loudly. Dark circles bruised the skin beneath her eyes. "I'm sorry. I've slept plenty, yet it's not enough. I could sleep all day and night right now." She yawned again, unable to stop herself.

"You should both get some rest." *While you can*, I didn't add. "Have you made arrangements to hide in the grotto?" I asked Katalini.

Her eyes held a defiant glint I admired. "I refuse to hide away when I can shoot. My father put a bow in my hand when I was six."

My stomach coiled, hoping I could prevent her from having to draw the string again. Prevent Breaker from plunging an arrow in the sand for her and their hatchling.

My ears pricked to hear Crest's voice from inside. He was speaking to his grandmother; I wasn't sure about what.

"Goodnight, Elira," Breaker told me. He wrapped an arm around Katalini's shoulders and steered her away.

I ducked inside. Magma looked me over. I wondered if she could tell I'd been crying. Were my eyes red?

"The Salt says we can rest well tonight," I offered.

"No trouble will befall us before dawn, then," Magma said, a tightness in her tone. "Well, the two of you go and enjoy the peaceful moments that come before the worst storms." Crest hugged his grandmother and placed a kiss in her silver hair before telling her he'd come and see her tomorrow if he was able. "You have to. I have arrows for you both," she said pointedly.

He gave a grim smile.

She tried to smile. "Goodnight, you two."

Crest pushed out the door with me and we took the path that led home. Aderyn and Jorun were sitting on the small porch outside my tent. Their eyes tracked my every step, along with Crest's as we stepped into his tent. The tension was palpable.

Our people were preparing for a battle far worse than any we'd ever fought. We would lose friends. Some would lose family.

It was different seeing things from the sand when you knew the sky, too.

I threw a log into the fire pit, laid down my bow and quiver, and crossed the room to wash my face in a basin of fresh water.

Crest started to prop his trident alongside his other weapons, but took it back up. "Do you trust me?" he asked out of nowhere.

"Of course," I answered without hesitation.

"Will you come with me to the sea?"

My brows pinched. "What for?"

He let out a heavy sigh. "I need the brine. I need to wash the ash from my face and hair. Most of all, though, I need you."

"You want me to enter the ocean?"

"I know it's dangerous and I'm not asking you to go far, but the shallows are safe for you and you're safe in any depth with me."

"You're awfully sure of yourself," I teased.

"When it comes to you, lacuna, yes I am."

Calm waves gently lapped over my feet as I stood on the shore. Every wave's facet caught the cool moonlight and the sea sparkled like a glittering, dark gem. Stars wheeled overhead. They moved so slowly that if you looked directly overhead a few hours from now, you'd see a different sky than the one looking down upon us now.

"Is this Talay's doing?"

The Shark's lips twitched into a grin. "I might have asked him for a favor."

He'd waded out before me and sunk into the waist deep water. Now he serenely floated over the barely-there swells. The salty water scrubbed away the sweat and ash from his face.

The ash was so fine I hardly noticed it raining down until I saw it in his hair and on the broad, emerald leaves of plants earlier today.

On the other side of the Isle, the mountain still bled. The ocean still burned.

I took a step toward him. Then another. Until the water swept against my knees and the gentle waves brushed over the tips of my wings.

Another step…

Crest slowly rose as I walked to him, knowing I trusted him despite my fear of the crushing blue. He took my hand in his and studied the two of them, intertwined. The knot in his throat rose and fell like it floated over its own wave.

"What do you see?"

"How your hand fits with mine." He looked up and met my eyes. "It's perfect."

"Wouldn't anyone's hand fit yours just as well?" I rasped.

"No," he said adamantly. "No one else's could feel like this."

He dragged a finger along my palm as he opened it and goosebumps spread over my skin. That finger made a path over the inner part of my wrist, then my forearm. He clasped my elbows and eased his hands up my biceps. They slid around to my lower back, then cupped my bottom.

"Let me carry you."

I flapped my dampened wings and wrapped my legs around him. His pupils flared at the sight of my wings. "Why do you like my wings so much?"

"For the same reason you rake your nails over my scales. Because they're different and so unabashedly you. They're beautiful."

I traced the pattern of his tattoo as it coiled over his heart and crept over his shoulder. It was as dark as the fabric of the night sky stretching between the stars, making their light shine more brilliantly. "This is part of you," I told him.

He nodded. "And you are part of me, lacuna."

I swallowed thickly. "But you don't love me."

He leaned in to claim a kiss so searing, I suddenly knew what it felt like to be the sea when the mountain's fire spilled into it. My hands suddenly couldn't touch him enough. They raked through his hair and roamed over his strong back and shoulders, then rose to his jaw.

Crest gave a pleased hum and pulled his lips away.

It was only then that I realized he'd walked us deeper into the sea. The waves brushed our chests now. My wings were mostly submerged. Just the top curves jutted from the water. If he set me down, I might be dragged under.

I tightened my arms around his neck.

"I won't let anything happen to you," he quietly vowed, his gaze dropping to my chest before he met my eyes again. I shivered against him, unused to such unabashed attention. His hands clamped onto my hip to raise me higher and I let out a sharp yelp. We'd both forgotten about the bruise I'd collected today.

"I'm so sorry!" he immediately apologized, moving his hand away. "I forgot you were hurt."

"It's just a little tender." I took his hand and brought his fingers back over the skin, a gentle glide. He nodded, his eyes drifting closed as I maneuvered his hand over my skin. I worked my sarong's knot free. The fabric floated delicately around us, tickling my skin and his. "I don't want to lose my clothes in the sea…"

His stare sharpened. His hand ghosted up my side to where my top's tie stopped him. "We wouldn't want that."

Overwhelming need blazed wherever he touched me. When he looked at me like I was something precious, priceless.… *His.*

Unknotting my top at the back, then the neck, I held it between us, gathering the sarong after a little maneuvering to free the fabric trapped between us.

Crest took the garments and tossed them up onto the sand. A moment later, he set me down so he could remove and add his to the strewn, soaked fabric. My toes curled in the soft, wet sand.

He walked around and settled behind me, stroking his fingers over my feathers.

A shiver spread up my spine. My feathers made the water around us tremble.

Crest's hand spread across the flat plane of my stomach while the other slid between my breasts to clutch my throat. He tugged me backward until only my wings separated us and eased me further into the sea with him. The fingers on my stomach slid lower…lower, until I vibrated with need. A need he immediately worked to satiate. As he pleasured me, The Shark kissed the column of my neck, using his broad hands to cover my mouth when I cried out and came undone in his arms.

His hand peeled from my mouth as I panted, trying to calm my racing heart, heady with the promise of more. More touches. More of our bodies joined. More of Crest.

More moments we had to take now in case we couldn't have them later.

"Turn around. I want to see you," he ordered.

I faced him, my knees weak from what he'd just wrung from me, as well as from his commanding tone. His hands wrapped around the backs of my thighs and hiked me up, arms like vices under my bottom. Crest nipped and licked at my breasts and I arched my back to give him more, loving every husky moan he let slip through his defenses.

He hiked me higher and threaded one of my legs over his shoulder, the other around his back, spreading me. He kissed me as the waves washed up and over us. Crest moved in time with them as though he were one of them. I closed my eyes and reveled in the feel of him, of this, of us.

His finger teased my opening, then pushed inside. My lips parted and a mewl escaped. My hands dented his sun-kissed skin and to the rhythmic cadence of the sea, Crest worked my body until it was ready for more…

I whispered into his ear. "I want you, lacuna…"

A growl. His hands clamped onto my hips, bruise be damned, and dragged me down and onto him as he thrust upward and into me. We joined with such force, I could swear the sea and air around us rippled.

CHAPTER TWENTY-FIVE

I laid with Crest in his hammock until his breathing was steady for a long while. When I was sure he wouldn't wake, I slipped out of it. For a long moment, I lingered. Considered climbing back in. But then I thought of Neera and her demand.

Return to Empyrean and face me…

There was no other choice but to do exactly that. A piece of Neera was manipulating the Oracle's body and it would be the goddess, not Talon, who would wage the coming war.

Neera always kept her word. *If you do not come to me, I will come to you. And when I reach the Isle, I will rend that wretched swath of sand and kill every soul upon it.*

I'd fought her a thousand times before, in just as many lives, but remembered only the last battle. Per the goddess, per the shells, she'd found a way to tip the scales and unmake my soul. I feared there would be nothing to be measured against her might. Her will would tarnish the sky and ruin the sea. And the hope that still lingered like the last wisp of smoke from a sage bundle would be swept away by her Great Wind.

I padded across the floor and found my clean sarong and top, quickly tying them on. Holding the arrows tight to the wall of my quiver so they wouldn't rattle, I grabbed my bow and stepped outside.

Pausing, I wondered if I should tell him. Was this how Aderyn felt the night she left? I was completely torn, not sure if it was better to leave to keep him safe or tell him I was going, knowing he would try to stop me. Knowing what would happen if I stayed. I couldn't allow it. I had a chance. A single opportunity. And the time was now.

The path toward Magma's stretched before me. Beyond that, a greater trail. One I hoped would not forsake me.

One foot in front of the other, I left The Shark behind. I didn't allow myself to look back, though I desperately wanted to run to him and gather him in my arms and tell him I was sorry.

Something scurried in the underbrush as I passed by. Otherwise, there was only insect song and the quiet, clear sky. Barely a breeze stirred the cool night air.

The Mender's overturned wash tub still concealed the top of my leather armor. I just needed the bottoms. I slipped quietly into Magma's workshop.

I hadn't expected that someone would be lying on her cot.

It was North. He was asleep, lightly snoring. Even in the dim light, I could tell he was still far too pale.

Wide awake, Magma sat before a lit, half-consumed candle. Streams of pale yellow wax trailed down its bumpy sides and pooled at its base. My blue leather bottoms were folded and laying on her lap. Her arms were folded, lips pursed tightly, and her brows were drawn. "Were you going to wake me?"

"I gave you my word that I would."

She harrumphed. "Yes, well I'm certain that Crest has no idea you're leaving. If he did, he would storm in here to say his goodbyes, just in case. Fully willing to die for his lacuna – the one so eager to abandon him when he needs her most."

The words were red hot lava streaming over my heart. Cruel. Consuming. And yet true, at least in part.

I carefully considered my words and fought the anger welling in my voice. Fought and lost the battle with it. "Magma, I'm not leaving because I *want* to. I'm leaving because I *must*. To *protect* my lacuna and all of you – his people. Did The Salt tell you what I've done?" She shook her head, her silver hair glimmering nearly gold in the candle's warm light. "When I used the wind to save Koa, I unknowingly freed a part of Neera's essence."

Her thin lips parted. "How large a part? What does that mean, exactly? Is the goddess free?"

"The Salt says that most of her is still bound in the sky, but it doesn't matter because Neera is incredibly strong." Magma's breathing went ragged. "She has taken over the Empyrean Oracle's body. She overwhelmed The Salt and took over *her* body for a time last night. Even Talay's Seer bent to Neera's will." I let that sink in. "I called for you when Neera left her in a heap on her sand floor."

"Talay help us," she whispered, hands clamped together over her mouth now. "I didn't know. She didn't say."

"I have a chance to stop her, Magma. So you can judge my actions if you must and say I'm a wretch for sneaking away, but you know he would die if he went into the sky with me. You must know that."

Magma sniffled as tears spilled down her face. "I know it. I know he would. And I'm glad you're protecting him, but at what cost to you?"

The cost to me did not outweigh the risk to the people of Kehlani, or even to the decent Empyreans who were pushed into roles and lives they did not want and would not choose if given the choice.

I walked to her and patted her back as lovingly as I could, mimicking the motion she'd done for so many others. Then I crouched so she could look into my eyes. I needed her to see the truth in them. The truth in me.

"How could I not try?"

I loved him, more than my own life.

"I see," was her simple reply, because there was no more to say.

I might have gotten a lot wrong in my life, but not this. About this, I was right. I could feel it in my heart. I could feel it in the soul I bore.

"You shouldn't go alone," she argued, still crying for me.

I tried to smile. "The only friends I have in Empyrean are being held against their will, so it seems I must be the one to face her."

"Are you not afraid?" she gasped.

Truthfully, I was petrified to square off against the goddess and lose. But not because I was worried for my life or soul, but because I worried for Crest's and Magma's. Breaker's and Katalini's and that of their babe. Frey's and Koa's and Wade's. Even Nori's and North's. The soul of The Salt… I could go on and on. There wasn't a soul on Kehlani who deserved the fate Neera would deal them if I failed.

She leaned forward, still shaking her head. "I have a terrible feeling about this, Elira. It's haunted me since I made you promise to fix this. I was wrong for putting such a burden on your back."

My wings flexed to ease the ache I felt. Not from her, but from worry. "My back is strong, Magma."

"Strong is *not* the same thing as unbreakable," the Mender argued.

I looked at her. "If I don't return, it's not because I don't want to," I told her. "Make sure he knows that. Make sure he knows I only left because I love him."

"Have you told him how your heart feels?"

I shook my head. "He would know," I croaked, then cleared my throat and tried again. "He would know I was leaving if I did. We've never told one another that with words."

But our hearts knew. I could feel it when he looked for me in a crowd, when he encouraged me to be myself, when he marveled over me despite my sharp edges, and when he decided my flaws were no worse than his.

Our lives, upbringings, and experiences were vastly different. We'd tried to kill one another far longer than the days we treaded this sand together. I just hoped I'd have the chance to come back to him and resume our walk on this beautiful isle.

"Can I do *anything* to help?" she asked.

"I need my leathers," I said, tapping the garment draped over her legs. "And sky fire arrows – as many as you can spare."

"Take them all," she told me, gesturing to the pile.

"Crest will need his portion – in case I fail."

She stood and the candle's flame guttered in her wake, bathing flickering light over the tent walls. She extended the blue leathers to me and waited as I stepped into the legs, drew them upward, and fastened them at the waist. Watched as I pushed my arms into the sleeves The Salt had reattached and tightened the buckles around my body to secure it all against the wind and anything else that might stand against me.

I looked down at my bare toes.

Magma reached under the table and held my boots out for me to take.

I tugged each on and laced them tightly.

She was ready with a tattered scrap of fabric. I bound my hair into a braid before coiling it into a bun at the base of my neck.

Moving to the door, I took as many arrows as my quiver could hold, while leaving Crest at least half.

With a sky fire arrow in my left hand and my bow in my right, I straightened and faced Magma. She'd put me back together in more ways than one. More times than she would've liked, thanks to my stubbornness.

"Magma, I'm grateful for all –"

"No," she interrupted. "I'll see you when you get back." She nodded profusely and crossed her arms, unyielding and resolute. "Yes. When you get home, I'll be here waiting, and we can talk then. If you need patching or bleeding, so be it. I'll see to your mending."

I wanted to thank her and thought about giving her a hug, but knew she wouldn't allow me to do either. She'd dismissed me with her blessing.

So I inclined my head and fought to swallow against the knot forming in my throat as I pushed out her door. I walked toward the shore, passing The Salt's home where the tormenting shells' slow rhythm made me want to fire an arrow through the top of her tent.

I ducked my head inside and found her cozy home dark and empty, immediately knowing where I would find her.

On the shore upon which Talay delivered his cowries, The Salt stood.

And she wasn't alone.

Aderyn's dark hair waved in the breeze. Jorun positioned himself at her side. Both wore mangled leathers. Aderyn's sleeves had been reattached like mine and Jorun's were scarred and stitched at the shoulder. Along with their Empyrean armor, they donned Kehlani blades, bows, and quivers full of poison-tipped arrows.

Their expressions were stony. Aderyn and Jorun were ready for battle, one in which they were determined not to lose. They were ready to risk it all.

"Why are you here?" I asked Aderyn.

It was the same cruel question she'd posed to me when I came looking for her after the quaking earth dislodged the rocks and sent them tumbling, crushing their way into the hollow where she'd lived.

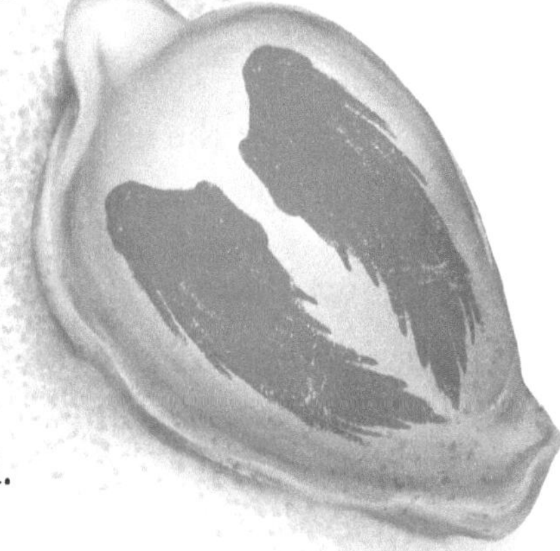

"I'm your second," she answered. "You don't go into battle without me at your side."

"You gave up that position and privilege," I told her.

She stepped aggressively toward me. "I am your second and I will fight at your side until the day one of us truly falls."

She left the sky the same as I had, though under vastly different circumstances, yet here we stood. Having fallen, yes, but also having risen again as new creatures. Aderyn buried her old life on the land she claimed as her own, while mine drowned in the sea that fateful eve.

Our lives in Empyrean were merely memories now. If we tried to fit back into our former roles, it would never work. Was that how a soul felt each time it was reborn into new flesh, at least for a time?

"I appreciate your fervor, but you can't fight with me, Aderyn. You have the hatchlings to think about now. Besides that, you have no idea what lurks in Empyrean."

"Care to enlighten us? There have been murmurings, but rumor isn't rooted in truth," she replied, tipping up her chin a notch. Jorun added his agreement.

"Who have you been eavesdropping on?" I asked.

Neither would tell.

"Busybodies…" I hissed. "Conjecture could get you killed."

"I prefer the term *spy*," Jorun corrected. "And whether or not your assertion is correct is highly dependent upon whose conversations I've listened to."

"Well, I hope you haven't spied on me and my lacuna lately," I advised sharply.

Aderyn scoffed. "No one could stomach the two of you for that long. I tried and failed within seconds."

My lip curled with the tension of a thousand curses that wanted to leap from my tongue.

She looked skyward. "I'm going with you. We all know that if this isn't stopped, the hatchlings won't survive the goddess's wrath."

"You can better protect the babes from the ground," I argued. She'd never vexed me as much when she was my second.

"I'm going to Empyrean to flank *you*," she corrected. "You are my first. My sister. My best friend. And you *need* me now, just as I have come to realize with your absence in my life that I need you. I was wrong, Elira, and I'm sorry for hurting you. I'm sorry I didn't *see*…" Her voice shattered.

If she finished her sentence, I might throttle her. I didn't want or need her pity. I needed her compliance right now. I needed her safe.

"Then rest well knowing that I forgive you," I said, forcing the words out. "But you can't return to Empyrean now that your wings are gone." I looked at her companion. "You should stay with her, Jorun," I told him. "You came here to find her and now you can fight together – from the sand."

"Then by that logic, you should stay here and fight at Crest's side," Jorun proposed.

"You have no right to tell me what I should and should not do!" I snapped.

"I made a promise to your father –" he argued.

The trouble with insubordination was that it spread like an insidious vine, robbing and choking everything under it until nothing survived. "Then I release you from your obligation in my father's stead," I interrupted.

Aderyn bristled. "I know the peril and accept my fate should I fall from the firmament."

I thought of the shells. Of the meaning of the sound they made and whether her dying heart's beat might align with mine if I allowed her to ascend.

"The moment you approach the sky kingdom, the goddess will sense you. Then you'll be glad you listened to reason," Aderyn added.

"She's right, Elira," Jorun advised. "There is a reason The General insisted upon quads instead of letting us fight alone. There's strength in numbers."

I smiled, then looked to The Salt. They had no idea what they were trying to get themselves into. My brow arched. "Have you told them what must be done?"

"No," she answered, crossing her arms and digging her toes into the sand. "I wasn't sure you would want me to. It's your truth if you'd like to offer it to them."

"Has Talay imparted any further wisdom?" I asked the Seer.

She tossed her thick, dark braids over her shoulder. "Only that he will help where and when he is able."

"What are you two talking about? What must be done?" Jorun asked.

I held Aderyn's stare. "I have to kill the Oracle – and fast."

A shocked breath tore from their chests. The Oracle was Neera's chosen Seer, but this Oracle was special. She was her conduit, the one blessed with a direct connection to the far-away goddess. Or so they thought. They didn't know just how deep and direct that connection now was…

"Still want to ascend and fight with me?" They were silent. Probably debating the wisdom of their plan.

"Why her?" Aderyn finally choked out.

"Because I accidentally released a piece of Neera and now that tiny sliver of the goddess is dwelling within the skin of her conduit. But that piece is infinitely stronger and scarier than anything I've seen or known before – in *any* lifetime."

I'd rendered Jorun speechless, but saw his mind working.

"She'll know when you return," he finally said.

"The Oracle's body still requires sleep. That's why I want to go now." Before the sun rose. Before a new day began.

"The Elders sequestered her in the sanctum," Jorun stated, punctuating the impossibility stretching before us with a high-pitched laugh. "How could we possibly sneak into the sacred hall?"

"The Elders hold no power now." I tightened my fingers around my bow, carved and curved to fit my hand. "She's probably already slaughtered them. As for the rest, I haven't smoothed the details of my plan as of yet."

Smoothed the details, Jorun mouthed.

"If you lure the Oracle out of the sanctum, Elira, I'll put an arrow through her heart," Aderyn promised. "She might see *you* coming, but she won't see me."

Hope once again stirred within my heart as hot and urgent as the fiery blade hidden within its walls.

She turned to Jorun. "After you fly me onto the firmament, I want you to go to Elira. Flank her and guard her until I can get a clean shot."

"Neera knows everything. There's no lying about where we've been or what we've been doing," I warned. "She'll brand us traitors and use the scale to weigh our hearts if we're caught." *After she tears them out…*

"If I could destroy that blasted scale, I would," Aderyn cursed.

I nodded grimly. "If I agree to let you come with me, you both have to give me your word on one thing."

"What's that?" Jorun asked hesitantly.

I turned my attention to him. "If I tell you to take Aderyn and go, you do it without question. Without arguing. You scoop her up and fly her as far away as your wings will carry you." And to Aderyn, I demanded, "And you let him. There's more you don't know."

"Then tell us! The more we know, the better we can prepare," my sister adamantly demanded.

It was the same thing I'd told my quad since the moment I became first.

I looked at The Salt. Her eyes again said that the truth was mine to gift or keep. So, I gave it to them.

"Talay's shells foretell my death."

Aderyn's chest heaved. "No! You can't die in this battle."

"I'm not immortal."

"Your soul will just return. What would be the point in killing your body now?" she insisted.

I turned to face the sea, taking a moment to calm my breaths and the fear coursing through me. After this moment, The Salt and I wouldn't be the only ones who knew. Just speaking it made the ominous sounds of the cowries fill my ears.

Aderyn stepped closer. "Elira? Your soul will be reborn. Won't it?"

I turned my head to meet her eyes. "No. Neera seeks to kill my soul and end the war between us so she will finally be free. Without me in the way, she'll claim the sea and sand as her own and have dominion over anyone who survives her wrath."

"Then you can't go," she said, her voice rising as she flung a hand toward Empyrean. "You can't go up there. You have to hide!"

"Where?" I shouted. "Where would you have me go? Where can I possibly hide from her? She took over The Salt's body. She made it clear that if I don't go to her, she'll bring the fight to me. She'll come *here*, Aderyn. Neera threatened the soul of everyone on the Isle, our siblings included. I can't allow that. I couldn't live with myself if I cowered, knowing that all of Talay's souls would be slaughtered because I was too weak to fight her."

Emotion overwhelmed Aderyn's face. "Then we stick with the original plan. You tempt her from the sanctum, and I'll kill the Oracle."

We'd barely thought this through, didn't have any true plan other than the vague one Aderyn just spouted. But there was no planning out every aspect of a battle. There were too many variables to consider to ever fully prepare.

Aderyn continued, "You shouldn't go into her sacred hall alone. She could trap you in there and kill you, slowly if she liked. You need to draw her outside and onto the square at first light. Challenge her to a fight if you must. She wouldn't squander the opportunity to cut you down in front of everyone."

"If she touches me, my soul will die," I told her.

"Then don't let her touch you," she growled.

"Where should I fly *you*?" Jorun asked Aderyn.

A sinister grin spread over her face, one that promised retribution. "Take me to the roof of the House of the Clipped."

"There's a lot that could go wrong here," Jorun cautioned. "Watch out for the Warriors. They'll fight for *her*, and against us, out of fear."

"If there is trouble before we reach the firmament, we flee," I told them both.

Neither argued – surprisingly. When all was settled and we were ready to fly, Aderyn stood before Jorun, prepared to let him lift her.

The Salt pressed a finger to my chest. "Don't forget where your sword is sheathed, or how hot it burns."

"I won't," I told her, the resolve in my voice masking the fear in my heart.

"Talay keep you all," she whispered.

I flapped my wings and tore into the sky.

I could still see the mountain spilling its molten fire into the sea when I heard his shrill cry from the sea below. My tears splashed into the brine, carrying a plea to Talay.

Comfort him. Keep him safe.

CHAPTER TWENTY-SIX

I kept flying.

Didn't stop, despite the overpowering ache in my chest or the tension in the roots of my wings. Didn't dive to explain myself, though he deserved it. Or beg his forgiveness, though it was all I wanted in that moment. That – and for him to be safe.

No, if I descended an inch, I wouldn't be able to leave him to fight her. It needed to be done and I was the one who had to do it. The one she chose. The one she elevated. The one who picked this unending fight with her.

I bore her blood and power and hatred. No one deserved her wrath more than I did, and I welcomed it. I wanted the aching fury to tunnel her vision so she wouldn't expect the blow we intended to deal her.

Every intention I ever presented to her was a lie.

This was my truth.

My soul wanted to kill the goddess and end the ceaseless suffering she caused, and the scale would demand far more than mere feathers or freedom as payment. I knew it. I accepted it. But I couldn't accept death unless I knew Crest would live and the island of Kehlani would be the haven my loved ones needed and earned by sacrifices far too great for many to bear.

The further we flew, the more I thought about sending Aderyn and Jorun back to the Isle, but they came prepared to fight and wouldn't leave me now. I'd led a quad into many battles, but none as dire as this.

The night faded quickly.

Soon, the sun would rise and cast its golden light over the sky city. An ill feeling settled into my belly as little by little, the thick clouds obscuring Empyrean soaked with crimson and began to flicker with Neera's power.

"They're like the sanctum's cloud," Jorun observed, flying close enough that we could speak.

A heavy weight filled my chest.

"She knows I'm near." That meant we needed to adapt our plan. A new order was necessary. "Take Aderyn straight to our nest." It was on the outside edge of the firmament, and they might be able to sneak in from there. "Then, move carefully together until you reach the square," I told them.

"But he's supposed to go with you!" Aderyn argued.

"I need you two to strike as I draw her out. It was *your* plan, remember?" I reminded her. "And it's the best we have."

"The best isn't good enough," she argued. "What if this piece of the goddess doesn't die with the Oracle? What if it simply moves and takes over another host? We can't kill them all. What then?"

"I don't know!" I shouted in frustration.

I didn't know what to do then, nor did I know what to do now to ensure victory. I simply *didn't know.* And I hated it. It was driving me mad. I'd always prided myself on thinking one step ahead of my enemies.

No wonder The Salt couldn't see through the clouds. They were drenched in Neera's power and held not so much as a sprinkling of Talay's brine. She'd gathered them in a protective sphere around the sky city and we had no choice but to fly through them. Thick and viscous, copper-scented and flashing with forked warning, we made our way through the sanguine maze.

The impure Empyrea seeped into our leather armor with every cloud we entered, saturating our skin and hair. The blood-rich vapor thickened the closer to home we flew until it felt more like we were struggling against the confines of the heavy sea and not sky mist at all.

I wiped blood from my eyes and found Aderyn staring at me as Jorun held her beside me.

"Did you hear him call out to you?" she asked of Crest.

I nodded once, unable to speak.

"Don't forget him."

I bristled at the suggestion. I could never.

Sensing my ire, Aderyn rushed to explain, "I *mean* that whatever happens, remember that you rose to the top when a false sense of clout was all there was to gain. Now that you have something real and everything to lose, don't let her part you from him."

"I thought you hated him."

"No, I resent him," she corrected.

"For what?"

"For cleaving my wings."

I bristled. "You asked him to."

She gave a nod. "I know."

We met no resistance as the blood-laden clouds spat us out, drenched and freezing on the other side. Empyrean emerged before us and Jorun peeled away, flying Aderyn around to where they could easily access the nest as long as it, too, was unguarded.

The sun rose in a flash of brilliance as I flew toward the empty piazza, but the light lent none of its warmth to the kingdom of the frigid sky goddess.

Empyrean was still. Unusually so.

I nocked a sky fire arrow, pointing its hammered, deadly tip to the threat I sensed but could not see.

At dawn, Warriors were expected to arrive at the Quarter to meet with their commanders and collect any orders meant for them or their quad. If there was no duty to which they were bound, they would train, spar, and hone their skills. But the Warrior Quarter was empty.

Not a single person moved within the nests of the general populace.

The Scholars' Village was eerily still.

None of the Clipped walked about. None of the younglings or hatchlings, either. It was like the citizens were gone and Empyrean was nothing more than a forgotten tomb.

The sanctum's towering doors were shut tightly. Aderyn was right. Going in there by myself wouldn't have been wise… I would much rather fight where I could fly rather than be hindered by ceiling and wall and the goddess's oppressive, shadowy presence.

I landed in the middle of the piazza and turned a tight circle, waiting for something or someone to emerge. A few moments passed before the tall sanctum doors parted with a creak, pushed open by two individuals I didn't recognize at first glance.

When I did, I couldn't believe what – or whom – I was seeing.

Their once-pristine robes were tattered and filthy, spattered with blood. Their wings had been torn from their backs. The ragged, bloody roots still protruded from the slits in the garment's back.

Tanu and Idris… The silver-tongued serpent and the owlish shrew had neither mouths nor eyes, but pale, concave flesh where the organs should be.

Tanu stooped low as he moved, his neck bent forward unnaturally as if something heavy laid upon his shoulders and to straighten would cause far more pain than he endured with it bowed. Idris was hunched, too, but to a lesser degree. She was older and her brittle body did not fold as easily as his. If Neera forced *her* spine into such a severe angle, it would have broken.

Each paused before the door they'd opened.

I kept quiet, unsure what to expect next or how to prepare for it.

In an orderly fashion, the people of Empyrean quietly marched from the sacred hall. They teemed onto the landing, spilling down the opulent staircase and onto the piazza where they surrounded the square. None of the Warriors were armed as far as I could tell, but I watched to see if bowstrings would be drawn, swords would sing from their sheaths, or knives would cut through the air. No member of the general populace would so much as steal a glance from me. The youngling children clustered together near the Clipped who carried and guarded the hatchling brood.

Movement flashed between nests, revealing a familiar, long brown wing.

Aderyn and Jorun had made their way forward. Now, they just had to advantageously position themselves. I begged them to have the foresight to remain together. Separating could be catastrophic for one or both if it became necessary for them to flee.

I almost gave the command for them to…

Usually when my quad kept close in a fight I was comforted, my confidence bolstered, but their proximity today just reminded me of the danger they were both in. The closer they crept, the greater risk they took.

This was not the Empyrean we had left behind.

"Where is she?" I asked to anyone who dared answer.

Several shoulders flinched at my tone. Children cowered near anyone who would allow them, some clustered and clung to one another.

No one replied. No one even looked up. No one was brave enough to. Not even the Warriors I'd once flown beside.

What had Neera told them about me? Did they think I was a traitor? A deserter? Did they lose hope when she overtook the Oracle and her insidious reign began anew? This was the influence of only a sliver of the goddess who remained imprisoned, but it was enough to destroy us all anyway.

"Neera!" I shouted.

Hundreds of doves that built their nests on our rooftops took to the sky. Their heavy flapping and the sporadic shrill whistle of wind filled the otherwise noiseless space.

The bloody clouds beyond the House of the Clipped parted as Neera breached them, her jade wings beating as she crouched within the body of her Oracle. My heart stopped. Because along with the jade, I saw a flash of glistening copper. Crest was slung over her shoulder. His arms swung limply like braids down her back.

He wasn't dead.

He can't be dead! my heart screamed. I started forward.

Her amethyst eyes dared me to inch closer and look as she landed and dumped him onto the firmament between us.

I pulled back my bowstring and fired the poisoned arrow at her head, my eyes blurring with tears. A gust of wind sent the arrow off its trajectory and it lodged in the thigh of a boy who couldn't have had more than ten of his intentions weighed.

His screams ricocheted off the nearby buildings.

A Clipped woman crawled to him despite the risk to her person. She held him close, comforting him the way only a mother could. The Clipped knew their offspring, even if we didn't recognize them. Even after we were torn away.

I nocked another arrow to keep Neera's focus on me.

"Your friends are next," the goddess promised with wide, bloodthirsty eyes. "They creep like vermin through the hollows of my city and think I'm ignorant of their scampering."

My yellow eyes fastened onto hers. "You didn't make the firmament on which you stand. *I* did. Empyrean is mine."

Her pearly teeth gleamed in the sun. "The sky belongs to me, as does everything and everyone in it." She used her half of the wind to roar through the city, dragging Jorun and Aderyn to the piazza. "Move!" she commanded the people standing in their way. The people, frightened, obeyed.

Jorun and Aderyn hurried to flank me, their bows drawn.

Aderyn gave a subtle nod to Jorun.

Jorun fired, Neera's wind again sending his arrow flying over several ducked heads.

Aderyn and I breathed the same curse at the same time, neither taking our eyes off the goddess. Both trying to figure a way out of this situation.

Neera used the wind as her shield. I couldn't do the same, or use my gusts to nullify hers, without risking a greater piece of the goddess's essence escaping.

The only choice was for us to fight her hand-to-hand.

Aderyn lowered her bow, glancing at me for a command that might work. I had none, and worry settled into her eyes. "Is he dead?" my sister whispered of Crest.

Crest's chest rose and fell. He was unconscious, but alive. When I glanced from him back to Neera, from high over her shoulder, a gleam of bronze caught my eye where the sunlight illuminated her ponderous scale. Patina trickled over its weathered seams, but the green did not detract from its beauty. If anything, it magnified it.

"Distract her again," I breathed to my second, who gave a scant nod.

Aderyn drew a trident from the arm of her leathers. It was small, no longer or wider than a chopping knife, but Neera sneered the moment she saw the small, darted blade. Aderyn drew back and hurled it toward the goddess's feet.

"You dare defile my city with Talay's filth?" Neera gritted. Her golden eyes flashed with wrath.

When she bent to pluck up the offensive weapon, I aimed and fired at the scale itself. My arrow struck one of the pans, tipping one side. The head did not lodge into it or break the chains that held it up. Neera hurled the trident over the firmament and back to the people of the sea to which it belonged.

She wheeled on me, something strange shining in her golden eyes. "You cannot ruin the scale with your paltry weapons and attempts," Neera seethed.

She started toward me, stepping over Crest's calves. I looked down to see his shoulders flex. He planted his hands on the firmament, raised his head, then kicked out and caught her ankle, sending her sprawling. She hissed, glaring back over her shoulder at him.

The three of us fired at once, but our arrows found nothing but wind. She wasn't even watching us; she was busy preparing to tear The Shark to ribbons. She shouldn't have been able to thwart our attempt… then I realized she wasn't simply knocking away our projectiles. She'd wrapped herself in a thick, invisible stream of wind to keep us from striking her.

Our arrows were as useful against the scale as they were against the goddess who made it. But after I'd struck it, something flickered in her eyes and voice that made me wonder if she might value it despite the trouble its perfect balance had caused her.

I took off flying toward the apparatus, drawing a poisoned arrow from my quiver just in case I was right.

A crushing blow landed hard on my side and knocked me away from the device just before I reached the pans.

I tumbled, my vision spinning and blurring until finally, I struck one of the sanctum's columns and landed at its base with a pained groan. At least it wasn't the same side that hit the tree…

My hand lay empty. Instead of in the Oracle's soft flesh, the wax-coated arrow was lodged in the firmament too far away for me to gather it again. The goddess hovered above me. The Oracle's jade feathers bled into a golden sheen that belonged only to the goddess. Her amethyst eyes were completely overcome with pupils of the purest ichor.

"You're wondering why I haven't destroyed it," she observed like she knew me when she knew nothing.

I slowly rose to stand before her.

"It cannot be unmade," she informed me.

"You've already tried, haven't you?" *And failed.* I let out a mirthless laugh. "You crafted it too meticulously," I told her. "Just as you did me. I cannot be unmade, either."

She bared her teeth. "We'll see."

I dove, not for the scale, but for the firmament beneath it, melting it away at a touch. *Unmaking* it. The scale fell into the void, but Neera dove after it and brought the scale back up through the hole I'd made, holding it like she might bludgeon me with it.

Crest's harried gasps made my heart race. His gills flared wildly. Shivering, he crawled toward me, despite the thousands of Empyreans surrounding him. Despite the goddess standing between us as she always had.

Lacuna… I'm trying.

I locked eyes with Jorun, who had moved in tandem with Aderyn to protect Crest. To him, I mouthed the word, *Go.* It was the command he'd agreed to follow when given. It would be difficult for him to carry them both, but he was strong. He needed to gather Aderyn and Crest and get them off this firmament. *Now.*

Neera fixed her attention on my fourth, then narrowed her eyes at Aderyn before focusing on Crest, who'd dared call out my name. Her wings snapped angrily. She was going to end them before they could escape. Her intention slammed into me as hot as a thunderbolt.

That was when I remembered that I had one to use against her.

"Don't forget where your sword is sheathed, or how hot it burns," The Salt said…

Quickly, I tore at the fastenings of my leathers and bared my scar. It called to her and she swiveled her head, forgetting my lacuna and my friends. In my periphery, Crest writhed on the ground.

My mark flashed with the indignant anger of my heart. She caught The Shark, but forgot that I had caught him first. He was *mine*. My lacuna. And I would do anything to protect him. I would guard him with my last breath.

I pressed a palm to my skin and called forth the lightning bolt sword. The power in that streak of fire thrummed against my hand.

Neera's golden eyes flared when I withdrew the fiery blade. She looked skyward and reached to the heavens with her free hand. Energy crackled around us as she unsheathed her own bolt, pulling it down from the blood-drenched clouds.

I swung hard and cut the scale in half, severing the chain, pans, and balancing post. The apparatus's top flopped over, hanging from the bottom. The bronze melted, then cooled instantly. Pans flailed, swinging wildly.

Neera, with her hand still gripping a thunderbolt, went completely still. Her gaze slid to the ruined apparatus held out before her. I wished the arc of my weapon had severed the hand with which she held it.

A quick glance over her shoulder confirmed that Crest, Aderyn, and Jorun had fled. That was all that mattered, for now. *They* were all that mattered.

When my eyes landed upon the goddess again, my mouth fell open. In her hand, the scale sat whole. The beam's solid brass mast stood proud and strong. The chain links were mended. Its pans rocked gently as though they'd been jostled and not intrinsically destroyed only seconds ago.

The scale will never set us free.

"Release me, Elira," Neera demanded, jerking the bolt from the cloud as easily as a Kehlanian child plucked a flower. She tossed the scale onto the landing and brought her fiery sword down on me. I blocked the blow, sparks and flame flying from our matched weapons.

She turned her head as if her ears pricked and offered a sinister smile before darting into the air.

I flew down the steps, stopping short when she reappeared seconds later with Aderyn. The sky goddess clutched my sister by her long, dark hair as she dangled, wingless in her hands. My heart thundered. The sky roared in perfect matching rhythm.

Why hadn't they reached the sea? Had they truly left, or did they regroup to help me when I specifically ordered them to go?

"Your second. Your sister," the goddess gloated. "Yet also a liar and a traitor, not only to her kind, but to you. She severed her wings, yet still returned to Empyrean knowing full well that she could not fly back to her refuge. Do you think she longs to soar through the air again? Do you think she regrets cleaving her only connection to her home and to you?"

"Don't," I asked, taking a step toward her. *Don't hurt her.*

"Cast away the sword," Neera ordered.

"No, Elira!" Aderyn shouted. She hissed when Neera gripped her hair tighter. Blood droplets slid from her scalp, painting her pale skin crimson. "It's your only defense." She yelped when Neera tightened her grip. "She's not capable of showing mercy."

"Cast away your sword and I'll let her go. I give you my word," Neera purred.

What choice was there? I tossed the bolt. It clattered down the steps like it was made of metal and not fire at all.

Satisfied, Neera flew near with Aderyn swinging painfully below her. She darted past me and soared over the Scholar's Village to the firmament's edge.

"No!" I gave chase.

Aderyn screamed, kicked, and clawed at her hands, but the goddess would not be dissuaded. She finally stopped over the sea. Then she relaxed her hold on my sister's hair and grinned. "I gave you my word."

I dove for my sister.

Tucked in my wings and arms.

The cold wind tore at my eyes and tangled my hair, squeezing tears from my eyes as I let out a guttural scream.

I couldn't seem to fly fast enough to catch her.

She fell faster and faster and I realized Neera was using her wind to propel Aderyn into the sea. She was trying to kill her in front of me.

And knew I wouldn't – couldn't – let her die.

I pressed my eyes closed and did the only thing I could, even though it was the last thing I should've done.

I called upon the Great Wind.

It roared around me, catching Aderyn and gently lowering her toward the sea. She fell into the water, making a foam circle, but emerged, bobbing on the sea's surface.

She reached out for me. "I'm okay. Take me back with you!"

I shook my head. "I can't. It's too dangerous for you now. It's my turn to leave you behind."

"NO!" she screeched. "Elira, the shells…"

I nodded rapidly. "I know." I knew what they foretold. Tipping up my chin, I returned her prior words. "I know the peril and accept my fate should I fall today."

"Please," she begged, "don't do this."

Tears blurred my vision. "Get the hatchlings to safety!"

Frey's burgundy hair surfaced next to my sister. The sea's Guardian would see the sky's Warrior safely to the shore.

I hurried to find Crest and Jorun before they faced the full wrath of the goddess I had just fully freed from her windy prison.

CHAPTER TWENTY-SEVEN

Just before I reached the saturated blood clouds, I was met by Era and Zura who were both soaked crimson after fleeing Empyrean, struggling to fly while supporting Jorun's weight. Era had his arms hooked under Jorun's and Zura held his feet. "Is he dead?" I asked, my heart pounding.

"Alive," Era grunted. "For now."

"And Crest?"

A crystalline tear carved through the gore on Zura's cheek. "They have him. We could only reach and help Jorun."

Breathless, I instructed, "Fly to Kehlani. There's a large tent on the southern shore. Do you know it?"

Era nodded. "I do."

"Hover above it and tell them I sent you. Tell them that Jorun needs Magma's help."

"But they'll shoot us!" Zura protested. She'd grown several inches since I saw her last. The curves of her youthful face had sharpened, as had her spirit.

I shook my head authoritatively. "You won't be targeted if you do as I say. Magma is a friend and so is The Salt. They know Jorun and will recognize his wings."

"The Salt?" Era mouthed, puzzled.

"Go," I told them. "The wind will see you there." I sent a sliver to support Jorun's weight and pushed it toward home, then flew through the sanguine clouds, nearly choking on the Empyrea they held. I reached the firmament's edge and raced back to the piazza. The Empyreans lining the square now lay prostrate, their foreheads pressed to the ground.

In the center of the space stood Neera. Not even a sliver of her was encased in the flesh of her conduit; she stood as the goddess herself.

The scale had forced her into flesh that looked startlingly like mine in its proportions, but you could see that the feel and fit of it was wrong. Barely contained power wafted from her like heat from a fire. Or perhaps that was the shifting currents of the wind streams with which she protected herself.

The whole of the sky, the kingdom, and even the hollows of my bones filled with the energy she exuded. She let it pour from her, not to flood us with comfort, but to drown us in fear.

What I felt of her in the sanctum that day was nothing compared to this. A speck of sand on a shore of infinite grains.

The Oracle's body lay discarded a few yards behind Neera.

Her amethyst eyes were lifeless now, staring at everything and nothing at all. Her beautiful jade wings were broken, the feathers jutting in odd angles.

Having the gift of a Seer made her special. Being chosen as the Oracle made her vital. Being Neera's conduit had proven fatal. Neera did not value the Oracle's gift, roles, or life, only what she could provide for her.

She needed no conduit now.

Neera's indigo hair whipped on the wind she ruled. With a simple command the Empyrea-laden clouds emptied into the sea. The vapor that remained dissipated like wisps of fog in warm sunlight, here one moment and gone the next. Her unscarred, golden armor shone. Her matching eyes glowed from within. Not dull from being hidden and dimmed within flesh that wasn't hers, but bright with righteous anger.

I would pay for caging her.

The irony wasn't lost on me. Her punishment was my greatest fear back when I didn't know I was already in a prison she'd constructed just for me.

From behind her, Crest was dragged forward by Talon and Soraya.

He gasped over and over and shivered so violently his teeth crashed together as he huddled forward to try and warm himself. His skin was pale blue, his beautiful lips a deep purple. The same currents that shielded her were draped around him. She was freezing him to death, breeze by breeze. Wrapping him in frigid air when his body desperately needed warmth and water. To breathe the brine.

Rivulets of blood slid from his gills. More flowed from his nostrils. Fresh bruises blossomed on his jaw and cheek and stomach.

Despite the fact that he was suffocating, he'd fought. Talon's nose was crooked and bleeding, the bridge already purple and swollen. Soraya's hair was torn from her braid and her chest heaved.

"Take your wind away from him," I demanded as I deftly nocked an arrow. Did she think I was foolish enough to try to strike her again?

My former quad members knew better. They knew the arrow was meant for one of them.

Talon cursed and released Crest to grab Soraya's arm. He jerked her in front of him, using her body as a shield. My arrow's tip cut through the center of her chest just as he slid her into place. It would have soared clean through her had my blue fletching not caught against her skin.

She doubled forward, her mouth agape and fingers wide as she considered what to do. "Healer," she wheezed. "I need a healer."

Talon ignored her plea for help, of course. Paid no mind when she sank to her knees.

He dipped his fingers into a fresh cut in his leathers. When he withdrew them, blood coated his fingertips, Empyrea jerking through the scarlet. I wasn't sure if the arrow left all its sky fire in Soraya's middle, or if just enough clung to the arrow's tip to affect him, too.

He wasn't about to let me take another shot. He jerked Crest upright and positioned The Shark in front of him.

Crest's eyes never left mine.

The sky held many shades of blue, but none the color of the brooding, beautiful sea. He wasn't made to thrive in this vast hollow where only wind dwelled. He was meant for a land filled with warmth and beasts and brine.

He mouthed something to me, but I couldn't make out what he was saying…

My brows furrowed.

He tried again, but I still couldn't understand him.

One of Talon's hands twitched and fell from Crest's bicep. He lifted it with great effort and shook his head as if clearing his vision. His breathing shallowed, his chest puffing and falling so fast I couldn't believe what I was seeing. I looked at his mouth, wondering how long it took sky fire to turn the tongue of an Empyrean into the mocking color of the sea.

Laughter bubbled up from that dark presence swirling in my belly. Her favorite flavor was retribution and she lapped up the panic that began to pour from Talon.

There had been *just* enough sky fire left for me to kill two traitors with one arrow. I wanted to kiss Magma's cheek, and Wade's, and even Koa's for good measure.

"Do you also need a healer, Talon?" I taunted him.

Talon's knee buckled. He swayed toward Soraya's limp form but righted himself. Soon, there would be no fighting Tella's toxin as it coursed through his veins. Soraya wasn't quite dead beside him. Her eyes still searched for help she wouldn't find in our people. For a mercy she'd neither given nor deserved. But her body would no longer obey her commands. It succumbed to the will of a goddess whose corporeal form might long be dead, but whose soul still craved justice.

A commotion came from atop the staircase of the sanctum. Elder Magnus, his back somehow bowed further than it was before I left, had stumbled and fallen. With no eyes, he couldn't see what impeded him. And with no mouth, he couldn't cry out for help.

Neera sneered and called him pathetic.

I fired another arrow at her in case she'd dropped her wall of wind when the scale forced her to take on this form. It was immediately batted away, but it did not strike anyone as they were all bowed in supplication.

"Why were you so adamant that I free you when you prefer the wind's embrace?" I chided. "But you're wise to be wary of my aim. If the wind wasn't guarding you, you'd be lying beside Soraya right now."

"The sky is my shield, Elira. It's my home. My heart, and my impenetrable skin."

She sent a frigid gust barreling toward The Shark and I watched as it cut into him like a thousand sharp knives.

Crest gasped wildly, his eyes going wide. He collapsed onto his side, clutching it. I started toward him, but Neera pointed a sword of Empyrea at my heart. "Don't," she warned. "He now knows where he belongs, and where his kind is not welcome. It's time you learned the same."

A powerful, unexpected explosion from somewhere beneath Empyrean rocked the firmament so violently that it tilted on its side. I wondered if the kingdom might topple. Wings fluttered, ready for flight, but no one took to the air, too afraid to move without the goddess's permission.

A harried shriek tore from Neera's chest as she looked at her damaged kingdom. She flew to the sanctum's platform and grabbed Elder Magnus by his tattered robes, who'd been struggling to stand back up after having been thrown by the blast. His back straightened with a series of painful pops.

"What have you done?" she screeched.

I hurtled over the thick line of Empyreans and ran to retrieve the lightning sword I'd cast down the steps earlier. The bolt sent a brutal shock rippling through my flesh when my fingers tried to curl around its handle. I was thrown back, landing against the backs of the Warriors I'd once fought alongside and led, knocking three of them over. Shaken, I stood as soon as my feet would carry me, wondering what happened and why I couldn't hold the lightning bolt anymore.

My eyes darted to Neera to see if she'd watched it reject me, but thankfully, she was preoccupied with Magnus and whatever he'd done to anger her.

With trembling fingers, I moved my leathers aside to look at my scar. The forked mark no longer glowed within my chest. The light in it had bled away like that in Soraya's eyes.

I pushed into the air to better see why the goddess of the sky was so flustered, gasping when I saw a wide chasm gaping in the firmament.

I searched the platform for her scale, but there was nothing but the landing, the Elder, and the hollow gash *he* had torn into the foundation of her sacred hall.

The scale was gone.

And if I was right, Talay had taken possession of it.

Sending it to a watery grave was Magnus's final, quiet act of defiance. I wondered if he bent to listen as it fell. If it made a shrill whistle as it raced toward the water. Was the thunderous explosion a trumpet of Talay's exuberance, a warning to me, or both?

Magnus could not speak through the flesh knitted over his mouth, but he tried. Rusted, muffled sounds grated from his throat. I imagined him telling her that the balance she so fervently valued was no more.

My heart sank.

I lifted a hand to try to pull away the wind still tightly encircling Crest, but it didn't obey. I couldn't help him now. And I couldn't help anyone who fell from the firmament, because the scale no longer lifted my powers and lessened hers. The pans had tipped, and Neera was not only free of her cage, but she was also free of the limitations she'd imposed on herself by demanding I become her equal.

That was why I couldn't touch the bolt without being shocked. Perhaps the purity of my blood was what kept it from killing me, but I wasn't confident it would help a second time. Without the magical balance with which she set her scale, Neera was greater than me again in all things. The first soul was reduced to flesh and bone. The goddess just hadn't realized it yet. But when she did…

Roaring in response to his deadened words, Neera plunged her hand into his chest and squeezed his heart until it burst in her hand with a sickening squelch. She pulled out the shredded flesh and dropped the lump to the firmament, her hand and forearm soaked with Magnus's blood.

She tossed the Elder's body down the sanctum steps, his skull cracking on the sharp edge of one…

two… of them.

A gasp slid from between the lips of everyone she hadn't yet muted.

Neera had destroyed the Oracle and now she'd killed a revered Elder.

In brushing our attempts at killing her away, the innocent had died. How many more of us would she see fall? Better yet, how many would she allow to live?

Just beyond Magnus's prone body, a group of brave younglings peered up at me from their downcast faces. Their gazes urged me to do something to stop her. Talon, their new General, had done nothing to stop Neera. He'd probably bent the knee the moment she took over the Oracle.

Their Commander, Soraya was dead. I was the top-ranked quad leader. The successor to their highest roles. And the final hope.

Some moments were powerful enough to alter the course of fate in a place where clarity and decision entwined. Moments that echoed through your mind in such a cacophony, you weren't sure which thought was yours or if all of them were. Times when the path of your life came to an abrupt stop because the path you treaded upon forked. One direction led to destruction, while the other… the other led to prosperity. Victory. Freedom.

I just had to choose correctly which divergent path to set out on.

The scale was gone now.

The scale was gone, and so were its demands.

Its balances.

And my advantage. Neera was right about that.

I was no stronger than any other Warrior whose foreheads dented the square.

The goddess stretched, groaning in relief as she grew and stretched out of the skin the scale had forced her to wear.

I couldn't allow her to get to Crest. Couldn't let him die here when Talay was just beneath us, waiting. I dove for him before she finished her transformation, and like I'd pushed Koa through the core of the tightly twisting funnel, I pushed The Shark through the firmament, melting it beneath my hands. It, thankfully, still recognized me and my blood and obeyed, giving way immediately and allowing us passage.

Crest gasped and clung to my neck as best as he could. His skin was so cold and flying this fast would only make it worse, but I had to believe that Talay could thaw him and preserve his best warrior if I could set him in the sea. He would defend the souls he had made.

"I failed," I choked. "She's free and she's coming. I'm sorry." Neera would end us all. Her fury built in the sky behind us until it crackled. Thunderheads built and boomed so loud, my eardrums were nothing but a loud buzz.

I felt the Empyrea clawing at me with its fiery, forked claws, but there would be no taking hold of a thunderbolt now. Like my poison-tipped arrow had pierced Soraya and Talon, it felt like the goddess intended to strike both me and The Shark as we fled from her.

Crest's teeth chattered in my ear. "Your featherssss."

I glanced back to see a thick trail of blue gray tearing loose from my wings. I held my lacuna tighter to lend him what warmth I had left. My feathers, my wings – they didn't matter now. All I cared about was ferrying him into the waiting arms of the sea god.

I flapped harder toward the deep blue. My wings felt as thin as the hope that plummeted with us. The Salt said that Talay would help where and when he could…

"Talay!" I screamed, the briny salt spray finally rising to meet us. "I need you. *He* needs you!"

"She's here!" Crest gritted, tightening his hold on me.

I flapped my wings harder, barreling toward the plume of smoke that poured from Tella's molten heart. "We can lose her in the smoke, but you cannot breathe it, Crest. Can you hold your breath?"

He chattered a 'yes' into my ear.

Turning my head, I saw the goddess following my feathered trail. People used to say that my father, The General was the fastest flyer in Empyrean, though they claimed I'd taken the title when he was awarded his illustrious position and I was elevated into the top-seated rank. But neither of us had ever flown as fast as the goddess that ruled the great blue sky.

"Deep breath!" I panted.

We entered the dense cloud, and I adjusted our course to fly through it toward the sea. I could see nothing. The hot air, along with noxious gas and ash bit my exposed flesh.

Crest's back would be blistered.

A deep ache filled the follicles that were achingly empty in the skin and bone of my wings. With what remained I tried to push harder, emerging from the plume to fly alongside it so we could breathe, using the smoke as cover. I needed to see the ocean we were about to slam into. My movements were becoming more and more difficult to control. It was harder to veer one way or another, and I knew that when I tried to slow us, there would be little left of my wings to flare. Flesh was not the same as feathers.

Tears squeezed from my eyes. "I'm sorry," I told him again. I was sorry that I wasn't strong enough. Fast enough. Fierce enough. That I couldn't save him, and that I wouldn't reach the sea before she caught us.

"I feel Talay…!" he shouted into my ear.

Suddenly, the sea that was too far beneath us began to rise to meet us.

Before I could tell him that I loved him and thank him for loving me, an enormous swell swept over us like a mighty hand. Water swelled to my neck, then drained away as the god of the sea caught his Shark in a giant, cresting wave.

I let him go. I'd gotten him home.

As the water sank back into the ocean, I heard a loud snap from behind my neck followed by a splash. A small circle of bubbles rose beneath me. I desperately felt for my bow and looked down to find it missing.

My bowstring had snapped under the water's weight. It had been taken into the water with Crest, and now the only weapon I possessed was a single sky fire arrow rattling alone in an otherwise hollow quiver. I reached over my shoulder and found its fletching, then held it before me like a blade, careful of the tip, knowing that the goddess's unrestrained power would snap it and me like insignificant twigs.

Crest shouted beneath me. He called my name. He called for his guardians. Fully willing to risk their lives for mine.

I stared at the tip of the arrow and considered my father. Then remembered that Crest was watching me…

"No!" he screamed. "No, Elira."

Time seemed to slow. The salt spray ate away at the blood staining my leathers. Neera was coming. The Great Wind whipped my blood-saturated hair as it parted the smoke and ash, eager to make a path for the ruler of the sky.

My wings were nearly empty. Would barely hold me.

But if I was to die on this day, it would not be by her hand.

And I would remind her that it was *she* who cut me into sharp facets and placed me amid the Warriors, knowing what and who I was. That sometimes we choked on the bitterness of our own truths and failed to honor our intentions. That we forgot what lay dormant in our blood.

I stared at the sea, then looked at her.

Decision made, I curled my hand tightly around the arrow's shaft, tightly tucked in my ruined wings, and dove toward the water.

Neera shrieked behind me. I could almost feel her breath on my neck, her wind desperately trying to curl around me when I surprised us both by breaking the surface with my hands outstretched and breath trapped in my chest – for now.

The sea burst into bubbles all around me. They slid silkily over my skin and then up, up to the surface. I fought the terror and blind panic clawing from my chest, heralded by the crush of waves rolling over my head. I was as powerless against them as I was her.

I tilted my head and looked up through the waters to see Neera circling above in the place where she thought I'd died. She searched for me amid the circle of foam. Water filled my ears and nostrils, the salt stinging my eyes as I fought to stay beneath the glassy surface.

Like a vision pouring from the sea's dark heart, I saw the glint of copper. Inhumanly fast, the Shark came to me, a short, but sharply barbed trident clenched in his steely grip. He wasn't alone. Koa and Frey were there, just as well-armed and ready to help their leader – *and* his lacuna. Ready to do their duties as Guardians of the sea, the people of Kehlani.

But there was something else. *Someone* else.

I'd felt Neera's dreadful shadow move within the sanctum on my last Intention Day and beheld the power in the very walls of her sacred hall answer to her commands.

Talay felt *nothing* like her. Where Neera's shadow was a formidable specter, Talay's presence was as full, wise, and ancient as the sea, his heart just as fathomless. He appeared from the darker water beneath me, his body formed of the creatures he kept.

The god of the sea was comprised of starfish and crabs, octopi and sharks, rays and turtles, and colorful, glistening schools of fish. They formed a crustacean crown upon his brow, his mighty hands, and an immense tail that stretched so far into deeper water, I could barely see the fins at its bottom.

Talay swam between Crest, Koa, and Frey, appearing before me as my lungs began to burn and ache for air. As I fought to stay beneath the waves.

He gestured toward the shore where lava still flowed into the sea, its stubborn fire pushing inch by inch through the water that cooled it. From this place, steam rose into the sky. Not from the caldera but from the clash of hot and cold, new and old.

I nodded to indicate that I understood him.

We had landed in the place where oceans burn and where skies fall.

The voice of the sea roared in my head.

Crest tilted his head to Talay, listening, then extended the small trident to me. I dropped the sky fire arrow I'd clung to and tightened my fist around the trident's copper shaft.

The sea god guided me upward with my back to the surface. I let my entire body fall limp, allowing only my fleshy wings to bob atop the swells that Talay calmed so that they gently rocked me.

Relax and stay still, I told myself. *Don't take a breath yet. Don't move a muscle.* My legs felt heavy drifting beneath me.

Reaching out for Talay, begging him for help, I flinched and hoped she hadn't seen.

Bubbles bled from my mouth. I needed air desperately. My vision began to blur, but he was there with me.

The heartbeat thumping in my head began to slow until it fell into a cadence I immediately recognized. It was the same pulsing rhythm that the shells in The Salt's home had played to mark my last breaths.

Talay reached out both of his hands and brushed his fingers over either side of my neck. Pain flared from his ministrations, incredibly sharp, but short-lived. The jolt startled me and the breath I'd kept trapped bubbled away.

Panic rose. I fought the urge to turn my face toward the goddess of the sky and breathe in her air and face the fate she had planned for me – body and soul. Crest moved close and ran his hands over the places Talay had just touched.

My lacuna calmed me like nothing else possibly could have.

Crest pointed to his gills and then to me. I lifted my hands to find that Talay had slitted my skin. I pressed a hand to my chest and felt my heartbeat growing stronger. The sea god had rearranged my body in one touch to allow the sea to give me life in the way that it did his people. Now, I was wholly one of his own. Now, I could breathe beneath the waves, swim and not drown. And in them, I could finally see a clear path to victory over the oppressor from the sky.

I felt *her*, as close as one's reflection in mirrored glass, hovering just above me. The waves were no danger to her now that the sea had gone as still as I kept my body.

She thought I had died.

She saw my ragged, lifeless appendages bobbing on the water atop the bejeweled sea. *She* swept low, but rose again just in case… Testing… tempting…

More minutes passed. Crest and Talay stayed with me. Koa and Frey flanked us three. The brine filtered through my body and my strength returned, then built.

I held the trident close to my forearm, concealing it as best I could.

She swooped low again. Until finally, the beating of her wings buffeted the air just above mine. When *she* pushed *her* hands into the cold water, the sea thrummed with Talay's advice…

Not yet.

Frigid, cruel fingers curled around the strongest of my wing's bones, but I stayed limp, holding my breath and allowing *her* to think *she* had killed me. That *she* had won and I'd chosen to drown rather than face *her* wrath now that the scale favored *her*.

She dragged me from the water, starting back toward Empyrean. I could envision her tossing my listless body on the piazza and forbidding any soul from touching me. My people would watch as the sky slowly and cruelly decayed and consumed me – a warning to anyone else who would dare stand against her.

Now, Talay instructed.

Neera looked skyward, her grip tightening on my bones. Slowly, I maneuvered the trident into position and gripped it tightly. Mentally bracing myself for the pain I was about to cause myself, I twisted fast and hard and thrust the short barbs deep into her chest.

My wing bones had snapped the moment I rotated, and still she held their broken frame. Fiery pain erupted and I suddenly knew why Tella's mountain burned. A guttural scream tore from my chest, but Neera didn't let go. I didn't thrash. I wanted her to *see me* as she held me there in front of her, broken but not beaten.

She stared at my hands now both firmly wrapped around the weapon's handle, until her golden eyes rose to meet mine. A myriad of questions swam in the molten gold.

Did this actually happen? Is it real? Is this truth?

That she'd lost the war.

Her power over me had ended.

The sky was free of her just as I was.

That the goddess of the sky could perish by the soul she'd crafted to rival her own.

She coughed and pure Empyrea slid from her lips, trailing down her chin. It sizzled when it met Talay's water.

"You were right, Neera. The war ends in the place where oceans burn."

Her eyes slid sideways to the steaming water, trailing over the red-orange streams of lava, rising to the miles-high plume of smoke and ash and steam.

A look of horror marred her face as she realized where we were. She tried to push me away but could not free herself of the trident's barbed tips. Her ability to fly faltered.

"Release me, wretch!" she gasped. More Empyrea spittle bubbled from her lips.

"A wretch I may be, but as your soul flies into the hereafter, I hope you remember me as Elira. Your first soul. Warrior of the sky. Guardian of the sand and sea. And most appropriately, I hope you forever know me as your ruin."

She bared her ichor-coated teeth and released my broken wing bones to clutch my wrists, not trying to break my hold on the trident's handle.

No, if she was going down, so was I. But she didn't know I was already home. My lacuna waited just beneath the waves. I felt my gills flare and heard her gurgling gasp.

Several more of my wing bones cracked as we spun toward the water. Our legs slapped, then cut into the brine, but that was all Talay needed. She pleaded, to whom I wasn't sure. But the goddess of the sky begged for her life in the moment before it was taken.

Neera sank, the sea consuming her inch by inch.

Her legs…

waist and wings…

chest and neck…

her mouth and nose and head…

I refused to release the trident embedded in her chest until Talay came.

Neera finally released my wrists. Like Talon's grip on Crest had failed under the weight of the sky fire toxin, Neera's faltered under the weight of the water.

What was the one thing that could kill a goddess?

Neera had given us all the answer when she slew Tella.

Only another of equal power could end her. I could drag her into the water, but only Talay could truly destroy her. A god among the gods.

I watched alongside The Shark, Koa, and Frey as Talay took the trident from me and dragged Neera into the dark depths, as far from the sky as he possibly could. A watery wake spread out behind them as they descended. I wondered if he would bury her in the soil at the bottom of the world. In Tella.

I pushed to the surface, needing to breathe the air and see the sky. It wasn't that I didn't appreciate Talay's gift, I just needed to prove to myself that I was still alive.

Crest surfaced at my side, the reflection of the silvery gray above us like velvet over his wet skin. "It's over now," he rasped, gathering me in his arms.

I clung to him, because though he kept me perfectly safe, I felt like I was sinking. Like Talay was dragging *me* to a watery grave instead. He very nearly *had* taken me into the burial trench. I nearly lost this battle. This war.

But now, it was over and I felt like collapsing. A tent succumbing to the power of a gale after withstanding years of battering.

I now intimately knew how Neera felt when she looked at me and questioned whether any of it was real and true and actually happening.

A sob tore from my chest and I wept, clinging to my lacuna. Because the sky felt empty. Calm and serene. And though I was broken and my wings were ruined, I was free. We all were.

CHAPTER TWENTY-EIGHT

On the shore, Aderyn anxiously waited with Magma. Just behind them stood Breaker and Katalini, Wade, The Salt, and more Kehlanians than I could count. Zura was among them, too.

My legs wobbled as Crest helped me out of the rushing waves.

Magma clapped her hands over her mouth at the sight of my wrecked wings. I winced, still crying as the breakers bent my broken wings even further. She hurried to me before I left the water behind. Her skirt soaked immediately. I lost my footing and stumbled forward.

"Don't touch her!" Magma cried. "You'll hurt her worse."

Crest, though his injuries were nearly as severe as mine, did what he could to help ease my fall, but I crashed onto my knees in the gritty sand. My palms indented the soaked grains. I caught my breath, wondering how my shattered wings could make breathing so painful. Then I realized it wasn't my lungs that hurt, it was that when they expanded, they moved my back and the roots of my wings were pure agony.

Water surged around my body before Talay pulled it back into the sea.

With great effort and trembling shoulders, I raised my head to look at the healer, unable to speak around the boulder in my throat. I could only mouth the word, *Help*.

Wade, wearing his new leg, rushed forward with Aderyn.

I accepted their help, sobbing when I could barely push myself into a standing position.

Frey and Koa helped The Shark stand, and someone threw a blanket around his shoulders. His skin was still blue despite the warm sea. The brine scrubbed away the blood that had slid out of his gills, but was he hurt beyond what I could see?

Beside me, Wade and my sister each supported a forearm because the moment I tried to lift my arms to brace over their shoulders, I nearly buckled from the pain.

Aderyn asked people to move so I could pass. My ankles felt weak and wobbled when I trudged forward. I gripped their hands, mine shaking from the effort it took to even take a step.

"Jorun?" I asked her through teeth that chattered, not from cold, but from the excruciating pain lancing through my wings and back.

Another step…

Then another…

Would we ever reach Magma's workshop at this pace?

"Jorun is alive. Era is with him," Aderyn answered.

I breathed a fraction easier. Then I wondered what his injuries might be and whether he would survive them.

Just when I opened my mouth to inquire about his state, I took a step into the downy soft, deeper sand and swayed. The world tipped exactly like Empyrean had and a buzz of dark spots filled my vision. A commotion of voices, all undiscernible save for one… Crest was in front of me? Beside me? I couldn't tell.

Strong arms lifted me. "I've got her," Breaker's voice announced.

He and Crest argued, but Breaker won.

"Brother, let me carry her for you right now. I promise not to hurt her."

I felt like I was flying… but that wasn't possible now.

A tear slipped from my eye and slid into my hair, warm and wet.

No… I wasn't flying at all. I was floating, my face turned to the surface, long arms outstretched and limp.

"Mind her wings, Breaker," Magma warned as the buzzing in my ears drowned her out.

I woke laying on my stomach on the Mender's cot, groggy and confused. Scared until I recognized the room and its familiar contents and scent. Magma's counter lay piled high with ingredients for her pastes, teas, and tinctures. But I didn't recall what landed me in it – at first. When I did, panic set in.

"Calm down, Elira," Magma warned. "Breathe. You're safe."

Why was it that the words 'calm down' always evoked the opposite of their speaker's intent?

"My wings," I croaked, feeling the absence of them on my back. Their reassuring comfort and weight, their strength… they were gone now.

With a sigh, Magma carefully sat on her stool at my side and brushed the hair from my face. My skin should've been crusted with dried blood, but it felt soft and clean as she ran her hands over it. "Aderyn and I bathed you," she told me. "We had to be sure there were no injuries overpowered by those you sustained to your wings."

"Can I sit up?" I cried, unable to stanch the flow of tears.

"If you feel like you can, then yes."

She hovered as I maneuvered until I sat facing her.

Glancing over my shoulder was a mistake. The roots of my wings were bandaged tightly, drawing attention to the fact that my once luxurious wings – a source of pride – had been sheared away, leaving only nubs. A deep, unnatural ache pounded through them with every beat of my heart, but I wouldn't call it pain. It was more like the blood that pushed through my wings was now impeded and broke against the new and unexpected wall. I wondered if The Salt's shells throbbed to this new rhythm.

"Why don't they hurt?"

"Because Aderyn formed a cauterizing cloud with your blood."

Surprised, I asked, "Is there still Empyrea in my veins?"

Magma nodded. "As pure as the day you were born."

For now. Would it dissipate now that Neera was gone? Or would we be the last generations to possess it?

Her lightning, her wind – they fully belonged to the hollow sky. It was a lot to take in, but as acutely as I felt the absence of my wings, it was a relief to feel the absence of the goddess.

"Where is he?" I asked of Crest.

"I'll get him," Aderyn offered. "The Salt sounded her shell and he left to attend her. Before she called, I couldn't pry him from your side, and believe me I tried."

Magma stood from her stool and started toward the door.

I looked to the tent's top, hoping that focusing on something, anything, might take away this misery, but I wasn't sure anything could.

"Your wings were part of you, and you have every right to mourn them," Magma said softly. "But they weren't you, Elira."

Tears slid down my cheeks, diving off my jaw. "Would you say the same of your scales?"

"I think so, eventually."

Then perhaps she should check back in a few weeks and see if I'd come around.

Magma studied me for a long moment. "If you feel unsteady, lay back down."

"I will," I promised.

Satisfied with my vow of compliance, she set out to fetch my lacuna.

Moments later, Crest and The Salt entered Magma's tent with Aderyn close on their heels. The moment he walked in, I slowly stood. His hair had been cut. It was short now. My fingers twitched with the need to touch it and him. The muscle in his jaw jumped as he ground his teeth.

There was concern in his blues, but anger shone in them, too. Hot and glassy, like the emotion could melt the eye from within.

Whatever restrained him snapped and he rushed to me, carefully wrapping me in his arms. I clung to him, pressed my face into the crook of his shoulder, and bawled. Neera tried to kill him slowly in front of me and I was powerless to save him. "I'm so sorry!" I pleaded.

Beneath my hands, his shoulders hardened. "Why would you say that? You have nothing to apologize for."

I fought to catch my breath. "I couldn't help you."

"You helped *everyone*, Elira," he said adamantly, even as his voice crumbled. "You saved us all."

"I just want to go home," I told him.

He looked over my head at his grandmother to get her permission. She sighed. "Alright, but I want to see her tomorrow and every day after until she's healed."

The Salt lingered near the door with Aderyn. I inched toward them. The Salt wore all white, her dark skin glistening and smelling of coconut. Her hand was fisted at her side. She extended it and unfurled her fingers. My cowrie sat in the center of several others. Boldly formed on the back of my shell were my outstretched blue wings.

"Just moments ago, Talay called me to the shore." She gestured to one shell at a time. "These are for Jorun, Aderyn, and your hatchling siblings."

I nodded my thanks, unable to speak, then eased her palm closed.

She hugged me as well as she could. "I never lost hope, because I knew it was the one thing you held within your heart. We find our greatest strength in the moment when all seems lost," she sagely whispered, releasing me from her careful embrace.

I nodded my thanks to Aderyn for helping me from the shore, but didn't move to hug her or even extend my hand. Something held me back.

Crest and I walked slowly home beside one another. It was nearly dark, the sun setting in a brilliant wash of the most spectacular hue of orange I'd ever seen.

"Tella is settled," he told me, pointing to the Green Mountains. The volcano was scarred, but quiet. No steam or ash billowed. No lava flowed.

In Crest's tent, I noticed that the cache of weapons he normally kept by the far tent wall was gone. Only the single, small trident I thrust into Neera's chest lay on his wooden floor.

I padded to it, picking it up and running my thumb over one of the barbs that had cut into the heart of the goddess of the sky. Glancing at Crest, I waited for him to explain how he'd gotten it back. Had he gone into the deep?

He cleared his throat. "Talay returned it to the shore."

The bed he'd given me sat against the far wall. The last time I'd seen it, it was in my tent for Jorun, Aderyn, and the hatchlings to rest upon.

Crest saw me looking at it. "Aderyn insisted that you have it so the hammock doesn't hurt you as you heal."

What had she slept on while healing after her wings were cut away? Without having her wing roots cauterized, how long was it before she was able to leave Magma's tent? How did she bear the pain during the long walk to the hollow?

"How long was I out?" I asked him.

"Most of this excruciatingly long day."

"All days are equal," I told him.

"They're not. The ones where you're in danger or hurt, or anything but blissful, are far longer," he replied in a clipped tone.

I tilted my head sideways. "You're angry with me."

"Furious," he sharply corrected.

I knew he would be. If I were in his shoes, I would be upset, too. His footsteps fell heavily over the floorboards. His breathing turned ragged as he moved closer.

If he thought I would apologize, he was wrong. I did what I felt was right; I did the same thing he would've done. I narrowed my eyes at his angry blues.

"Would you have me lie and tell you I'll do it differently if the need arises in the future?"

"Lacuna," he breathed, capturing a strand of my long, pale hair between his fingers. "I intend to make sure it will be *impossible* for you to imagine leaving me behind again."

Well, then. I swallowed thickly, heat flooding my body.

"And how will you manage such a feat?" I croaked.

He left me with only that dark promise, though I was thrumming with need by the time his fingers trailed my hair to its tip, then fell away. "You'll see – once you're healed. And not a moment before."

"Lacuna…" I tried, finally touching his shorter hair, raking my fingers and nails through it. His eyes fluttered closed. He breathed through his nose, trying to keep calm. To restrain himself.

Still… I craved his unleashing.

Crest caught my wrist and moved it to my side before he left me standing there alone to think about what he'd said, and what I could expect. I decided to make my own plans for when he finally gave in to me.

CHAPTER TWENTY-NINE

I pushed faster, holding tight to Crest, desperately trying to control my nearly-bare wings, begging Talay to do something – anything to save him. When he sent up a towering wave, I nearly cried as I released Crest into his care.

That was when Neera caught me by the shoulder and shoved a sword of lightning through my chest.

The Shark roared from below, watching, his eyes wide with horror as my goddess waited for me to die. She would not give me over to Talay. Would not allow anyone or anything to resurrect me.

"I unmake you, first soul," Neera seethed. "Before your beloved, before the god you would choose over me, before all the sky, sand, and sea. I unmake you…"

The nightmares made sleeping difficult because in my mind, the goddess who hated me still lived on. Still tormented me. Still sought to end me in every imaginable way.

Her memory was a cage in which I was trapped, and I had no idea how to truly break free of it and her. Neera was gone. I knew that while I was lucid, but it was as if my mind had not clasped the fact and refused to release the fear she imparted when I slept.

Dawn brushed the sky in streaks of lavender and gold. The hues were softer, but they reminded me of the Oracle's and goddess's eyes. Tender waves slowly rolled ashore, then took their time dragging over the sand to return home. Gulls squawked as they flitted from spot to spot along the shoreline to gobble up tiny fish gathered at the sea's edge.

I kept having to remind myself that I was alive and on Kehlani.

That Crest was here. Safe.

That everyone I cared for was.

On a more selfish note, I tried to distract myself from the reality that my wings were gone. At that, I failed miserably. To say the least, my emotions were difficult to temper today.

Crest dipped his hands into a small tide pool and plucked a red starfish out of it. He carried it to the water while its arms curled around his fingers.

"I can't thank Talay enough, Crest."

Maybe it was my tone, but he looked at me from over his shoulder, his eyes unguarded. I watched his dark sarong flutter against his calves. "He knows you have a grateful heart. He just hates that you have to endure this sadness before the joy comes."

I tried to smile, hoping the joy he spoke of so confidently would hurry.

We were on the way to meet one of his Guardians. Crest hadn't said which one to expect on the shore. We left a long line of footprints in the sand before we saw someone approaching in the distance. I couldn't make out his face at first, but the moment the wind carried his humming to me, I knew him.

Wade.

My chin trembled as he made his way closer. His brown skin glistened as the sun grew stronger, rising higher.

Crest mumbled an excuse about needing to see The Salt and jogged up the dune path, disappearing a few steps later. The sea oats bent and bobbed alongside him.

"You look well," Wade told me encouragingly, his icy blue eyes warm despite their cool hue. It was the same thing I'd told him when he woke after his leg was taken by the shark.

"When will I feel like I truly am?" I asked.

"It takes a bit. Longer for those of us who are stubborn."

I muttered a curse, fighting the tears building in my eyes.

"Elira… when you carved this leg for me, you didn't give me the ability to walk again."

My brows met, because that was exactly why I'd carved it. And exactly what the leg was for.

"The walking only came because you gave me the push I needed to live again. The life I knew was over, so I thought *everything* was. I didn't think I'd walk, or swim, or be lacuna material. I didn't think I'd get to be a father one day, because who would want someone who's mangled? But you showed me I was wrong. My life didn't end when the shark took my leg. That's why I kept my promise and immediately donned the leg, even though I was terrified it wouldn't work, or that I'd fall in front of everyone. At that point, I didn't want any more pity. You know?"

I nodded. I knew exactly what he meant, already dreading the stares and whispers I knew would erupt when I garnered the courage to enter the crowd in only a handful of days, my back bandaged where my beloved wings used to sit.

Breaker had come by earlier to make sure I was up to celebrating our victory. We would all contribute to a grand feast and sup together as one in Talay's temple. There, Breaker and Katalini would announce their happy news now that nothing sinister lurked in the sky above them.

The vision he had of the future, the one he shared with me when we first met, was coming to fruition and I could see the spark of hope in Breaker's eyes. When he spoke. When he looked at his lacuna. When he peered into the faces of his people.

Wade stared at the sea. "I can't carve a functional set of wings for you. I would if I could, believe me. But I *can* give you one thing, and that's my friendship. And I vow to remind you every day that your life didn't end because you can't soar. The sky still brushes you, even on the land. The wind still plays with your hair." He gestured to where pale strands lifted from my shoulders. "You survived her against all odds, Elira. Life can continue for you here on Kehlani and it can be beautiful. Far more fulfilling than the one you left behind."

I gave a slight smile. "And here I thought you hated me, Wade."

He laughed. "I did. Believe me. But things change, and so do people." He jutted his chin resolutely toward the water. "You need to have Crest teach you to swim. Then you could earn the title of *The Scourge of the Sea*."

I tried to smile. Tried to envision swimming as fast as Crest, of conquering the sea's currents as I once had the sky's. My gills flared and my fingers raced to smooth them, not because I wasn't grateful, but because the feeling was so foreign.

"Thank you, Wade."

Before we could feast, we needed a reason to celebrate. Peace had to be negotiated and a threat made, and I wanted to be the one to make it.

I donned my leathers, careful of my bandages as I tightened the buckles, and waited for Jorun to finish doing the same. My pale hair blew sideways in the soft breeze blowing off the waves.

It still seemed strange that malice no longer pushed the regal wind now that Neera was gone. The sky had claimed its inheritance, so forever the weather would just *be*. Storms would come and go. Clouds would build and fade. There would be days of quiet and nights of torrents, but none of it would come from Neera.

She was gone, though well-worn fear made me question the truth at every turn.

Even now as we prepared to go skyward, I reached out to feel her and my heart and mind found nothing. Not a shred of her lingered.

Other than a few lacerations, Jorun's injuries consisted of internal bruising. Most of it came from the attentions of Talon and a few close friends he kept. They'd beaten him unconscious, then kicked his prone form some more for sport.

If I hadn't already killed Talon, his death would take precedence over any negotiation for peace.

I didn't even have to ask Jorun to carry me. And though I hated the discomfort my added weight would add to his battered body, it had to be done and it had to be him. Era and Zura would struggle to carry me that far, though I was sure they would try if I asked. Aderyn was willing but *couldn't.*

Before Jorun volunteered and before I accepted his offer, I'd already checked with Magma about his condition. When I asked our Mender if carrying me so far would kill him, she'd reluctantly admitted it wouldn't cause long-lasting harm, but emphasized that it would be *markedly unpleasant* for him.

She also forbade me from asking him to do so before he was fully healed, but this couldn't wait. This conversation was one that if put off too long could prove catastrophic amid such a fragile time.

The war had ended in *our* eyes, but I needed to know it was over to those in power in Empyrean. The Kehlanians needed to impose limits to our tenuous peace and make clear the consequences of breaking our new trust.

Aderyn stood nearby, her arms crossed and a fierce but concerned look on her face. "I wish I could go with you," she said for the fourth time.

"Jorun and I will be fine." Small tridents were strapped to my arms and thighs. I held a larger one in my hand.

She flung a frustrated hand toward the weapons I'd borrowed from Crest. "What good will those do you in

Empyrean? You need your bow. You can't even wear your quiver!"

"My bow is gone, Aderyn," I reminded her. "Besides, I likely won't need it."

"When did you become an optimist, Elira?" she demanded, seeing through my false bravado.

Crest and Breaker lingered nearby. The leader of Kehlani had worn a path in the sand into which the sea had begun to seep.

I sighed. "Out with it, Breaker. Stop pacing and say what you need to."

His pacing stopped and the request fell from his lips. "*Please* be cordial, Elira," Breaker begged.

I raised my chin defiantly. "I will do no such thing."

"They have to know we want peace," he argued.

"They have to know we want peace, but that we're willing to bring forth a greater war if they breach the terms of our negotiated treatise."

Crest smiled proudly, brilliantly, ignoring the way Breaker rubbed the stress away from the corner of his eyes.

"I'll be back as soon as I can," I told my lacuna.

He hadn't called me that. Hadn't told me he didn't love me since I landed on the shore. Last night, he laid in the bed at my side, but barely touched me. I couldn't help but wonder whether leaving him behind hurt him far worse than I realized. Maybe it had caused irreparable damage. Perhaps I had wounded him in a way that couldn't be mended.

The very thought turned my stomach.

"Ready?" Jorun asked.

I nodded and waited as he gently lifted me into his arms. Pain glossed his eyes as he smothered a sharp wince.

But he pushed through the discomfort, and soon his long wings flapped and carried us into the sky.

The sky city of Empyrean was still tilted. Jorun flew me beneath it where a simple push of my palms set it straight. My blood had made this firmament and it still knew me and obeyed.

Jorun brought me to the square next. He landed in the middle and eased me down so I could stand. There was no need to shout or announce our arrival. When I set the city right, the people of Empyrean poured out of their nests and homes and into the streets. They saw and were drawn to us, cautious but curious.

"Who is in charge?" Jorun asked a nearby Warrior. Her eyes were fastened – not on my eyes, but on the absence of my wings.

"He asked you a question," I snapped at her.

She startled and promised to return quickly.

Murmurs and shouts came from every direction and soon we were surrounded. The Warriors of the sky were armed as I expected, but they didn't point their arrows or draw their bows or swords. Instead, one-by-one, they raised their fists. As did those I recognized from the general populace.

The brazen younglings.

The clutch of hatchlings.

The Scholars.

And the Clipped.

This wasn't the first time Empyrean's people had raised their fists to honor me or Jorun, but it was the first time that truly mattered.

Jorun's jaw worked and my heart thumped with an emotion I couldn't name.

Pride and shame warred with me. We had set things right because we'd found something worth fighting for. Something worth dying for. They just reaped the benefits.

They didn't know I'd prepared their enemy to fight them, to kill them with the sky fire they'd first aimed at the souls on the shore.

I once lavished in their respect and garnered their praise because it bolstered my ego. Fed my pride. My hunger for power. The person I was before falling would have loved to see their tribute, but I found I didn't want it anymore. All I wanted, all I cared about, were the opinions of the people I loved – my lacuna's paramount to all the rest.

There were moments that severed a person's past from their future, and though we rarely recognized them when they happened – they were far easier to spot after distance was applied – I knew I was standing in the middle of such a consequential divide.

Jorun straightened his back and glanced in my direction. Was he as uncomfortable as I was?

"I don't see the Elders," he quietly observed.

He was right. I'd searched for pale wings and eyes and found none. Were they who the girl went to collect?

The crowd parted before the sanctum and from between the wings of the Empyreans, the Seer-Archivist Gamut emerged. The first thing I noticed was her humble walk and the hand pressed to her heart. The second was her unexpectedly kind eyes. Their hue was a soft green, the color of blades of sea grass. Her snowy hair was braided and delicately wreathed her head.

"You, Elira, have set things right in far more ways than one, I see." She spoke of the kingdom, and of the goddess.

Jorun let out a pent-up breath at my side and flashed a hopeful glance.

Gamut walked to me and leaned in to quietly whisper, "Did Era and Zura survive?"

I nodded. "Both are safe on the shore."

Her eyelids pressed closed for a long moment. "I'm glad to hear it. I could use his help as we rebuild."

"I'll give him your request," I promised. "I came to discuss the peace we've dwelled in during these past days."

"Of course," the Seer answered. "We would like to ensure it continues."

"Then we need to come to an agreement on certain things, Gamut."

Her head bobbed. "I wholly agree. As do the other Scholars."

"What about the Elders?" I inquired.

"As a people, we have decided to remove the elect from power. Moving forward, in order to fairly represent all of Empyrean, a committee will be formed. Each walk of life will elevate one to represent and speak on their behalf. The committee will vote on matters of importance – the peace process being the most vital, of course, as a new era of tranquility is forged in the smoldering cinders of a war that burned far too long." She looked from me to Jorun and back again.

Jorun shifted uneasily at my side. He cleared his throat and raised his voice. "I appreciate that you are working hard to institute the sort of change that will echo through generations in a very short amount of time. But know that in time, things will likely have to be tweaked and corrected. Nothing is perfectly formed the first time. I have no say in Empyrean's future, as I want no part of it. I plan to live out the rest of my days on the Isle of Kehlani. But if I could offer you one piece of advice that might prevent immediate strife and discord, I would suggest that you avoid binding yourselves with past prejudices and allow equal representation to the formerly oppressed Clipped, and those you might seek to punish for Neera's actions. Both her Seers and those who fought in her name were as powerless against the goddess as the rest of us were."

"Well said," I told him, proud of his astute observation and the eloquence with which he delivered it.

I made them aware of Breaker's allowances, leaving no room for negotiation on those. They included where the Kehlanians would and would not allow fishing, what would happen if anyone from the sky fired upon or harmed one of Talay's people, and how the grove's bounty would be managed. A time and day were agreed upon for no more than six Empyrean Gatherers to descend to collect bushels of fruit from the grove. They would bring no guards or weapons as a show of good faith. We would send a small delegation – Jorun and myself included – to help them collect what they needed and would do so unarmed.

I proposed one final matter for them to consider.

"I could lower the firmament so that it's perched nearer to the sea. At a lower altitude, the warmth of the sun may allow you to grow crops of your own," I offered.

"But… so close to the ocean, the firmament itself would disintegrate…" Gamut breathed.

"No, it wouldn't. I didn't know it until very recently, but the firmament will hold because I made it. My Empyrea doesn't yield to the brine. I don't suggest that you make it an isle by any means, but perhaps lowering it enough that you could supply some of your needs moving forward would be best. It's something to consider."

Gamut slowly nodded. "We will certainly discuss it. Would you both be willing to return in one week's time so that we can deliver our answer and arrange the first harvest?"

We agreed to do so.

Facing so many people we used to know and who knew and looked up to us, whose fists once again were raised to honor our efforts, Jorun carried me from Empyrean, back to my home near the sea.

Koa found me one evening, cooking fish over the fire in front of Aderyn and Jorun's tent – formerly mine. My sister and friend were dining with the twins' nursemaid and her family tonight.

While Crest's indoor firepit was nice, sometimes I just liked being outside. The view of the empty sky was one I often sought.

His gilded scales lit in the firelight as he sat down, gently placing a basket, its top covered by a thick cloth, beside him. As outlandish as he could be, he was one of the best swimmers and Guardians the sea had ever seen. I wondered what color scales Talay would have given me if I'd been born to him, then imagined a thin layer lining my thighs in the same blue gray hue my feathers had held.

He surveyed the state of my fish. "You should flip them now."

I slid my knife under them and gave them each a little flip. He was right. They were charring on the other side and drying out far too quickly.

Crest was busy with Breaker. The two men were consulting Era about the needs of Empyrean to better prepare for our next meeting. Jorun and I would return, but this time, we would ask for someone – Gamut, perhaps – to come with us to the sand. If we were to be good neighbors, we needed to try to know and understand one another's pasts so that together, we could forge a new future.

"If you've come to belittle my skills with a fillet knife, you should know I'm well aware of my deficiencies. If you've come, instead, to berate me for hurting him, I'm still not finished berating myself, so you'll need to wait until I'm through to begin." My nonexistent feathers were ruffled.

He offered a slight smile. "And if I came for a completely different reason?"

"I'm not sure I'd believe it," I grumped.

He smiled. "Well, allow me to prove it to you, Elira. I brought you something very special. It's no perfect wooden leg, but I made it myself."

I narrowed my eyes at him. He removed the cloth from the basket with a flourish, then extended his gift, gracing me with a full, proud grin.

"What is this?" I asked, studying it, noting its sweet, fruity smell. Set in the hollow of a palm-sized copper pan, it was small, round, and crusted on the top, but something dark and red like ripe pomegranate lay under the surface.

"It's a pie. I made it for you," he said incredulously.

"What do I do with this pie? Is it edible?" I spun the small copper dish around to look at the pie's dimpled edge.

"Is it *edible*?" he scoffed, looking properly offended. Perhaps angry. I held the pie's copper pan tightly so he didn't tear it away. "It's a dessert. Cooked fruit trapped between layers of delicious crust. I can't believe you've never had pie!"

Still unconvinced, I pressed, "What fruit does it contain?"

He choked out a laugh. "You're not kidding."

I arched a brow and waited for him to reveal the contents of this… pie.

He sighed. "It has cooked berries and plums, pomegranates, even apples in it." Without another word, Koa walked inside the tent to get a fork, then placed it in my hand and sat beside me, watching me like a hawk.

"Why are you staring at me like that, Koa?"

"Because I want to see if you like your first bite."

I was getting more and more leery of eating it.

"Please?" he begged. "There's no sky fire in it. Not even a smidge," he added with a wry smile.

I *thought* he was teasing…

I plunged the fork into the flaky shell and dug out a bite of what looked and smelled like cooked fruit.

"Pie is best when served hot," he declared, "but I couldn't stand to hold it while it was still bubbling, so I had to let it cool before bringing it over, but it should be warm enough."

I slid the pastry onto my tongue. Flavors and sweetness burst upon it and I groaned delightedly. "This is delicious." Proud, he leaned back and braced his hands on the ground. "What did I do to deserve such an offering?" I asked around another bite.

He shrugged. "You saved everyone I love." I stopped chewing, but he waved it off. "Don't go getting a big ego about it, though. All you'll get from me is this tiny pie."

"Must you always be so difficult?"

He smiled. "Absolutely."

Crest appeared through the shadows, his copper scales glinting with the fire's warm light. Suddenly the bite I'd just taken lay forgotten in my mouth. "Hey," he greeted Koa. The Shark's dark blue eyes met mine. "Why are you out *here*?" He looked back at his tent, a question denting his brow.

"I wanted to see the stars," I answered, resuming my chewing and focusing hard on the pie Koa had baked for me.

Crest crouched across from us with a playful grin tugging at his lips. "You made a pie for her?"

Koa shrugged. "She deserved one for what she did."

"Koa's pies are famous across the Isle and highly coveted because he rarely makes them," Crest explained, staring into the fire.

Koa held up his hands. "To be fair, I rarely have the time or an occasion to go to all the trouble. But I couldn't *not* reward you for utterly kicking Neera's ass."

The three of us laughed, but after it died away, Crest and Koa spoke to one another without words. Aderyn and I knew each other well enough to do the same.

Koa gave a fake, dramatic yawn and announced his intention to fall asleep early and sleep late tomorrow. To his chagrin, Crest told him they had things to do at dawn.

"What things?" Koa asked in a disappointed tone.

Crest gave him another look I couldn't decipher.

Koa slowly nodded. "Oh, *those* things…" Either Koa had no clue or Crest had jogged his memory. I wasn't sure which.

Crest waited until he was out of earshot. "I brought honey and new dressings, but my grandmother said she can help you if you'd rather she do it."

"If you wouldn't mind, I'd rather have you change them."

"Of course," he said, staring at the sizzling, half-burnt, too-dry fillets.

I gestured to the fish. "Hungry?"

"Starving."

So he sat and we ate. He had the most unfortunate meat I'd ever cooked, and I ate the pie Koa brought. I offered Crest part of what was left but he declined, pretending the fish I made was delicious when I knew better.

Later that night, his fingers brushed my skin as he began to unwrap the bandages that bound my back and chest. A shiver scuttled up my spine and he noticed. "Cold?"

I was seated by the fire pit, so close its warmth spread over me like a blanket. Crest needed its light. "No, I'm not cold."

He was quiet as he peeled the last cloths from the roots of my wings. The Empyrea had singed them and stanched the blood, but there was still a risk that the burn would get infected, Magma said. Honey would keep that from happening as the skin fully healed – even from the cauterization.

"How do they look?" I rasped.

"They're healing well."

He dabbed some honey onto the wound. It was cool and wet, sticky and thick as it settled over the wound and slowly oozed downward. Crest hurried to finish both roots and then pressed a new bandage against my skin. He wrapped several layers around back and breast until my torso was covered with pale strips, then knotted the ends beneath my ribs and finally met my eye.

"Hey," he said softly, dropping to his knees.

I looked up at the ceiling, cursing the damned tears that welled and fell.

"Did I hurt you?" he asked.

I shook my head.

"Do you miss them?" he guessed, his worried chest deflating. There were things that could be mended with honey, and others that no amount of honey could help.

I nodded, my throat sore with unshed tears.

He leaned forward and wrapped me in a tender hug. "Lacuna," he breathed.

The fact that he finally said it made me cry harder.

In that moment, I knew he was right and I shouldn't have left him without saying goodbye, no matter how well intentioned my motives were.

He pulled away just enough so I could see him. "The Salt told me what you asked her to tell me if you didn't make it back. She told me that you wanted me to have your shell."

I went still, watching as he carefully repeated the words she'd given him, my words…

"That you thought you never deserved me, but knew you had to try to make things right. That you wanted to prove to me you were more girl than eagle. That you went to try to save your lacuna."

He went quiet after that, looking away from my eyes and face to stare at the bandages barely holding me together.

"She left the most important part out," I croaked.

"What's that?"

"That I love you with every sharp shard of my soul."

His hands clasped my hips and he rose, eyes flashing a moment before his lips crashed into mine.

Demanding.

Punishing.

Perfect.

The Shark was done. Done with being careful, and I loved it, moaning when his teeth caught my lower lip and dragged it toward him. His strength roared and mine rose to meet it. My lacuna reminded me who I was at the core, proving with every kiss that he still wanted me.

His strong hands, his lips and tongue, said I wasn't damaged beyond repair or too fragile to be his equal. His ocean eyes burned for me despite the fact that my wings were gone. He dragged me forward to the edge of the chair. The legs screeched across the wooden planks.

He was so tall standing on his knees that when I wrapped my legs around his waist, I felt his longing at the juncture of my thighs. His scales raked deliciously down my skin as he leaned in to capture another harsh kiss.

Crest's broad hands slid up my thighs, dragging my sarong higher up my hips. He leaned in, kissing the curve of my neck, my chest…

"Lacuna," he whispered against my skin, dragging his lips over my collar bone.

I waited, my breaths shallow, for him to prove it.

"You're the missing part of my heart," he breathed over the hollow of my throat. He placed a kiss there, followed by a sharp bite.

The sound that escaped my chest could only be described as a mewl.

"I'm your lacuna, and you're mine, Elira. That means we fight together as a duo instead of a quad. We don't leave one another behind."

"I know that now," I quickly promised.

His stare sharpened. "You don't, but you will. I'll make sure of it."

He jerked me forward, off the chair's edge and onto him, as he sheathed himself deep inside me.

CHAPTER THIRTY

Crest and I laid beside each other on the beach on our stomachs with the gloriously warm sun on our backs. What skin wasn't encased in bandages was likely burning and Magma would grump when she found grains of sand in my dressing, but I didn't care. This felt too good to do anything else in the moment.

"Would you come with me somewhere this evening? There's something I'd like to show you," Crest said out of the blue.

I lifted and craned my neck to see him, curious. "But the celebration is this evening, and I'm supposed to see The Salt beforehand."

"It's not too far. We won't be long," he offered vaguely.

"What is it? Or where?"

Crest taunted me with a grin. "I can't tell you."

Frustrating, infuriating male. "You're being intentionally vague and evasive."

Crest laughed. "And *you're* being stubborn and far too curious."

I narrowed my eyes at him.

"It's a surprise, Elira. I won't give into your needling and ruin it."

Just then, Koa's shrill call sounded over the dunes. He buried his head back into his arms and groaned. My body went rigid. I looked at him.

"Not urgent," he grumbled, anticipating my question. "But maybe you should go see The Salt now so we have plenty of time later..." Again, he didn't spoil whatever surprise he'd concocted. "I'll catch up to you soon," he promised with a quick kiss.

He pushed up from his blanket, the sand that had stuck to his skin falling away. He started toward the water where Frey and Koa's voices could now be heard – arguing, of course.

I hurried past Magma's tent. The pinned-back door flap's bottom ruffled in the breeze, but I heard no voices emerging from the dark interior. I didn't want her to see me. I hadn't gone to see her like I told her I would, so she'd given Crest the supplies to keep my wound clean and wrapped. She didn't push the issue because North was back in her workshop, and I wasn't going anywhere near him if I could avoid it.

But it appeared there was no avoiding Magma forever. She stood in The Salt's tent when I arrived. They were deep in discussion when I stepped inside, startling the

Mender when she turned and found me standing behind her.

"You are too quiet!" she yelled, clutching her chest.

I looked at my feet and wiggled my toes. "No boots."

She made a displeased sound in the back of her throat. I'd missed hearing it.

"You wanted to see me?" I addressed The Salt.

Magma tutted. "I know why you haven't been to my tent. I haven't been able to leave North for long, but still I need to check your back." She glanced at The Salt. "Do you mind if I take a few minutes?"

"You should look at her wounds while you have the chance," The Salt graciously allowed.

Feeling chipper, I turned and presented my wounds to her.

She gave me a wary gaze. "What's gotten into you?"

It wasn't appropriate to tell her that her grandson had. "Nothing in particular," I lied instead.

She shook her head as she unknotted the wrapping and began to unfurl it. I covered my breasts as The Salt chuckled at Magma's grouching. Apparently, there was a lot of sand in my bandages. Also her grandson's doing, but I spared her that knowledge. Again.

"It's stuck in the honey," she griped. "What have you been doing, rolling around in the sand?"

The Salt covered her mouth with her hand, smothering her laughter. I couldn't contain mine.

Magma's hands went still. "Talay's breath! The two of you are ridiculous," she grumbled.

"We're lacunas," I reminded her.

Magma deadpanned, "Yes, the entire Isle is aware." She cleaned the honey off my roots and looked them over carefully. "I think you can leave them uncovered now. They need some air. I wouldn't go rolling around in the sand with them bare, though. For the next few weeks, use common sense."

Still holding an arm over my chest, I stretched my back, still unused to the feeling of my wings not responding to my commands. At least there was relief to be found in being unbound.

The Salt gave me an empathetic smile. There was no pity in it, though. Only an understanding that came from the culmination of more lifetimes than I or anyone else could possibly imagine.

"I have something for you," she quietly spoke. The Salt pulled out a soft dress and handed it to me. It was blue with a hint of green, like the edge of the sea that hugged the Isle. Along its skirt, The Salt had added feathers, forming them with strands of thread a shade lighter than the fabric itself.

"Thank you." I turned and slid it on, quickly knotting the top at the nape of my neck. "It's beautiful."

"The back is open and won't brush your scars," she delicately told me.

I took her hands and squeezed, hoping she knew how much her thoughtfulness meant to me. "It's perfect."

After catching up with Crest we crossed paths with Aderyn and Jorun, each carrying one of the hatchlings. The babes had grown significantly. They were no longer skin and bone, no longer gnawing their own fists. In fact, their cheeks were nearly as puffy and dimpled as their little hands. "You're attending the celebration, aren't you?" Jorun asked.

"Of course," Crest answered. "I just need to handle something real quick and then we'll be right over."

Aderyn quirked a brow as if to ask what – exactly – he intended to handle.

"We'll see you soon," I told her as Crest tugged me away, toward the Guardian's Hall.

If his slight touches to my exposed lower back were any indication, The Shark appreciated the dress The Salt had given me.

We passed the hall he frequented and took a path that had been recently trampled, judging by the barely decayed leaves underfoot, through a section of dense vegetation and palms on the western side of the Isle. "What's out here?" I asked, craning my neck to try and see over his ridiculously broad shoulders.

"Other than the best view of the sunset, your gift is just ahead."

Hmm. I looked around him again to no avail.

The vegetation thinned and fell away into the sand. On the shore, there was one palm that bent toward the water more than all the other tall, straight ones. From this bowed tree, a hoop of twisted, dried vines hung. It was lovely. "What is this?"

"Surprise," he softly said, kissing me gently. An ache built in my chest.

The setting sun cast an orange hue over sky and clouds, sea and sand, painting us in auburn shades. His copper scales matched the evening sky. "Come here," Crest said. His hand met my lower back and he guided me in front of the hoop.

He sat down on one side, the rope that held it tightening under his weight. He reached out for my waist and brought me over to stand before him. "Straddle me," he said.

I carefully seated myself on his lap to face him, not realizing he was about to lift his legs and push us into the air. My arms wound around his neck as I gasped, tensing to keep my balance.

"What *is* this, Crest?" I asked as he rocked us back and forth toward the sea and sun before the rope drew us backward.

"A swing."

A swing?

He offered shyly, "I just thought that whenever you missed flying, this might help a little."

My heart nearly burst. "I don't know how to thank you."

"You don't need to thank me, lacuna. I know it's not the same, but maybe if you close your eyes and rock high enough, it might remind you of it. I can't tell you how sorry I am about your wings. I know what they meant to you."

I took a deep breath. "You don't think I'm hideous now?"

He traced my back with his fingertips. "I could never think that. I didn't think that even when you were tracking me and tried to shoot an arrow through my heart."

My mouth curved in a crooked grin. "It's mine all the same now, isn't it?"

He smiled. "Every sharp shard." Moving his hand behind my knee, he hiked me closer until my chest was flush with his. Our lips touched, but only barely. "I just want you to be happy, Elira. I hope I can be that for you.

A place you love more than the sky. I hope I can be your home one day."

"You already are. Who do you think I fought the sky goddess for? It wasn't only for me."

"I know that," he breathed, pressing a pained kiss to my lips. "I've never been so scared than when I thought you might die. You pushed us toward the water and I didn't know if I could save you from it. I was so cold."

"How did she catch you at first?"

"Well, I didn't exactly make it hard for her," he answered sheepishly. "I could think of nothing else but reaching you."

"She could've killed you." I remembered Elder Magnus's burst heart. The sound of his skull cracking, then cracking again against the marble stairs, the sound of his lifeless flesh as it landed.

"None of that matters now," he said. "You know that path we wanted to blaze together?"

I nodded.

"We're on it." His hand ghosted up my back to graze the tender skin where my wings once extended in glorious bursts. "I love you, lacuna."

"I love *you*, Crest," I breathed.

I'd never considered what loving someone might feel like, but now I knew. And I knew what it felt like to feel someone's love in return. Lacunas completed one another in a way nothing else could. This hoop swing was just one of the countless ways Crest taught me that.

"We should start toward Talay's Temple," he suggested, resting his forehead against mine and breathing deeply.

"Can we come back after?" I asked.

"We can come here any time."

Katalini glowed as Breaker stood among Talay's people in the sea god's temple and announced that his lacuna was carrying their first child. Cheers erupted. Smiles abounded. And there was joy.

Joy that wasn't forced forward by the threats and fear of the future, but was born of an easy, hopeful tide rolling up onto a comforting, familiar shore.

Era and Zura sat with The Salt in places of honor, along with Aderyn and Jorun. They would return to their home in the morning to meet with Gamut and help the Empyreans prepare for Jorun's and my return later in the week. They would discuss the advantages and disadvantages for lowering the firmament, though of the latter, I could think of few.

The hatchlings were being passed around by a clutch of older women, one of whom was Magma. She'd helped raise Breaker and Crest and she would help raise her grandchildren as they learned to live and love on the Isle and conquer the sea of Talay.

I spotted the tattooist Vasa across the room and skirted it to make my way over. He beamed when I stopped in front of him. "Elira!" He bent at the waist in greeting. "I owe you my thanks."

I brushed off his words, embarrassed each time someone offered them. "You don't, but I wonder if I might ask a favor of you."

"Anything," he easily agreed.

"Can you give *me* a mark, or is it forbidden? I'd like a tattoo. I know it's not the right day or time, but…"

He held up a hand. "Whenever you're ready, consider it done. Do you know what you want?"

"I want a lacuna mark," I told him, finding Crest watching us across the room with a curious look on his face. "And on my back extending from my scars, I want wings. Blue wings, if you can do that. I'm still healing, so I won't be ready for several weeks. I just saw you and wanted to ask."

"I'm honored," Vasa replied, placing a hand over his heart before offering another bow.

After I left Vasa and began drifting back to Crest, someone touched my elbow. I turned to find Nori there.

"Elira, I give you my word not to bother you or Crest again. But that's not why I came to find you tonight. I need your help."

"Help with what?"

She nodded across the room to where North sat in a chair, far too sick to attend tonight's feast. "Magma can't mend him."

"What do you mean?" I asked.

"He's wasting away. He's dying," she said, her voice shattering. She looked down at the cuticles she'd torn at until bloody before ripping another away. "He won't tell us what you did, and I won't breathe a word, I just need to know the cure."

My brows kissed. "Nori, I didn't do anything to North."

"During the fight, you must have!" she insisted. "Just tell me how to make him better." Her voice raised so that the people around us quieted and turned their attention to us.

"She did nothing," The Salt crisply informed her, stepping between two men to stand with us. "North's suffering is a punishment from the sea god himself. Talay is the only one who can deliver him from its grasp."

"Then ask him to!" Nori begged, tears flooding her eyes.

The Salt's face was impassive, imposing. "North must be the one to ask. Not you. And before Talay will hear him, your brother must rid himself of the darkness swirling within his heart. Talay will not suffer murderers, those who would rip through the choice and defile the wombs of women, those who would torture and maim, and laugh as they did it. Your brother's thoughts are no better than the terror of the sky that Elira ridded us of. North will suffer *his* fate, not by her hand, but by Talay's if he does not alter his course – and quickly."

Nori turned rage-filled eyes upon her brother before wiping her cheeks and nose and stalking toward him. She demanded that someone help her remove him from the temple. Two Guardians jumped to help and Nori followed her brother outside.

Crest's hand found the small of my back. "What was that?"

"The Salt just informed Nori who's causing North's malady and the reasons for it," I answered.

After the feast, Crest went to North and tried to persuade him to see reason, if not for his own sake, then for Nori's. Koa talked with him, too. But North would not yield.

And neither did Talay.

After ushering his former friend into the deep, Crest told me that North had cursed the god of the sea as he lay on Magma's cot, drawing his last breaths.

I didn't step foot on the sand as his people gathered to offer him to Talay. Didn't wear blue to honor or mourn him. Instead, I walked to the grove and climbed into the canopy to touch as much of the air as possible.

Crest was pensive for days after his death. Upset at North, yes, but also for his inability to sway him. I didn't know of the guilt he harbored until one night as we lay under the stars, he cleared his throat and said, "Part of me is glad he's gone. He's no longer a threat to you now."

I didn't crane my neck to see him. I imagined Talon alive and living on the Isle, and of the constant threat he would pose to Crest and his family and friends. I was glad Talon was dead. Soraya, too.

I wasn't sure what it said about either of us, that we took comfort in the absence of someone we both once respected, but I loved him more for being so open about his thoughts. No one had ever fully trusted me. Not even Aderyn, I realized.

The twins, having attained a proper weight and strength for hatchlings their age, began to crawl. Crest, Aderyn, Jorun, and I spread out to corral them as they explored the area between our tents. They were deceptively fast despite the fact that their wings didn't assist their movements.

The nursemaid kept them quite often. She had grown to love the babes as her own and insisted that Jorun and Aderyn spend time together when she took the boys for the afternoon or overnight. Not that they squandered a moment.

Aderyn and I… were trying. That was all I could say.

The Salt noticed the strain that lingered and predicted that time would heal the wound between us. I wasn't sure if Talay told her or if she just assumed we would work things out. Things would never be the same as before she left, because we weren't the same people. But I still loved her, and I knew she loved me. She returned to the sky wingless so I wouldn't face Neera alone. You certainly didn't risk your life for someone you hated.

I thought of the Empyrean souls who had recently made their lives on the Isle. Jorun, Aderyn, Era, and Zura. I rested easier knowing the four of them had cowries, proving that Talay welcomed and accepted them. Since the battle, the people of the sea had accepted us, too; the ones who left the sky to tread upon the sand and build a life beside the swells with them.

Bellen and those who had chosen to separate themselves from the villages trickled back into their sliver of land, but they did not rebuild the homes that were crushed within The Hollow. Jorun was glad he was gone.

There was a lightness to his laugh. He smiled wider, more genuinely. He laughed as he played with the hatchlings, and he watched Aderyn, not with fascination, but with a newfound contentment I understood to my marrow.

Maybe The Salt was right after all. Things were slowly changing among us.

The peace forged with Empyrean held. Era and Gamut came to visit regularly and were open with the state of things in the sky. The council members had been chosen – all walks of life represented among their number, even the former elect – and were making a sincere attempt at governing fairly. Jorun and I had plans to meet them all the morning after the next full moon.

Magma once said that we should enjoy the calm moments that came before the storm, but there was a calm that descended afterward, too. As if the world and everyone who survived the gale collectively breathed a grateful sigh when the sun shone for the first time again.

The sun shone for us now, reminding us that we'd come through it.

Weeks later…

I lay on my stomach in the heart of Talay's Temple as Vasa tapped indigo ink into the flesh on my back. I could feel the shape and contour of every feather he formed, each quill and shaft, barb and vane. The skin over my heart was tender and raw, covered by four concentric circles formed of shark's teeth. Vasa did not have to ask The Salt to reveal the pattern Talay would have me bear. I saw the pattern in my mind so clearly that the artist accepted my word immediately.

I didn't tell Crest I was coming here, or what my plans were. He'd surprised me with the swing, and I wanted to do the same by keeping my lacuna mark private until I could reveal it to him in a special way.

When we parted earlier that morning, we made plans to meet at dusk at the swing. He promised to provide the fish for dinner. I was bringing pomegranate, plums, berries, and chopped apples – in the form of Koa's pie. I'd asked him to make Crest one after I saw the way he stared longingly at the one made for me.

I'd tried to share it and Crest wouldn't take a single bite. Koa's pies were too precious a gift and he'd made it for me, he argued.

Smiling to myself, I didn't realize Vasa noticed.

He didn't comment or muse about what, or who caused it. Likely, the artist knew. He just offered a soft smile of his own and continued his work until late in the afternoon, when he stopped adding the final touches and was satisfied with the wings on my back. Wearing a knitted shawl over the strapless top The Salt helped me make in preparation for this very day, I gingerly made my way to the swing, hurrying down the path to see Crest and excited to show him my new mark.

I passed the Guardian's Hall before veering off the path to the trodden trail that led to the ocean and Crest. His back was to me, facing the sea as he tended the skewered fish cooking atop the fire he'd built. He glanced my way and thanked me as I sat the basket that contained Koa's pie beside him.

"I'll come back and slice it," I promised, "but first I'd like to swing."

His eyes widened as the enticing aroma of the rarely baked pie seeped from the basket, then his head swiveled my direction as I sat on the woven loop and let my shawl sink from my shoulders.

"There's no…" his eyes caught on my mark, "rush…" He slowly stood, then came to me. "Vasa did this?" he croaked, climbing through the hoop to sit beside me as he took it in. He faced the foliage and I took in the spectacular sea – not the one before me, but the one glittering proudly in Crest's eyes.

"He did."

"They're shark's teeth," he noted, his eyes tracing the concentric pattern splayed across my chest.

"They are," I replied. With bated breath I waited for more.

"Your hair is up," he observed, eyes catching on the woven strands.

"It is."

Crest scrutinized the mark on my chest, his eyes lit with fascination. "I thought you only wore it up in battle or when you sparred?"

"Except today," I told him.

His eyes hungrily traced every serrated tooth.

"There's more," I told him, twisting my shoulder so he could see it.

He stopped my gentle swinging and asked me to lean forward. "Your wings!" he marveled. "They're perfect."

His thumb tenderly brushed the tattoo. It stretched from arm to arm, shoulder to shoulder. Crest vowed that once it was all healed, he would trace every mark with his tongue. I vowed to let him, toes curling as he began to rock us, pulling me over to straddle him.

That night, the fish burnt on the spit as we rocked together.

And it struck me that the joy I'd hoped to find had found me first.

EPILOGUE

I ran to the shore and paced as I waited for The Shark. He was near. I could feel it.

In the distance, a painful shrill made me clamp my hands over my ears. Only one beast made such a terrible sound. *Hydra.* My stomach dropped. I started toward the water.

"Elira," a sharp voice warned, halting my advance.

Magma and The Salt had caught up to me, cresting the dunes before coming to stand with me.

"Crest is fine," The Salt soothed. "The hydra won't harm him."

"Are you sure?"

She gently inclined her head.

Just then, Koa surfaced, laughing, of course. Frey, too. Then there was a flash of copper scales. I shook my head and fought the grin that crawled onto my lips. Crest was fearless, leading the beast away from the Isle to keep his people, especially the younglings that were far too daring for their own good, safe.

The Guardians ushered the serpent to deeper water, but not before I counted at least three distinct heads.

"Were you just going to run out here and tell him?" Magma chided. "You don't want to do something romantic to surprise him?"

My brows furrowed. "It's none of your business."

The Mender laughed in response.

"Magma?" She hummed a response, fondly watching her grandson and his closest friends do what they loved the most. "Will our child be winged or scaled?"

Magma's brows furrowed. "I honestly don't know." She looked to The Salt for help. "Do you?"

The Salt smiled, then posed, "Why must he have one feature or the other? Why can't he have both?"

"He?" I breathed, brushing a hand over the small, hard swell of my lower stomach.

Waiting for Crest to return from his adventure with the hydra, I fell asleep in the shade of the trees that lined the beach near the swing Crest built for me. He settled on the blanket beside me, still wet from the sea. Water dripped from his dark hair and slid down his skin. I watched them for a few long moments before sitting up.

"Sorry to wake you."

"I'm glad you did."

He smiled and ran his fingers over the tattooed wings on my back. I sat up, unsure how to go about telling him. I'd planned to run to him and blurt it out, but Magma's comments about telling him in some grand, romantic way made me reconsider. I wanted him to know so badly I was nearly bursting, but I wasn't sure what to do that would be great enough for the news I carried.

"Crest…"

He twisted to see me, worry marring his brow. "What's the matter?"

"Nothing," I promised. I cupped his face and kissed his lips, slowly pulling away. Then I took his hand and placed it on my stomach, smoothing it around in a circle. His fingers stilled and slightly tightened.

"Elira?" he choked.

I wasn't sure what to say, if he was happy or horrified.

He calmed my worry immediately by pulling me onto his lap and laughing, kissing my lips so that I could taste his joy. "I love you. How long have you known, lacuna?"

"I just confirmed it this afternoon."

"With my grandmother?" he asked.

I nodded. "The Salt also knows. She happened to be there when I went to Magma."

He shook his head. "There's no keeping anything from her. She's likely known since conception."

He peppered me with kisses that were only interrupted by tender hugs and exclamations of uninhibited, pure and radiant joy, once more reminding me that he was a part of my heart as much as I was the missing piece of his.

"Crest," I interrupted his happy moment, "The Salt said he might have scales, gills, – *and* wings."

His ocean eyes caught fire. "Then he – or she – will master the sand, sky, and sea."

Our child would be exactly that. A product of a love that bridged two worlds.

I was excited for this new chapter and whatever the next might hold. Happy to write it with him.

The Shark of the Sea and Scourge of the Sky began as enemies. Became unlikely friends. Ignited into lovers. Were soon to be parents… and all that just served as proof that the two of us had dared to blaze a new path that no one else could see or believe in. We were walking it along Kehlani's shore just like Crest said we would. His footsteps beside mine… I hoped the impressions we left would last far after Talay called our souls into the deep.

The End

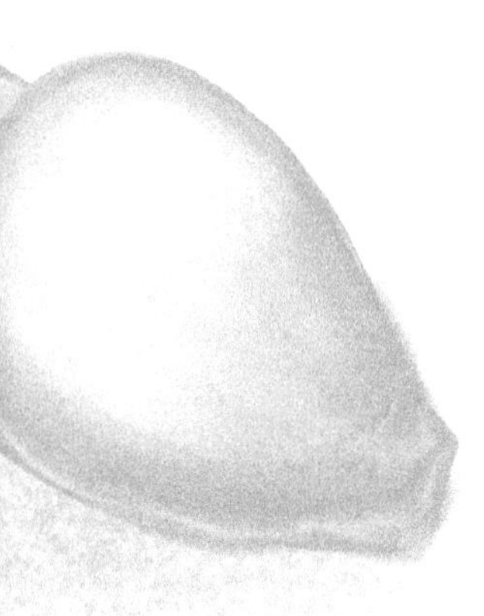

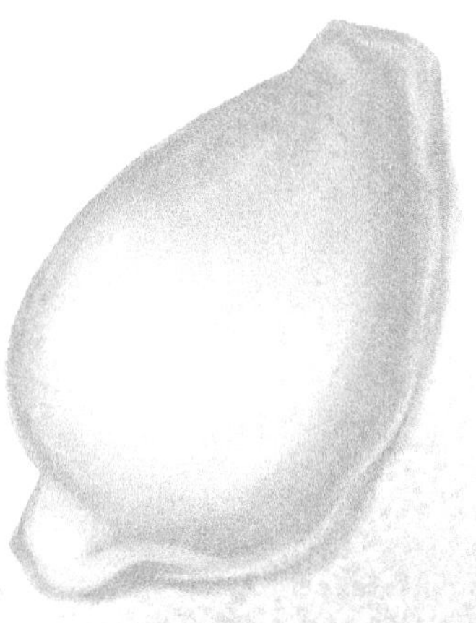

ACKNOWLEDGEMENTS

I'm ever thankful to God for his mercy and blessings in my life. I thank my family for their constant encouragement, my friends for their support, and fans for loving my characters and stories as much as I do.

Thanks to Melissa Stevens for the beautiful covers, interiors, trailers, graphics and for generally pouring magic and love into this duology. Love you tons.

Thanks to Stacy Sanford for waving her magic red pen over my manuscript and polishing it until it is as sharp as the tip of Elira's arrow.

Thanks to Steffani Christensen for illustrating one of the most beautiful scenes that emerged from this story for the hardcase and art prints.

Thanks to Cristie Alleman and Amber Garcia for reading this book before anyone else and helping me make the story better. I appreciate your time and keen eyes.

Thanks to Angelina J. Steffort and Alisha Klapheke for reading this while it was still being polished and offering endorsements to make her soar.

Lastly, thanks to you, the reader. Whether you're a member of the Bondtourage Reader Group, social media stalker – er, follower – or this is your first Bond book, I appreciate you reading the story that bled from my soul.

ABOUT THE AUTHOR

Casey L. Bond lives on a rural farm in West Virginia with her husband and their two beautiful daughters. She writes phoenixes – gloriously flawed and morally gray characters that fiercely rise from the ashes of their circumstances. World building is one of her favorite hobbies, along with stamping metal jewelry, swimming, and enjoying the beauty of nature. She thinks thunderstorms are better than coffee and that watching a meteor shower is the closest thing to magic you might ever see. She's a firm believer that every amazing book needs a world you want to wrap yourself in, a character you want to win, and a love you would fight for.

www.ingramcontent.com/pod-product-compliance
Lightning Source LLC
Chambersburg PA
CBHW020242030826
48979CB00030B/2484/J

* 9 7 8 1 0 8 8 0 1 2 4 8 2 *